TAPPED OUT

MAPLE SYRUP MYSTERIES

EMILY JAMES

STRONGHOLD BOOKS

Emily James

authoremilyjames@gmail.com

www.authoremilyjames.com

Editor: Christopher Saylor at www.sayloroediting.wordpress.com/services/

Cover Design: Deranged Doctor Design at www.derangeddoctordesign.com

Published October 2017 by Stronghold Books

Ebook ISBN: 978-1-988480-11-4

Print ISBN: 978-1-988480-12-1

ALSO BY EMILY JAMES

Maple Syrup Mysteries

Sapped: A Maple Syrup Mysteries Prequel

A Sticky Inheritance

Bushwhacked

Almost Sleighed

Murder on Tap

Deadly Arms

Capital Obsession

Tapped Out

Bucket List

End of the Line

Rooted in Murder (Coming Soon!)

Cupcake Truck Mysteries

Sugar and Vice

Other Mysteries

Slay Bells Ringing

(contains a Maple Syrup Mysteries novella and a Cupcake Truck Mysteries novella)

For Christine. When I think of what it means to be a true friend, I think of you. I also think about you playing a piano in the back of my pick-up truck in the street.

Who lies for you will lie against you.

— Bosnian Proverb

*T*he look on Erik's face said that whatever he'd come to talk to me about wasn't good.

So did the fact that he'd cleared his throat three times in the last minute. We'd been friends long enough that I knew what that particular tic meant. He was nervous.

I nudged the cup of coffee I'd made him across my kitchen island and waited.

He wasn't in uniform, so at least I knew this wasn't official police business. No one was dead, and I hadn't somehow gotten myself into trouble without realizing it.

For a second, I considered clearing my own throat. The silence was getting uncomfortable, but Erik wasn't the kind of man you rushed. He'd tell me when he was ready.

"Do you want some maple syrup popcorn?" I asked. "I've been testing recipes for Stacey's baby shower."

Stacey Rathmell, Sugarwood's bookkeeper and all-around fix-it woman, was due to have her first baby in a little over a month. I was throwing her a shower, and she'd decided she wanted maple-syrup themed favors, but not something we sold in the shop because she didn't want me expending Sugarwood resources on her. I'd have gladly spent the money on tiny bottles of maple syrup or bouquets of maple syrup candy if it got me out of my kitchen.

Erik looped a finger through the handle of his coffee mug, but didn't bring it any closer to him. "I'm not hungry." He cleared his throat again. "I need advice about Elise."

Was he thinking of proposing already? Erik and Elise started dating after Mark and I did. I thought they weren't considering marriage yet—especially since most people waited longer than Mark and I had to get engaged. But maybe I'd been wrong. If he needed help planning a proposal Elise would love, I could give him some great ideas. I had to be better at planning a proposal than planning a baby shower. Or a wedding. Without Mark's mom, I'd have been lost.

I didn't want to come straight out and ask if that were it, though, and embarrass Erik even more. "Is something wrong?"

I casually popped a couple kernels of maple syrup popcorn into my mouth. This batch was only marginally better than my first attempt—it practically glued my jaw shut, it was so sticky.

"Maybe. She's keeping something from me, and I'm not sure what to do about it."

Crap. That was the opposite of where I'd hoped this conversation was going. It fell more into the *I'm not sure this relationship is going to work* category.

He'd probably come to me because, as far as I knew, I was his only female friend, but asking me for relationship advice was like asking a toddler to quiz you for a spelling bee.

"I've only had two serious relationships. One was a borderline psychopath who murdered his wife and tried to kill me. The other was Mark. Maybe Mark or Quincey would be a better choice to talk to this about."

"I can't talk to either of them. They're both county employees."

Erik was so by-the-book sometimes that he made me want to color outside the lines just to be contrary, but he'd lost me this time. "You're going to have to be a bit less cryptic if you want my help."

He sighed and finally took his first sip of coffee. "Elise has been suspended, and she won't tell me why."

Even if he'd let me guess, that wouldn't have crossed my mind as a possibility. Elise wasn't quite as strict as Erik, but she was a good police officer. "You're sure this isn't a mistake?"

He shook his head. "I asked her about it. She didn't deny deserving the suspension, and she said that it's not something I needed to worry about."

If I had to make a guess about why she was keeping this from Erik, I'd have said it was one of two things. The first was that she didn't want him getting in trouble trying to help her. The second seemed more likely. "Maybe she's embarrassed. It was probably an innocent mistake, and Chief McTavish had to give her a slap on the wrist."

"I asked the chief," Erik said. "He wouldn't tell me what was going on either, and he suggested it'd be better if I left it alone."

That explained why he felt he couldn't go directly to Quincey or

Mark, even though Mark was the county medical examiner and not a police officer like the rest of them. If Chief McTavish found out that Erik continued to dig even after he'd shut Erik down, Erik and whoever he went to could be in trouble. Besides, if Erik didn't know the truth, it wasn't likely Quincey or Mark would, either. Mark wasn't a police officer, and Erik outranked Quincey.

It also sounded ominous, like this was more than a small disciplinary action.

Erik had to be thinking what I was now thinking. Fair Haven's former chief had been involved in all kinds of cover-ups. Chief McTavish came here in part to uncover whether the corruption stopped with the former chief or went deeper. If he'd suspended Elise and warned Erik off, it could be because he suspected Elise of being dirty.

No way was Elise a dirty cop. "You know she's not—"

"I know." He pushed his cup back away from him. "It's not that I think she's actually involved in any of the things the chief's investigating, but that doesn't mean circumstantial evidence won't point to her. That could end her career."

Or at least end her career here in Fair Haven, where the court of public opinion sometimes mattered more than the actual law. Even if she was cleared in the end, it could mean she'd have to start over somewhere else. Leaving Fair Haven meant leaving her family behind, and I knew how close the Cavanaughs were. One of the items in the con side of the list Mark and I were making as we tried to decide whether to move back to DC after we got married involved leaving his family behind.

And then there was Erik's job. Would they even be able to get employment in the same county, or would a forced move for Elise mean the end of their relationship?

I dumped my half-finished cup of coffee in the sink. "I'll go talk to her. Maybe it's not as bad as we think."

I DECIDED NOT TO CALL AHEAD AND GIVE ELISE A CHANCE TO SAY *no*. The whole drive, my parents' voices yelled in my brain about how rude it was to show up unannounced. Fair Haven had that small town *drop by anytime* attitude, so hopefully Elise wouldn't be too annoyed.

Or, at least, not annoyed by me showing up on her doorstep. Based on what Erik had told me, she wasn't going to love me poking into her private situation.

But that's what family did. In a few months, I'd officially be a Cavanaugh, and Elise would be my cousin-in-law.

I parked behind Elise's car in her driveway. The high-pitched squeals of happy kids playing drifted from the backyard.

Elise's kids were young enough that she'd probably told them she was on vacation rather than that she'd been suspended. She wouldn't tell me anything around them. If I wanted the truth, I'd have to draw her away.

I detoured from my path to the backyard and rang the doorbell instead.

Elise answered a minute later, her dark hair pulled back into a ponytail rather than the ultra-strict bun she wore for work.

She scrunched her lips together. It wasn't quite a scowl, but it came close. "He told you."

I didn't see a point in playing dumb. As soon as I tried to come around to the topic of her suspension, she'd know I'd been lying. "He did, but coming here was my idea."

She lifted her eyebrows in a way that seemed to say *I wasn't born yesterday.*

I crossed my heart. "I offered to come. I was worried, too, once he told me what's going on."

An expression flickered across Elise's face too quickly for me to figure out what it was or what caused it. "You mean you came because I wouldn't tell him what was going on."

Ouch. That made it sound like I was simply being nosy. No denying an abundance of curiosity was one of my flaws, but it hadn't entered my motives this time.

I felt like I was back talking to the Elise I'd met when Noah, Sugarwood's groom and mechanic, was attacked. The rumors floating around Fair Haven about me had made her more than a little confrontational. We'd moved past that once she realized rumors were all they were, but all her barriers were firmly back in place now.

This time I had the upper hand. We weren't strangers now. We were close enough that she was standing up in my wedding in a few months. Plus, I had insider knowledge. I knew those barriers came up when she was scared or trying to protect someone she cared about.

"It's not about curiosity," I said softly. "It's about people who love you wanting to have your back. Erik's worried this is about Chief McTavish's investigation and that you'll be blamed for something you had no part of."

That same expression crossed Elise's face again. "And what if I tell you that it's none of your business, either, and close the door in your face?"

It almost felt like she was testing me. "August in Fair Haven is close to the perfect temperature for me, and I ate enough popcorn in the past 24 hours that a fast wouldn't hurt me. I can probably wait you out."

One corner of her mouth twitched. She stepped out of the doorway and motioned me in. "I don't want the rest of the family to know."

I tripped on the doorstep and caught myself. The Cavanaughs were a family where *privacy* was practically a swear word. We'd both be in bigger trouble for keeping a secret than we would for whatever Elise had done to get herself suspended. Mark's mom still brought up how Mark and I had fudged the number of times I'd almost been killed.

I straightened up, kicked off my sandals by the door, and scurried to catch up with Elise. "It's a small town. They'll find out eventually."

She stopped so suddenly I almost rear-ended her. "Not this time. I asked the chief if we could keep it quiet."

That put a whole new spin on things. Erik assumed the chief warned him away for his own reasons. Elise made it sound like she'd asked for discretion.

"They'll know you were suspended, though. It's only a matter of time, and then they'll want to know why."

Elise was shaking her head before I finished. "Chief McTavish said he'd tell anyone who asked that I needed to take some personal time. The only other person who knows—knew—was Erik, and clearly I shouldn't have even told him."

She had every right to be miffed. I would have been too if the roles were reversed and Mark went running to Erik about something I'd told him in confidence. That explained why Erik had seemed so conflicted and had sat in my house for a long time before telling me what was going on. But—

Elise raised a hand. "I can see what you're thinking. I don't need to be told he only did it because he's worried and he cares."

At least she'd forgotten about getting an actual promise from me about not sharing this with the family. Though, given how betrayed she already felt by Erik's breach of confidence, I might have to work on convincing her rather than telling Mark behind her back. First I needed to figure out exactly what was going on.

"Is this about Chief McTavish's investigation?"

Elise leaned backward and glanced over her shoulder, as if checking that the kids were still outside. "Not directly. He said he had to suspend me to keep me from coming under suspicion. Besides, if he didn't, it'd look like favoritism and then all the work he'd done could come into question."

This was getting cloak-and-dagger enough that maybe I didn't want to know more until I knew I wouldn't be pressed into keeping it a secret from Mark. "I know you don't want the whole family to know, but I'm going to have to tell Mark whatever you tell me."

Elise pulled a face that made her look eerily similar to her five year old. "Only Mark. And if I tell you, you have to promise to help me."

2

$\mathcal{A}$s soon as Elise wanted a promise from me, I knew I wasn't going to want to agree to whatever she was about to ask. That was the only reason she'd want a promise ahead of time. If the help she needed was something I wouldn't normally object to, she'd have had no reason to insist on a promise up front.

But I also knew Elise well enough to know she wouldn't ask me to do anything immoral or illegal. Whatever she wanted might make me uncomfortable, but it wasn't likely to get me arrested.

I'd promise, with one caveat. "I promise I'll help as long as it doesn't require me to lie to Mark."

Elise's lips narrowed to the point where they almost disappeared. She hadn't wanted her family to know anything about what was going on, but she'd also hated me when we first met, in part because she thought I'd mistreated Mark. She couldn't hold it against me that I wasn't going to lie to my future husband about whatever she was bringing me in to.

Her lips relaxed. "Fine. It's not something you'd be able to hide from him anyway."

She didn't reiterate her request that I keep this a secret from the rest of the family, so hopefully she'd given up on that idea as well. Fair Haven was too small a town to expect anything to stay top secret for long anyway.

"What do you need me to do?" I asked.

"Mom?"

Elise spun around, and I leaned sideways to see past her. Arielle bounced on her toes through the kitchen doorway, hair plastered against her face and a limp towel around her shoulders.

"Hi, Aunt Nikki." She waved at me, then turned her attention back to her mom. "Can we have popsicles?"

Elise's expression softened. It was almost like magic, watching her with her kids. All the hard lines in her face disappeared, and she always looked ten years younger.

Not that it surprised me. Her kids were smart, precocious, and two of the best-behaved munchkins I'd ever met. Even though I'd never met Elise's ex-husband, they seemed to take strongly after the Cavanaughs. It still melted my heart hearing them call me *Aunt Nikki*. They'd begged for the privilege as soon as we announced our engagement.

Elise held up a finger. "You can split one. I don't want you full for lunch."

Arielle grinned and sprinted off. The towel flapped behind her like a cape.

Elise leaned against the wall. The fine lines were back in her face, more noticeable now than they had been before Arielle's appearance. "Chief McTavish had to suspend me because I used police resources for personal reasons."

She stated her infraction like she was reading from a police report.

Since she didn't try to defend it, it had to be true. Using police resources for personal reasons could mean a lot of different things, though. "I get the feeling you weren't photocopying coloring book pages on the copy machine."

Elise shook her head. "I was looking into a case where I think the person charged with the crime is innocent."

It could have been a lot worse. Basically, she'd gotten a slap on the wrist because she was spending work time and, potentially, other officers' time to continue investigating a case the county believed no longer required police involvement. She'd probably also done background checks on other possible suspects. She must have spent a lot of time digging for it to result in a suspension rather than a reprimand—though, as she said, Chief McTavish also wanted to protect her from coming under suspicion of worse.

More interesting to me than what she'd done to get in trouble was why she'd done it. She'd have known she was taking a risk.

Elise liked to make things right. If she'd missed something or felt she'd been biased against the person they arrested, it made sense that she'd try to fix it now.

"Were you involved in the original investigation?"

"I wasn't," she said.

I waited for more, but nothing came. She'd angled her body subtly away from me. The blank expression of a trained police officer who wanted to give nothing away covered her face.

That line of questioning, clearly, was closed.

I'd leave it be for the moment. She still hadn't told me how I played into all of this, but I had a sneaking suspicion. "Since you can't investigate anymore, you want me to."

"In a manner of speaking. He needs a lawyer."

If I didn't know better, I'd have thought it was a conspiracy, that my parents had bribed Elise. I did know better. She did *not* want Mark and me to move to DC. When we told her about Mark's job, I thought she might cry, and Elise cried even less than I did.

My parents' involvement aside, if she felt the man was innocent and she wanted him acquitted, I was the wrong person to hire.

"I'm not a good lawyer, Lise. I was never the lead on a case when I worked for my parents. I couldn't string two coherent sentences together in front of a jury."

Her left eyebrow arched up. "Everyone in the family knows your parents offered you your job back. They wouldn't have done that if you're as bad at it as you think."

"They think I'll get better with practice, which isn't the same as saying I'm competent now."

Her eyebrow stayed triangled. "Even if I believed that, which I don't, any lawyer is better than him defending himself. That's what he's threatening to do. He says he can't find another lawyer who'll take his case, and he doesn't trust the public defenders to believe he's innocent and dig up the evidence to prove it. They're too busy and jaded."

Everyone was entitled to representation, but the number of things Elise had already withheld from me made me even more certain taking this case would be a terrible idea. "Why doesn't he have a lawyer?"

"His lawyer quit. He said the case wasn't one he could win."

That I didn't believe. No criminal defense attorney I knew turned down a paying client because they didn't think they could win the case. In a lawsuit where you only got paid if your client won, maybe. But this wasn't a lawsuit.

Elise hadn't shifted position an iota, though, so she believed his story at least.

It seemed I wasn't going to get the answers I needed from Elise. Nor was she going to be swayed by my arguments. "I'll talk to him. I can't take someone on as a client without their consent anyway. But that's all I'm promising for now."

Elise ran a hand over her ponytail as if she wished it was in a work bun. I'd always suspected the neatness of her attire for work gave her a sense of security and control.

"That seems fair," she said.

"I want one more thing though."

Elise's eyes narrowed. "What?"

"One of those popsicles."

3

*E*lise must have called the man as soon as I was out the door, because I'd barely gotten home and put the dogs on their leashes for a walk when my cell phone rang. I didn't recognize the number.

Given who I suspected it was, I opted for a professional opening. "Nicole Fitzhenry-Dawes."

"Hi," a man's deep voice said on the other end. It was the kind of voice that made you think the owner had to be over six foot, muscular, and in the running for sexiest man alive. "I'm Dean. Elise said I need a lawyer, and I should call you."

The way he phrased it, and the tone he used, made me think he hadn't wanted to call. He probably thought I was a criminal trial version of an ambulance-chaser and that I'd approached Elise about taking his case.

Having a client who didn't trust me might actually be worse than having one who did. When a client trusted me more than I trusted myself, at least it motivated me to live up to their expectations. With a client who didn't even want me on the case, the best I could hope for was to prove them wrong.

I was far enough into the bush that I felt safe letting Velma and Toby off their leashes to run around for a bit. That'd give me one less thing to split my concentration, and Velma didn't tend to run off on me the way she did Mandy.

"Elise told me close to the same thing," I said.

He chuckled. Even the man's laugh was sexy, which meant he was probably five foot and paunchy with acne. No one could have a voice like that and a physique to match.

"Before we go any further, how about you tell me about your case."

"Elise didn't tell you?"

Velma gave a sharp bark, took off running, and treed a squirrel. For some reason, I felt a bit like the squirrel. "Even if she had, I'd want to hear it from you."

A sound like he'd let out a breath. "Okay. Well, I've been accused of killing my wife."

I'd expected it to be a murder case, so his blunt pronouncement didn't shock me the way it otherwise might have. Elise wouldn't have risked her job for anything less. "How?"

"Well, first they read me my rights, then they asked me some questions, and told me I was under arrest for Sandra's murder. After that, the exact steps get a little fuzzy."

Great. A smart mouth. He'd be a joy to represent in court. That might be the real reason his last lawyer quit. Losing came with the territory, but being humiliated by your own client was another thing entirely.

"I must have made the question too complicated. I'm sorry about that. Let me simplify it. How do they say you killed your wife?"

I couldn't quite keep the bite from my voice. Your wife just died, dude. Show some respect. If he'd tried to be a comedian with the police, it was no wonder they'd suspected him.

"Suffocation." He sounded a little mollified. A very little. "Someone put a plastic bag over her head and duct taped it shut."

A shiver ran over my arms. Toby pushed his cool nose into my palm, and I dropped to one knee and draped an arm around him.

That would be an awful way to die. Hopefully they'd drugged her first so she didn't know what was happening to her. I wouldn't ask him that, though. I'd wanted to deflate him a little, not be cruel. I could find out the gritty details from the reports.

"And where were you when this happened?"

"Passed out on the couch downstairs."

And right there was why the police didn't believe him that he hadn't killed his wife. Setting aside whatever other evidence they might have against him, it was a stretch to think he hadn't heard what was happening upstairs. But he had said *passed out* rather than *asleep*. "Were you drunk?"

"Yeah."

No more jokes from him at least. "Do you remember anything about that night?"

He made a negative grunt.

Even though Elise insisted he was innocent, I still had to ask him. Because people did things all the time when they were drunk that they didn't remember the next day. "You're sure you didn't hurt your wife while you were drunk?"

"Now you sound like the police."

That most definitely wasn't an answer. For a second, I thought he might hang up on me. "I have to know. I can't defend you if you lie to me."

"Yeah, I'm sure I didn't kill my wife."

All the humor was definitely gone from his voice. It was all snark now. Why in the world would Elise care what happened to this jerk? Since she hadn't botched his investigation, she must have known his wife. I could see that. I'd want to be sure the right person went to prison for murdering a friend, even if that meant I had to help a jerk be acquitted of the crime in the process.

And because this was important to Elise, it was important to me. If I didn't love her so much, I'd hang up on this man and never look back.

"Okay. Since you didn't kill your wife, can you think of anyone who might have wanted to hurt her?"

"The prosecution won't ask that when I'm on the stand."

I kicked a stone off the trail. Never a straightforward response, it seemed. Elise should have given me the whole box of popsicles. I was going to need the sugar.

Despite his claim that he hadn't killed his wife, I wasn't convinced. Wouldn't an innocent person be more forthcoming? "If you're innocent, one of the best defenses we can build is to show that other people had motive and opportunity. It helps create doubt in the mind of the jury."

"Everyone likes..."

His voice cracked, and I felt it like someone stepped on my heart. It was easy to dislike him when I thought he might be guilty. When he showed a moment of genuine love for his wife, it was hard to think he might have killed her and even harder to push him for answers.

Of course, I might simply be gullible. Just because I'd never met anyone who could fake a crack in their voice didn't mean it couldn't be done. Actors could do it.

"Everyone liked Sandra. She always wanted to help people. She volunteered at her sister's business all the time to help them out, and she was worried out of her mind when our neighbor Ken was sick. She even took him chicken soup."

"Even nice people have flaws and enemies."

"Her only flaw was that she didn't like kids. I wanted more, and she refused."

I mentally logged the fact that he had children. We could counteract his sarcastic nature with the family man image if we had to.

But we were going to be in real trouble if I couldn't find another person who might have wanted her dead. Juries wouldn't believe *random home invasion* or *silent serial killer* when Dean looked like such a lock for the murderer. I'd dig deeper into who might have had a grudge against her or who might have wanted to hurt her to get back at Dean. All of that, though, would have to wait until I was officially on the case.

"Elise wants me to represent you." Hopefully he'd hear the unspoken *and I'm willing to do it for her sake*. "If you agree, I'll contact the prosecuting attorney and request the discovery package so I can bring myself up to speed on your case."

"What's the catch?"

I let out a silent scream. Toby twisted back to look at me. I patted him on the head. The poor boy should be off playing with Velma, and instead he felt the need to stay and comfort me.

"If you call the need to pay your bills a catch, then that's the catch."

Elise or no Elise, this guy needed to pay, if for nothing else than the pain and suffering I was certain he was going to cause me.

"Money's no problem."

He hadn't even asked how much. Was he independently wealthy or planning to stiff me?

I swallowed down a grumble-sigh. No way to tell which it might be ahead of time. "We'll have to meet to talk about your defense once I've had a chance to go over the evidence, but that's all I need from you for now."

I confirmed his phone number before disconnecting. Given his confrontational attitude, I passed on asking for the name and number of his previous lawyer. I texted Elise instead. She'd known enough about this case that it was worth a shot. His last lawyer didn't need to give me anything, but I was hoping he would fill me in on any work they'd already done on the case as a professional courtesy.

I threw a ball for Velma while I waited. It was the kind that was as big around as my head and had a handle on it. She loved the added challenge of chasing it through the trees. I didn't like the added challenge of trying not to hit a tree and have the ball rebound into my face, but Velma had so much energy that we had to burn it off somehow. Thankfully, Mandy seemed to have finally figured out how not to lose Velma when she walked the dogs. I was glad for the extra legs to take them out for some exercise, especially on days when I was busy.

Toby opted to sit next to me while Velma ran around, his tongue lolling out of one side of his mouth. I didn't often remember that he was already heading into his senior years, but the hot weather made it more evident than even his winter limp.

A text buzzed in my pocket. Elise had sent me the name and number of the former lawyer.

I heaved the ball for Velma again and dialed while she galloped after it. The receptionist put me through.

"Anderson Taylor," a man's voice answered.

Voices were never a good indicator of age, but if I had to guess, I would have said the man who belonged to it was early to mid-forties.

"This is Nicole Fitzhenry-Dawes. I've been retained as defense counsel for your former client..."

Whose last name I didn't know. I slapped my forehead with my free hand. He'd introduced himself only as Dean, and I'd never asked. I was going to sound like a complete idiot when I had to admit I didn't know his full name. What kind of self-respecting lawyer took on a case without even knowing her client's name?

The best I could hope for was that he only had one client with the name Dean. Assuming that was his first name. Maybe it was his last name.

Oi, I was an idiot sometimes.

"Your client who was accused of suffocating his wife. Dean."

Lame, Nicole. Completely lame.

"Anyway, I was hoping you'd be willing to pass along anything you'd already dug up that could help in his defense."

Velma dropped her ball at my feet and cocked her head as if to say *nice save*. Hopefully it's sounded like I figured he'd know which case I meant.

"Happy to, but I should tell you there isn't much. I wasn't on the case long."

A hint of hesitancy entered his voice near the end. I didn't think it was because he didn't want to share, but I couldn't think of anything else that would cause it, either.

"Fitzhenry-Dawes?" he said. "You're not related to Edward Dawes, are you?"

I cringed. Maybe that was it. My parents tended to be polarizing even within their profession. Other lawyers either looked up to them or despised them. Perhaps Anderson Taylor fell into the latter camp. But I wasn't going to lie. My parents were my parents, for better or for worse.

"My dad, yes."

"I didn't know his firm practiced this far north. You *are* with your dad's firm, aren't you?"

I might soon be again, but for now I wasn't. Meaning I was kind of in no man's land for an answer. "I'm soloing this one as a favor for a friend."

He umm-humm'ed. "We analyzed case studies from some of your dad's trials when I was in law school. He's a beast in the court-room. If lawyers had fan clubs, I'd be president of his."

I chuckled. All other things aside, it was nice to hear my dad spoken of in admiring terms.

But it raised other questions. Why the hesitant tone to his voice earlier, and why had he backed out of this case? If my dad was his idol, he wouldn't have dropped a client because he felt he couldn't win. Based on what Dean said earlier, it didn't sound like payment was the issue, either.

"What address do you want me to courier the package to?" Anderson Taylor was asking. "I'll send it out today."

I gave him my address, and the silence stretched a beat like he was trying to decide whether or not to say something else before signing off.

The skin on my arms felt tingly, like the hairs were deciding to stand on end or not.

"Listen," he said. "I wasn't going to say anything, but knowing you're Edward Dawes' daughter, I won't feel right if I don't. Part of your dad's reputation is that he pushes the lines but never crosses them."

The hairs on my arms made their decision. The ones on the back of my neck rose as well. With an intro like that, I had no doubt I wasn't going to like what came next.

"I don't know what Dean told you about why I chose not to continue representing him."

It was a statement, but it ended on a question mark, like he wanted me to tell him but didn't want to ask. "I was told you thought he was guilty, and you figured you couldn't win the case."

A huff of air. "I'm pretty sure he is guilty, but so are a lot of my clients. That's not why I quit. He wanted me to tamper with the jury after selection. Even though I told him flat-out I wouldn't do it, I didn't want to risk it. Like your dad always says, reputation and image are everything."

Anderson Taylor really *had* studied my dad.

Part of my mind knew I'd focused on that element because I didn't want to face the meat of his pronouncement.

I'd taken on a client who was likely a liar and a murder, and willing to do anything to get away with it.

By the time the dogs and I returned to the house, I still felt like molten rocks were rolling around in my stomach. What had Elise gotten me into?

I yanked my phone from my pocket. *We need to talk without the kids around,* I texted her.

I'm heading to the park with the kids, she texted back almost immediately. *We could talk privately while they play.*

She responded so quickly that it felt like she must have been waiting to hear more from me. She wasn't going to like what I had to say.

I made it to the park in ten minutes. I hadn't had to ask Elise which one. I'd gone with Elise and the kids a couple of times already this summer. Tourists took their kids to the park by the lake with the giant, flashy splash pad and the children's-sized rock climbing wall. Locals took their kids to the smaller, quieter park on the other side of town. It was filled with the more traditional swing sets, slides, and jungle gym.

Elise's kids weren't the only ones on the playground equipment when I arrived, but Elise had chosen a bench on the opposite side of the equipment from the other parents. No one tended to sit on this side if there was free space on the other side because these benches were older and creaked like they might collapse underneath you when you sat.

I eased carefully down next to Elise.

She kept her eyes on the playground equipment like she was worried about one of the kids disappearing. "Did you and Dean come to an agreement?"

She must have meant it to sound casual, but her slightly higher pitch gave her away.

I angled on the bench as far as I could to face her. "His last lawyer quit because Dean asked him to tamper with the jury. That's jail time and massive fines, Elise. Not only does this guy look guilty, but it puts my professional and personal life on the line if he tries to manipulate the jury on his own and I'm implicated in it."

My voice rose in volume unintentionally. Just saying what the repercussions could be made my stomach lurch.

Elise went vampire-pale. "I didn't know."

As much as my parents wanted me back practicing the law, I could almost hear my mom's voice in my head telling me to drop this case. One paycheck wasn't worth your entire career. Hopefully Elise would see logic and tell me it was okay to walk away from this, or she'd have some compelling reason she believed Dean was innocent and worth defending.

"I never thought you did know," I said. She needed to understand that I believed in her and her motives. Whatever they were, they had to be pure.

"I still need your help."

Cross logic off the list. That left a compelling reason. "And I need a good reason to take the risk. What's going on? Who is this guy to you?"

She pressed two fingers into the space between her eyes. "My ex-husband."

The words were almost inaudible, but they stung like a slap.

While Elise was pregnant with her five-year-old, Cameron, her husband was out at strip clubs and eventually ran off with one of the dancers. They divorced when Cameron was only a few months old. Elise had full custody, and her ex had visitation rights. His name was never mentioned among the Cavanaughs. The only reason Elise hadn't gone back to her maiden name was because she wanted to keep the same last name as her children.

A few years later, her ex-husband re-married. No one had mentioned whether it was the dancer he left Elise for or if he'd found someone else. Not that it really mattered. Whoever he'd married was dead now, and he was no less a jerk.

I planted my elbows on my knees and buried my face in my hands. "You should have told me from the start. The whole Cavanaugh family is going to hate me for even considering defending him. Why do you even want me to?"

"Aunt Nikki!" Arielle called from somewhere in front of me. "Watch me slide!"

I lifted my head and waved at her so she'd know I was paying attention. She sprinted to the ladder, scurried up, and went down with her arms in the air.

Once she hit the ground, I glanced at Elise. She wore a translucent smile.

"They're why. All last year, Arielle came home from school crying at least once a week because she had a girl in her class who teased her about not having a dad. And Cameron counts down the days when he knows his dad's going to visit. What'll it do to them if Dean goes to prison? They shouldn't suffer because I picked a crappy dad for them."

I knew the effect a child's relationship with their father—and their father's reputation—could have on them well into adulthood. Maybe better than anyone, I understood.

But if he'd done what he was accused of, he deserved to go to prison. "If he's guilty—"

"I know." She ran both hands over her hair. "I know you won't defend him if he really did this. You shouldn't. I don't want the kids around a murderer, either. But I don't think he did."

She had no idea how much I wanted that to be true. I wanted it to be true almost as much as I believed it wasn't. "I haven't seen the evidence yet, but from what Dean told me, this would be a hard one for anyone to win, even my parents."

"What's his motive?" Elise asked. For a second, she sounded like a police officer again, rather than like a woman under too much stress.

If it made her feel better, we'd play it like two professionals running down a case, as if this wasn't personal and important. "A lot of cases where one spouse kills another are domestic violence taken to the extreme."

"Exactly." Elise's posture straightened. "Dean's not violent. Even during our worst fights, he never so much as threatened to hit me."

"That might have been because you're a cop. He knew you could defend yourself, and he knew you wouldn't let him get away with it."

"We could easily prove I wasn't the exception by calling his other girlfriends as witnesses."

I let the *we* slide for now. I'd brainstorm with Elise right now because I needed to decide if I took this case or not. If I did, she'd need to back off and let me handle it. She couldn't put her career in further jeopardy.

I made a mental note to ask Dean for the names of his previous girlfriends.

Elise's lips drew into an *I'm right, and I'm not backing down* line. "Once we can show that he wasn't the kind of man who beat his partners, the prosecution doesn't have motive. He's already shown he has no problem leaving wives if he wants out. He didn't have to kill her for that reason, either."

"No prenup that you know of?"

"No money that I know of. Sandra worked at a gas station, and Dean hasn't been consistent about helping with the kids' expenses. He's been better the past year, but he hasn't made extravagant purchases for them or anything."

That didn't match with Dean's nonchalance about paying me. Of course, based on what I knew now, he probably planned to never pay me.

I'd still want to check that Sandra wasn't some sort of closet heiress. Or that they hadn't come into any money post-marriage through a lottery win or gambling. Depending on how much cash a windfall like that garnered them, he might have been willing to kill to keep all of it rather than lose half in a divorce. The prosecution would have already subpoenaed their bank records, though, so all of that should be in the discovery package.

Arielle and Cameron were coming across the grass toward us, looking like they were both ready for a nap.

"Please," Elise said quietly. "For them. They love their dad, and for how much of a crappy husband he was, he loves them, too."

I bit back a sigh. Maybe my parents were right. Maybe I did have *Easy Mark* tattooed on my forehead. Though they seemed to think that less these days than they had in the past. Recently, they'd shown more confidence in me. I needed to have confidence in myself too. I had to trust that I could make good decisions, and that I could find a way to rectify things if I made a bad one.

"I'll look into the bank records and talk to a couple of his previous girlfriends. If I come up empty on a motive, then I'll give him the benefit of the doubt that he's innocent, and I'll take the case."

The material Anderson couriered to me arrived the next morning, before I'd finished my first cup of coffee. If he was this on top of everything, he might manage to become the northern version of my dad.

I ripped open the package. It included the prosecution's evidence against Dean and a list of former girlfriends, which made me think he'd been building a defense against domestic violence as well.

I'd put in a call to the prosecutor's office after my talk with Elise, and they were sending me a discovery package anyway, but having Anderson's copy would help me get started right away.

He'd attached a handwritten note. *If there's anything else I can do, give me a call.*

The number underneath had to be his cell. It didn't match the number I'd called yesterday.

I put the number into my phone and texted him a thank you.

Just as I hit Send, a text came in from Russ. *Hope you remember our meeting this afternoon.*

I rubbed my temples and glanced over at the coffee pot. I usually limited myself to two cups in the morning, but today might end up being a three-cup kind of day. My to-do list had already been long between following up on Dean's case and planning Stacey's rapidly approaching baby shower. I hadn't forgotten the meeting with Russ as much as I hadn't wanted to remember. Discussing orders and purchases and the health of the maple bush was better than sleeping pills.

Can we postpone? I texted back.

Really need to discuss Stacey, he wrote.

I rubbed my eyes, but I hadn't misread his message. What did we need to discuss about Stacey? As far as I knew, she'd been working miracles with our accounting and organization. Hopefully Russ simply wanted to figure out what we were going to do when she needed time off after her baby was born. I might melt down if he wanted to fire her. All the work she'd been doing would land back on my desk.

Or what if Stacey had told him she didn't want to stay after her baby was born? Originally she'd asked for a job at Sugarwood because she didn't want to work around the fumes at her dad's car repair shop while she was pregnant. She might have handed in her resignation now that fumes soon wouldn't be a problem.

The knot that formed in my throat was so big I couldn't even swallow a sip of coffee around it. I wouldn't be able to concentrate as well as I should on Dean's case if I was wondering what Russ needed to say regarding Stacey.

I punched half his number into my phone. It rang before I could finish.

I hit the Answer icon. "Russ?"

"Sorry to disappoint," Anderson's voice said from my phone. "Is Russ your boyfriend?"

It wouldn't be the largest age gap between a couple, but the thought of dating Russ was about as appealing as the thought of kissing my cousin. If I had a cousin. Besides, I wouldn't have traded Mark for anyone, not even Russ.

I grinned even though Anderson couldn't see me. "Russ is my business partner."

"Am I interrupting something, then? It sounded like you were expecting a call from him."

I definitely didn't want to go into complicated Sugarwood business with a near stranger. "Nothing that can't wait."

"Good." His voice sounded like he was smiling as well. "I thought I'd call to make sure you got all the material I sent."

"I texted you. I guess it didn't go through. It wouldn't be the first time. I live in Fair Haven. It'd be easier to find the Holy Grail than a stable cell phone signal here."

Anderson chuckled. "I'll remember that. Did you want me to walk you through the high points?"

The quicker I got up to speed, the better. "Please."

"Based on the grocery store receipt in the bag on the kitchen counter, they know the victim was still alive at 9:00 pm."

I flipped past the first few pages of written material until I came to the crime scene photos. The bag lying on the counter was the reusable kind. "They confirmed with the clerk that she was the one buying the groceries, not Dean?"

"Yup. The night clerk ID'd her from a photo, and she'd left food out on the counter that spoiled by the time the police arrived in the morning. It couldn't have been out any longer or someone would have thrown it away. The receipt in the bag also came from the same store that the bag used to suffocate her was from, and the items on it matched the ones out on the counter."

Those photos would be further back, but I didn't need to see them at the moment. The last thing my pride needed was to get woozy while talking to another lawyer.

Something niggled at the back of my mind. "She was suffocated with a plastic bag?"

"The photos should be in there."

"I see them now," I lied. "Most people either use all plastic or all reusable. It's strange to mix and match, so where'd the plastic bag come from?"

"It might have been from a different trip, or she could have purchased too much to fit in the reusable bags she brought. But that's a nice start to reasonable doubt."

There was real admiration in his voice. He was probably thinking about how I took after my dad. In laying the groundwork, maybe I did. I'd always been good at putting the puzzle pieces together. It was in the courtroom where it all fell apart.

I turned to another photo. It was of a beige carpet with mud stains that looked like they might be footprints across it. Because of the way they were smeared, it'd be impossible for the police to have gotten a boot print or even a shoe size from them. "Did they test the dirt on the bedroom carpet yet?"

"They did, and they took samples from the boots Dean still had on when they brought him in, and from the other sets in the closet. The results were inconclusive. There wasn't anything special in the mud, so it could have come from him or anyone else who walked through their neighborhood. Which, of course, would be anyone who entered their house."

I grabbed a pen and jotted notes. "Did you look into the weather that day?"

"Rain until late evening."

Mud dried fairly quickly, so whoever had killed her hadn't been in the house long before it happened. "Anything else I should know heading in?"

"Like I said, I really hadn't gotten far. I got a list of Dean's former lovers to try to establish that he wasn't violent with his romantic partners the way the prosecution wants to claim, but I'd only spoken to one so far. My notes are in there, but she said he never hurt her."

A strange knot formed in my chest. Elise might be right about Dean's innocence after all. "I talked to his ex-wife already, and she said the same."

I glanced through the other photos, but it seemed like we had all the key points except for one. "Dean said the person who killed his wife duct taped the bag on. Did they find the rest of the roll of duct tape?"

"No, but if I were the prosecution, I'd argue that he had time to get rid of it. According to the medical examiner's report, the latest her TOD window could stretch was 2:00 am, and that's a long shot. They figure it was closer to 11:00 pm, shortly after she arrived home."

If that was the case, why did Dean leave her body in the bedroom rather than disposing of her along with the duct tape while it was still dark out? "Who called it in?"

"Her sister. She got worried when Sandra wasn't answering her cell the next morning, and she came over. She says she walked past Dean, asleep on the couch, and found her sister's body in the bedroom. She assumed he'd done it, locked the bedroom door, and called the police."

I added Sandra's sister to the list of people I needed to talk to, along with Dean's former romantic partners.

Stress pooled above my eyes, and I kneaded my fingers into the spot. Dean's lack of a violent past and the missing duct tape alone wouldn't be enough to create reasonable doubt for a jury, but they were for me because of what was at stake for Arielle and Cameron.

"Thanks for bringing me up to speed," I said.

"Call me any time," Anderson said. "It's fun working with a Fitzhenry-Dawes."

I couldn't help myself. The little imp inside me grabbed hold of the reins controlling my mouth. "My dad's not always right, you know. As excellent a lawyer as he is, sometimes people are innocent."

"Yeah, sometimes they are." There was a short pause. "But the guilty ones usually pay better."

I was still laughing as we disconnected. It died quickly.

My next step in the case would be visiting the murder scene myself to see if I could poke any more holes in the case. But first, I needed to talk to Russ "about Stacey."

"lease tell me you don't want to fire Stacey," I blurted as soon as I was through the door of Russ' office.

His caterpillar like eyebrows drew down over his eyes. "Why would I want to fire Stacey?"

I flopped into the chair across from him. "Then is she wanting to quit after the baby's born?"

Russ slowly shook his head. "This is why I tell you not to listen to the rumor mill. It never does no one no good."

I hadn't realized people had been suggesting the same things as I'd been thinking, but it didn't surprise me. "Those ideas are all mine. I started to worry when you said we needed to talk about Stacey."

Russ brought a hand up to his head and ruffled his thinning hair. My heart tried to scramble up into my throat.

He hadn't called me here to talk about either of those things, but he was still nervous about something. Maybe Stacey needed a raise now that she'd be a single mom. That wouldn't be so bad. We could afford to raise her salary.

"It's not even so much about Stacey as it is about you and me and Sugarwood," Russ said.

I clenched my hands around the arms of the chair, bracing myself. That didn't sound like Stacey asked for a raise, either.

If he hadn't said it was about Stacey, I would have thought he wanted out of the partnership. But that couldn't be it. Stacey was too young to have enough money to buy him out.

The only thing I could think to say was, "Okay."

Russ had both his hands in his hair now. When he laid them back on the desk, his hair stayed spiked out like a mad scientist.

"Thing is, I'm getting old. In another five or ten years, I'm gonna wanna retire. With you and Mark talking about moving to DC, where does that leave Sugarwood?"

I saw where he was going, but it didn't make me feel any better. I'd been told so many times that Sugarwood needed to be owned and run by someone who was here and involved and understood the town and what Sugarwood meant to the community. I might as well tack a scarlet T for traitor on my chest.

And I still didn't see how it applied to Stacey.

"Mark and I aren't sure we're moving yet. We still might stay in Fair Haven."

We'd been putting off having *the talk* about it, but we only had a few weeks left until the deadline they'd given Mark for his decision, and I had a Skype interview with the prosecutor's office in a couple of days. They wouldn't want to wait long for an answer if they offered me the position.

While we could always move back if we absolutely hated it in DC, it wouldn't be the same. Mark probably wouldn't be able to step back into his job as county medical examiner, and Sugarwood would have been restructured to run without my direct participation. If we moved, we'd have to sell Mark's house and rent mine out since we couldn't sever it from the rest of Sugarwood.

Russ wagged his head. "Even if you stay, are you gonna want to make Sugarwood your full-time career?"

That was, as my grandma would have said, the sticky wicket. Move to DC or stay in Fair Haven, I still needed to decide what to do career-wise.

What I'd learned about myself since coming to Fair Haven was that—all things being equal—I loved being a lawyer. I loved helping clients. I loved solving puzzles. If I could stick to defending innocent people and somehow channel my parents' skills in the courtroom, I'd be content with my job for the rest of my life. I'd be happy working for the prosecution as well, minus the whole speaking-in-front-of-people thing. Thinking about it, I understood what the person who came in fourth at the Olympics must feel like. It was the thing I loved doing, but I fell shy of being good enough.

"I don't think your Uncle Stan left you this place to tie you into another person's dream for you," Russ was saying.

I forced myself to focus back on him. "Why do you think he left it to me?"

"I think he wanted to make sure you had options. He knew I'd be here to run the business one way or another. 'Sides, he loved you a lot more than he loved this place."

Pressure that felt a lot like tears built behind my eyes. I brushed a hand over my face.

Why Russ brought Stacey into this finally made sense. "You want to apprentice Stacey to take over for you when you retire."

Russ nodded. "Sort of like an assistant manager for now. She already handles the books and record-keeping better than I ever did, and she seems to love the place."

She loved fixing cars too, though. "I'm good with offering her the opportunity." I shot him a sidelong glance. "I still want to be able to get in the way around here anytime I please, though, especially when the sap starts to run."

Russ laughed in that way that always reminded me of Santa Claus. It came from deep in his gut and shook his whole body. "I expect you to make a nuisance of yourself."

His smile sagged a little at the edges, probably with thoughts of Noah. Having Stacey here meant Russ would get to see Noah's son or daughter grow up first-hand. He'd lost a lot in the short time I'd known him, and he deserved to have something good in return.

He dropped his gaze to the papers on his desk, examining them like they were essential...except they were upside down.

"We should probably offer her a raise too," he said, flipping through the papers as if his request was an afterthought.

It wasn't. Russ always thought about others. I don't know why he felt he needed to hide it. "Let me know what you think we can manage."

Russ gave me a thumbs up.

I left his office, but I headed out into the bush instead of going straight back to my house. The wind rustling the leaves overhead sounded almost like water lapping at the shoreline, and three distinct bird calls echoed above it all. Maybe if we stayed here, I'd even learn what birds they belonged to.

Deep inside, I'd known for a while that I wasn't cut out to run Sugarwood the way Russ did or the way my Uncle Stan must have. It still stung a little to be so easily replaced. Though it probably said something that it didn't sting as much as it should have.

And, as Russ had said, giving me the opportunity to choose that for myself was probably what my Uncle Stan wanted. Besides, stepping back from the roles I'd taken at Sugarwood and allowing Stacey to fill them didn't mean Sugarwood wasn't still fifty-one percent mine. I could still help during the busy maple season and walk the trails and care about the people.

The real problem was how I could be a lawyer when there were a few key parts that I didn't do well.

Before I could contemplate that, however, I still needed to break the news to Mark that I'd agreed to take the case.

***

The last reaction I'd expected from Mark when I filled him in was laughter. It took me a minute to figure out he thought I was joking.

"Don't try to play that one on Elise," he said. "I don't think she'd appreciate it."

My throat tickled enough that I almost took a page from Erik's book and cleared it. "I'm serious. Elise is the one who asked me to represent him."

A beat of silence. "This isn't funny anymore." His tone of voice said *Please tell me you're still kidding.*

I wished I could. "It wasn't funny for me even from the start. Think about it. How would I know his name if this wasn't for real?"

Another long silence. When I first called him, I could hear him opening and closing drawers in the background. Now even his surroundings were vacant.

"Elise asked you to do this?"

"I wouldn't have agreed if she hadn't." I told him what she'd told me about the kids.

"I know you wouldn't have." The sound of a mouse clicking and him typing on the keyboard started up. "The murder must have happened while we were in DC. I'd have been the ME called to the scene otherwise. I'd have had to decline due to possible conflict of interest, but at least we'd have known about it."

Elise shouldn't have had to face this alone. Not for months. Not even for a day. "She's mostly embarrassed right now. She was worried about the family learning about it. I'm hoping that'll wear off."

"No one liked Dean, but the more we opposed him, the more she defended him. I wish we hadn't pushed her so hard. Maybe she wouldn't have married him."

An image of Elise and the way she looked when she was with her children jumped into my mind. "Maybe, but then we all wouldn't have Arielle and Cameron. Everything happens for a reason, right?"

His mumbled assent still sounded half-hearted. "When you get the autopsy report, let me know. I'll go over it with you. As much as I wouldn't mind seeing Dean in prison, I want to do something to show Elise that we're behind her no matter what."

I'd have kissed him if we were in the same room.

"But Nikki?"

The heavy tone in his voice sent a shiver down my spine, and not the good kind.

"Be careful. Dean's a master manipulator and a user. He'll do whatever it takes to get what he wants, and he won't care who he hurts to do it."

*T*he next morning, I drove half an hour to the town where Dean lived. Once I realized he didn't live in Fair Haven, it made a lot more sense that Erik didn't know Elise's ex had been arrested and that she'd been suspended for poking around in the case. The murder wasn't even in the jurisdiction of the Fair Haven police.

Dean's lawn was a little too long, like he stretched the time between cuttings as far as he could get away with. The front porch looked like it'd been white at one point, but the paint had mostly peeled away, leaving it looking like it had a bad case of eczema.

The car in the driveway, however, was brand-new. I'd seen the same model last week when Mark and I casually walked through a lot and chatted with a salesman. My car had been in enough accidents that I wanted to replace it before winter.

I peeked in the window on my way by. Dean's car had leather

seats and a sunroof. Those only came in the top-of-the-line package. The floor of the car was clean, making me think he hadn't owned it long.

While that was a good sign for me when it came to him being able to pay my fees, it was a bad sign in terms of the case. I'd have to check whether Dean had a large life insurance policy on Sandra. If he'd gotten himself into debt, he might have killed her for the life insurance. Or, at least, that's what the prosecution would argue if I destroyed their *wife abuser* motive.

The porch wobbled underneath my feet as I climbed the stairs. The doorbell didn't seem to be in working order, so I knocked.

The man who answered the door was nothing like what Dean was supposed to be. He was supposed to be a former jock who was now fat and balding, his sexy voice the only thing remaining of his former glory.

The glory of the man who answered the door was anything but former.

To make it even worse, his chest was bare.

Heat crept up into my ears, and I averted my eyes. It was no wonder Elise married him. She'd probably still been young enough that she didn't realize good looks didn't make a good man.

Out of the corner of my eye, I caught his I-know-I'm-good-looking grin. He didn't make a move to put on the t-shirt in his hand.

He leaned casually against the doorway. "How can I be of service, darlin'?"

The way he said it turned my stomach. Whatever little bit of power his appearance had given him faded away. In the back of my head, I could almost hear my dad telling me that if we could get him to keep his mouth shut in court, his appearance would work in our favor. No one expected handsome people to be killers.

But that was something we'd deal with once we finally got to court. Right now, I had to deal with the fact that he apparently had the memory of a goldfish and forgot our appointment. "I'm your lawyer."

I kept my voice deadpan. Hopefully he'd feel at least a little bit of shame.

His gaze moved slowly down me in a way that made me wish I'd worn a muumuu instead of the tailored blouse and skirt I'd chosen because I wanted to look professional.

He stepped out of the doorway, but still made no move to dress himself. I spelled Arielle and Cameron's names slowly in my head. Maybe if I focused on them, I wouldn't be so tempted to give their dad a black eye.

The door swooshed shut behind me, and big hands grabbed my waist. Tight.

My heartbeat kicked up into my throat, and I couldn't breathe.

I tried to pull away from his touch, but he closed his grip.

"Stop it. What do you think you're doing?" My voice came out a lot more freaked-out than I'd intended.

His lips hit my neck with wet kisses. "I prefer naughty nurses," he said, "but a naughty lawyer fits the situation better. You'll have to tell me who to thank when we're done."

Calm washed over my brain, and I stopped squirming even

though his lips kept moving over my neck like a slug leaving a trail of goo.

The man was an idiot, with the self-control of a cat in heat, but thankfully, it seemed he wasn't a predator. He really thought I was a call girl sent by one of his skeezee friends.

"You can thank your ex-wife." I managed to bring my voice into a passable imitation of my mom now that I wasn't panicking. "And if you don't take your mouth off me, I'm going to place a knee on you in a spot you won't enjoy."

He stilled and cursed none too gently. "You're actually my lawyer."

"That depends on how quickly you take your hands off me and put your shirt on."

He jerked away, and I turned around. His head was already halfway through his shirt.

"You don't look like a lawyer." His voice came out muffled. He yanked his shirt down into place. "If Elise wasn't the one who found you, I'd think you won cases by doing special favors for the judge." He winked. "Not that I'd have a problem with that as long as you get me off."

Images of me kneeing him in the groin anyway danced in my vision, nearly blinding me.

Arielle and Cameron. I was doing this for Arielle and Cameron. Though, honestly, they might be better off if this guy was in prison.

I clenched my teeth, then forced my jaw to relax. The worst thing I could do was let him know he was getting to me. It was like how the bullies in school got worse the more they upset you.

I would not be bullied. We clearly needed to establish who was in charge here and what the ground rules would be.

"As long as you stand accused of your wife's murder, you're not allowed to go to any strip clubs, hire any prostitutes, or accept any *gifts* from your friends that show up at your door. You're not even allowed to date. Your wife just died. You want any chance of being acquitted of her murder, you need to at least act like you're a grieving husband."

His face twisted up like he was going to cuss me out and kick me out of the house. Instead, he fisted his hands. "I guess I don't have much choice. Elise said I had to listen to you, 'cause if I end up in prison for this, she won't bring the kids to visit."

An emotion rippled across his face that I couldn't quite catch. It almost looked like...fear? Regret?

Even the worst examples of humanity loved someone. For Dean, it seemed like that some was two someones—Arielle and Cameron.

Oddly enough, his motivation was the same as mine. Perhaps this would all be easier if we established some common ground.

"Arielle and Cameron are why I agreed to represent you."

"What are my kids to you?" He crossed his arms over his chest, making his biceps into chiseled bars. "Elise switch teams or something?"

Lord give me patience. I held up my left hand, back facing him so my engagement ring came into view. "I'm a few months away from becoming a Cavanaugh."

"Bobby?"

"Mark."

His arms loosened slightly. "I always liked Mark. It was a shame about his first wife."

Everybody liked Mark, but it softened me a bit to Dean. If he'd said something snide about Mark, I might have dropped him as a client regardless of the other factors.

I checked the buttons on my blouse. Thankfully they'd survived his manhandling, and we shouldn't have a repeat. "We're all working toward the same goal, so try to cooperate with me. When I tell you to do something, it's for the good of your case."

He gave a half nod.

Since that was probably as close to agreement as I was going to get, it was time to move on to what I'd come here for. "One of the strongest pieces of the prosecution's case against you is that you were apparently in the house during the time of death window. I'd like you to show me around outside. I need to see if I can argue that the killer could have gotten in another way."

He led me into the living room. The couch sat in the middle of the room, the TV up against the wall in front of it. Behind the couch were the stairs. The house wasn't large.

I could see why it looked condemning to the police. "Is that the only way upstairs?"

The cockiness drained from his stance, and he suddenly looked more like a normal man than an underwear model. "Yeah. Whether they came in the front or the back door, they'd have had to climb those stairs." He pointed to the couch. "But in my defense, I was wasted. I wouldn't have heard a car crash into the house."

That wasn't much of a defense. We couldn't prove it. It was easy for him to claim he'd been too drunk to hear an intruder, but without evidence, it wouldn't stand up in court. It also wouldn't endear him to the jury any. "Do you have receipts from whatever bar you were at? If we could show how much you had to drink, I might be able to use that. Or do you remember what taxi service you used to bring you home?"

If he'd driven himself home drunk, we'd have zero chance in court. Juries, in my experience, had very little patience for drunk drivers.

He shook his head. "I was drinking with a buddy at his house, and he brought me home."

"What time?"

"Around 10:00 or 10:30 I think. I don't remember exactly. I'd planned to come home and have a late supper with Sandra, but then she wasn't downstairs when I came in. I figured she was already asleep."

Well, that was just great. "How did you get your car back?"

The look he gave me said he'd been lying about the friend driving him home.

I headed toward the back of the house. "Why don't you show me around the outside?"

Dean's backyard wasn't much tidier than his front. A two-foot wide swath of plants that had to be nearly four feet tall grew along the back fence. They'd bloomed in a showy presentation of purple flowers that looked like little hoods.

I didn't recognize them, but they were planted among holly-hocks, clematis, and some sort of daisy. At least, I thought they were hollyhocks and clematis. This had been my first summer with gardens to tend, and I'd basically tried to keep up with what my

Uncle Stan planted the year before. I'd been slowly identifying the varieties in his gardens, so I could figure out how best not to kill them. I was certain the little white flowers with yellow centers in Sandra's garden were daisies, at least. I used to buy bouquets of daisies for my apartment back in DC.

The hollyhocks and purple flowers matched the ones that were in a tall vase on the kitchen counter in the crime scene photos. Sandra must have spent some of her last hours cutting blooms.

I gestured toward the garden. "Did Sandra like to garden?"

Dean hardly glanced in the direction I indicated. "Not really. Her sister was the one who liked plants. Nadine might have helped Sandra plant those, or they might have been here when we moved in. I can't remember."

Dean was shaping up to be the most difficult client I'd ever dealt with, and that was saying something, considering my parents' stable of clients. "Where's the bedroom window?"

Dean led me around the side of the house.

Just when I thought it couldn't get any worse, it did.

The side of the house practically butted up against the fence. I could walk through the space, but anyone with wider shoulders or hips wouldn't have been able to. The neighbor's house on the other side of the fence seemed equally close. If the fence wasn't there, I could have stretched out my arms and touched both houses at once. The placement of the windows on the neighbor's house meant they'd have had a good view of anyone trying—I couldn't see them succeeding—to set up a ladder and climb into the bedroom window of Sandra and Dean's house.

But their bedroom probably wasn't the only room on the second floor. The killer hadn't necessarily needed to come directly into the bedroom. Maybe he'd come into the bathroom or another bedroom window.

I blew out a puff of air. "Maybe we ought to look at the other windows."

I continued on to the front of the house. It would have been dark out when Sandra died, so theoretically, the killer could have come in through one of the windows above the porch. They'd have even had an easier time because of the porch roof.

I took out my phone and made notes to interview the neighbor across the street. The police should have already done so, but if they were sure Dean was their guy, they might have skipped a step. I also wrote down all the other items I'd been keeping on my mental list. I'd been spoiled working for my parents. I'd always been part of a team. On this case, anything I wanted done, I'd have to do myself. The police certainly weren't going to help.

"The screens don't come out," Dean said.

I glanced up. "The screens don't come out of what?"

"The windows on the front. It's an old house, and the screens on the front windows are in a metal frame. He'd have had to cut the screens."

And clearly the screens weren't cut. The killer hadn't gone in those windows, either.

We walked the rest of the house, though by the end, it felt like I shouldn't have bothered. The windows in the bathroom were too small for anyone other than a child to climb through, and the windows on the back that were large enough were also painted shut.

"Old house," Dean said with a shrug.

How he could be so nonchalant was beyond me. What we'd managed to prove was the killer had walked right past him and killed his wife while he was downstairs.

Or he was the killer after all.

a tension headache bloomed in a line across my forehead. "You could have told me from the start that the killer couldn't have gotten in through a window."

"You're the boss. I'm supposed to follow orders. You wanted to see the windows."

I decided to ignore the touch of snark in his words. If a bit of wasted time was the price for him to do what he was told as a client, I'd pay it. "I need to see the bedroom next."

Dean walked me to the bottom of the stairs. "It's the first door, but you can look in the others if you need to. We use the second bedroom to store stuff."

That sounded like… "You're not coming up with me."

He shook his head. His expression had gone flat, and for the first time, I noticed fine wrinkles starting in his forehead. "I haven't been up there since it happened. There's a second toilet down here, and I shower at the gym."

He must also be sleeping on the couch. All my desire to hit him with something heavy faded. Maybe he had loved his wife after all. Maybe he hadn't killed her. Not everyone knew how to deal with grief in a healthy way. Russ was a prime example. He hadn't wanted to talk about the loss of my Uncle Stan and Noah. Instead, he'd put on an additional ten to twenty pounds and ended up on blood pressure medication.

"I'll let you know if I have any questions once I take a look around."

The stairs creaked on my way up, like I was an elephant rather than a person. I'd have to ask Mark's medical opinion about whether a person could be passed out drunk to the point where they wouldn't hear someone on the stairs or a fight taking place in a bedroom right off the stairs.

My *look around* was even quicker than the walk around the house had been. The bedding was gone, probably removed by the police as evidence. The mattress lay bare.

Dean had been telling the truth about not sleeping up here anymore.

Nothing in the room looked to have been broken or disturbed by a fight, either. That fact gnawed at me.

The mud smears were still on the bedroom floor. I crouched down as well as I could in my skirt and heels. There was only one set of prints, so there'd only been a single attacker.

The stairs groaned underneath me again as I went back down. I wouldn't have been able to sleep through their noises, but then again, I'd never been fall-down drunk. I'd never even been drunk.

Dean sat on the couch, his feet propped up on the end table, and any humility gone from his expression.

That was my cue to leave. There wasn't anything more I could do here anyway. In fact, I felt further behind than when I'd come. *Always leave your client feeling confident in your abilities, no matter how hopeless the case seems,* my dad would say.

"I'll be in touch soon so we can discuss potential strategies for your defense. I need to talk to your neighbors first and see if they noticed anything they didn't report to the police."

I chose my words carefully to make it sound like we still had a chance to win. Unless I came up with something better than *he was passed out asleep and a random person broke in and killed his wife and he didn't hear it,* a win wasn't likely.

Dean hopped to his feet. "Don't you need me to introduce you to my neighbors?"

Had he hit his head while I was upstairs? "I'm more likely to get unbiased answers from them if I go alone." Anderson's warning about how Dean tried to convince him to tamper with the jury flashed into my head. If Dean was willing to tamper with a jury, he'd have no qualms about bribing or blackmailing witnesses, either. "You shouldn't talk to them at all from this point on until your trial is over."

Dean's gaze flickered to the side just enough for me to catch. I'd been right to be concerned. He had been planning on influencing them somehow.

I pointed a finger at him like he was a naughty child. This was definitely going to be a situation where I needed to follow my mom's lead and lay down firm ground rules that couldn't be argued with later on. "If you do anything illegal while I'm your lawyer, you'll be back to defending yourself. Is that clear?"

I held back a shudder. I'd swear I'd even sounded like my mom.

Dean snapped a salute. I turned on my heel and left him there. I'd have to hope that my warning, along with Elise's threat to keep the kids away from him if he ended up in prison, would be enough to keep him from doing anything stupid enough to sabotage his case.

I wasn't optimistic. The sooner I could find solid evidence that someone else killed Sandra, the better. If this case went to trial, not only would we be handicapped by my bumbling courtroom abilities, but we'd have to cope with Dean's flippant attitude and blatant disregard for the rules.

I stopped in the middle of the driveway and tapped my foot. Because of the way the road curved, Dean and Sandra only had four houses that could be considered neighbors. One was the house behind them, whose back yard butted up to theirs. Unless the murderer came through their back yard to enter Dean and Sandra's, it wasn't likely they'd have anything useful to say, though I would want to ask them if a roll of duct tape magically appeared in their backyard one morning.

The other three neighbors were the houses on either side and the one across the street.

I headed left. There weren't any cars in the driveway, and no one answered the door. That wasn't unusual, considering it was the middle of the day. I'd come back on an evening or weekend.

I went back to the house on the right and rang the doorbell. The man who answered had the lean, sun-spotted look of someone who'd spent their whole working life outside. At this point, I would have put his age at around 65 to 70.

He only opened the door a crack, and I had the feeling like he'd planted his foot behind it in case I tried to force my way in.

"I don't need any tracts on salvation," he said.

I peeked down at my clothes. I suppose I could be mistaken for a Jehovah's Witness. They always came to the door nicely dressed.

"Actually, I'm Dean's Scott's lawyer. My name's Nicole Fitzhenry-Dawes."

I held out my hand, but he ignored it. I lowered it back to my side.

"I was wondering if you could give me a few minutes for a couple of questions. Right here is fine." His body language clearly said I wasn't getting an invitation into his house, so right here would have to be fine.

His gaze shifted from the left to the right. "Which one is Scott?"

I pointed back toward Dean's house. "His wife, Sandra, was killed." I gave him the date and time.

He nodded along. "I did see the police crawling all over the place, and they asked me if I'd seen anyone lurking around. I thought there'd been a break-in. Didn't realize someone had died."

At least he remembered that much. That should mean he would also still recall if he'd seen anything suspicious. "I have to do my own investigation, so forgive me if it seems repetitive. Did you see anyone entering or leaving the Scotts' house the day before?"

I left it broad. We had to allow that the murderer could have sneaked into the house at any point. He or she might have even been waiting for Sandra when she came home from the grocery store.

"I spend most of my day in my shop." He hooked a thumb back over his shoulder. "Like I told the police, my hearing's going, and my saws are too loud to hear anything else."

This interview seemed like it was going to be a dead end, but I'd try one more route. "What about that night, after you came back into the house? Did you see or hear anything then?"

He gave me an are-you-stupid-or-something look. "I sleep at night like normal people. Can't see anything with my eyes closed."

Fair enough. I had one question left that the police might not have thought to ask. "You didn't happen to find a roll of duct tape in your back yard the next morning, did you?"

He closed the door in my face. I would take that as a *no*.

The driveway of the house on the other side still sat empty of cars, so I crossed the street.

As I passed in front of Dean's house, a figure stepped back from the window. Had he been watching me?

My skin went cold despite the warmth of the day. Why would Dean be watching me? If he'd been anyone other than my client, I'd have thought he was worried about what I'd find out from the neighbors.

I straightened my back and lengthened my stride as much as I could without risking wiping out thanks to my heels.

The front door of the house across the street swung open when I was only halfway up the driveway.

"Are you a real estate agent?" The woman standing in the door wore a sequined t-shirt and mom pants—the kind with the high waist that would make anyone look like they had a paunchy belly. "Are they selling the house?"

Did normal people not dress up in this town? First I'd been mistaken for a call girl, then a Jehovah's Witness, and now a realtor.

I didn't want to yell across the driveway, so I waited until I was almost at the door. "I'm a lawyer actually."

Her face still held the anxious-hopeful expression it had when she first opened the door. "A property lawyer?"

"Criminal lawyer."

"Does that mean the police think he killed his wife? If he ends up in prison, they'd probably sell the house instead of letting it sit empty for decades."

The instincts I'd developed from years of listening to my parents interview witnesses both on and off the stand came to attention. This woman was much too interested in seeing Dean and Sandra's house sold. "Are you interested in buying the place? I could talk to my client and see what I can do if you are."

Her lips pulled together in a way that made her look like she was puckering up for a kiss. "I don't have that kind of money. It'd just be better for the neighborhood if they weren't part of it anymore."

She narrowed her eyes as if to say I should be ashamed of myself for taking on someone like Dean as a client.

I knew that look well. It was the one that meant the person I was interviewing was about to shut down and wouldn't tell me anything at all if they thought it would help my client. I needed to derail her before she got that far.

"I don't think he plans to stay here now that his wife is dead."

On the color spectrum of lies, that one wasn't exactly white, but hopefully it didn't count as completely black, either. "What makes them such bad neighbors?"

"Besides the motorcycle that races into their driveway at all hours? I don't know how anyone can sleep through all that racket, but I certainly can't."

The way she'd phrased it made it sound like the motorcycle didn't belong to Sandra or Dean, but rather to someone else who regularly visited their house. "Did the motorcyclist visit the night Sandra died?"

"Thankfully, no. It was the first good night's sleep I'd had in weeks."

Her *thankfully* was my *drat*. If the person who rode the noisy motorcycle wasn't here that day, it seemed unlikely they'd played a role in Sandra's murder.

"What else made them bad neighbors?" I said, stalling for time so I could figure out another way to come back around to asking if she'd seen anyone going into the house during the day.

She gave me a litany about the unkempt lawn and washing his car during a drought warning a few years back. None of what she said should have resulted in Sandra's murder unless I wanted to try to argue for the jury that an environmental activist wanted to stop his water waste, or that this woman had killed him because she couldn't stand looking at his weeds anymore.

Still, she seemed like someone who paid close attention to what went on in the neighborhood. I might want to come back and ask her more questions later when I had a better idea of what might have happened. The man I'd spoken to before her would probably never open the door for me again since it was clear he thought I was either crazy or stupid.

"I'm so sorry for all the trouble they've caused you," I said. "I'll encourage him to sell the house one way or another, for the good of the neighborhood, and I'll let you know if he does."

The last thing she said before she closed the door was "You seem like too nice a girl to be a criminal lawyer. You really should consider a career change."

9

I sat in my car in Dean's driveway for five minutes to organize my notes. Short of finding anything unusual that the police had ignored, the only way I saw of getting Dean acquitted was to find the person who'd really killed Sandra.

Since the neighbors hadn't seen anything, that left me without a clear direction except the clichéd catchphrase *follow the money*. Not only did he have a rundown house with an expensive, new-looking car in the driveway, but Elise had said he'd recently begun contributing to the support of the kids.

I couldn't shake the niggling feeling that he wasn't completely innocent. If he was involved in some criminal activity, that could have ended up in Sandra getting killed. Maybe she threatened to turn him in, and he killed her. Maybe Dean crossed the wrong person, and killing Sandra was retribution. Maybe Sandra had money, and Dean killed her for it.

Following the money seemed like my best option at present for figuring out who really killed Sandra, whether it was Dean or someone else. Besides, if Dean was involved in something illegal—whether or not he killed Sandra—Elise might let me quit this case. Talking to Dean left me feeling dirty in a way that even defending guilty clients hadn't. I didn't like him, and I didn't trust him.

I started my car and pulled out of the driveway. Dean's head appeared in his front window, then vanished again, and the neighbor across the street stood in her front door, openly staring. I was beginning to understand what a prey animal felt like.

A yawn cracked my face even though it was only early afternoon. Investigating a case on my own was turning out to be exhausting. In the past, I'd always had help from my parents' firm and extensive resources or from the Fair Haven PD.

I certainly couldn't ask for help from either of those sources now. Neither Elise nor Erik should put their careers on the line to run things down for me.

But I would need outside help to check in to Dean's background and financials. The financial reports that came in the discovery package were a start, but I wanted to dig deeper and look into areas the police might not have.

I instructed my phone to call Anderson's cell phone.

"Well, if it isn't Ms. Fitzhenry-Dawes again. If we're not careful, I'm going to look forward to our regular chats."

His tone was light-hearted, but my throat squeezed shut a little bit. Had I given him the wrong impression at some point?

Egotistical much, Nikki?

He'd never even seen me in person. For all he knew, I was twenty years younger or twenty years older. I shouldn't read too much into someone being nice. I was the daughter of his role model, after all, and he might not get a chance to talk to other criminal attorneys much.

I'd follow suit with the banter.

"You might not look forward to the calls if I keep making requests on your time."

He chuckled. "What can I help you with?"

"I need to hire someone to poke around in a person of interest's personal life and financials"—probably best not to tell him I planned to investigate my own client—"so I was hoping you could recommend someone."

"That's an easy one. I'll text you the contact info for the guy I use. He's not cheap, but he's thorough. If your guy or girl is hiding anything, he'll find it. Tell him I referred you. He can be picky about the new clients he takes on, and mentioning my name will ensure you a spot."

Since I could only be in so many places at once, I might also have him check into a few of Dean's other girlfriends as well. "Much obliged."

I was about to say goodbye, but he didn't give me a chance.

"You really are flying solo, then?" he asked.

I couldn't remember exactly what I'd told him the first time we'd spoken, but I'd likely been vague. "Entirely solo. I have a job at my parents' firm waiting for me in DC if I want it, but I'm also considering...other options."

That was the best I could do to keep from lying without also going into my whole complicated situation. Not only did I not want to share that with someone I'd never met, but it would have required divulging my weaknesses to a colleague. Not happening.

"I bet you're thinking of starting your own firm, aren't you?" Anderson said. "Expanding into new territory."

Starting my own law firm would mean I'd be able to take on only the clients that I believed were innocent. Since those would be less frequent, I'd also be able to continue working at Sugarwood, as long as Stacey agreed to become assistant manager and shoulder the administrative work. When Mark and I had our own children, it'd allow me more time to spend with them. I didn't want my kids spending more time at Grant and Megan's house or at Elise's house than they did at their own the way I'd spent more time in my Uncle Stan's office growing up than I did with my parents.

Running my own firm didn't give me a solution for my trouble speaking in the courtroom, though. I didn't agree with my mom that I'd grow out of it in time. It wouldn't be fair to clients to take them on and build a strong case, only to be unable to stick the landing in court.

A squeak sounded like Anderson was swiveling around in his chair. "Why don't we grab a coffee someday next week? I could tell you about my experience, maybe answer some questions you might have. I imagine you weren't alive when your parents were building their firm."

Be careful, a voice whispered in the back of my head.

I promptly told it that was silly, and then wanted to smack myself for talking to and answering myself. There was nothing wrong with meeting another lawyer to talk shop, and maybe I *should* consider launching my own firm. It wasn't any more outlandish than going back to work for my parents, and I was considering that.

Besides, I'd tell Mark about it so that everything was legitimate.

"That'd be a big help. Thanks. Where would you like to meet?"

***

I woke up on my couch the next morning to Velma eating maple syrup popcorn out of my hair. The case files were scattered on the floor beside me, many of the pages under her paws. I must have dropped them when I'd drifted off last night, and I'd been so tired that I hadn't woken up enough to go to bed. Or to put the dogs in their crates, apparently.

I batted Velma away. The bowl I'd filled with the latest test batch of the maple syrup popcorn for Stacey's baby shower lay empty on the cushion beside me. Velma must have started there, because the inside was still a bit moist.

I couldn't blame her. This batch finally met my expectations. I'd take a sample that hadn't been snuffled by a dog over to Stacey for her approval, but I finally had hope that the last detail for her shower might be ready.

I picked a piece of popcorn that Velma had overlooked off my phone and flipped it over. Five missed texts.

Yikes. It'd been a long time since I'd slept soundly enough to not even hear my text notifications. Mark said the fact that I'd been sleeping better the last few weeks was a good sign that I was starting to cope better with my PTSD. He might not think so if all the missed texts were from him.

The first was from Elise, asking if I thought she should tell Erik everything. She'd been feeling guilty. That one was an easy yes. If they were going to have a future together, she needed to trust him with everything, even the yucky parts of life.

Text two was from Anderson, letting me know his availability for our coffee business meeting next week. With the way this week was headed, it looked like I wasn't going to be able to find a spot in my schedule until a week from Saturday.

One was a photo from Ahanti from her belated honeymoon, and another was from Mark telling me he might be hard to reach today—he had an autopsy to do and then he had to head to the next county. The medical examiner there wanted him to consult on some strange results. And could we postpone our lunch date since he needed to be out of town? The text ended with an apology since he knew I'd wanted help with this case.

The final text was from Russ. *Stacey said no. Can u talk to her and try to change her mind?*

I groaned and tossed the phone aside. Life would have been so much simpler if Stacey had just said yes. I wouldn't try to change her mind if this wasn't what she wanted, but I would go talk to her. Since she'd moved onto Sugarwood's grounds, she'd become a bit like the little sister I'd never had. Setting aside the needs of Sugarwood and my own selfish interest in her learning the role of manager, I wanted to be sure she was making the choice that would be best for her long-term. Whatever that choice might be.

But I couldn't go now. Stacey had this morning off for a doctor's appointment, and I had my Skype interview with the prosecutor's office this afternoon.

Since Mark wouldn't be able to meet for lunch and cover the

medical examiner's report with me the way we'd planned, I might as well press ahead on Dean's case.

Last night, I called the investigation company Anderson recommended, and one of their investigators was digging into Sandra and Dean's finances. I couldn't sit around and wait for him to call. In the meantime, my next logical step seemed to be to continue retracing the police's steps by talking to Sandra's sister since she was the one to discover Sandra's body.

According to the case files, she worked at a garden center outside of the town where Dean lived.

The drive there gave me a lot of time to think and pray about whether Mark and I should stay in Fair Haven or move to DC, but I didn't feel any closer to an answer when I arrived than when I'd set out.

I shoved the decision to the back of my mind as I got out of my car.

The image I'd conjured in my mind when I read *garden center* online didn't match the reality at all. I'd thought it would be like the fenced-in room of plants that some of the major chain stores put in their parking lots in the summer in DC.

The parking lot was gravel and butted up to a building that looked a lot like a barn crossed with a warehouse. The large doors on the front were thrown open, and a teenage girl stood behind the counter. A line of six people stretched out in front of her. Behind her, inside the warehouse, packages of berries sat on wooden pallets like they were waiting to be transported to the grocery store.

I might have cut the line in DC to ask where I could find Nadine, Sandra's sister. I knew better than to do it here.

I tucked in at the back, and when my turn came, the girl directed me to follow the gravel path until I reached the first greenhouse.

The greenhouse was half empty, showing the effects of the planting frenzy for pots and hanging baskets that must have happened in spring. Not many people would want to plant flowers in August, so the garden center wouldn't have had any reason to replace their product. Most of the plants I walked by had a yellow sticker on them, declaring them to be fifty percent off.

The place seemed empty except for a woman partway down, re-potting a plant with red flowers that I didn't know the name of. As I walked up, she tucked a smaller pot inside a plastic bag and tied it loosely at the top. I couldn't be sure of the purpose for it, but it looked like she was creating a mini-greenhouse around each cutting, probably to make it sprout better.

"Excuse me. Are you Nadine?"

She turned around with a surface-deep smile on her face. "What can I do to help you?"

I might not have seen how shallow her smile was if I wasn't trained to notice small details. It was the smile of someone who was out of the initial shock of grief and who was now learning how to live again with a hole where someone important used to be. I knew from personal experience what a hard journey that was. At the start, smiling could feel awkward and disloyal.

And I was about to make it worse by asking her about Sandra. Assuming, of course, that she'd even talk to me once she found out who I was.

My dad would say I shouldn't tell her, but the way she looked—

like she just wanted to get through the day—made lying to her feel slimy. I was going to go with honesty. It wasn't always the best policy, but it did make it easier to sleep at night.

Besides, she hadn't killed Sandra. She was one town over, picking her daughter up from a party she wasn't supposed to be at, during the time of death window. Her daughter confirmed it when the police checked with her. Nadine also had a gas station receipt still in her purse, and the waitress at the all-night coffee shop where she'd taken her daughter for a serious mother–daughter talk after picking her up vouched for her. They'd been there for hours.

"I'll let you decide if you even want to help me once you know who I am," I said. "I'm defense council for Dean Scott."

Angry disbelief flashed across her face, like she thought I was playing a cruel trick on her. Straight anger quickly replaced it. "I have no reason to help someone who's defending Dean. I gave my statement to the police, and I'm pretty sure I don't have to talk to you."

Based on her reaction, I'd have to ask that she be treated as a hostile witness in court. "You'll have to answer my questions at trial, but you don't right now. I'm still hoping you will. Dean says he didn't kill Sandra."

Nadine snorted. "Of course he does." She turned around and shoved a plant into the new pot so hard I thought it might snap.

Definitely a hostile witness.

Now's when you lie to her, the voice inside my head that sounded suspiciously like my dad said.

I blew a mental raspberry at it. There had to be a way to win her over without lying to her.

I moved to the end of the table. I wasn't directly in front of her, making myself seem confrontational. I wasn't behind her, either. She could look at me if she wanted, but she didn't have to. It should allow her to feel safe and in control.

"You don't know me, so I understand why you wouldn't want to answer any of my questions. To you, I'm someone who's trying to strip away the one thing your sister has left—justice for what happened to her. But I'm picky in my clients. I only work with people who are innocent. If you can convince me that Dean killed your sister, he'll have to find himself a different lawyer."

Her hands stilled, her fingers partly buried in the dirt. "All I have to do is convince you?"

"That's it."

She turned from the pot, dragged a stool over, and sat. "I still feel like this might be a trick to get me to answer your questions."

I'd have wondered about her if she didn't. If she'd been ready to convince me without any skepticism, I probably wouldn't have believed anything she told me. It could have all been lies made up to get me to drop Dean as a client.

Her continued reluctance meant she wanted to share the truth, but was worried it wouldn't be enough. She wasn't sure she wanted to risk helping Dean.

"It's not a trick," I said. "You can stop at any time or refuse to answer any questions I have. Is there somewhere else you'd rather talk, or do you need to ask your boss for a short break?"

Her mouth moved at the corners like a real smile wanted to break through. "I own this place. My husband and I do, I mean. So I don't think my boss will mind."

It seemed strange that Sandra would be working at a gas station when her sister and brother-in-law owned a garden center. Dean had said she volunteered here, but they clearly had employees. Why wouldn't they have simply hired her? If she had a tendency to steal from her employers, that could have gotten her killed. It was a long shot, but Dean wasn't the easiest client to defend. I had to take every shot I could get.

"How about we start with something easy, then? I'm trying to get a better idea of Sandra's life. Would you mind telling me why she didn't work for you?"

"She did." Nadine pulled the pot toward her and pressed the dirt down tighter, as if the feel of it comforted her. "For years. She was the last full-time employee we let go. We've been struggling to bounce back from a few challenges, and Sandra needed a full-time job. It broke both our hearts." She shrugged. "Life does that sometimes."

It sounded like Sandra did like plants. Dean had said she didn't. I suspected he didn't know his wife as well as he thought.

I brushed my fingers along the leaves of the newly potted plant. "Did Sandra have your green thumb?"

Nadine touched the leaf I'd brushed moments before. "Not really. She didn't spend any time here in the greenhouses. She worked with the pick-your-own fruits. I think she liked talking to the people who'd come to pick." She wiped at her face, leaving a streak of dirt behind. "I don't see what that has to do with the case, though."

I'd forgotten about the case. "It doesn't directly. But I like to remember that cases aren't just cases. They're about people."

She nodded. Her shoulders hunched forward slightly, and she'd swiveled to face me. She crushed in her fist the bag she'd been about to slide the plant into. "I guess you probably want to know about how I found her."

My knees locked. I'd planned to come around to that at the end, but if Nadine wanted it out of the way now, we'd talk about it now. It seemed like she felt more comfortable being in charge, anyway, rather than letting me lead the conversation.

I might have been, too, if I were in her place. I wouldn't have wanted to risk the conversation going in directions I didn't want it to. Not that I could be sure those were her motives.

"It would help me to understand, yes."

She wrapped her hands around the pot and drew it close. "I'd been calling Sandra for a few hours. She'd volunteered to come early in the morning and help pick blueberries." She pointed back over her shoulder. "You probably noticed we sell pre-picked baskets out front for people who don't want to do it themselves and for a deal we have with other fruit stands in the county."

She stopped abruptly. I moved another stool over. This story would be hard for her. I didn't want her to feel rushed because I was standing, hovering. If I sat, it should help her feel like she could take whatever time she needed.

"I don't remember how many times I tried to call her, but it was a lot. Sandra always answers my calls. I got worried."

The statement she'd given the police said she'd walked past Dean sleeping on the couch, so he hadn't let her in when she arrived. At least if the door hadn't been locked, I could argue the murderer sneaked in quietly enough not to wake him. "Was the door unlocked when you got there?"

She shook her head. "I have a spare key."

Crap. Now I had to explain how a random intruder or serial killer had not only murdered Sandra while her husband slept downstairs, but also how he broke into a locked door without leaving any marks or making any noise or getting spotted by the neighbors.

"Dean was on the couch, snoring and smelling like a still." Nadine's upper lip twitched as if she could smell him again. "I thought maybe Sandra was sick and he was too wasted to take care of her."

She shook her head in that really slow way people have when their minds still don't want to accept the truth.

"When you entered the room, did it look like there'd been a struggle?" I asked gently.

She shook her head. "Sandra was on the bed...I knew..."

She pressed a hand over her mouth.

A rock settled in at the bottom of my throat. It felt cruel to push her for details I could see in the pictures about what Sandra looked like.

I'd come at it a different way. "Did you notice anything strange? Anything that stood out to you?"

I immediately wanted to grab my words back. The strangest thing in the room would have been her dead sister.

Her eyes glassed over. "I don't remember. Sandra was there. I knew it was her even though I couldn't see her face. She was so still." She jumped from the stool and backed a step away. "I can't. Maybe some other time, but I can't right now. I have to work."

I slid from the stool. I'd found bodies before, and it'd been hard enough even when they weren't family. "It's okay. I'll come back another time."

She dipped her head. "Call first. I'll answer more questions, but now isn't a good time, so call first."

Hopefully that wasn't her way of saying *don't call us, we'll call you.*

*T*he next morning, I packaged up the maple syrup popcorn and headed for Stacey's house. Since hiring on, she'd taken over the two-bedroom house that used to belong to Noah. Sugarwood's grounds had three houses on it—mine, Russ', and Stacey's. Part of her salary was that she didn't pay rent, only her utilities.

I knocked on her door, and my phone rang in my purse. I pulled it out. The name on the screen belonged to the investigative company I'd hired on Anderson's recommendation.

Worst possible timing.

Stacey opened the door, and I let the call go to voicemail.

I held up the bag of popcorn. "Test batch number...uh..."

Stacey laughed and stepped out of my way. We'd eaten enough popcorn together that it was a miracle I wasn't waddling the same way she was. Still, if I had to fail at creating the popcorn for her shower a hundred times just to make her laugh, I'd do it. It'd been months after Noah's death before I even saw her smile.

Between handfuls of popcorn, she filled me in on her doctor's appointment. When she finished, she held up the half empty bag. "This one's exactly what I wanted."

At least one thing was going right for me. I let the silence stretch for another breath, but I couldn't wait too long. If Stacey started into another topic, I might lose my nerve to come back to this one.

I filled my hand with more popcorn, studiously taking my time and keeping my gaze on what I was doing. "Russ said you weren't interested in a long-term position here."

I'd learned that, with Stacey, leading statements were often better than questions. She still had moments of that teenage defensiveness toward direct questions, but if I made a statement, it was like she was a mouse who smelled cheese in a trap and couldn't resist it.

She moved back on the couch and tried to pull her legs up to sit cross-legged. Her belly blocked her progress. She settled her feet back on the floor. "That's not exactly what I said."

I chewed a piece of popcorn. I hadn't been around many teenagers, so I didn't know if Stacey was normal or not. She seemed to be a walking contradiction at times. She was more responsible than most forty-year-olds when it came to business, but in her personal life, she had a stubborn, sometimes irresponsible, streak.

It was possible Russ came on too strong and made her feel like she didn't have a choice in her future. "Russ must have misunderstood, then. I'd love to know what your plans are. If you have any."

Stacey twisted a strand of hair around her finger. "Everyone else seems to have plans for me, and they expect me to do what they want."

And there it was.

As much as I wanted her to stay, I didn't want to be another person telling her what to do. If she felt forced to work at Sugarwood, she wouldn't stay. Eventually, she'd move on and then we'd potentially be in a bad spot. And with all the challenges she'd already faced, fighting to be allowed to be with her fiancé and then losing him, only to find out she was pregnant and would be a young single mom...she'd survived all that. She should have a chance to pick the kind of future she wanted for herself and her baby, even if it was only picking her job.

I didn't want her to feel trapped the way I had before Uncle Stan left me Sugarwood.

I pulled one leg up under me so I could turn on the couch to face her. "I don't care about what anyone else wants you to do with your life. What matters is what *you* want to do with it."

She tugged the piece of hair up to her mouth but stopped short of actually chewing on the ends. "My dad wants me to come back to the garage once the baby's born. I'm not sure I want that anymore."

I could understand the pressure of wanting to please your parents. "My dad wants me to come back to work at his business, too."

Stacey lowered the hair away from her face. "In DC?"

I nodded.

"What are you going to do?"

"I don't know yet, either. Why don't you want to go back to your dad's garage?"

"Part of it's Noah. I can't go in there without seeing him everywhere." She ran a hand over her belly. "Part of it's how hard it's always been to get anyone there to accept me. I don't know whether it's because I'm a girl or young or what. The employees wouldn't respect me even if I was their boss."

Her words bounced around in my head. The employees wouldn't respect me even if I was their boss. I hadn't been able to put it into words before now, but that was one of my fears about returning to my parents' firm. I'd been liked, but never respected. Every new person my parents hired thought I only had my job because of my parents. And I couldn't say they were wrong. They were probably right.

But not working for your parents and not working in the same field as your parents were two very different things. "Do you think you'd still like to work in *a* garage?"

"I like fixing things, but I can do that here. Or I could save up and buy an old classic car to fix up the way Noah and I always talked about. I liked balancing accounts for my dad, and here I get to do that and manage the online orders."

"But you turned down Russ' offer."

Stacey crossed her arms and shrugged. It was one of her tells—protecting herself and trying to shrug off something important as if it weren't.

Earlier Stacey had said that everyone was making plans for her life. Her dad was only one person. "Did Russ ask you, or did he lay it out for you like it was a done deal?"

The way she shifted her gaze to the side gave it away completely. She was balking the same way I had when my dad demanded I come back.

Poor Russ. He always felt like he was doing the right thing by "protecting" people. He meant well.

"Why don't you want to go back to work for your dad?" Stacey asked. "Did you not like being a lawyer?"

Ugg. I had brought that one on myself. "I didn't like defending people I knew were guilty. It made me feel sick inside. It felt wrong."

"You have to do that if you work for your dad?"

At the start I would. Maybe in a few years, once I became partner, I could be choosier, but even then, I'd have to pull my own weight. "Yeah."

"Then you can't do it." Stacey's face had taken on that immoveable-mountain-meets-unstoppable-force look that seemed to be trademarked by toddlers and teenagers. "Remember how much Noah and I wanted to be together, but he said we couldn't until I was eighteen and legal. He was right, even though I couldn't see it then." She twisted a strand of her hair around a finger. "Besides, defending guilty people when you feel it's wrong doesn't seem to fit with all the stuff you've been telling me about from the Bible."

Stacey had come to my baptism last month. Ever since, she'd come out with questions about my faith, usually when I least expected it. I did my best to answer her questions, though a couple of times we'd had to call Mrs. Cavanaugh because I didn't know the answer. I could tell by the way Stacey's questions built on each other that she listened carefully and thought about what I'd said.

This only proved that even more.

And the way she said it, so matter-of-factly and Stacey-ish, it seemed silly that I'd been considering it at all. No amount of money was worth selling out my integrity for.

I felt like I could take a full breath for the first time since Mark and I came back from DC. If we moved there, I'd have to take the job with the district attorney's office, assuming they offered it. Whatever else happened, I had to do what I believed was right.

I was halfway home when I remembered the call that came in while I was standing on Stacey's doorstep.

"Ms. Fitzhenry-Dawes, this is Hal from Frontline Investigations. I found some items that raise red flags for me. Please give me a call back."

He left a number.

My hands went cold, and I wished I still had something sweet to drown the empty feeling in my stomach. The first task I'd assigned Frontline was to look into Dean's financials. I wanted to know if there was a possible financial motive for Sandra's death, either by Dean's hand or someone else's due to something Dean was involved in. Too many things hadn't added up where money was concerned.

I dialed the number Hal left. He answered quickly, and I told him who I was.

"Sandra didn't have any hidden money that I could turn up, and Dean has a life insurance policy, but Sandra didn't," he said. "It looked like she made about the same as she spent and had nothing left to save. No recent lottery win, either, and no extravagant purchases. She didn't have enough to fully pay off her credit cards each month, but she wasn't in serious debt, either."

Dean's supposed motives for killing Sandra were getting thinner all the time. Since he had the life insurance policy, it would have made more sense if he'd been the one found smothered to death. Combined with the glimpses of grief he seemed to want to hide, I had to admit he might be innocent after all.

Though Hal had mentioned red flags. "That doesn't sound concerning. Did you find something else?"

"It's nothing concrete," he said. "But he paid cash for his car three months ago, and within the last two months, he's cleared off all the creditors who were bringing down his credit score."

He was definitely getting a sudden influx of money from somewhere. Based on what Nadine said and Hal confirmed, it also wasn't because Sandra had a lot of money in savings that Dean suddenly gained access to upon her death. A woman with a lot of money in savings could have afforded to continue working only part-time with her sister.

"You want me to keep digging?" Hal asked.

"Please. And do a little light surveillance on Dean."

Even if Hal didn't turn up anything suspicious, a tail would tell me if Dean was obeying my orders to stay away from women. I'd have no chance at showing the jury he was a grieving husband if the prosecution had pictures of him cavorting around so soon after Sandra's death. If he wasn't following my orders, I wanted to know who the woman was. She might end up as another avenue I could use to cast reasonable doubt.

While Hal worked on his end, I needed to have a talk with Dean about money. I finally had enough information that I could go into it with the advantage.

I punched Dean's number into my phone. Literally. I had to remind myself that the phone wasn't the one causing me headaches.

"Scott," he answered.

It was a bit eerie since Elise answered her phone the same way when she was on duty.

If I came right out and accused Dean of anything, it'd be about as useful as trying to cut a diamond with my teeth. He'd never be forthright with me.

I'd have to come at it from a different angle. My dad liked to say that the best lies used the truth. In this case, I wouldn't be lying, exactly. I'd simply be collecting information for multiple reasons and only telling him about one.

"It's Nicole. I've been working on putting together your defense, but I need to ask you about a couple of things I think the prosecution might try to use against you in court. I need to make sure I have all the information so they're not able to surprise me."

"You don't like surprises?"

There was too much smirk and innuendo in his words for my comfort. His tendency to turn everything into a joke or a come-on was really starting to irk me. It wasn't at all like the Cavanaughs, who teased each other but somehow always understood where the lines were and managed not to cross them.

"Not in court I don't, and that's the only part of my life that you need to be concerned about."

He let out an exaggerated sigh. "Fine. What do you need to know?"

"Your financials show recent large deposits, and you've been making purchases with cash and paying off a lot of debts recently." I didn't know all that was true. He might not be depositing large amounts into the bank, but it seemed like a fair assumption. "The prosecution could spin that in a lot of different ways, but my guess is that they're going to say you're into something illegal and Sandra threatened to expose you."

The silence on the other end of the line stretched too long, like he was trying to make up a believable lie to tell me.

My throat burned. I couldn't shake the feeling that he was guilty, but because I couldn't prove it, I couldn't leave the case. Once we got partway into the trial, if it became clear he had murdered Sandra, I'd have no way out.

He still hadn't answered me.

"How do you explain the money?" I asked.

"I run a business. I take payment in cash because I don't want to risk a check bouncing or a credit card being declined."

That sounded...reasonable. Except everything I'd heard about him from the Cavanaughs before I met him had made it sound like he couldn't hold down a steady job, let alone run his own successful business. "What business? How long have you owned it? Those are questions the prosecution will ask if that's how we explain the money."

"Construction. I've been at it for a year with a buddy of mine."

Even if he only took cash payments, he'd need records for tax purposes. "I'll need your friend's name and contact information, as well as copies of all your invoices for the past six months."

Another long silence. "Okay."

"By tomorrow." Which shouldn't give him time to fabricate fake records.

I thought I heard him swear, but I couldn't be certain. If he had, I'd want to look closely at whatever records he gave me.

The next morning, I picked up the files from Dean, drove to the nearest fast food restaurant, and turned my car into a mini mobile office. I didn't want to drive all the way back to Fair Haven only to drive back here to interview his clients if I decided I needed to talk to them. Today was Saturday, so more people would be home over a weekend than on a weekday, making it the ideal time to try to reach them.

The stack of invoices Dean gave me seemed to have no order to them, either alphabetical or chronological. It was almost like he'd printed them off, shuffled them up, and tossed them into his box. Hopefully his partner kept better records or they'd be in trouble come tax time.

There also weren't as many as I'd expected for a company that'd been in business a year and was making enough for Dean to start paying off all his debts and helping Elise with the kids' expenses.

I sorted the invoices by date, and wrote down each client's

name, address, and phone number on a separate sheet of paper. I'd start with the most recent and work my way back.

I added the contact information for Dean's partner at the top, then I went through the invoices one more time. This time I didn't care about the names. I paid attention to the amounts billed and the description of the work.

The work descriptions themselves looked legit. Repairing water damage, replacing a roof, building a gazebo, building a porch.

The amounts though...I wouldn't have paid those prices even in DC.

The prices explained how they'd made such a large profit without working a higher number of jobs, but it created the new question of why people hired them at all. I could see Dean and his partner duping a customer here or there into paying an exorbitant price, but *every* customer?

Calling them was an option, but my instincts said I should go in person. I needed to see the work Dean and his partner did and read the reactions of the people I spoke to.

I plugged the first five addresses, including Dean's partner, into my GPS. It set out the most efficient route. I'd keep track of anyone who wasn't home and swing by again some weeknight evening.

Then I sat in my car for a few minutes even after the GPS told me to drive to the highlighted route. I needed a game plan. Anytime I tried to operate by the seat of my pants, it ended in embarrassment for me.

I had to be careful, too. If Dean was doing something illegal under the front of his construction business, I didn't want to tip his clients off to my suspicions. My knowledge of building things was limited enough that I couldn't pass for a building quality control inspector. It seemed like my best tactic would be another version of the truth. I'd be Dean's defense attorney, trying to establish that he was a reliable, conscientious businessman.

Putting that spin on it should make them believe that all I cared about was whether Dean showed up on time and did a good job.

The first two clients didn't answer their doors when I rang the bell, and they didn't have cars in the driveway. I lucked out on the third.

A woman whose wrinkles put the lie to her dyed black hair answered the door.

"Can I help you?" she asked.

I'd worked out my spiel carefully on the drive. I handed her my card—I'd had some printed specifically for this case at Fair Haven's print shop. "I'm representing Dean Scott against an accusation made against him, and I was wondering if you'd be willing to talk to me about the work he did for you."

Hopefully she'd assume I was representing him in a lawsuit having to do with his business.

She squinted at my card in a way that said she normally wore reading glasses. She kept holding the card in both hands even after she looked up. "What do you need to know?"

Her voice had the same hesitation people tended to get when they answered a call and weren't sure if the person on the other end was who they said they were or a scammer.

I gave her a calculated smile—not too small, because that would make me look nervous, and not too big, because that'd make me look like I was trying too hard. My mom called it the Goldilocks smile.

"Nothing invasive or personal. I'm only interested in whether you were satisfied with his work." I flipped through the notepad I'd brought with me as if I were looking for something even though I already knew the answer. "What exactly did he do for you?"

She glanced up. "Our roof. New shingles." She looked down quickly and examined my card again.

That part of my questions shouldn't have made her nervous, but it had. "About how long did the work take?"

"I don't remember." She worried the edge of my card with her fingers. "It was a while ago."

Theoretically, she could be having memory issues. I'd have placed her age somewhere in her early seventies. But I had a feeling it was something else. "Were you happy with the quality of his work?"

"No problems."

I wrote that down as if I actually needed to take notes, so as to give myself a little time. There wasn't anything obviously wrong with her answers, but they were so short that I couldn't read much into them. It was almost like she kept them brief on purpose.

"He completed the work with integrity?" I asked without looking up.

A slight hesitation. "Yes."

I pasted my smile on again and met her gaze. All my training, all the years watching my parents work, told me there was something more here, but what? It all sounded legitimate on the surface.

I stopped myself in time to keep from chewing on my bottom lip.

"Would you be willing to testify if we need a character witness?"

She shook her head rapidly. "My husband supervised the work, really. I only met Dean Scott once. I don't know him well enough to vouch for him."

Her voice edged a little toward panic. Not far enough to be obvious, but her tone was higher-pitched than before.

"If your husband supervised, then it'd be better to have him testify anyway—"

"My husband's too busy. I'm sorry, but we can't help any more than we have."

She raised a hand in goodbye and closed the door.

The impish part of me wished I'd thought to wedge my foot in the door so she couldn't close it on me. Then again, I didn't want to end up arrested for harassment, either.

I shuffled slowly back down the walkway. I stopped halfway to my car and looked up at the roof.

It seemed like a good roof as far as roofs went. As far as I could tell, it was relatively new as well. Though, a roof probably looked new for years.

Maybe I was also reading too much into her reaction. It was possible somewhere deep down I wanted to prove Dean guilty rather than innocent. Even though I loved Mark and wouldn't trade him for anyone, it still hurt when I thought about what my ex-boyfriend Peter did to me. Cheating husbands pushed my buttons in a way few other things did. It felt like Dean should have been punished more than he had for what he did to Elise.

Maybe it was time I checked my motives so that I wasn't chasing figments of my imagination. If Dean was doing something that might have resulted in Sandra's death, that was one thing. If I was now on a witch hunt to punish him because he reminded me of Peter, that was something entirely different.

I hadn't ever had work done on a home, so maybe I was underestimating what things should cost. And perhaps the woman was nervous because she wasn't convinced I was who I said I was. She had kept checking my card. I couldn't blame her for not trusting me. I was a stranger who showed up at her door, and I had been kind of lying to her.

I pulled out my cell phone and texted Russ. *What's the average price for a new roof?*

I went to put my cell phone away, but it chimed before I could. *What happened? Which building needs a new roof?*

Oops. *It's for the case I'm working. House looks like it's about 1600 sq ft. Rancher with a basement.*

The number he sent back was half what the woman I'd just spoken to paid Dean.

I was halfway through writing a reply to Russ, asking if there was any reason he could think of why a roof would cost double, when a large white square of cardboard-like material in the garden caught my attention. It had metal rods sticking out of the bottom as if it were supposed to be standing up. Dead leaves, dirt, and a few fresh weeds hid it, as if it'd fallen over and been forgotten sometime during the past winter.

It reminded me of the signs construction companies often asked their clients to display after a job. If Dean had asked them to advertise his company, then he couldn't be doing anything shady.

I sent the text to Russ, and wriggled the sign out of the dirt to make sure it was what I thought it was.

His text came back. *Rush job maybe. Short notice. Or higher quality materials.*

I flipped the sign over. It was for a roofing company alright, but not Dean's.

And if another company installed their new roof, that meant Dean and his client had lied to me.

I went back to the front door and rang the bell again, but the woman didn't answer.

I snapped a picture of the sign with my phone and headed on to the next "client." The young man who showed me the gazebo in his back yard had a strong Hispanic accent. The fact that he answered the door in the middle of the day, wearing pajama pants and a t-shirt, made me think he worked the night shift somewhere and didn't want to disrupt his sleep schedule on the weekends.

After some of the same questions I'd leveled at the first client to warm him up, I asked why his gazebo cost so much.

He gave me a convoluted story about special wood and extra foundation and the long hours Dean put in himself and on and on until I could barely keep his reasons straight in my head. One thing I knew for sure, the gazebo looked like plain old normal wood to me. The varnish job wasn't even that great. I could see spots where it'd dripped and dried without anyone bothering to smooth it out.

I ran a hand along the rail. "It's a very pretty gazebo. I've been thinking of building one. What kind of wood is it?"

He raised his shoulders. "I don't know the word in English."

I flashed a smile that I hoped would make him think I believed him. I pulled my phone out. "I'll get a picture then and ask someone else."

I snapped the shot before he could object and backed away. "Thanks so much for your help. I'll be back in touch if I have any more questions."

I turned around, waited two steps, and peeked back over my shoulder. He was striding toward the house like he was late for an appointment. He probably wanted to get away before I asked anything else.

I couldn't prove it, but Dean wasn't running an honest business. Something else was going on here.

Dean had agreed not to lie to me. Or, at least, I thought he had. That meant he was more afraid of telling me the truth and what would happen if he did than he was of being caught in a lie. Or he was cocky enough to think I wouldn't catch him.

Why would a man who wanted to see his wife's killer brought to justice hide information that could solve the case?

I slowed my steps. Maybe I'd been looking at this wrong even though Mark had tried to warn me. Dean cared about Dean. He didn't care about justice for Sandra or finding her killer. He cared about not going to prison.

A shiver wracked my body like someone had dropped an ice cube down my back.

The most logical explanation for it all was that whatever Dean was hiding would also result in him going to prison if anyone found out.

Time to give myself a back-up plan before I talked to Dean's partner. I sent Hal a text.

I'm headed to the office of Dean Scott's construction firm to talk to his partner. I think their business isn't what it seems. Could you look at his partner, as well as these clients?

I attached the names of the two I'd spoken to. It'd be next week before he'd get me anything on them since it was the weekend, but at least the process was underway.

Even though I should be safe in a public place like an office building, texting Hal also covered my back. Someone now knew where I was and what I suspected—phrased in a way that wouldn't make me seem weird and paranoid if I turned out to simply be weird and paranoid.

I reached the front of the house. Sometime since I arrived, the mailman had delivered the mail. A couple letters stuck out the top of the box on the front of the house.

I glanced around. No one from the house had followed me or seemed to be spying on me from the windows the way Dean tended to do. It wouldn't hurt to take a quick look at the letters to see if anything unusual jumped out at me. It was a long shot, but I had to do something to unravel this.

It wasn't like I was doing anything wrong, either. I didn't plan to steal their mail or open it. There wasn't a law against touching someone else's mail, after all.

I edged sideways, hopped up the two cement steps, and grabbed out the mail. One looked like a credit card bill. It was addressed to the same name as was on the receipt.

The other piece was to a Wendy Steel. Her name wasn't Hispanic like the client's, but the letter to her was post marked from Mexico.

I dropped the letters back into the box. I'd become a mail peeper, and all I'd really learned was that Jose was probably living with a girlfriend or fiancé who wrote letters to his family in Mexico.

I texted the name to Hal as well, just in case.

Not my finest piece of detective work, but hopefully I'd have better luck when I talked to Dean's partner.

***

Pulling into the small parking lot for G&D Construction immediately answered one of my questions. A black motorcycle rested in a spot marked for the owner.

That was a letdown. I'd secretly been hoping that Dean's business partner was the one who killed Sandra so I could be done with this case. Unfortunately, the woman who lived across the street from them was certain the motorcycle hadn't shown up the night Sandra died.

Of course, that didn't mean he wasn't our guy. He could have parked his motorcycle somewhere else and walked, or he could have driven a car that night. Even checking to see if he owned another vehicle wouldn't be definitive. He could have borrowed one from a friend.

For now, I'd keep him on my list of suspects.

I checked the information Dean had given me. His business partner's name was Griffin Podleski. G&D Construction—Griffin and Dean. Not the most inventive of names, but every town couldn't be Fair Haven.

Another car parked on the opposite side of the door from my car and Griffin's motorcycle. That meant Griffin had a customer.

I hesitated with my hand on the door handle. I had two options. I could go in quietly and hope to overhear something incriminating, or I could go in boldly, announce who I was, and watch the reaction of the customer.

If their construction business was legitimate, the customer should express curiosity or concern about hiring them, but they shouldn't look scared or guilty.

It'd be too much of a gamble to hope to overhear something pertinent.

I drew my shoulders back and strode in.

The building felt smaller on the inside than it'd looked on the outside. The door opened right into an office with a desk. Two other doors led off from the back. One bore the label *Restroom*. The other must lead into a room that made up the rest of the depth of the building.

The men sitting on either side of the desk stopped their conversation and looked up at me. Even if I'd intended to sneak in, it wouldn't have been possible.

I marched straight to them and held out my hand to the man behind the desk, since he must be Griffin.

"I'm sorry to interrupt. I'm Nicole Fitzhenry-Dawes, an attorney working on Dean Scott's criminal case. Do you think you'll have time to speak to me after you finish this appointment? I'd be happy to wait."

I left out that I was Dean's defense attorney and kept my face serious.

Griffin's face gave nothing away. His handshake, however, moved the bones in my hand.

The customer pushed his chair back. It screeched across the concrete floor. "I was leaving anyway."

No question about what Dean had done, and he avoided eye contact like he didn't want me to be able to remember his face.

Not the reaction of a man whose conscience was clear.

I took the seat the man vacated without waiting to be asked.

The door whapped shut behind him, and the silence in its place felt almost heavy. I'd expected there to be other people here. A receptionist, maybe, or another employee. Or for the office to be part of a shared building.

None of those things turned out to be true. Instead I sat in a building alone with a man who might be a criminal. I could scream, and no one would hear me.

I'd have to pray that the fact that I was Dean's lawyer would mean that I was safe even if I might otherwise not have been.

Just in case, I'd have to be careful how I played this. I couldn't come across as a threat to him. I had to be a co-conspirator. As much as it made me want to slither out of my skin, I'd approach it as if I knew all about the true nature of their business and I simply wanted to make sure they'd thought of everything to cover their butts.

To start with, that meant throwing Dean under the bus. "You look like you didn't know I was coming. Dean was supposed to inform you."

Griffin had the kind of low, heavy brow line that made people look like they were scowling even if they weren't. It made it harder to tell if my words had any effect on him.

All he said was, "He didn't."

I rolled my eyes to make myself seem less threatening. "He should have told you. Basically, my job is to either disprove or cast doubt on each piece of the prosecution's case against Dean. If the prosecution subpoenas your tax records, whether personal or business, will they be in order?"

I tried to give him a wink-wink-nudge-nudge look without going over the top.

The man had mastered the deadpan look. "The IRS hasn't had a problem with us so far."

In a way, it was like trying to interrogate a rock. A tickle of panic clawed at my throat.

Woman up, Nicole. You've dealt with scarier, less accommodating people. You can handle this. "Great. I'll just need your accountant's name."

"I do our taxes."

There went that idea for figuring out what was really going on here. And clearly I wasn't going to figure out anything useful by talking to Griffin. "I just need to see your back room, then."

I made sure to say it casually, like it was perfunctory. If the back room was full of wood, tile, and granite samples, it would be. At that point, I'd have to admit that I was seeing animals in the cloud shapes.

He got up without a word and headed for the back.

I trailed along behind him. That he hadn't hesitated about

bringing me to the back room made one of two scenarios likely. He either figured I was safe because I was Dean's lawyer or he figured there wasn't anything there to incriminate them, either because they were a legitimate construction business or because he figured I wouldn't know what I was looking at. He might be right about the second.

Or maybe he planned to murder me and dump my body in a large freezer. But that was probably simply me being paranoid. He hadn't showed any signs of wanting to hurt me, and I'd become pretty good at recognizing them.

He unlocked the door to the backroom and moved out of the way.

I stepped inside. The room was almost...sterile. No samples. No obvious signs of nefarious activities, either. It looked more like I would have expected a technology start-up to look than a construction company. Two top-of-the-line computers rested against one wall on separate desks. Other equipment that I couldn't name sat nearby.

"Satisfied?" Griffin asked from behind me.

No, but I had to play my part. "Thanks for letting me cross my I's and dot my T's."

It wasn't until the words were out that I realized I'd mixed it up. I internally shrugged. In this case, having him underestimate me probably worked in my favor. The last thing I wanted to become was a threat to another criminal.

Especially since I didn't actually know anything concrete at this point. I knew Dean was up to something, and seemed to be extorting money from his "clients." It might be electronically based, if their office was any indication, but beyond that, it was all still question marks.

They could be hacking people's computers and stealing their dirty secrets, using them to blackmail them. I doubted they were hacking people's bank accounts and straight-up stealing the money, but I couldn't come up with any other options at the moment. Once Hal provided me with some background information on Griffin and their clients, that might help generate new possibilities.

I stopped beside my car and reached for my keys, but my purse wasn't hanging on my shoulder.

I cringed. I'd hung it on the back of the chair when I sat. If I wanted Griffin to think I was an airhead, I was probably doing a great job of it. Forgetting my purse wasn't a professional move.

He wasn't in the front room when I entered. The door didn't seem to have a bell—electronic or otherwise—so hopefully I could sneak in and back out without drawing too much attention to myself.

"What were you thinking sending her here?" Griffin's voice drifted from the back room. "She scared away a potential client."

A pause.

Griffin cursed. "She can't turn you in to the police, but she's not my lawyer. She doesn't have to protect me."

He had to be talking to Dean. Their conversation confirmed my suspicions about their business. It also meant I needed to get out of here before Griffin caught me unintentionally eavesdropping.

I grabbed my purse strap and edged toward the door. My purse snagged on the chair and dragged it an inch across the floor. The screech sounded like I'd scraped glass over a chalkboard with a microphone next to it.

Griffin appeared in the doorway, phone still to his ear.

My heartbeat hit a syncopated rhythm, and my head felt full of air. I had to pull it together. He assumed I already knew too much, and he hadn't said anything on the phone to Dean, at least that I'd heard, that could send him to prison.

I had to take back control. What would my dad do in a situation like this?

Stupid question. My dad wouldn't have gotten himself into a situation like this in the first place.

I'd been playing this like I was here on Dean's behalf to make sure nothing here could be used against them. The best plan I could come up with was to stick to that.

I shook my head like I was disappointed in him and pointed toward the door. "Get a bell. This time it was only me. Next time it could be anyone."

I pivoted on my heel and strode out the door, back straight, like I wasn't afraid of him. I climbed into my car, and it took me two tries to get my keys into the ignition.

He stood in the doorway of the building and watched me drive away.

As I reached the edge of town and hit my signal to turn onto the highway that'd take me back to Fair Haven, a tingle went down my scalp. The faint drone I'd been hearing got closer, and what had been a black dot in my rearview mirror grew large enough that I could make out what it was.

It wasn't a car. It was a motorcycle.

*W*hen I first saw the movie *Minority Report*, I'd rooted for the main character as he struggled against a society where crimes could be predicted in advance and people were incarcerated before the crime happened.

Now, watching a black motorcycle identical to Griffin's follow me down the highway, I wasn't so sure a world where crimes were stopped before they happened was such a bad thing.

The only positive I could find was that a motorcycle couldn't run a car off the road. If he'd been driving anything larger, that's what I would have feared.

Sweat slicked my grip on my steering wheel. He'd know that as well as I did, so he had to have a different purpose for following me —like finding out where I lived.

Thankfully I hadn't been stupid enough to hand him one of my business cards. Since I didn't have an office, I'd put Sugarwood's address on them.

I had to lose him before I could go home. I wasn't a stunt driver, and a motorcycle could outmaneuver my car anyway. Plus, he likely knew the roads around here better than I did. My GPS wouldn't be able to recalculate my routes fast enough to make taking random detours a viable possibility. I'd only end up lost and being followed by a potential murderer.

That narrowed my options to...well...one. I'd have to go somewhere with a lot of other people and wait. Hopefully he'd give up.

Strike that. I wouldn't go just anywhere. I'd drive right up to the Fair Haven police department and walk in. If any of the officers I had a good relationship with were working today, I'd explain the situation and ask for an escort home. Griffin would have to be pretty bold to continue to follow me if I had a police car along with me.

All the spots in front of the station were filled when I pulled up. I parked along the curb in a spot that wasn't technically a parking spot and hurried inside.

Sheila sat behind the front desk, her gaze focused on the computer. She glanced up, and a smile bloomed on her face. "Hey, Nicole. You won't believe it. I finally got Royal to stay."

Sheila and her border collie Royal had been in the same obedience class that I'd taken Velma to. Royal had been one of the smartest in the class, but his kid-on-a-sugar-high levels of energy meant he'd never been able to hold a stay for longer than fifteen seconds.

I congratulated her and casually asked which officers were on duty, giving the lame excuse that I had a question about No Trespassing signs. Neither Erik nor Quincey nor anyone else who wouldn't think I was blowing this out of proportion were in. Even Chief McTavish was off.

Since I was sure Griffin wouldn't shoot me, I'd go back out to my car and take a look around. If I didn't see him, I'd start off again on a circuitous route through Fair Haven. Now that I was on my home turf, I might even be able to lose him.

A piece of paper tucked under one of my windshield wipers fluttered in the breeze. At first, I thought it was a parking ticket. Then I got closer. Someone had ripped one of the yard sale flyers off the nearest lamp post and had scrawled something across it.

Friendly town you have here. Sugarwood sounds like a nice place. I might visit sometime.

I sagged against my car's hood. I'd underestimated him. His note was smart. It could as easily be a friendly message as the threat I knew it was. I'd figured that as long as I didn't lead him to Sugarwood, I'd be safe.

But instead I'd led him close enough. All he'd had to do was ask someone where he could find Nicole Fitzhenry-Dawes, and after that, Sugarwood was easy to locate. We had signs plastered all around town.

Griffin knew where I lived.

And there was absolutely nothing I could do about it.

***

The look on Griffin's face, the memory of that black motorcycle following me, and the thought of his note continued to send shivers over my scalp the rest of the week.

I'd made sure to lock my house up tight, and I'd kept Toby in the bedroom with me each night. I even shoved a chair under the front and back doorknobs. I didn't know if that actually worked to block a door, but it couldn't hurt.

To make matters worse, Dean's case felt like it stalled out. Hal hadn't been able to find anything useful on the names I sent him. Griffin had a background in IT and a sealed juvenile record. The names of all of Dean's clients turned up clean, and Dean himself seemed to spend most of his time at the gym or at G&D Construction.

By the time Friday came, I was thankful for the hustle of final prep for Stacey's baby shower to take my mind off of it for a bit.

I hadn't believed Stacey when she'd warned me what a baby shower in Fair Haven would be like. I'd thought we could hold it in my house until the guest list swelled to nearly a hundred women. I'd ended up renting a tent that Mark, Russ, Dave—who worked our rental shop—and Stacey's dad, Tony, set up in the clearing where the antique sugar shack used to be until it burned down. In a way, it was a blessing that the contractor couldn't fit us in until fall to build a replica since it gave us a spot to put the tent. Mandy, Stacey, Stacey's mom, and I spent all of Friday making the maple syrup popcorn and putting together the favors.

But it was worth it to watch the outpouring of love for Stacey. Some of the local gossips might have come mainly to see how she was handling becoming a young single mom. Most of the people were there because they cared about Stacey and her family.

When what I'd expected to be a two-hour event stretched to four, I was also glad I'd given in when Mandy insisted that I let her cater. The finger foods I'd thought we could manage with wouldn't have been nearly enough. I was clearly not cut out to be an event planner.

It took us another hour to transport all the gifts back to Stacey's house, even though Mark, Russ, and Tony all returned to help.

I leaned on Mark on the walk back to my house and stifled a yawn. "Eloping is looking better all the time. Planning a party is more exhausting than dealing with criminals."

"Too late now." Mark squeezed my waist. "We'd have to move to DC if we did it now, because we'd never be able to face my mom again."

I started to laugh, but it turned into another yawn. "Does it mean I'm old if I want to go to bed now even though it's only six o'clock?"

"Before supper? I could run into town for something if you don't have anything in your fridge. We still need to look over the ME's report for your case."

My fridge had been holding everything I'd put together for the baby shower. Now it probably had a bag of apples and a carton of orange juice. Not exactly supper fare. I might have a pizza in the freezer, but I couldn't make any promises. I'd been so busy with Dean's case and Stacey's shower that I hadn't had time to shop.

"I can stay awake long enough to eat and go over the report."

"I'll pick someplace close."

When we reached my house, he climbed into his truck, and I headed up the steps. My key turned too easily in the lock, which meant the door hadn't been locked at all.

My heart beat in my chest like it was having a boxing match with my fear. I knew how it happened. Russ was last out of the house this morning in our food caravan, and he'd never locked a door in his life as far as I knew. We'd had multiple conversations about how he needed to lock my door if he was in and out of my house, but he insisted Fair Haven was safe. Half the population didn't lock their doors.

Half the population hadn't been attacked as many times as I had and hadn't been recently followed by a potential criminal and left a threatening note. I was keeping my big-city habits even if we stayed here twenty years.

I should have checked that he'd locked the door, but I'd been so distracted with making sure we hadn't forgotten anything we needed.

Despite the wasted air conditioning, I'd just leave my door open and stay within sprinting distance until I could get my dogs out of their crates. And I'd have Mark check the house to be on the safe side once he got back.

I stopped three feet inside the door. The house was too quiet. It gave me the same feeling as when I woke up in the night and the white noise had vanished because the power had gone out. It'd only happened a few times this past winter, but I couldn't sleep when it did.

I could hear the fridge humming this time, so it wasn't that.

It had to be that my dogs weren't squeaking and howling to be let out. Toby's hearing had been going lately, but Velma should have still heard me come in.

I headed for the laundry room. The door stood open. That door I knew I'd closed when everyone was here. Mandy must have come by to take the dogs for a walk again.

I poked my head in the door. As expected, both crates were empty.

Good thing I hadn't sent Russ an angry text about leaving my door unlocked. Mandy would have left it open because she hated juggling a key and leashes. Given the current situation, I'd need to ask her to lock up when she went out as well.

In the meantime, I'd leave my front door open. Not exactly energy-efficient, but better than growing a stomach ulcer because I was afraid someone would sneak up on me and I wouldn't be able to escape in time.

While I waited for Mark, I pulled out the medical examiner's report on Sandra and refreshed my memory on the items I wanted to check with Mark.

Mark came through the door, his arms full of bags from A Salt & Battery. He kicked the door shut with his foot and looked around. "Where's my furry welcoming party?"

I closed the file and slid it to the side until we finished dinner. "I think Mandy must have taken them for a walk after the shower. They've been gone a long time, though. I'd better call and make sure Velma hasn't escaped again."

Mandy was convinced Velma did it on purpose, that it was a game to her, like the dog version of hide and seek. That might be true, but the one time I'd almost lost her, she hadn't been trying to hide from me. She loved to run, and it seemed like she took off and then forgot how to get back. I was more careful than Mandy about keeping watch on her and calling for her when she got too far away. Mandy got distracted, and by the time she looked up, Velma was gone.

I plugged Mandy's number into my phone and prayed she wasn't in one of the dead-zone pockets.

"Hello?" Mandy sounded out of breath.

If I hadn't known that she'd lost ten pounds since she started borrowing my dogs, I'd wonder why she kept taking them out. She always came back red-faced and sullen.

"It's just me. I wanted to make sure Velma hadn't run off on you again."

More wheezy breathing. "I'm not out with the dogs. I just finished unloading all the leftovers from the party."

I know I'd put them in their crates so they weren't underfoot while we took the food out for the baby shower. They were smart dogs, but they didn't have opposable thumbs. They couldn't have let themselves out. The only other person who took them without asking was Russ, and he'd been with us the whole time post-shower until Mark and I left to walk back here.

"Why are you asking about the dogs?" Mandy said.

I hung up on her. My body felt like it belonged to someone else, and I'd borrowed it. It didn't want to respond to my commands the way my own body should.

Mark stopped beside me, silverware in his hands. "What's wrong?"

"Mandy doesn't have the dogs."

Mark laid the silverware down slowly, as if he didn't want to spook me with any sudden moves or loud noises. I couldn't blame him. I felt like I was about to shatter, sending body shrapnel everywhere.

"Maybe someone else borrowed them," he said. "Like Dave.

Remember you told me that customers have been asking to see the dogs ever since that article about Sugarwood turned her into your mascot."

That part was possible. The reporter had asked to do a piece on Sugarwood because it was one of the oldest sugar bushes in Michigan. I'd been teaching Velma a few tricks to keep her mind engaged in non-naughty behaviors, so I showed the reporter how she would hold a wooden bucket in her mouth. It ended up as the largest photo with the story, and since then, Dave had told me the most common question he got from visitors was whether they'd be able to see the dog from the article carry the bucket. We'd even framed the article and photo, and it now hung in the Short Stack, our pancake house.

But even with my door unlocked, it seemed far-fetched. "Dave would never enter my home without permission. Besides, he's allergic to dogs."

I dialed his number just in case.

"I wouldn't take them without asking, but I wonder if I could work that into my mystery. Maybe it could be a mystery-fantasy and the dogs teleport from—"

I hung up on Dave as well. "He doesn't have them. I feel sick."

"Someone has to have them." Mark's face had lost enough color that I could see the blue veins near his temples. "Did you check for a note?"

I did a mental forehead slap. If I hadn't been so panicky, that would have been the first thing I did. Whoever took them probably didn't want to bother me with a phone call while I was busy with Stacey's baby shower.

I walked to the laundry room.

When I'd glanced in before, I'd seen Velma's crate hanging open. Toby's crate nestled farther back in the room. It hung open as well, but a note was taped to the door.

I slumped against the door frame. "Whoever it was left a note." Whoever it was would also get what my grandma used to call a *tongue lashing* for not at least texting me to ask permission, interruption or no. Even in a small town, you shouldn't traipse into someone's house. An unlocked door didn't constitute permission.

Someone should also suffer a little for the fact that I felt like a doofus because I didn't check for a note.

I yanked the note off the crate hard enough that the tape stayed behind and the top of the paper ripped.

It was typed.

We have the dogs. They're safe. If you want them back, you'll stop poking around in other people's business and make Dean Scott plead guilty rather than going to trial.

he paper slipped from my hand.

Mark caught it before it hit the ground. His gaze skimmed the paper. "I'm calling the police."

I grabbed his wrist. "You can't call the police."

"It doesn't say that."

It hadn't said that? I read the note a second time to be sure. "What type of kidnapper doesn't specify not to call the police? Isn't that a given? Don't these people watch TV?"

My voice jumped in pitch, but I couldn't seem to control it. Not only had someone been in my home, they'd taken my dogs. Even though the note promised they were safe, they didn't have Toby's bed or his glucosamine for his joints or Velma's toys. And there was no way they'd walk them properly because they couldn't risk being seen.

If I didn't comply, who knew what they'd do next? Whoever had taken my dogs had probably killed Sandra as well since they wanted Dean to take the fall for it. If they'd killed a person, they wouldn't hesitate to kill my dogs. Maybe next time they'd kidnap me, too.

You need to calm down and think, the voice in my head that always sounded too much like my mom said.

I didn't want to calm down and think. I wanted to panic and cry. But calming down and thinking made a lot more sense. As my dad loved to remind me when I was a little girl, crying didn't achieve anything. And I knew that panicking didn't, especially as an adult.

"Call the police," I told Mark. "I'm calling Dean."

I dialed his number, but he didn't answer. Instead of leaving a message, I ended the call and dialed again. And again.

Finally, on the fifth try, he answered—with a curse word strong enough that I would have hung up on him if the situation were different.

"Someone took my dogs. Either you get them back to me, today, or you'll be finding yourself a new lawyer tomorrow."

"What makes you think I can get them back?" Dean said. His tone still had a snarly quality to it. "I didn't take them."

"Because they know you well enough to know I'm your lawyer, and whoever took them wants you to go to prison without a trial. You didn't take them, but it's a good bet you're connected to the person who did."

A sound like fabric rubbing over the phone filled my ear. Given his tendency to go around shirtless, he was probably getting dressed.

"How do you know that?" he asked.

To his credit, the sniping tone had vanished. I filled him in on the note.

"The note said *other people's business*? It said that's what they wanted you to stop nosing around in?"

Yarg. If my dogs hadn't been involved, I never would have missed that. That meant this likely wasn't about Sandra's murder at all. It wasn't the real murderer who'd taken my dogs. This happened because I'd been poking around in Dean's construction business. Then again, Griffin might be both the one behind the kidnapping because I'd been poking around and the one behind Sandra's murder. "That's what it said. So I'd start with your business partner."

"I don't think it was Griffin. I'll handle this. Don't call the police."

Don't call the police? He had to be kidding me. I might have listened to that if the kidnappers had demanded it, but I certainly wasn't doing it to cover Dean's hind end. "Mark's already called the police."

He swore again. "You just made this worse."

That did it. "It's not my fault if you get caught doing something illegal. And it's time I talked to Elise about it. I want off this case."

"Don't call Elise." Now his voice had a frantic tone. "I'll tell you everything once we get your dogs back, but don't tell Elise. She'll use it to get my visiting rights to my kids revoked."

She probably should, depending on what he was involved in. People who would snatch my dogs might also kidnap Arielle and Cameron. Granted, they'd seemingly only come for my dogs because they thought I was on to them, which meant Arielle and Cameron weren't in immediate danger.

Still, if Dean was involved in something illegal, Elise should know. Her job—my job as their future "aunt"—was to protect those kids.

"You'll tell me everything, and then I'll decide whether Elise needs to know or not. For now, get my dogs back."

We ended the call. Just in time, too. A Fair Haven police cruiser stopped in my driveway.

Please be Erik. Please be Erik.

I pocketed my phone and met Mark at the door he'd already opened.

The man who climbed out of the police cruiser wasn't Erik. It was Grady Scherwin.

His gut hadn't gotten any smaller than the last time I saw him and still looked out of place with his oversized arm muscles. Maybe he took steroids. I gave myself a mental pinch. There was no need to be mean, even in my mind, and even if I was under stress. Grady was mean enough for the both of us.

I turned to Mark. "I'm not trusting Grady Scherwin to find my dogs. He won't even take this seriously."

Mark hit a button on his phone. "You're not. Don't worry. I'll handle this."

He stepped away from the door, and I went out onto the front steps. I placed myself on the top step so that Grady Scherwin couldn't come up without pushing past me.

He squinted up at me even though the sun was behind him. "I hear you need to report a theft."

A theft. As if my dogs were nothing more than stolen property. "My dogs were kidnapped." I emphasized *kidnapped*. "Is Sergeant Higgins working today?"

"If you want to make a report, I'm willing to take it"—he crossed his arms, making his biceps look even larger—"but don't waste my time asking about other officers. This isn't *The Bachelor* or something."

From the corner of my eye, I caught movement behind me. I glanced back, and Mark motioned for me to join him.

I held up a finger to Grady. "I'll be right back."

I might have taken a bit too much enjoyment from the annoyed look on his face.

Mark led me to the far side of the room. "Erik and Quincey are both off today, but I talked to Chief McTavish. He's sending Troy."

I pressed a hand into my forehead. Troy was at the bottom of the Fair Haven police totem pole as far as seniority was concerned. He'd only been out of the academy for two or three years, and Fair Haven had been his first posting. Because I'd never worked with him on a previous case, I didn't know if he was even any good at his job. In fact, this might be the first serious case he'd ever worked. If I was remembering correctly, he mainly worked traffic. I didn't even know him on a personal level the way I did many of the other officers.

"There's no one else?"

Mark shook his head. "Everyone else is busy. Quincey's back in tomorrow, and McTavish promised to give him the case then, but today our choices are Troy or Scherwin."

"Troy it is."

"I figured as much. He's on his way."

I leaned around Mark. Grady Scherwin's ears were now a reddish-purple, like the only thing keeping him from throwing his proverbial weight around was Mark's presence. Other than Chief McTavish, Mark was the only person I'd ever seen Scherwin show respect to. Given that the man seemed to think wearing a badge made him better than everyone who didn't, that was saying something. Mark wasn't an officer.

"What do we do about Scherwin?" I asked. "Do we wait for Troy and hope he takes the hint?"

"McTavish said he'd have him called back to the station, but I'll talk to him anyway."

My phone vibrated in my pocket. Maybe Erik had heard about what happened—Fair Haven shared news faster than Facebook or Twitter—and he was going to offer to come in.

The screen displayed Mandy's name. I should have known better than to think I'd get away with hanging up on her. I shouldn't have done it. It wasn't a nice way to treat a friend. Dave, thankfully, would assume I'd walked into a cell phone dead zone. We'd been disconnected that way more than once before.

I touched the screen to answer. "I'm sorry about earlier," I said in lieu of hello.

"Are the dogs okay? What's going on?"

Her voice had the same tone to it as when she'd discovered a puddle of blood in one of the rooms of her bed and breakfast. It was that my-sanity-is-held-together-by-Scotch-tape sound.

I was a horrible friend. She loved me, and she loved my dogs, and no matter how scared I was, I shouldn't have left her hanging. I filled her in on what had happened.

"I'm coming over."

That was the last thing I needed. Mandy would have a bunch of crazy theories about who took my dogs, from a rogue taxidermist to kids pulling a prank. None of them would be anywhere close to accurate, and all of them would only make me feel more like throwing up all the food I ate at Stacey's shower than I already did. "You don't need to come. Mark's here, and the police are on their way."

No need to feed the rumor mill by telling her I'd rejected the first police officer who showed up. Grady Scherwin already didn't like me, and his pride wouldn't take a public slight well.

"I can find them," Mandy said. "I'm coming. Don't let the police leave until I get there."

"Mandy, you can't—"

The line went dead. For a second I fantasized about throwing the phone across the room. But that wouldn't do me any good. Then I wouldn't have my dogs or my phone.

I sank down onto one of the stools by my kitchen island, lowered my head onto my arms, and prayed. Praying should have been the first thing I'd done if I'd been thinking more clearly.

I must have lost track of time because, the next thing I knew, a hand that could only belong to Mark rested on my back.

"Scherwin's gone, and I showed the note to Troy. He'll need you to give him the names of anyone you think might want to see Dean go to prison without a trial."

So far, that could be almost anyone. His partner might want to see him skip the trial because that would keep attention off of their possibly illicit business. Any of their "clients" would have the same motivation. If the trial had been going in our favor, I might have even suspected Nadine of trying to make sure justice was done for her sister. Since we hadn't started the trial, she seemed the least likely. It could also be whoever had killed Sandra, a list that could include one of Dean's clients or his partner but wasn't exclusive to them.

I slid from the stool. My front door still hung open. Troy waited at the bottom of the steps, his notebook in his hand.

Before I could reach him, Mandy's car wheeled into my driveway. Stones shot from under her tires.

For a second, I thought she was going to slam straight into Troy's cruiser. I flinched backward, but her car skidded to a stop less than a foot from his bumper. Troy lunged forward at the same time as Mandy half jumped, half tumbled out of her driver's side door.

She held her phone in the air. "They're not moving." The words came out in a huff. "We can catch up to them."

Troy glanced back at me with a look that said he wasn't sure whether to talk to Mandy or arrest her. I had a suspicion that if she'd been clocked driving over here, it'd be the latter.

But she seemed so certain. My heart took a flutter-step into my throat. "How do you know where they are?"

She waved her phone in the air. "You know how Velma is. She gets away from me almost every time I walk her, and you said I couldn't keep walking them if I couldn't control her."

That had been an uncomfortable conversation. Mandy loved walking the dogs, but twice we'd lost Velma for over two hours. Mandy stopped walking them for about a week, came back with a gift of another new collar for Velma and a chew toy for Toby, and we hadn't had problems since.

Maybe that should have been my tip-off. It wasn't like Mandy would have been negligent with Velma before and suddenly responsible after our talk. It also wasn't like a single lesson from a dog trainer would have improved matters. I'd convinced myself that she simply stopped letting either dog off their leash since Velma would have yanked away if she released only Toby.

Now, though, the itch at the back of my mind that had warned me something was wrong leapt to the forefront. "And how does that help us find them now?"

Mandy sucked one edge of her bottom lip between her teeth, making her look more like a sixteen-year-old who'd wrecked her parents' car than like a mature, independent sixty-year-old. It was quite a feat given Mandy was taller than most men.

"I didn't tell you before because I knew you wouldn't like it. I bought a collar for Velma with a GPS tracker in it. She's still been getting away from me, but I've been able to trail her until Toby and I catch up."

That also explained why Mandy's walks got longer. Normally, I would have been angry, but if it gave me a chance of getting my dogs back, I'd take it, and I wouldn't lecture her. "Show me."

She passed me her phone. Mark and Troy moved in as well.

A small red dot blipped on the screen, on a map that looked a lot like the GPS built into my car or like the Map My Walk app I'd been using to track how many calories I burned while walking the dogs. Mandy introduced me to that as well. Her penchant for enjoying mysteries also meant she liked to keep up-to-date on technology that could have multiple purposes.

"If you tap the dot," Mandy said, "it gives you the closest address, too. I've been watching it since I got in the car, and they haven't moved in the last five minutes."

I tapped the dot. White Cloud, the town where Dean lived. And

I knew the street address. I'd been there only a few days ago, talking to a man who I'd stupidly given one of my cards to. I'd practically drawn him a map to get to me. "This is the home of one of Dean's construction clients."

Troy already had his phone out of his pocket. "That's outside my jurisdiction. I'll call Chief McTavish to get in touch with the local police."

"We're not going to wait here, are we?" Mandy asked. She rocked back and forth like she wanted to speed down to White Cloud and take the dogs back by force.

While I wouldn't go that far—I'd had more run-ins with killers than Mandy, and I wasn't interested in inviting more—I also didn't want to wait around here and have the police put my dogs into a kennel somewhere. They might not even be properly equipped to transport them.

I shook my head.

"I'll drive," Mandy said.

"No," Mark and I both said in unison.

I pointed at Mark's truck to stop the inevitable argument. "He's set up for the dogs, and I'll want you to be watching the GPS in case they move them. If they do, I can call it in while you continue to watch."

That, and we both wanted to make it there alive.

Mandy's concern for the dogs must have overruled her tendency to micromanage, because she headed for Mark's truck without another word in argument. She climbed into the back behind the safety screen for the dogs, and I took the front seat. If—no, when—we had the dogs back, we'd have to flip down the center console to form a third seat up front. That would be a tight squeeze, but I'd try to climb into a cardboard box right now if it meant having my dogs returned to me safely.

Before I climbed in, I arranged to call Troy if anything changed. Since I didn't have a contact on the local police force in White Cloud and Mark didn't have any authority unless a death was involved, that was as good as we were going to get when it came to communicating with the police there. They probably wouldn't take a dog kidnapping any more seriously than Grady Scherwin had unless an officer from another jurisdiction was asking them to look into it, anyway.

"Make sure they realize this is connected to an active murder investigation," I said over my shoulder as I scaled up the running boards.

I made a point of not looking at the speedometer while Mark drove. If he was speeding, I didn't want to know. If he wasn't driving any faster than normal, I also didn't want to know because I'd have been tempted to pressure him to go faster.

Ten minutes from the address, Mandy sucked in a breath. "They're moving again."

It took all my self-control not to drop a curse word. I wasn't someone prone to swearing, but right now it was more tempting than it probably should have been.

Mark took his foot off the gas. "Do I keep going or change direction?"

If the dogs weren't there anymore, we had no grounds to even look in the house at the original address, and we couldn't prove they'd had anything to do with it. They must have, but our proof was leaving. The only person we could prove as guilty was the person who had them.

"We follow the dogs. I'll call Troy. Hopefully the police will still question Dean's clients."

I dialed Troy's number and put him on speaker phone.

"Good timing," he said. "The chief just called me. They're sending someone, but they don't think it's a priority. It could be a while before they get there. You should hang back."

I explained what was going on.

"Which direction are they headed?"

Mandy leaned toward the dog grate and linked her free hand through the wires. "Fair Haven. Or at least generally that way."

She listed the road. Mark threw on his clicker at the last second and swung into a sharp turn. It was a good thing we weren't being videoed. Mandy and I probably looked like actors on an old science fiction show who jerked to the left and right when the ship was supposed to be taking fire.

"If you can catch up to them," Troy said, "give me the license plate number. I can stop them if they come into Fair Haven."

For the next few minutes, I gripped the arm rests while Mark took poorly signed gravel roads. He finally pulled back onto the highway and accelerated.

The dog grate rattled as if Mandy were tugging on it. "They should be right ahead."

Mark pressed the gas pedal and the truck lurched ahead, making up ground. A dot of another car appeared on the road in front of us.

I started praying that they'd head into Fair Haven...and that another police officer wouldn't spot our vehicle and pull us over for speeding before we could get the license plate number.

The car grew as we gained on it.

A prickle went up the back of my neck. The car could be the identical twin to the one sitting in Dean Scott's driveway.

J swiveled to see Mandy in the back. She watched the screen of her phone like I watched magicians, not wanting to miss the sleight of hand. "Are you sure the dogs are in that car?"

Her head bobbed. "The dot turns from red, to yellow, to green as you get closer. It's bright green now."

I tapped Dean's number into my phone.

"You might want to wait until we're a bit closer before calling Troy," Mark said without taking his gaze off the road.

That crazy peripheral vision of his would come in handy when we had kids. "I'm not calling Troy. I'm pretty sure I know who's in that car."

"Scott," Dean answered. His voice had the loud, tinny quality that told me I was hearing him through the car.

"It's Nicole. We might know where my dogs are."

"Listen, I've been thinking about that, and I bet this was all a practical joke. I'm sure your dogs'll be returned by the time you get home."

So that's how he'd planned to explain the sudden reappearance of my dogs. We were close enough now that I could see the license plate, but I was more confident than ever that I wouldn't need to give it to Troy. "Do you know who might have taken them?"

"I'm guessing here. But I can't imagine someone would want me to go to prison enough that they'd steal my lawyer's dogs. That's pretty risky and stupid."

The last part, at least, was true. I could, however, imagine quite a few people who seemed to dislike him enough to meddle with his freedom. I was done with this charade. I wanted my dogs back. "Pull your car over."

I would have sworn his car swerved a touch, and my heart whacked into the front of my chest. My dogs had no safety harness or anything in his car.

"What?" he said.

"We're right behind you. I know you have my dogs. I want them safely in Mark's truck, and then you're going to follow him back to Fair Haven and tell me where you got them from and why that person took them."

Dean didn't answer, but his brake lights blazed.

Mark turned his hazard lights on and followed him over to the edge of the road.

I unsnapped my seat belt as soon as the truck came to a stop. "I'm going to let you and Mandy take the dogs. I need to ride with Dean and have a lawyer–client chat."

Mark's lips thinned. "I'm going to follow you back just in case."

Given that Dean had somehow figured out without a GPS tracker where my dogs were in time to beat the police and us there and then planned to smuggle them back into my house to make this all disappear, I couldn't blame Mark for not trusting him. I didn't trust him, either. The difference was that I didn't feel he was a physical threat to me. He still needed me too much to hurt me.

After I hugged both dogs long enough that Velma, my little attention hog, started to squirm, Mark and Mandy loaded them into his truck.

I climbed into Dean's car without asking permission. "You're driving me home."

My dad always said that silence was one of our greatest tools if used properly. I let it stretch after Dean pulled back onto the road. I wanted him to worry about what was coming next. I didn't let it go on long enough that he could come up with guesses for what I might say and work out lies that would pass for truths.

"I made the rules clear when I took your case. If you did anything illegal, you were on your own. My dogs wouldn't have been taken as leverage for me to throw your case if you were an innocent man. You have until we get back to Sugarwood to convince me that I shouldn't drop you as a client and sleep better tonight for it."

His hands tightened on the steering wheel, his knuckles bulging out.

All at once, I was thankful that Mark was overprotective Mark and had insisted on following us rather than going on ahead. Even though Elise insisted Dean wasn't the violent type, I couldn't help noticing the strength in his hands and how easy it'd be for those hands to hurt me. How easy it would have been for those hands to strangle Sandra.

He kept his gaze on the road. "I haven't done anything illegal since you took my case."

That was very specific wording. Specific enough that I believed him because it basically told me that he had done things that could get him arrested prior to me becoming his lawyer.

"And yet someone still went into my house, took my dogs, and threatened me. I need to know that won't happen again. Especially since your business partner followed me the other day. Elise wouldn't want me on this case if it puts me in danger. And if these people took my dogs, are you sure they didn't kill Sandra?"

He tapped a finger along the top of the steering wheel. "How far does lawyer–client privilege extend?"

Ugg. In all my time as a lawyer, on all the cases I'd worked with my parents, nothing good ever followed those words. In fact, some of the most disturbing revelations came once clients were sure they were safe telling you absolutely everything related to their case.

Privilege didn't cover everything, though, which some people didn't realize. My parents had occasionally had to stop clients before they learned something they'd have to disclose. "You can't tell me anything about future crimes you plan to commit. You can't ask me for advice on avoiding prosecution for crimes not yet committed. You also can't tell me about anything you might be thinking of doing that would harm someone else. And, obviously, if you waive privilege, then everything is fair game."

I'd always hated having to tell clients about the limits of privi-lege. For some lawyers, it might not bother them. But a large part of me wanted to know if my client was planning anything more. I would have rather been able to tell the police so they could stop them.

Yet another sign that Stacey was right. I wasn't cut out to defend guilty clients. Because of his other criminal activities, Dean flirted with the line even if he was innocent of Sandra's murder.

"My construction business isn't a construction business," Dean said.

I barely kept myself from snapping out a sarcastic *no kidding*. Once again, it was unfair that I didn't have the Cavanaugh ability to control my eyebrows. It would have at least let off some steam if I could have arched an eyebrow at him. "And what type of business is it exactly?"

"You might call it identity theft. I prefer to think of it as a consulting business that helps people start a new life."

Given how much cash Dean seemed to have access to, I doubted he sold his wares only to people looking to start a new life. Dean likely dealt with clients here in Michigan, but I suspected Griffin took a lot of their business online to the Darknet.

A hot shower and a lot of soap weren't going to be enough to erase the slimy feeling this case gave me. *It's not your job to parent your clients or comment on their life choices,* my dad's voice chimed in the back of my head. *Your only job is to win their case.*

I mentally scowled at my dad all the way back in Virginia. "And you didn't think that was pertinent information when I wanted to know who might have killed Sandra?"

The car sped up slightly, and I instinctively clenched the armrest. Speeding up was a jerk move if it was intended to scare me, but it might be a subconscious reaction to being questioned on topics that made him uncomfortable.

He shook his head. "My clients were perfectly happy with my work until you came around asking questions and making them think the police were going to come around asking even more. They wouldn't have hurt your dogs. They're good people."

"Stealing my dogs wasn't the way to stay hidden. The police are still on their way to your clients' house."

"They won't be there."

"The police will wait or come back."

He took a curve in the road much faster than the posted limit. "They won't be back. I told them to grab what they needed and go. They were only renting the place anyway."

Maybe it was best he hadn't told me all this before. "I'm afraid to ask, but I need to know to be sure your business didn't get Sandra killed. What type of people are the clients you've dealt with? You're not helping criminals hide from the police, are you? If people feel like their secrets are in danger, they'll kill to protect them. They might have thought Sandra knew their true identities and that she might turn them in."

His shoulders bunched. "Not real criminals. Illegal immigrants. Draft dodgers. That sort of thing. It's mostly people who want to start over. I'm telling you, they were all fine. No complaints. We're careful about who we work with."

"What about the people whose identities you stole?"

Dean's foot came off the gas slightly. "I don't think so."

"You don't *think* so."

"Griffin handles that end of it. But he's only supposed to take the identities of dead people or people who aren't using them anymore, like old folks and people locked up for mental health stuff. He's careful."

My whole body wanted to cringe away from him. "So basically he preys on the most vulnerable segments of society."

Dean opened his mouth, then closed it again.

Smartest move he'd made in weeks not to argue with me on that one.

I gave it a couple of beats to let that sink in. Maybe at least part of it would reach whatever conscience he had left. "If Griffin isn't following those rules, you could have someone who wanted to get even with you for stealing their identity. It's not a victimless crime. It can make it difficult for the person whose life you've hacked to get a mortgage, to get credit cards, to pass background checks."

"He set the rules for who we'd target, so I don't think he'd break them. Like I said, he's careful. But I'll talk to him. You have to leave him alone."

He might as well have said *I can't control what my business partner will do if you make him feel threatened.* "Would he have hurt Sandra?"

"Sandra didn't know that my business wasn't legit."

Something hard and hot formed in the pit of my stomach. His current wife didn't know that his business was actually a cover for his illegal activities. His ex-wife wouldn't, either, which meant she also wouldn't know that he'd suddenly started paying child support thanks to money Elise would never take if she knew where it came from.

"Is your *construction* business your only source of income?" I tried to keep my voice professional, without a note that would tip him off that I was going anywhere else with it than trying to sort through sources for Sandra's killer.

His silence said everything. Even with his relaxed interpretation of right and wrong, he had to be able to guess what I'd think about him lying to his wife about how they were paying their bills.

I speared him with a firm look. "I know that Elise can't know, either."

His took his gaze off the road and fastened it on me. "Elise doesn't need to know. I'm taking care of my kids. Isn't that all that matters?"

His voice wasn't angry. It was more...resigned. Like what I'd have expected from someone who really wanted to be a good parent, but felt they didn't have the capacity to do it—at least not through traditional means—and felt the criticism of those around them deeply.

It was the opposite of what I'd have expected, especially from Dean.

Part of me wanted to leave it be. Dean providing financial support meant Elise had to struggle less to take care of Arielle and Cameron. My dad would say meddling in Dean's personal life wasn't any of my business if it didn't affect his case, which, technically, it didn't.

I caught a glimpse of Mark in the rearview mirror. I knew what he would say. I knew what my pastor would say. I knew what my Uncle Stan would say, too, if he were still alive. And I'd long ago decided I didn't want to be like my dad. Accepting money, or allowing a friend to accept money, that came from an illegal source wasn't right.

What Elise didn't know wouldn't hurt her only as long as she didn't know. Someday, she might figure it out, and when that happened, she'd not only feel like she had to find some way to "give back" that money, but she'd feel betrayed by me, and our relationship would never be the same. If that wasn't enough, I didn't know what it would do to Elise's career if someone found out she'd been accepting money obtained from criminal activity. She could claim she didn't know how Dean got the money, but the stain of that would follow her around anyway.

"Elise needs to know. She won't want the money, knowing where it came from."

The sidelong glance he gave me made me think of a shark—cold and calculating. "If I refuse to tell her, you can't. Lawyer–client privilege."

I felt the cold of his gaze all the way down into my core. I hadn't taken Mark's warning seriously enough when he said Dean was a master manipulator and user. He'd made me think he asked about lawyer–client privilege so that he could answer my questions without it being used against him in court. Maybe that had been part of his reasoning, but clearly he'd also been making sure that he maintained control. He only let me think I was in charge. Even if I dropped him as a client, I couldn't reveal what he'd told me while I was his lawyer.

I narrowed my eyes slightly. With most people, he'd have won. But I was a Fitzhenry-Dawes. I might not be the lawyer my parents were, but I hadn't been raised by them for nothing.

Every building had a backdoor if the front one seems locked, my dad loved to say.

"You're right. I can't tell her. I can refuse to represent you, though, and you won't find another lawyer who'll be able to get you acquitted. There's enough evidence against you that the prosecutor who has your case probably cracked open a beer and put his feet up the day it landed on his desk."

Dean's gaze flickered slightly.

I leaned toward him. "And once I'm not your lawyer, I can have a friendly chat with my soon-to-be cousin-in-law Elise and recommend, as a friend, that she shouldn't accept any more money from you and that her kids would be safer if they weren't allowed to spend time alone with you. Elise is intelligent. If you think she won't read between the lines regardless of how vague I am, you're wrong. And you'll still need to find a way to pay my already-accrued fees that doesn't involve dirty money."

We hit the outskirts of Fair Haven and Dean dropped his speed. It seemed like the fight came out of him with the speed drop as well.

His broad shoulders hunched. "How do you expect me to pay you or help out my kids then? I don't have any other money."

It felt like something clicked into place in my head. Mark had said Dean was manipulative, and he was. But I suspected that under all that bravado hid someone who was much more scared and wounded little boy than evil supervillain. What had he experienced in his own childhood?

I settled back in my seat. The shift in the air was almost palpable. I could turn this around now so that we were working together.

I wouldn't go so far as to call us allies since I still didn't trust him, but I had a chance to win him over so he trusted me a little more.

To do that, I had to figure out a legitimate way he could support his children and pay me.

I ran my fingers along the car's leather armrests, then looked down at my hand. He might not have cash, but he had assets. Some of what he owned had probably been paid for with his ill-gotten gains, but the rest of it would have come from Sandra or from money he'd gotten prior to opening his new "business" a year or so ago.

"You could sell your car and your house and downsize. And then it'll be time to dissolve your partnership with Griffin and find a real job."

The veins on the back of his hands bulged, but he nodded his head. "Griffin won't like it, but I'll do it."

We passed through Fair Haven and onto the gravel road that led to Sugarwood. We were running out of time to talk privately.

I'd never been a parent, but I did understand the pressure of wanting to make the people in your life proud. I understood how motivating that could be. Dean had shown he wanted to support his children like a good dad would. His attempt to do it had been misguided, but his motives were pure. At least, I hoped so. The man was as slippery as a wet bar of soap.

"I'm going to do what I can to make sure you don't go to prison for something you didn't do, but I don't want to put in all that work if you're only going to throw it away getting arrested for something you did do. That won't help your kids. You're getting a chance to turn things around now. If you really love them, then they don't need fancy stuff. They need you to be a man they can look up to."

"I'm not sure I know how to do that."

His words were so soft I almost missed them under the sound of the tires on the gravel road.

Almost like he wasn't sure he wanted me to hear them.

He didn't strike me as the kind of man who was good at being vulnerable. Which meant that if I waited too long or said the wrong thing, I'd lose all the ground it seemed like we'd gained. He'd feel like he'd been too exposed and like he had to regain superiority.

I shrugged. "I think it's about trying to become the kind of person you'd want your kids to grow up into." I made sure to keep any pity from my voice, and I tried to wipe my expression into something professional. "We're almost there, and we can't talk about anything confidential once others are around. I need you to tell me honestly. Would any of your clients have had a reason to hurt Sandra?"

"No. I meant it when I said that."

"What about Griffin?"

His Adam's apple moved like he'd swallowed instinctively. It was a tell he couldn't hide. "Griffin couldn't have done it."

Was it a tell that he was lying or that something else about the answer made him uncomfortable? "How can you be sure? You weren't with him at the time."

He pulled his car to a stop in front of my house. "That's the thing. I was with him at the time. I was with him until nearly sunrise, working on our business. I'd told Sandra I'd be home before midnight. I didn't really pass out on the couch when I came home. I slept there when I came in 'cause I thought she'd be pissed at me for not showing up when I said and not calling."

I felt like throwing my hands up in the air. "Why didn't you tell the police that? You have an alibi. We wouldn't even have to take this to court."

"We weren't..." Dean squirmed in his seat like the seatbelt was choking him. "What we were doing wasn't legal, and Griffin said if I told the police I was with him, he'd lie and say I wasn't."

My mind ground around in a circle over the idea that both Dean and Griffin were innocent. Deep down, I think I'd sincerely believed one of them had done it, and I'd been leaning toward Griffin. Now I knew I was defending an innocent man—at least innocent of murdering his wife—and all the people I'd thought could have done it were off the list.

I undid my seatbelt but didn't leave the car. "My dad would say we should push Griffin in court, build our case around making him look guilty for Sandra's murder. Worst case, it'd create reasonable doubt. Best case, he'd admit he was with you. My dad rarely loses."

Purple smudges appeared under his eyes, and a white thread outlined his lips. "Griffin's not the kind of man I want to cross. I'm the junior partner. He's the pro. And if we go after him, he won't just come after me. He'll come after you, and Mark, and Elise, and my kids. When he does, he won't be stealing your dogs. I'd rather go to prison for something I didn't do. At least then my kids would be safe."

Monday morning, I showed up at Dean's house at 8:00 am. I'd warned him I was coming, that I'd even bring coffee and donuts, but he still wasn't wearing a shirt when he opened the door, and his hair sticking up on one side suggested he'd been asleep on the couch until I knocked. Based on the crumpled shirt lying next to his couch, I was beginning to suspect that he stripped them off as soon as he got home and didn't bother to cover up until he had to.

I pointed at his naked chest. He sighed and grabbed the shirt from the floor, but didn't argue. The rest of the morning went more smoothly from there. I helped him put together his résumé and figure out where to look for jobs. Those seemed like they should be skills every adult had, and yet he didn't. My argument for learning them wasn't only that he needed to be a better example for his kids, but also that we needed to be able to honestly prove he was a respectable member of society and gainfully employed. Even though juries were only supposed to judge based on the facts of a case, that's not how it worked in real life. They also looked at how a defendant was dressed and what type of a person they seemed to be.

After we finished with his résumé, I also helped him pick a real estate agent and call the office. She promised to come by that afternoon to assess the house and get it listed. Since we still had a lot of work to do on Dean's case, I offered to wait.

First, I had to grab my files from my car. We had to figure out who else might have had a motive to kill Sandra.

As I unlocked my car, a movement from across the street caught my attention. The neighbor I'd talked to before stood on her front lawn, a giant green watering can in her hands. She clearly meant it to appear like she was watering her plants, but the water from the can hit her shoes and driveway instead.

The neighbor I really wanted to talk to was the one who never seemed to be home, mainly because I wanted to know if he'd found a roll of duct tape in his yard. Last week, I'd checked with the neighbors at the house behind Dean's. They'd been on vacation that week, but they hadn't found a roll of tape when they came home. That left only the one neighbor I hadn't spoken to. With how little he seemed to be home, I doubted he'd noticed anything.

Now that Griffin wasn't a suspect anymore, though, I was back to square one. It wouldn't hurt to talk again with the woman who seemed to watch her neighbors closely enough that I questioned when she found time to weed her gardens. Though perhaps that's why they were so well tended. I bet she didn't have any gardens in the back where she couldn't watch who came and went from the houses around her.

I waved to her. The watering can slipped, and the stream of water doused her leg. She pursed her lips and set the can down as I jogged across the street. Today I'd decided casual was the best way to go, so at least I didn't have to worry about heels.

Her lips stayed pursed and her gaze slid over me from my sneakers to my ponytail. "You don't look like this visit was professional."

Apparently, I couldn't win when it came to my clothes. "Heels aren't very practical when you have a long day ahead of you."

Her lips relaxed. I wouldn't have called her expression friendly, but at least it wasn't openly hostile anymore. My dad would tell me to suspect everyone, and that she might have hated Dean enough to kill him, but I couldn't see her killing Sandra. Lecturing her about how she could do better, maybe, but smothering her with a grocery bag...it didn't fit. Though I'd been wrong before.

I pointed back at Dean's house. "I promised to tell you if Dean planned to sell the house."

The woman stopped swiping at her wet pant leg and looked up at me. "He's selling." She gave her pant leg one more squeeze, not even allowing me a chance to confirm that she had the facts right. "It's about time. I'm not one who likes to speak ill of the dead, but they've been keeping nice families from moving into the neighborhood, which hurts all our property values. No one wants to bring their spouse and children into a community with an open marriage like all those celebrities have."

I wasn't up-to-date enough on celebrity gossip to know which couples she meant, but this was the first I'd heard about Dean and Sandra having a non-monogamous relationship. That could mean a jealous third party had killed Sandra—either to have Dean to herself or because she didn't want Sandra sleeping with her man. It could also open up motives on the side of whoever Sandra was cheating with. If he asked her to leave Dean for him and she refused, that could be motive as well.

I started to ask the woman *why* she thought they had an open marriage, but stopped myself. *Why* questions could come across as accusatory if they weren't worded perfectly. I leaned forward, drew my eyebrows down, and opened my mouth slightly, pretending to be aghast. "You saw them with other people?"

She nodded. "Women would show up at their door when Sandra wasn't home. Sometimes men, too."

That sounded more like it related to Dean's business than him having affairs. He'd said Sandra hadn't known what he was really doing, so he likely met with clients at times when she wasn't around.

"And Sandra went next door to Ken's house more than was neighborly," the woman said. "At times when Dean wasn't around. She tried to be discreet at least, but asking to borrow a screwdriver doesn't take an hour."

I'd heard the name *Ken* before. Back in my original conversation with Dean, he'd said something about Sandra taking care of Ken when he was sick. The prosecution's list of witnesses they might call also included a Ken Vasel. In his statement to the police, he'd said Dean and Sandra's relationship was rocky. The prosecution never had to disclose how they intended to use what they'd uncovered, but I'd assumed—apparently correctly—that Ken would be called to the stand to present evidence for Dean's motive.

It was a good bet Ken wasn't the sixty-something man I'd spoken to before. He was more likely the neighbor who never seemed to be home during a weekday. His absence suggested he worked a regular nine-to-five job. Not that people who held down regular jobs couldn't kill the woman they were having an affair with —it happened all the time. But if he had done it, people would be much less likely to want to believe it than if I'd been able to find evidence that Dean's partner had done it.

Unfortunately, if Sandra was having an affair and Ken had an alibi for her time of death, I might not be able to save Dean. Given what Ken said in his statement to the police, the prosecutor had probably already spoken to him and likely knew about the affair. Even if Ken hadn't admitted to it, any decent prosecutor would know enough to push him about why he thought their marriage was falling apart once they put him on the stand and he was under oath to tell the truth.

The question then would be whether Ken was afraid enough of being accused of Sandra's murder that he'd lie about the affair even under threat of perjury. If he had an alibi, he'd tell the truth, and Dean would be sunk.

I backed up and casually waved to Ms. Nosy Neighbor so she didn't know how important what she'd said could be to Dean's case. "I'm glad I was able to convince him to sell. You'll hopefully see the sign up this afternoon, but don't worry if you don't. He's definitely going to sell."

She scurried for her house, presumably to call the neighbors and tell them the news. She left her watering can tipped over on the lawn.

I bypassed my car and headed straight back inside Dean's house. The files I'd brought wouldn't be necessary if it turned out that Sandra was having an affair. We'd then have another viable suspect to investigate. The question I needed answered now was whether or not Dean knew about it.

If he did, we had a lot of damage control to do where his case was concerned. Beyond that, I needed all the details about the affair he could give me. Proving Ken had killed Sandra could be the only way to prove that Dean hadn't.

Dean was still sitting at the computer where I'd left him, but when I stopped behind him, he was playing Minesweeper rather than searching for jobs.

It was amazing that Sandra had been the one to die. If I'd been asked to lay odds, I would have put them on her killing Dean. Elise must have more patience than I could even imagine.

At least now I knew Dean couldn't have killed Sandra since he had an alibi. It was nice to know one thing was a solid fact. Mark had asked me if Dean might be lying about the alibi and simply trying to scare me enough that I didn't ask Griffin about it. I'd wondered the same until I'd gotten a voicemail from a burner number late last night. It'd definitely been Griffin's voice, and all he'd said was *He was with me that night.*

Something about the way Griffin said it had also made me certain that Dean hadn't been exaggerating about what Griffin would do if we tried to expose him or the business.

Dean didn't even bother shutting Minesweeper down when I walked up. "You were gone a long time. Get lost in my driveway?"

I turned his monitor off.

He cursed at me and swiveled around in his chair. He leaned back and crossed his arms over his chest.

I pulled a kitchen chair over and sat across from him. It made me feel a bit like we were in a group therapy session and I was the counselor, but this case was turning out to involve a lot of protecting my client from himself.

"The prosecution will need to show that you had a motive for killing Sandra. Nearly half of all women murdered in the U.S. are killed by romantic partners. That means they're going to ask a lot of questions about your marriage."

"We had a good marriage," he said quickly.

Much too quickly, considering how evasive he tended to be when I wanted information out of him, and this time I hadn't even asked a question.

"Did you ever fight?"

"Yeah. Everyone does."

The sulky tone was back in his voice. He'd seemed a little scared when I asked about his finances before, like he was hiding something. It was part of what had tipped me off that his business might not be legitimate. Now he sounded like I'd hit a sensitive spot. He and Sandra had been having troubles in their marriage, and he didn't like to be asked about it.

His tone of voice wasn't angry, though. It wasn't the voice of a man who'd been having violent arguments with his wife and one of them went too far. It was more the voice of a hurt little boy trying to protect himself. That was good in one way. It meant they shouldn't be able to find witnesses that could say they'd heard them fighting. In another way, it made my eyes sting. I couldn't imagine what it did to you to have one failed marriage, let alone thinking your second one was heading the same way.

I softened my voice. "You know I have to ask because they'll ask you on the stand. What did you two fight about?"

"Normal stuff. Money."

Originally, I'd suspected Sandra's death might be connected to some shady business Dean was involved in. If the prosecution found out they argued about money, they'd say maybe she didn't like working so hard while he sat around—that'd been something Elise once confided in me happened within their marriage. Perhaps Dean finally got tired of the women in his life complaining about his laziness and he did something about it—something that resulted in Sandra's death.

The prosecution could still go down those paths, and I'd have to figure out how to block them without revealing Dean's alibi or the true nature of his construction business. Doing either would put Arielle and Cameron at risk from Griffin. Even if he ended up charged with a crime, he wouldn't be locked up immediately, and Dean seemed confident he'd take vengeance.

"What about money specifically?" I asked.

Dean gave what sounded like a mix between a huff and a growl. "Normal stuff. Not having enough. How we'd spend what we had. Are they really going to care about any of that? Every couple fights about money."

"They are going to care if they think it points to motive."

His sigh carried less confrontation this time. "Fine. When I started to make more, she wanted to give some to her sister, and I wanted to keep it for Arielle and Cameron."

The story I'd gotten from Elise was that Dean had been terrible about contributing to the needs of their kids until recently. "What changed? Why the sudden concern with providing for your kids?" I held back a flinch. That sounded more accusatory than I'd intended it to. "If the prosecution knows your history, they're going to push you on it."

Dean shrugged, his arms still across his chest. "Last summer, Arielle wanted to go to this horse camp. She was crying on the phone to me because Elise wouldn't let her go. I talked to Elise about it, telling her she should send Arielle, and she blew up at me about how she had to make sure they had shoes and clothes and that didn't leave money for expensive camps when I didn't send the child support I was supposed to. Arielle was mad at her mom, but it was my fault she couldn't go."

My mind bottomed out, and I had no idea what to say in response.

"I wasn't going to give money to save a stupid garden center when my kids needed it. Arielle was crying because I let her down and blaming her mom for it. Is that what you wanted to hear?" He sucked in a long breath. "Are we done?"

Boy, did I wish we were. Not only did this whole conversation make me feel like I was digging through Elise's underwear drawer, but I'd genuinely upset him.

But I had to ask him about the neighbor's assertion that one or both of them was cheating. I'd be negligent to omit it since the prosecution would likely find out and bring it up. "Your neighbor said people would come to the house when Sandra wasn't home. Did you have a girlfriend on the side who might have wanted to get rid of Sandra?"

"No. The only people I had come by when Sandra wasn't here were Griffin and clients."

His response wasn't too fast or two slow. Drat. I believed him. I had to make sure, though. "You cheated on Elise."

"Yeah, and look where that got me. By the time I realized how stupid I'd been, Elise wouldn't take me back, and now I get to see my kids a couple weekends a month."

"What about Sandra?"

"What about Sandra what?"

"Do you think she might have been seeing someone else? If she was, and she refused to leave you for him, he might have been jealous enough to kill her."

His Adam's apple jerked in his throat like he wanted to swallow and couldn't. His breathing turned ragged. "She might have been. One time when we were fighting about the money, she said she didn't have to stay with me. She had other options."

On one hand, an affair by Sandra gave us a viable person of interest in her murder. On the other hand, if Dean suspected an affair, it strengthened his motive, at least in the eyes of the prosecution and jury. Based on his history, if he'd been sure, he probably would have simply left her for someone else.

"I'm done talking about this for today," Dean said. "This is still my house. I'll talk to the real estate agent myself. You can get out."

Staying wasn't going to do me any good. His reaction told me he didn't know who it was. If he had, he would have said so. He'd want me to try to pin Sandra's murder on him.

I headed out to my car. The driveway to the left still sat empty.

With Dean's confirmation that Sandra might have been having an affair, now I had an even larger problem.

Based on what Ms. Nosy Neighbor told me, Sandra was most likely having an affair with her other neighbor Ken. I needed to talk to him.

But I didn't feel safe doing it alone.

hy anyone would want to be a lone wolf was beyond me.

I'd been back to my house for fifteen minutes, and I still had no idea who I could ask to accompany me to talk to Dean and Sandra's neighbor.

Elise and Erik were obvious *no*s. Not only was it out of their jurisdiction, but I hadn't talked to Erik since I took Dean on as a client. He hadn't called me, either. Erik was a born avoidist, so the lack of communication meant he was annoyed with me and had to work through it in his own head first.

I also couldn't ask Mark. He'd been working long days, and when we did have time, I needed him to look at the medical examiner's report more. We'd lost our opportunity thanks to someone stealing my dogs. Besides, I'd have a hard time explaining who he was and why he was there without raising the neighbor's suspicion.

My phone dinged with a text message. I scooped it up.

We still on for lunch on Saturday? Anderson wrote.

I stared at his name and the message for long enough that when I closed my eyes I had colored dots on the back of my eyelids.

I did have one other person I could ask to come with me —Anderson.

Problem was…actually so many problems popped into my head that I would have had trouble ranking them. Asking for his help put me more in his debt and might give him the wrong idea if he did have more than a professional interest in me. I barely knew him, so I'd have to explain why I wasn't capable of going alone. Or, more specifically, why I refused to go alone into the home of someone if there was even the remote possibility that they were a murderer.

I could let him think I was incompetent and needed help with the interview, but I wasn't my father's daughter for nothing. That was too humiliating even for me.

On the what-kind-of-a-mess-have-I-gotten-myself-into scale, embarrassment over him taking my request wrong seemed less daunting than having another person try to kill me.

I called Anderson.

"Not that I'm complaining," he said, "but you could have texted me back."

"It would have been too hard to explain over text."

"You're cancelling on me?"

Unless I was reading him wrong, he sounded a lot more disappointed than a simple lunch with a colleague merited. Crap. Double crap.

A thought flitted through my head that the best way to get what I wanted was to pretend to flirt with him.

My dad might have no problem manipulating people to get what he wanted, even if it hurt them in the end, but I did. It wouldn't be fair to Anderson, and Mark certainly wouldn't like it.

The straightforward approach it was.

"I'm not cancelling, but I'm hoping we can take a detour to talk to a witness in Dean Scott's case."

"Okay."

The way he drew the word out made it clear he didn't know how to interpret the request. Like maybe he thought I was presuming too much and taking advantage of his good nature. I had already asked for two favors.

"It's not what you think," I blurted.

Smooth, Nicole. Real smooth.

"I think there's no way I'm taking Dean Scott back as a client."

Absolutely not what I guessed he thought. "Not that I wouldn't love to be done with this case, but, believe me, I'm not trying to pass him back to you." There was just no way to say what I needed to without sounding paranoid, so I might as well dive in. "I need someone to come along so the neighbor doesn't try to kill me."

I smacked myself in the forehead. That could not have come out worse if I'd spent time coming up with the most awkward way to say it.

"And why would the witness's neighbor try to kill you?"

Great, now he was using the same tone of voice I would if I thought someone was off medication that they should definitely be taking.

"Not the witness' neighbor. Dean and Sandra's neighbor. Who is the witness. Arg!"

I glared at the phone and considered hanging up on him, bailing on Saturday's lunch, and never speaking to him again. I was making such a big fool of myself you'd think I was a medieval court jester. Or in a court room trying to argue a case.

A soft chuckle came through the phone. "Want to start over?"

I let out a long breath. "Please." I took a second to focus on my breathing. I was smart. I was competent. I was this man's equal. I didn't need to get courtroom jitters just because I was trying to win another lawyer over to my side and get his help. "I have reason to believe Dean's neighbor might have been having an affair with Sandra. If he was, that gives him a possible motive. And I have a bit of a track record of people wanting to kill me when they realize I know they're a murderer."

Three full seconds passed, enough that I thought he might have hung up on me.

Then he said, "I'll go with you on the condition that you tell me the full story behind those statements."

I barely stopped myself from saying *stories*. After all, if he knew how many times it'd happened, he might think twice about going with me.

*I*f Ken had murdered Sandra, not only shouldn't I go alone, but I needed to be better prepared to talk to him.

I texted Hal to have him run a background check on Ken, and crossed my fingers that he'd be able to get me something useful in time. If Ken secretly had some weird fetishes, a lot of past relationships that ended badly, or a criminal record, I'd know better how to approach the interview.

Even though I'd read the medical examiner's report myself, I also wanted Mark's trained eyes to look it over and make sure I hadn't missed or misunderstood any of it. I called him and told him I'd wait to eat as late as necessary to have dinner with him. It was eight o'clock before his text came saying he was on his way. He picked up our favorite fish-and-chips dinners from A Salt & Battery since our meal from there from last weekend went cold.

The dogs met him at the door with a level of wagging and wiggling that I didn't even get.

Mark handed me the food and stopped to give out ear rubs to the dogs. He moved more slowly than I was used to seeing, and day-old stubble covered his chin, as if he'd been too tired this morning to get up in time to shave.

I opened my cupboard door to grab plates for the food, but closed it again. Using plates meant washing plates. As much as it would have been nice to pretend this was a meal we'd cooked, I didn't have the energy, either.

"Table or the couch?" I asked.

"Table." Mark eased his way through the dogs, who seemed intent on blocking his path. "If we sit on the couch, I won't stay awake long enough to go over the case files with you."

Mark had the same confidentiality constraints on him that I did when I worked a case and couldn't reveal what a client told me. Because of that, I didn't normally ask for too many details about his job, but it seemed like he was working an unusual number of hours lately. "I haven't seen anything in the paper that would leave a lot of bodies in the morgue. What's going on?"

"I had a fire victim come in where the chief wanted confirmation on whether the victim had died in the fire or before. Then that consult I told you about turned out to be more complicated than I thought. There'd been a complaint against a nursing home about an unusual number of deaths, and the other ME wanted me to go over his autopsy reports to make sure we didn't have an angel-of-death situation. Obviously, we had to do that as quickly as possible. And

Chief McTavish dropped another load of old cases on my desk to look through. He's sure now that former Chief Wilson wasn't working alone, and he thinks he's closing in on who his associate was."

He wouldn't be allowed to tell me what he'd found out in any of those cases. Part of why we worked so well as a couple was that I understood that, and I wasn't intimidated by the parts of his life that he had to keep from me because of his job. I knew he felt the same about what I had to keep confidential when I was working with a client.

Mark chewed a French fry so slowly it almost seemed painful. "Other than the obvious, how was your day?"

I'd already updated him on all the new information—at least the parts I was at liberty to share—involving Dean's case and the situation with Anderson.

There was one thing I hadn't mentioned yet—our purple elephant, the one both of us seemed to be ignoring at all costs. It'd been weeks since we'd brought it up in more than passing.

"A call came in after I talked to you earlier." I pushed my last bite of fish around. "From DC."

Mark double-dipped his next fry in the ketchup. "And what did they say?"

No question about who'd called. There'd only been one call I'd been waiting on. "The job at the DA's office is mine if I want it. They said what put me above the other candidates in the end was my experience as a defense attorney because it'll help me identify ways the defense counsel could cast doubt on the cases I'd be handling."

Mark nodded and dipped the already-saturated fry again. "How's Stacey feeling? Has she managed to sort all the baby items?"

Whether it was that he was too tired tonight to deal with it or whether he hadn't had time to think about our decision with his busy week, he clearly didn't want to go into it now. I let it slide, and we instead spent the rest of our meal talking about how Stacey set up the room she'd be using for the baby. I showed him the pictures she'd texted me the day before.

The color came back into his cheeks by the time we finished supper. He smiled at me, his dimples peeking out. "I think I just needed time with you to recharge."

Maybe the research position in DC would be better for Mark than staying here in Fair Haven. He'd have regular hours.

But I wouldn't. Working as a prosecutor meant long hours and heavy caseloads.

I laid a hand on top of the pile of files. "I don't know how restful it is when I'm dropping another case on you."

Mark collected up the take-out containers and tossed them into the trash. "It's not the work that tires me out. I love the work. It's having so many cases where it seems like we're not going to find answers."

That I could understand. I scooted around the island and wrapped him in a hug. He leaned into me like he could borrow some of my energy. I would have gladly given him some if it worked that way.

He kissed my forehead. "Show me this case."

I laid the autopsy report out in front of him, along with the pictures. I'd slowly worked myself into being able to look at all of them.

I gave Mark time to go through it. When he finished reading, he pulled the pile of pictures closer and flipped slowly through them.

"No mention of defensive wounds at all, and it doesn't look like there was a struggle. Is that part of what's bothering you?"

Even tired, he didn't miss a thing. "If someone put a plastic bag over my head, I'd fight them. It doesn't seem like she put up a struggle at all. Did she have a sedative in her system?"

"Not according to this report, and he did test for it."

I edged one of the pictures of Sandra closer to me. My head felt disconnected from my senses, but I forced myself to look again.

It didn't even seem like she'd tried to rip the bag off her face, and there weren't any bruises on her wrists suggesting she'd been restrained.

I shoved the picture away again. "It can't have been some weird form of suicide. They didn't find a roll of duct tape in the room."

"Let me see the police report on the scene."

I handed Mark the folder. He pulled out the report and ran his finger down the page, as if it were the only way he could guarantee his eyes would focus.

If I'd ever doubted he loved me, I couldn't after this. Only love would bring such a tired man out here tonight to read more paperwork when he was supposed to be done for the day. It'd be so nice once we were married and living in the same house.

"Here." Mark jabbed a finger at the page. "It doesn't explain the lack of defensive wounds, but it's possible her killer smothered her with a pillow until she lost consciousness and then finished with the plastic bag. There was saliva on her pillow in about the shape and size I'd expect if someone pressed the pillow over her face or her face into the pillow."

I leaned closer. He was right. "How did I miss the connection?"

"I only thought of it because the ME's report mentioned a cotton fiber in her mouth."

Partially smothering her with a pillow first would have been quieter. It raised another question, though. Why not finish the job with the pillow?

"I think the report said no signs of sexual assault. Can you double-check?"

Mark flipped back. "None."

I slumped in my chair. Thank goodness. This case was dark and frustrating enough without adding that element to it.

I walked to the couch and picked up a pillow, turning it over in my hands. "The lack of defensive wounds is still a problem. How hard do you have to push a person's face into a pillow to smother them? If she'd been asleep, could someone have done it without waking her?"

Mark shook his head. "Doubtful. Not unless she'd taken a heavy sleeping pill, and we've already established she didn't have sedatives in her system. Besides, she's still wearing her shoes and she's wearing jeans."

She still had her shoes on? I came back to Mark's side and glanced at the picture, paying attention to her feet this time.

He was right. Sandra still wore her shoes and jeans. I'd been so focused on the plastic bag over her face and the seeming lack of a struggle that I hadn't paid close enough attention to her clothes. She wouldn't have gone to bed fully clothed and wearing her shoes, especially since the knees of her jeans were stained with what looked like mud. Besides, she'd left food on the counter. No one bought groceries and then went to bed, leaving them on the counter to rot.

I felt like I was running on a treadmill with this case, exhausting myself and getting nowhere.

I moved the picture closer to me. It wasn't only Sandra's knees that were muddy. The bottoms of her shoes were as well. Had she gone out in the rain, after dark, to cut the flowers in the vase on the kitchen counter?

I slid the pictures of the kitchen closer to me as well. If the flowers had been wet when she brought them inside, they were long dry by the time the police arrived to take pictures. Sandra had laid out the items she'd purchased on the counter next to the vase.

To me, it looked like more than a regular grocery run. It looked almost like she'd been prepping to cook. She'd laid out strawberries, mini angel food cakes, whip cream, t-bone steaks, haricot vert beans, packages of fresh herbs, and baby red potatoes. They all rested next to a cutting board and a knife.

A knife she could have defended herself with if someone broke in.

I pointed out the knife. "I think she knew her attacker."

"It could be the man you think she was having an affair with," Mark said. "This looks like she was preparing a special meal. Maybe this guy was into kinky foreplay and things went too far."

The food I'd eaten felt like it soured in my stomach. That would explain why she hadn't fought back and why she seemed to have been face down into her pillow at first. "But if it was an accident, why wouldn't he have stopped and waited for her to wake back up? Or why not just leave her there? He didn't have to put a plastic bag over her head and kill her."

Mark shook his head and shrugged.

I hadn't really expected him to have an answer. But at least I had what I needed. I now had a workable theory about how Sandra died —one that I could use tomorrow when I spoke to the man she'd been cheating on Dean with.

When I pulled into Dean's driveway, Anderson was already there, leaning against his car's back end. It struck me as something my dad would do—be there early and choose your position for maximum possible effect. To thank him for his help, I could arrange a meeting for him with my dad when my parents came up for the wedding.

Anderson wore khaki pants and a white button-down shirt with the sleeves rolled up past his elbows. I smoothed a hand over my royal blue blouse and blazer. My clothes might be why I'd gotten such strange reactions. It seemed lawyers dressed a little more casually here.

I slid out of my car and tried not to catch my heels in the cracks in Dean's driveway. It would have been just my luck to stumble at the worst possible moment and head butt Anderson in the stomach as I went down.

He was one of those people whose age was hard to guess. He

might have been thirty-five, but he could have been as old as forty-five. I suspected when he reached his fifties, he'd still look the same.

He smiled at me with teeth so white they looked like he should be modeling for a whitening strip commercial. His sun-bronzed skin said he spent his off hours outdoors. It was such a contrast to Mark's I-burn-from-watching-the-sun-on-TV skin that I couldn't help but make the comparison. But Anderson's nose was a bit too big, and noses grew until you died, so Mark still came out ahead in my estimation. Besides, I'd think Mark was the handsomest man on the planet even if he had buck teeth, a big nose, and ears that stuck out.

"Nice to finally meet in person," Anderson said.

He held out a hand. His handshake felt too warm for comfort. So did the look he gave me. I didn't linger in either.

Hopefully, after spending a few hours with me, whatever infatuation he felt would wear off. If it didn't, I'd have to find a way to flash my ring at him or bring Mark up in conversation that wouldn't be blatantly obvious as a shut-down. I still wanted to work with him in a professional capacity, after all, without any weirdness.

Anderson tilted his head in the direction of the house next door. "I'm guessing we're planning on talking to the neighbor on this side. The other one's been out working in his front yard, and he looks too old to be Sandra's choice. At least, if Dean is representative of the type of men she went for."

I snorted softly and turned it into a sneeze. My dad would be fainting back in DC if he thought his daughter snorted in front of a colleague.

"You guessed right," I said when my fake sneezing fit subsided.

Anderson's look was a touch too amused for me to think my cover held.

I headed for the neighbor's house. "Do we know if he's home?"

"His car's there, and someone's moving around inside," Anderson said from behind me.

I tottered along in my heels to the front door. Either the heels or asking Anderson along had been a bad idea. Maybe both. Thinking about him analyzing me was making me nervous enough to wipe out and face-plant even if I was wearing flats.

Not in an I'm-attracted-to-you nervous way. It was more that I hadn't had another attorney judging my work for a long time. All my old insecurities pounded on the inside of my chest like they wanted to make a hole for my heart to jump out of.

Anderson motioned for me to do the honors of ringing the doorbell.

The ding-ding echoed through the house, but no one came.

Before I could ring again, two cars pulled into Dean's driveway. The woman who stepped out of the first one carried a black folder. A couple in their early thirties climbed from the other car. It had to be the real estate agent showing Dean's house. Driving up, I'd noticed the new For Sale sign on his lawn, and there'd been one of those universal padlocks on his door that real estate agents used to show people around the house when the owner wasn't home.

A hand brushed my shoulder and I jumped.

"I hear the sound of a lawnmower out back," Anderson said.

We squeezed our way between the neighbor's house and the one beside it and stopped at a gate.

I wasn't tall enough to see over the fence, but Anderson was. He waved a hand at whoever was inside. The lawnmower's drone stopped.

If Dean was Sandra's type, then she hadn't been having an affair with the man who opened the gate, either. Dean had gym-rat muscles, while this man was ropey like a runner. His hair was red, and freckles peppered his cheeks. But he was a similar age.

And he looked like I would have expected the man matching Hal's report to look. According to the email I'd gotten just before leaving home, Ken had no criminal record. He didn't even have a speeding ticket. Heck, he didn't even have a parking ticket. His credit score would have gotten him a loan from any financial institution in the country.

Aside from what Ms. Nosy Neighbor told me, I was going in blind.

"Are you Ken Vasel?" I asked.

He pulled out his t-shirt sleeve and used it to mop the sweat off his forehead. He nodded, and his gaze bounced between us.

I needed to set him at ease—fast—or we weren't going to get anything useful from him.

"We're sorry to bother you. We're attorneys working on the murder case of Sandra Scott, and we need to confirm some of the details you gave in your statement to the police."

His Adam's apple bobbed rapidly. "Did I say something wrong?"

"There is no right or wrong," Anderson said. "We just want to make sure we understand the facts."

He was good. He'd made sure Ken wouldn't be afraid of his answers getting him in trouble.

Ken stepped out of the way and motioned us toward a picnic

table resting on a patio of concrete pavers. His appearance wasn't the only thing opposite of Dean. His yard and house were as well. Neither were big, but he clearly invested time in caring for them. If I had to guess, I'd say the differences in his personality compared to Dean probably outweighed the differences in his appearance. I know that, if I had to choose, I'd take a kind, responsible man over a handsome one any day. Thankfully, I hadn't had to make that choice the way it seemed Sandra had.

Voices floated over the fence as the real estate agent showed the couple the back yard first. The man complained about how run-down everything was for the price, and the woman responded with how they'd have a lot of work to get rid of the monkshood because it wasn't safe for the dogs or the kids if they ate it. Presumably the monkshood was the flower I hadn't recognized, but it was good to know they weren't safe for pets so that I didn't plant them at home.

The couple moved on to talking about how much of the sagging fence needed to be replaced. With the state of the house, I'd have to check that Dean hadn't listed it too high. I had no problem with listing higher than you expected to get to leave room for negotiation, but Dean hadn't shown a lot of common sense. He might have put the house unreasonably high so he'd have some money left over after my fees and helping out Elise with Arielle and Cameron.

Ken sat at the picnic table. I took a seat on the bench next to him at a friendly distance. Anderson slid in on the other side. It was textbook perfect framing.

It gave me a strange sense of déjà vu, as if I was working with a younger, less arrogant version of my dad.

I rested one arm casually on the top of the picnic table and gave

Ken an I'm-no-threat smile. Mark would have called it quasi-flirting. It was the smile I knew would soften Ken up enough that he might share with me things he wouldn't share with someone else.

"Before we start, I wanted to say how sorry I am for your loss."

Ken jerked slightly and his cheeks flushed, as if his heart rate spiked.

It told me all I needed to know about their relationship. They'd been more than friends. They'd also been trying to keep it a secret.

I'd taken a gamble in deciding to play it as if we knew and had evidence that he and Sandra were having an affair. Now I had to hope it worked.

"I've lost people I care about," I said, adding the next layer—the one where we had something in common. "So we'll try not to intrude on your grief for very long. In your statement to the police, you said you thought Sandra and Dean were having trouble in their marriage. Other than the obvious, did you have any reason to think that?"

He stared at me like I'd slapped him. "I don't know what you're talking about. I barely knew either of them." He stood to his feet and angled toward the gate. "Everything I told the police is accurate, so I don't know how much more help I can be. It'd be better if you left."

Crap. I didn't know which was worse, striking out so hard or doing it in front of Anderson. And basically wasting his time.

I trailed after Anderson out the gate and back around to our cars. I didn't even want to look at him.

I pulled out my phone. I could delay facing him for a few seconds and try to pull myself out of the embarrassment gutter.

Before I forgot, I needed to set Dean to work on fixing his place up some. "I just need to send a quick text."

Get rid of the flowers in the backyard asap, I wrote to Dean. *And fix the fence. Buyers are worried about both.*

I put my phone away and turned my keys around in my hand. I should offer Anderson an out. He might not want to waste his Saturday on someone who called him out here to botch an interview—especially when interviewing was supposed to be my strength. Had I pushed too hard?

I wasn't even sure if I should own up to my goof or pretend like it was nothing. My pride couldn't decide which was worse. With the former choice, it meant acknowledging my failing, and with the latter, I looked completely incompetent because I'd screwed up and didn't even know it.

I'd rather at least have him know I realized the damage I'd done. "I'm sorry for dragging you out here for nothing."

Anderson had his keys out as well. "It wasn't for nothing. That was gutsy. It's the kind of move your dad would have made. I don't know that I would have thought of it." His smile contained too much admiration. "Where should we go for lunch?"

My skin felt squirmy, like it wasn't comfortable on my body. His words came much too close to flattery. I couldn't risk a continued misunderstanding if there was one. This was even worse than the failed interview.

I licked my lips. "This is a business lunch, right?"

He ran a hand around the collar of his shirt and stretched his neck out. "I might have thought it could be dual purpose until I saw the ring."

I ran my thumb over the underside of the band. If I'd had more experience dating, I might have known exactly what to say. As it was, my mind had turned into a giant black hole.

He still had a hand behind his neck. "That's not your fault. I've modeled my whole career off your dad, and part of what makes his business so successful is your mom. When you called the other day, I thought it might be fate."

I let myself snort this time. "You might not have been so keen if you knew me. Interviews are usually my strength. I'm a mess in the courtroom."

He made a you're-only-trying-to-make-me-feel-better face.

"That's not my only failing either." I held my hand up beside my mouth like I was about to share a secret. "I won't defend someone unless I think they're innocent."

Anderson laughed. He lowered his arm to his side. "That's something I wouldn't have expected from Edward Dawes' daughter. How are you going to work with your parents if you won't defend someone who's guilty?"

For the first time since the initial call I'd made to him, it felt like he was talking to me, Nicole, rather than to Edward Dawes' daughter. "If you're still interested in grabbing lunch, I'll tell you all about it."

"*A*re you going to wait until the trial and question Ken then?" Anderson asked after we'd talked—and laughed together—about my predicament and the trouble I'd gotten myself into in the past year.

I twirled a piece of lettuce around on my fork. Since I had a wedding dress to fit in to in a few months, I'd opted for a salad instead of the burger and fries on Anderson's plate that looked much more enticing.

Setting aside the fact that I didn't want to argue this case in court at all, waiting until trial came with other difficulties. "I'm sure you know what my dad would say about that."

He grinned. "Never ask a question that you don't already know the answer to. Since you don't know whether he has an alibi, you're risking building a defense on something that could be blown away with a single answer. That undermines you with the jury. Juries only have so much patience for what looks like a lawyer fishing for information and playing guessing games."

Was there a handbook of my dad's philosophies out there that I didn't know about? Anderson hadn't been exaggerating when he said he'd studied my dad. He must have read everything he'd ever written and every article ever written about him, as well as studying the cases he'd tried.

Talking to him was a bit like being able to tap into my dad's experience without all the baggage attached to our relationship.

"I don't even have proof that Ken and Sandra were having an affair. I have the hunch of a nosy neighbor who didn't like Sandra and Dean. Dean suspected an affair, but not Ken. He even said something about Sandra caring for him when he was sick, and I didn't get the impression he thought it was anything more than Sandra being nice. I could make a royal fool of myself if I go in assuming there was an affair happening and it turns out there wasn't."

"I got the impression from Ken's reactions that they were more than friends."

I had, too. It was nice to have my interpretation confirmed. But that brought me back to how I could prove it. It wasn't like having Hal continue to dig into Ken would provide me with anything. Affairs often didn't leave a paper trail. Tailing Ken wouldn't show us anything, either, since Sandra was gone, and even a trip to the cemetery to leave flowers on her grave could be explained away as the gesture of a neighbor and friend.

I chewed a crouton. "I need someone who knew they had an affair to be willing to testify."

Not even willing to testify. That still put me back in court before I could follow up on whether Ken might have killed Sandra. I needed something to prove to Ken that I knew about the affair and I wasn't just guessing.

Anderson wiped his hands on his napkin. "Good luck. If his family or friends knew, they're not likely to turn on him because you ask nicely."

My fork sagged in my grip. Ken's friends or family wouldn't, but Sandra's might. Nadine hated Dean, but she hated the person who actually killed Sandra more. If I could convince her there was a reasonable chance Ken could have done it, she might be willing to help me.

I grabbed for my purse. "I have to go. I think I figured out a way to convince Ken to talk."

I fished enough money from my purse to cover my lunch and a generous tip and dropped the cash on the table.

Instead of waiting for the server, Anderson did the same. "Do you need me to come with you?"

Having another lawyer to bounce ideas off of had been helpful, but in this situation, I'd have a much better chance of convincing Nadine to talk if I went alone. Besides, I knew she hadn't killed Sandra, so I wasn't in any danger. "Not this time, but I might if I can get what I need. I won't want to be alone in private with Ken."

As soon as I got into my car, I called Nadine. Her phone went to voicemail. I tried again as I was pulling into the driveway of the garden center. Still no answer.

Even if she wasn't around, it wasn't like I'd come all the way from Fair Haven. I'd already been here. I'd have wasted only an extra ten minutes, and I could come back.

The girl at the cash register said Nadine wasn't working that afternoon, but I could try the house. I backtracked and drove down the fork in the driveway that went to the left instead of to the right. When I'd originally come, I'd followed the signs to the garden center. I hadn't realized Nadine and her husband also lived on the same land.

No wonder Sandra had been so adamant about wanting to use some of Dean's money to help them. If they lost the garden center, they wouldn't only lose their business. They'd lose their home as well.

My car rolled to a stop behind the car sitting in their driveway with the trunk open.

My breath caught in my throat, and for a second, I was back in Eddie's trunk, fighting to stay conscious and escape before I died of heat stroke. I could smell the air, heavy and hot, and my skin burned.

Along with all the work I'd been doing with my counselor and my PTSD support group, Mrs. Cavanaugh had suggested I start memorizing Bible verses and repeating them when I felt a panic attack coming on. She said it would help focus my mind back on how God was in control and I could trust him regardless of my circumstances.

I'd only memorized Psalm 121 and a passage from Romans so far, but I closed my eyes and recited them over twice, then three times. My heart rate slowly dropped back to normal, and I opened my eyes. I'd decided not long ago that I wouldn't live my life in fear. I couldn't give up now over an open trunk.

A tap sounded on my window.

Nadine stood outside. "Are you okay?" The glass of my window muffled her voice.

I nodded and opened my door. She moved back out of my way.

I made sure to close my car door to indicate that I planned to stay. Based on our last visit, I had a suspicion that if she thought she could brush me off by saying we'd make an appointment for later, she would.

After all, she had asked me to call first next time. "I tried to call, but I couldn't get you on your phone."

Nadine tilted the cell phone hooked onto the edge of her jeans and glanced at the screen. "My ringer must be off." She motioned back toward her car. "I just got home. I was out grocery shopping."

The way she did it, though, so fast she couldn't actually have read what her phone said, told me she'd recognized my number and hadn't answered on purpose. She could have answered my calls and told me she was too busy to meet with me today, but she'd chosen to avoid me entirely. If I couldn't get the answers I needed from her today, there was a good chance I'd never get them.

I slipped past her and headed for her car. "Let me help you carry the rest of your stuff inside."

I'd never agreed with the old cliché that it's better to ask forgiveness than permission, but in this case, if I didn't presume that she would invite me in, I guaranteed she wouldn't.

I snagged two bags, and the handles bit into my hands, more because of where they were from than because they were heavy.

Nadine shopped at the same store as Sandra. Her trunk was full of plastic bags that matched the one placed over Sandra's head.

How could she stand to look at them without thinking about that? I couldn't even handle seeing an open car trunk without flashing back to past trauma.

My dad would remind me that not everyone reacted to trauma the same way, but I couldn't shake the creepy crawly feeling running over my skin. If I hadn't been so sure she had an alibi, I would have suspected her of killing Sandra.

But she did have a solid-steel alibi complete with multiple witnesses and receipts, which meant I was grasping at straws.

Besides, did I really want Nadine to be the one to have killed Sandra? It'd be bad enough if Sandra's lover had done it, but to be killed by her sister, who she'd clearly adored, would be heart-breaking.

I needed to stay focused on finding someone who could have killed Sandra and would have wanted to.

Nadine came up behind me and took the last remaining bags from the trunk. She slammed it closed and led the way into the house without a word. I followed her around to a side door, and we entered into the kitchen.

She pointed at the table. "Just drop them there while I tell my husband I'm home."

Tell her husband she's home was likely code for *tell him they had an uninvited guest.* That could be innocent as well, though. Her husband might be the type who hung around the house in his boxers when they weren't expecting company. My dad had never been that kind of man—as casual as he got was khakis and a polo shirt—but I'd had a friend in high school whose dad stripped off his clothes as soon as he got home. I'd been over one day when he hadn't realized I was there and witnessed it firsthand.

That said, if I could overhear what Nadine planned to say to her husband, it'd help me understand how much of a battle I was about to have to convince her that Dean hadn't killed Sandra but Ken might have.

I tiptoed to the kitchen door and leaned in close.

"Tell her to leave. You don't have to talk to her."

The man seemed to be the kind of person who thought they were whispering even when they weren't, because Nadine's response was too soft for me to catch.

"No," the man said. "We know Dean killed her. All this is going to do is make you upset."

Nadine must have told him my belief that Dean was innocent. She might have even asked him if he thought they could be wrong.

Either way, he certainly wasn't wavering in his belief.

Does he protest too much? the suspicious lawyer voice in my head whispered. *Nadine has an alibi, but what about her husband?*

The thought had barely entered my mind before I tossed it out. I could come up with only two reasons why Nadine's husband might have murdered Sandra. The first was for money to save their business, but Sandra hadn't had a life insurance policy, let alone one where Nadine was the beneficiary. The second was if he'd been having an affair with Sandra. While that was possible, it didn't fit with what I'd seen so far of Sandra and Nadine's relationship. Sandra was trying to do everything she could to help her sister. To betray her by cheating with her husband would have been like asking a cat to bark.

Besides, Ms. Nosy Neighbor hadn't mentioned any men coming to the house to see Sandra. She'd only talked about Sandra going next door to visit Ken. While that didn't mean Sandra and Nadine's husband couldn't have had a tryst at Nadine's house or elsewhere, it made it that much less likely. They'd have had to find a time when Nadine wasn't home, Nadine's children weren't home, and Dean wouldn't be suspicious. Mark's favorite phrase of *possible but not probable* came to mind.

Their conversation ended—or at least I didn't hear anymore voice noises. I scooted back from the door. The door opened and Nadine came back in a half second after I reached my original spot.

She stopped next to one of the kitchen chairs and rested her hands on the back. She didn't ask me to sit. "My husband doesn't want you here. We know Dean did this. Anything we say to you, you'll only use to try to let him get away with Sandra's murder."

Her words sounded firm, but she didn't technically ask me to leave. The chair in front of her quivered. It was faint, almost not enough to see, but it made me think her hands were shaking. A little muscle twitched in her cheek.

Such small things, but they didn't say *angry* to me the way I'd read her the first time we'd met. They almost said *fear*.

If I eliminated the impossible, ala Sherlock Holmes, where did that leave me?

Nadine had an alibi, so she couldn't be afraid I'd find out she'd killed Sandra. Aside from that, I'd have expected her to expel me from the house the way her husband wanted if she were guilty.

She'd want to protect herself rather than take the risk. The same would be true if she wanted to protect her husband.

She must be afraid Dean hadn't done it. Our previous conversation had stuck with her.

That sense of uncertainty would be a horrible feeling. She'd been sure before I came around. More horrible than knowing the person who killed your loved one was not knowing who did it at all.

I eased a chair out from the table and lowered into it with the same care I'd use if a deer were in my yard and I didn't want to spook it. "It's normal for your husband to be worried, but he hasn't spoken to me the way you have. You know I want to figure out who killed Sandra because it wasn't Dean."

Her hands tightened around the chair. "You don't know that. He's not a good man."

"He's not a good man. His first wife is my fiancé's cousin, so I know what he's like." It was a slight exaggeration. I hadn't even known Dean's name prior to taking on this case, but now I knew more than I ever wanted to. Ignorance might really be bliss in some situations. "But I also know he didn't do it."

Her head was shaking. "You can't know that."

The way she said it had a desperate edge to it that seemed out of place. Dean was a jerk, no doubt, but he wasn't enough of a jerk that she should be so insistent on him being the culprit.

And I couldn't tell her how I knew without violating lawyer–client confidentiality. "I believe Sandra was having an affair and that her lover killed her."

A battle raged across her face. It confirmed for me that Sandra was having an affair and that Nadine knew about it...and that she didn't know whether to admit it to me or not.

"If you think I'm heading in the wrong direction," I said quietly, "I need to know. I just want the truth."

She sank into the chair. "Ken wouldn't have killed Sandra."

I slumped back. That wasn't even a vague suspicion. Not only did she know about the affair, she knew his name.

If she'd been a confrontational witness, I'd shoot her *you can't know that* back at her. But she wasn't. She was sad and scared and grieving. "You knew him?"

She scrubbed her fingers across her knees. "We had them over for dinner more than once. Sandra..."

Her voice broke, and she turned her gaze away, toward the window over the sink.

My eyes burned in sympathy. This part I hated. Intruding on people's grief. It never got easier.

She swallowed hard. "Ken was the opposite of every guy Sandra ever dated from high school on, but I think that's what finally appealed to her. He wasn't a bad boy that she was convinced she could reform and save. It was like she'd finally learned."

Tears slid down her cheeks. She leaned back and grabbed a paper towel from the holder on the counter. "I told her she should leave Dean and marry Ken. It didn't matter that Dean was finally making money. Sam and I didn't want Dean's charity anyway. But Sandra was so determined to help us save this place, and she thought she could talk Dean into giving us the money or loaning it to us at least." She gave the slow head shake that said *foolish girl* better than words ever could. "One of the last conversations we had, she told me Dean wasn't going to come around, and she'd made a decision about what to do."

All I could think was *oh, crap*. If she'd told the police that, then the prosecution was going to argue Sandra told Dean she was leaving him and he killed her in anger. I couldn't even argue that the reverse had been true—that Ken killed Sandra because she refused to leave Dean. Not if Sandra specifically told Nadine she was leaving him.

My stomach felt like I'd eaten a chunk of ice. "Did Sandra tell you she was leaving Dean and planned to tell him so?"

A beat of silence. "No."

Not that it mattered. That had to have been the decision Sandra made. Or, worse, she'd decided to take Dean's money first from their bank account—which I knew from Hal's report was a joint account—and then leave him. Hal hadn't said there was a large withdrawal, though, thank goodness, because unless Griffin decided to alibi Dean, we were in big trouble.

It was possible Ken still had some weird fetish and Sandra's smothering started as accidental at first, but dating "bad boys" wasn't the same as dating men who had weird fetishes, and Sandra hadn't likely switched from one to the other. Based on Nadine's description, she was someone who finally wanted to settle down with a normal and stable man. On top of that, Sandra was fully clothed. Although I'd never tried it, I had to imagine that re-dressing a dead body wasn't easy, especially if the clothes were wet or muddy.

"But she'd talked about leaving Dean before," Nadine said. "And this time she sounded different. She wasn't going to change her mind."

My mind snapped back into focus on Nadine. Ken wouldn't have killed Sandra if she was leaving Dean, but he might have killed her if she said she was going to and then changed her mind at the last minute.

Problem was, I had to be able to prove Ken was over at Sandra and Dean's that night. Since no one had seen anyone coming or going, that included Ken. The only way to prove he'd been there would be to get him to admit to it.

"I told you that if you could convince me Dean killed Sandra, I'd drop the case. I meant it. Help me talk to Ken so I can find out the truth. Is there something you could tell me that I couldn't have known unless it came from you? If he knows I have evidence of the affair, he won't feel like he needs to hide it anymore."

Nadine glanced back at the kitchen doorway. I could almost see her thinking about what her husband would say. "You think talking to Ken will help prove Dean killed Sandra?"

More or less. It'd help prove *which* one of them killed Sandra. "Yes."

Nadine did one more my-parents-will-be-home-any-minute type look over her shoulder. "I'll call him and ask him to talk to you myself."

I had Nadine set up a meeting for the next Saturday afternoon at a local café since I knew Ken would be harder to talk to during the work week.

Even though the meeting was set up for a public place, I didn't want to go completely solo. I also didn't want to call Anderson again, despite his offer. I couldn't expect him to keep bailing me out when there was nothing in it for him. Besides, he'd have expected to sit in on the meeting, and now that I had Nadine's seal of approval, Ken would be more likely to be honest with me if I seemed to be by myself. Nadine hadn't told him to talk to everyone who asked, only to me.

All I needed was someone who could sit at a table at the same café and then walk back to the car with me after we thought Ken had gone to make sure he hadn't hung around to kill or abduct me. It was essentially the same trick Mark and I pulled back in DC when we were investigating my best friend Ahanti's stalker, only this time Mark couldn't go. Despite it being Saturday, he had to work.

Which left me needing to find someone who wouldn't mind sitting in a café, doing nothing other than waiting for me to finish and making sure Ken didn't find some way to force me to leave with him against my will. The person wouldn't be in any danger, so that opened up a few options. I considered Mandy, but she'd be sure to find a way to butt into the interview. Russ wouldn't do it even though it was for a job, since he disagreed with anything that required me to even speak with a potentially dangerous person.

I decided to call Stacey. It'd be a free lunch, and we'd get to spend time together on the ride. I called her. We opted to spend the morning together as well, and were settled into the café in plenty of time before Ken arrived.

When Ken came into the café, his hair was wet like he'd recently gotten out of the shower. If I'd had to guess, he'd probably been working on his house or garden again before coming here.

As much as I hated to admit it, the fact that he bothered to shower for the meeting hinted, just a little, toward innocence. It showed a certain level of baseline respect for me as a person because he didn't want to come sweaty to our meeting.

He sat across from me in the booth. Stacey had positioned herself inside my peripheral version—her idea in case I needed to signal her to call for help because I felt threatened. She winked at me, the signal she'd come up with to say she was watching. If I was in trouble, I was supposed to wink at her. She opened her magazine in front of her, but she angled it in such a way that I could tell she wasn't actually reading.

In the six months I'd known her, I'd come to think she was born without a funny bone. I'd been proven wrong today. All the way here, she'd been calling herself 006 and me 007. Because there wasn't any danger as long as we stuck together in a public place, we'd been cracking secret agent jokes the whole way.

Ken didn't even say hello until the waitress filled his coffee cup and walked away.

He folded his arms on the table, a barrier between us. "I came for Nadine's sake, but I think you're a liar who's willing to do anything to get her guilty client set free."

If I could have physically reeled back, I would have. My brain felt like it turned to pudding, and my whole planned approach evaporated.

I sucked in a slow breath. "I guess Nadine told you I'm looking for evidence against Dean. The truth is I'm looking for evidence period, wherever that might point. If it points at Dean, I'll use it to convince him to plead guilty."

He raised his eyebrows in a way that said *do you think I'm stupid or something?*

Okay, if that's how we were going to play it, then I'd lay my cards out on the table and see how he reacted. At present, I wasn't going to get anything useful from him anyway. "Truth is, I think you might be the one who really killed Sandra."

His arms relaxed slightly. "Now that I believe. That's what I figured was going on when you and the other guy came to my house."

Go figure. I wouldn't have expected accusing him of murder to set him at ease.

Unless he's innocent, the little voice in my head said. *An innocent person wouldn't like you trying to trick them into admitting to something they didn't do.*

Innocent or not, he seemed to respect the straightforward approach. "So why should I believe you didn't kill her?"

He almost seemed to shrink in the seat. "I don't know. That's why I didn't want to talk to you. Sandra and I were having an affair, and I'd been asking her for months to divorce Dean and marry me. I don't have an alibi. I know how that looks. You could argue in court that I killed her because she wouldn't leave Dean."

"Did she say she wouldn't leave Dean?"

"No."

"Did she say she *would* leave Dean?"

"No." He looked down at his hands. "But Nadine told me after she died that she planned to."

Except she hadn't told Nadine that. Nadine guessed. It was a good guess, but a guess nonetheless, and it seemed strange that Sandra wouldn't have gone straight to Ken once she made her decision.

Unless she planned to make it special. She'd purchased ingredients for an expensive meal the night she died. Perhaps she'd intended to cook Ken a nice dinner and then accept his marriage proposal, such as it was.

If that was the case, he'd have had no reason to kill her. My "he accidentally killed her" theory looked pretty flimsy as well. Sandra wouldn't have told him her decision prior to dinner, and certainly not during the prep work for the meal.

It looked like I'd dragged Stacey along for nothing. All my instincts honed by my time working for my parents said Ken wasn't a killer, and Stacey looked suddenly exhausted. She hadn't even touched the cheese Danish on her plate. Stacey loved Danishes. She'd been craving them for months. The Burnt Toast Café back in Fair Haven practically kept a box at the ready for her. I'd pick her up a box on the way home so she could have them later when she wasn't so tired.

I watched Ken finally take a drink of his—probably lukewarm—coffee. One thing still bothered me. If Ken was supposed to go over that night, why hadn't he? If that special dinner was meant for him, he should have gone over and either found Sandra dead or encountered Dean or been worried about her because she didn't answer the door. The last option didn't seem likely. Had Sandra not answered, Ken would have called Nadine. They clearly interacted regularly before since Nadine had his cell phone number.

I thought about asking him if he'd seen Sandra that day, but that could sound like I was trying to trap him. This whole conversation had been frank so far. I might as well continue and see if his demeanor changed at all.

"Had Sandra invited you over that day?"

Ken shook his head. It happened so quickly that I was certain he was telling the truth. His body reacted the instant his mind processed the question. There wasn't a gap where he had to decide what the best answer was.

"I never went to Sandra and Dean's house. She always came to my place, or we went to visit Nadine and Sam."

That brought the finger directly back in Dean's direction. If Sandra hadn't planned for Ken to come over, she'd likely been preparing it to take over to his house and Dean came home and caught her. She'd told him she was leaving him for Ken, and he killed her. At least, that's what the prosecution could argue.

And unless I could produce Dean's alibi, I had no defense against it. While I could counter that Ken could be lying and he did go to Sandra's house that night, Ms. Nosy Neighbor had been specific. People came to see Dean at their house when Sandra wasn't home. Sandra went to Ken's house when Dean wasn't home. She hadn't said Ken came to Sandra and Dean's house. Any good prosecutor would know the avenue I'd try and be ready to block it by calling Ms. Nosy to the stand.

"Would you like another cup of coffee, honey?" the waitress asked from beside me.

I hadn't even heard her come up. I shook my head. We were basically done here, and I wanted to get Stacey home to rest.

The waitress looked at Ken. "How about you? Coffee? Or we have fresh strawberry-peach cobbler."

"Do you have any other kind?" Ken asked. "I'm allergic to straw-berries."

"Nikki!" Stacey's voice called.

I jumped in my seat, and my cup of coffee tipped over, sending the last quarter of a cup of liquid shooting across the table at Ken. He jumped to his feet as well. The waitress spun around toward Stacey.

"Nikki!" Stacey called again. Loudly. Her voice had a strained, panicked quality to it.

My first thought was that Ken had a gun on me under the table and Stacey spotted it.

Then I saw the way her hands clutched at her belly.

23

I pushed my car faster. I would have welcomed a police officer pulling me over at this point in time. He could have escorted us the rest of the way to Fair Haven, and maybe even delivered the baby if we didn't make it in time. The waitress at the café gave us the bad news that Fair Haven's hospital was the nearest one, and Stacey'd been too panicked to wait for an ambulance. She wanted to go. Immediately.

Stacey huffed in the passenger seat. "It's too early."

The memory of Mark's story about his first wife's premature labor and the death of their baby danced through my head. I definitely could not tell Stacey that. "Only four or five weeks. That's barely premature. It'll be okay. You'll both be okay. Why don't you try calling your mom again?"

Stacey's mom and dad had planned on taking a canoe out on the lake this afternoon. With how patchy Fair Haven's cell signals were in the center of town, I'd nearly hyperventilated when she told me.

But they'd thought it'd be safe. As Stacey kept repeating, she wasn't due for a month yet.

She held the phone up to her ear, then shook her head. "No answer. It goes straight to voicemail. Dad's phone, too."

Think, Nicole. Think. "Call Russ. He'll know someone with a boat, and he can go out looking for them."

My cell phone rang in my pocket, and the Bluetooth display showed Elise's name. I let it ring. Having Stacey in labor in my car while I drove was enough of a distraction. I couldn't talk to Elise as well without risking a wreck.

"Russ is going," Stacey said, "but the contractions are getting worse. Closer."

If she'd told me she'd gotten an arraignment date, I could give her an idea of where she was in the legal process and how long she'd have to wait. I had no idea what contractions meant, especially since we hadn't been timing them. I didn't even know if there was a standard.

"We're almost there," I said.

"We're not almost there!" Stacey growled. "And it hurts."

It was probably going to hurt a lot more before the baby came, but I wasn't about to tell her that, either. I added another ten miles per hour to our speed, and prayed instead that a police officer wouldn't spot us. At the speed I was going, he'd give me a ticket for reckless driving and then finish escorting us to the hospital.

Elise called me again as I made the final turn into the hospital parking lot and laid on my brakes. I shoved my phone in my pocket so I could call her back later—and, more importantly, keep in touch with Russ and Stacey's parents—and dashed into the hospital to get a nurse and a wheelchair.

When they had her moved over, she refused to let go of my hand. My phone vibrated in my pocket as we moved down the hall.

Elise usually left a message and waited for me to call her back. Something had to be wrong, but I couldn't call while Stacey needed me. Tears were running down her face, more from fear than from pain I suspected. If she lost this baby, it'd be like losing Noah all over again.

Nothing I could say would help her. All I could do was hold her hand until her mom got here, and I wasn't going to do anything to make her feel like she was alone. For the foreseeable future, Stacey had to be the most important thing.

Every few minutes—or at least that's what it seemed like—my phone rang. With every ring, my stomach tightened further until I could barely breathe. Not even Stacey turning the bones in my hand into pulp drowned it out.

At one point, I checked the call log to make sure it wasn't Russ calling. They were all Elise.

Stacey's mom arrived right as the doctor was telling Stacey she needed to push. I fled.

Russ sat with Tony outside the door. I nodded to them as I went by, and Russ mouthed the words *I'm going to stay with him.*

On any other day, I would have stayed with them as well. If it turned out nothing was wrong with Elise, I could come back. But my gut said something was very, very wrong.

Call me, I whispered back to Russ.

He nodded.

I went around the corner and took out my phone. The time on my screen couldn't possibly be right. It said I'd been with Stacey at the hospital nearly three hours. My phone now not only had missed calls from Elise—none with a message—but also a frantic message from Mark and multiple texts. He didn't know why Elise was trying to contact me, but he was worried that she hadn't been able to.

I sent him a quick text letting him know I was at the hospital with Stacey because she'd gone into labor early.

Then I called Elise.

"Where have you been?" she snapped.

A snarky response sprang to my lips, but I bit it back. She sounded odd. I'd expected the kind of anger that a parent feels when their child misses curfew and they don't know if they've been in an accident or not. I hadn't expected the kind of angry-scared that happens when you come home and find someone's broken into your house.

She sounded odd *and* she hadn't wanted to tell Mark why she needed to reach me. I could only think of one reason. Dean had done something stupid. "I'm at the hospital. What's wrong?"

"Oh thank God."

Her tone indicated it was an actual giving of thanks rather than taking the Lord's name in vain. It also wasn't at all the reaction I'd been expecting. Again.

I had to assume she didn't think I was at the hospital because I was sick or injured or her reaction would have been a lot different.

"I'm on the fourth floor," Elise said. "Please come. I'll meet you at the elevator."

She disconnected the call before I could get any more information.

If I hadn't been in a hospital, I would have sprinted. This sounded worse all the time. I silently willed the elevator to move faster, and this time not only because I hated riding in elevators. The fourth floor was the same floor where they'd put Noah after he'd been attacked and ended up in a coma. Had something happened to Erik? It couldn't be one of the kids because Elise would have called the whole family.

Elise practically yanked me out of the elevator when the doors opened and dragged me down the hall away from the nurses' desk.

"It's Dean," she said.

My first thought was that he'd hurt someone, maybe even Ken if he'd put the pieces together. But Elise's first call came in only minutes after I left Ken, so that couldn't be it.

Dean had to be the one in the hospital.

Elise was already rambling on. "He still had an In Case of Emergency card in his wallet with my name and phone number on it. It's the one I gave him back when we were married. The doctors won't talk to me because we're divorced, and they're trying to locate his official next of kin. I didn't know what to do."

So was I here as a friend, as her legal counsel, or as his? "Do you know what happened?"

She shook her head. "His neighbor called 911 because he collapsed on his front lawn. She'd been watching him carry plants back and forth. By the time the paramedics reached him, he wasn't conscious, and he was struggling to breathe. I don't know whether

he had some sort of heart attack or stroke or if someone intentionally hurt him."

All the heat rushed from my body, leaving a chill behind. It
couldn't be coincidence. Dean's warning about Griffin played in my
mind like a macabre soundtrack. Dean said Griffin wouldn't like
him quitting their business. It was possible this was his response.
He'd chosen to take out Dean and ensure that Dean wouldn't cause
him any problems in the future because he'd seemed to suddenly
develop a conscience. "Where are the kids?"

Elise twitched. "They're at my house with Erik. Why?"

"I think it might be a good idea if you went to stay with Bobby
in Detroit for a couple of days."

The look she gave me said she wasn't going to let it rest at that. I
told her my suspicion. "I'm going to call Chief McTavish and have
him contact the police force in White Cloud, but I don't know how
vindictive this guy is. Hopefully he'll stop if he thinks he's gotten rid
of the risk Dean represented, but Dean told me he threatened
Arielle and Cameron if Dean told the police that he was with
Griffin the night Sandra died."

A little bit of the police officer came back into Elise's stance.
Emotions flashed across her face. I couldn't interpret them all, but I
was sure part of them stemmed from the knowledge that Dean had
been willing to risk going to prison in order to help protect Arielle
and Cameron. It might have been the first time she'd felt respect for
him in years.

She dug her phone back out of her purse. "I'll call Bobby. You'll
let me know if Dean...I don't know how to tell Arielle and
Cameron."

I pulled her into a hug. "We don't tell them anything for now. For now, we keep them safe, okay?"

She nodded. "You stay safe, too."

I hadn't considered that I might not be safe, but Elise was right. Griffin knew Dean had told me that they were together the night Sandra died. He had to assume I knew they'd been engaging in illegal activities. He could easily guess I'd put the pieces together and concluded he'd been the one to harm Dean. And Dean had told me Griffin wouldn't stop at Elise and the kids. He'd come after me as well. Me and Mark.

I needed to call Chief McTavish, text Mark, and then I needed to get off this floor. Until the police had spoken to Griffin, I wasn't safe to go home. He could even be waiting there for me now or he could have broken into my home and planted some sort of poison in my food. He'd made sure to let me know he knew where I lived.

24

My best option seemed to be to go back downstairs and sit with Russ and Tony. Not only wouldn't I be alone, but I didn't want to go home until I knew Stacey and the baby were okay anyway.

My phone wouldn't pick up a signal in the elevator, so I waited until I reached Stacey's floor again. I called Chief McTavish, explained everything, and gave him Griffin's name and address. I also let him know that Elise was going to stay with her cousin.

He didn't even lecture me. Instead, all he said was "I've got kids myself. They're both off at college, but I understand."

I hung up, texted Mark, and came around the corner to where I'd left Tony and Russ. Tony's shoulders slouched forward, and Russ's hair stood on end as if he'd been tugging it.

My heart felt like it tumbled from my chest and hit the floor. "Any news?"

Tony didn't even blink in response to my question.

Russ set a hand on his shoulder. He'd probably been the closest thing Noah'd had to a real dad. It felt right that Russ had stayed, not only for Tony's sake but also for his own.

"They told us we could wait here," Russ said, "but they had to take her for a c-section. Her blood pressure was spiking, and the baby's heart beat had turned erratic."

A sudden weight in my chest pressed me down into the seat. The rational lawyer side of my brain knew there'd be some risk to the baby being born early, but I hadn't considered that Stacey might be at risk as well. Women had babies all the time. Many of them were much older and much younger than Stacey. She was fit. She was healthy. All her check-ups had been good.

I wanted to ask how much danger they were both in, but I didn't want to be the thing that pushed Tony over the edge. The man looked like he was barely holding it together as it was.

Tony's head turned in my direction. "Will you pray for them?"

As far as I knew, Tony and his wife didn't attend church. If someone had asked me, I couldn't have said whether they believed in God or not. But there was that old saying about there being no atheists in foxholes. Maybe the truth was closer to there being no atheists when the life of someone you loved was at stake. When your hands were bound, it opened your heart to the hope of someone more powerful who could do what you couldn't.

"Do you want me to pray out loud?"

***

Half an hour later, my phone rang. Tony had his head resting back against the wall, and he jerked hard enough that his skull made a thud.

I glanced at the caller ID. Fair Haven PD. That had to be Chief McTavish.

I signaled Russ. "I have to answer this. I'll be around the corner. Find me if there's any news."

I answered the call before it went to voicemail.

"I have bad news or good news depending on how you look at it," Chief McTavish said.

"Don't tell me he's dead," I blurted.

"Have you considered therapy, Dawes? That's not a normal response."

I was already in therapy, but I wasn't about to tell him that. He'd said there was news that could be either good or bad. Considering my history, that meant my suspect was dead—a good thing in that he couldn't hurt Arielle and Cameron, but a bad one in that Dean could go to prison for a crime he didn't commit...assuming he survived.

But I wasn't in the mood to argue with Chief McTavish or defend myself right now. I wanted to know the news and get back to waiting for word on Stacey. "If he's not dead, what happened?"

"He's in police custody, but he's been there over twenty-four hours."

This afternoon Dean was seen by his neighbor working on getting rid of the plants I'd ordered him to dig up. Griffin couldn't have attacked him. He might still have been able to poison his food. "Could you ask the officers in charge of the investigation to have the doctor test Dean's blood for poison? If Griffin poisoned him, he could have done it prior to going into custody."

Chief McTavish sighed. "I'll ask, but it's going to be a battle.

Your suspect wasn't brought in by the police. He came in to cut a plea deal for identity theft. He's turning over all the names of the other people involved and everyone they've sold an identity to in exchange for complete immunity."

Double crap. That made it look like Griffin was innocent concerning Dean's attack. Dean had told him he was leaving the business, and instead of coming after Dean or coming after Elise and the children the way he threatened, he covered his own backside. It was a much smarter move than following through on his threats would have been. I didn't know whether to be grateful or not that he was a smart criminal rather than a stupid one.

If he was spilling his secrets, now was the time to get him to alibi Dean, though. That would give Elise peace of mind, and she could honestly tell Arielle and Cameron that their dad wasn't a killer.

"If nothing else, please have them ask Griffin if he was with Dean the night of Sandra's murder. Dean claimed they were together, but Griffin threatened to hurt his kids if he told the police."

"I'll do what I can. The chief over there's not a reasonable man."

Russ called my name, and my phone slipped halfway out of my hand. I couldn't remember if I'd said goodbye to Chief McTavish or not, but I stuffed the phone and ran.

25

I'd only ever seen a shy smile on Tony's face before. His I-just-won-the-lottery look now went well beyond that. He was smiling, but he also looked a little like he'd had all the air knocked out of his lungs.

The smile, though, was all that mattered. Stacey and the baby must be okay. "Boy or girl?"

"Boy. Noah Anthony Rathmell."

Tony didn't sound at all put out by being the middle name instead of the first name.

"How are they?" I asked.

"The nurse said they're both going to be okay. Stacey's in recovery, and Noah's in the NICU. They want to keep him in an incubator for now because of how small he is, but it sounded like they're confident he'll be fine."

Russ threw an arm around my shoulders and drew me into a sideways hug. Mark had been texting every half an hour for updates on the case and on Stacey. I sent him a message and told him he could call me if he needed to. This had to be triggering some bad memories for him of losing his baby daughter.

"He'll be okay," Russ said.

At first I thought he meant Noah, until I saw that he was looking at my phone's screen.

My eyes burned, and I had to blink to keep back the tears. I didn't want to leave this. I didn't want to go back to a place where we were two among many. In DC, we could make friends, but in Fair Haven we had a community of people who knew us and cared. It'd never be the same in DC as it was here. Job or no job, I didn't want to leave. I'd rather spend the rest of my life patching broken sap lines than go back to the city.

P.S. I typed to Mark. *My vote is to stay in Fair Haven.*

A text dinged in before I could put my phone away. It wasn't from Mark.

Chief McTavish's cell phone number was attached. *Working on convincing them a full tox screen is needed. Doctor's initial assessment is stress and heat exhaustion. But your guy alibied out. They were together until almost sunrise.*

A second text from Chief McTavish dinged in.

Charges still not likely to be dismissed. They're confident no one else could have done it. Think G is lying to cover for him and will argue it in court.

My euphoria over Noah and finally making my decision about where I wanted to live dulled.

If they wouldn't move to drop the charges against Dean based on an alibi, I was back to needing to find the real killer.

I hadn't uncovered any evidence that Sandra knew about the true nature of Dean's business. She could have easily blackmailed him to get the money to save Nadine and Sam's business if she had. Since she didn't know about his business, none of Dean and Griffin's clients would have had any reason to hurt her. None of them seemed to have a grudge with the business that would have been severe enough to kill Sandra over. Besides, now that I knew Dean was innocent, I was sure he would have told me if any of his clients might have done it, however slim the chance. A client would have also needed the skills to pick the lock since Nadine said she'd unlocked the door when she arrived in the morning. Given the type of people Dean "helped," they might possess those skills, but it was a long shot.

Which brought me back to Ken, who also couldn't have hurt Dean because he was with me at the time. He might have had a key to their house, though.

Or Nadine's husband Sam, who had no motive that I could see, especially given that Sandra and Ken spent time with Nadine and Sam as a group and all seemed to get along well. The only things pointing to him were the plastic bags from the same store and access to a house key—except Nadine had her keys with her, so he didn't have any more access to Sandra and Dean's house than anyone else.

Maybe I was stretching and simply not wanting it to be Ken. Maybe Ken killed Sandra and Dean really did collapse from stress and heat exhaustion. Could heat exhaustion send a person into a coma?

Though considering it was getting close to five in the morning, it was also highly possible that my mind wasn't thinking clearly anymore.

Now that Stacey and baby Noah were safe and I knew I wouldn't go home to find Griffin crouching in my bushes ready to strangle me as well, I could get some sleep. As soon as I got up, I'd go back to Dean's neighborhood and talk to Ms. Nosy Neighbor. If anyone could tell me if Ken had lied and did sometimes go over to Sandra's house, it was her.

***

Mark had Sunday off. We'd decided to get up in time for church —meaning we'd probably each gotten no more than four hours of sleep—and head to Dean's neighborhood together afterward. The theory was that the passenger could keep the driver awake as we drove to White Cloud. I'm not sure how much of the sermon I grasped, however.

Once we were on our way, I wanted to know if Mark had gotten my text about settling in Fair Haven, but the conversation almost immediately jumped to Stacey, baby Noah, and Mark's deceased wife and daughter. We'd talked about them many times before, but what happened with Stacey and Noah had dredged up a lot of fears for Mark about us having children. It was something he wanted, and intellectually he knew the same thing wasn't likely to happen again. That didn't make the anxiety he felt any less real.

Midway through the drive, Elise texted to say that they were heading back home since the danger was past. She'd also been placed in charge of Dean's welfare temporarily. The hospital had reached Dean's brother out in Maine, and he'd asked them to speak to Elise and allow her to make decisions until he could fly in. Dean's condition showed no change.

I texted back, and she confirmed that the doctors thought it was heat stroke, but that she'd seconded Chief McTavish's request to run a full toxicology screen.

When we turned onto Dean's street, the gray garbage bin on Dean's front lawn still lay on its side, as if he'd tried to grab it as he fell and it went over with him. Wilted flowers littered the ground around it. I'd clean it up before we left.

We parked in his driveway and walked across the street to Ms. Nosy Neighbor's house. I couldn't see a reason not to bring Mark at this point. The woman seemed happy enough to gossip about Sandra and Dean to anyone.

She answered the door with a glass of lemonade in her hand. Her gaze darted to the glass as if she were afraid simply having it there would encourage us to ask for a glass.

"He hasn't changed his mind about selling the house, has he?" She leaned to one side, looking past us. "I've been watching, and the sign is still out front, but it hasn't sold yet, either."

The woman was the definition of impatience. The house hadn't been listed that long, and I doubted the real estate market was booming in this small town.

"He hasn't changed his mind." I left out that he currently couldn't change his mind. Since the first thing she'd cared about was the state of his house sale, she didn't deserve an update about his medical condition. I'd better jump straight to my question before I lost my patience with her, though. Lack of sleep could make me a bit grumpy. "When Sandra was alive, did Ken ever go over to Dean and Sandra's house?"

The woman shook her head. "Never. Ken and Dean are civil to each other, but they don't socialize. Sandra went to Ken's plenty of times, like I told you, though." She winked twice.

Her observation of their pattern didn't mean Ken hadn't gone over that night. It did mean my assessment that he hadn't killed Sandra was probably correct. She might have taken the meal over to him after she'd finished preparing it that night, but she hadn't likely invited him over to eat it at her house. Especially since, according to Dean, he'd told her he'd be home a lot earlier than he was.

I thanked Ms. Nosy Neighbor even though it made me want to gag, and we headed back across the street.

"Are you sure she didn't kill them?" Mark asked. "She seems desperate to get rid of them."

She didn't so much want them gone as she wanted a nice neighborhood, full of "good" people. "As sure as I can be about anyone in this case. Having a couple she disapproved of in her neighborhood upset her, but she'd know that two murders would mean fewer nice families would want to move here."

Mark hoisted the garbage container upright, and I gathered the plants. Dean had dropped only an armful, but it destroyed the curb appeal of the house. Now more than ever, Dean would need that money. Whether he lived or died, there'd be medical bills. I'd always hated that part of our medical system. It felt cruel to present someone whose loved one had died with a bill as well.

Tingling spread through my palms. I dumped the plants into the garbage bin, and shook my hands out. The sensation was disconcerting, like my hands had gone to sleep.

Mark closed the lid, then frowned. "What's wrong?"

My skin didn't look any different, but the sensation wasn't going away. "I think I'm having an allergic reaction to the plants."

He drew my hand toward him, touching only the back, not the palm. "I don't see a rash. What kind of plant is it?"

The lady who toured the yard with the real estate agent had called it something with a hood. "Monkshood, I think. Dean was cleaning it up because one of the people who toured the house was complaining it wasn't safe if their kids or dogs ate it. I thought it'd hurt the house's perceived value if he didn't get rid of it."

Mark tensed. "Is it just in your hands? Or are you having trouble breathing or a strange feeling in your chest?"

I hadn't been until he said that. "Only my hands. Why?"

"You're not allergic. Monkshood is aconite. It's poisonous, and not only if you eat it."

26

I felt like I was tumbling down a hole even though I hadn't moved. I'd survived multiple attacks from killers. Was I going to die because I picked up a plant? "How poisonous?"

"Fatal, depending on the dose." Mark took my elbow and led me toward the outdoor hose. I seemed incapable of making the decision to move on my own. "If you're only feeling it in your hands, you're going to be okay, but I want us to go to the hospital just in case. First we're going to rinse as much of the sap off your hands as we can."

I nodded dumbly. "Touching the plant can poison someone? Can it kill them?"

"You didn't handle enough of it." Mark turned the hose on. "You're going to be okay. I promise."

His calm tone of voice let me know he wasn't simply humoring me, but the tingling in my hands suddenly felt accusatory. "I'm not thinking about me anymore. I think I'm the one who sent Dean to the hospital. I told him to dig up those plants. Could that be what caused him to collapse?"

He checked the water temperature with a finger, then aimed the flow over my outstretched palms. "It's possible. The highest concentration of the toxin is in the roots. Yesterday was hot, so his pours would have been open. If he was chopping them out and carrying broken roots and stalks in his bare hands, he could have absorbed enough into his body."

Great. I'd almost killed Arielle and Cameron's dad. I might have killed him. We didn't know yet if he'd regain consciousness or what neurological damage there might be when he did.

Mark glanced sidelong at me as if he could read my thoughts. "That doesn't make it your fault. Most people don't realize aconite doesn't have to be ingested to be dangerous. Even people who garden. You said even the woman who toured the house and recognized it only mentioned eating it." He moved the spray back and forth. "Besides, Dean would have had to be an idiot and ignore the feeling in his hands. Or, more likely, the loss of feeling."

I could believe that of Dean. He hadn't shown the greatest judgment in anything he'd done since I met him, except for annulling his partnership with Griffin and agreeing to sell his house. This time, it might not have been complete poor judgment, though. "He probably thought it was an allergy the way I did, or that he was bitten by ants or grabbed a stinging nettle up with them or something."

"Either way, I'll let his doctor know. We might not be able to prove it. Without checking, I'm not sure how long aconitum alkaloids stay in the blood stream." Mark turned off the tap. "At least we know it's not likely someone intentionally tried to kill him. Sandra's killer is still out there, but since Dean's condition was an accident, you're safe, and so are Elise and the kids and Sandra's family. It turns her death back into an isolated case rather than a vendetta."

I stopped in the middle of shaking the water off my hands. Oh crap. Was it possible...? The sick feeling in my stomach told me it was. "Unless someone did intentionally try to kill him and it backfired."

Mark took my elbow again and moved toward the car. "That's not likely. We know he was digging out the monkshood. We could probably find out from the paramedics if his hands were bare when they arrived."

I followed along with Mark mechanically. I was sure Dean's hands were bare. It wasn't this time I was thinking of, but all the pieces were still trying to slide into place in my mind to confirm that I wasn't jumping to crazy conclusions. "I think Sandra's death wasn't a murder at all. It was an attempted murder that got her killed."

Mark's eyebrows lowered and he glanced at the garbage bin. One purplish-blue monkshood stalk stuck out of the lid. "You don't think..."

I did think. "Sandra didn't tell Nadine or Ken that she was leaving Dean. Everyone, including me, assumed that's what she meant. But what she *said* was that she'd decided what she needed to do. The meal she was preparing was for Dean. She planned to poison him and use the life insurance and money he'd collected

226 | EMILY JAMES

from his business to save Nadine and Sam's garden center. Once Dean was gone, she could marry Ken without a messy divorce."

That sounded like conjecture. I could tell by the look on Mark's face, one eyebrow raised a touch above the other, that he wasn't convinced.

"Humor me?" I asked.

"Talk it through." His tone of voice said *whatever it takes to keep your mind off your poison-hands.*

"Assume I'm right. That means the meal Sandra started preparing that night was meant for Dean." How had I missed it? I'd been distracted from Ken's conversation with the waitress by Stacey going into labor or I would have realized then that the meal couldn't have been for him. "Yesterday Ken turned down the strawberry-peach cobbler because he's allergic to strawberries. Sandra was making strawberry shortcake."

"Maybe she didn't know."

He had a point. I wriggled my phone out and tap texted Elise *What was Dean's favorite meal and dessert?* From what everyone had told me about Sandra, I could see her wanting to make Dean's last meal a good one, as weird as that was. Dean had originally planned to be home for a late supper that night before he got caught up with Griffin.

Steak, potatoes, and strawberry shortcake, Elise texted back.

I read it out to Mark and tried—unsuccessfully—to keep any gloating out of my voice. "Sandra started preparing the meal, and then went out to cut flowers in the garden."

"She might have simply wanted flowers on the table. We're

guessing based on what she bought and how much she spent on it that she wanted the meal to be a nice one."

I wanted to stick out my tongue at him, but I know he was only trying to prepare me for what any law enforcement officer would say. "That's possible too, but she worked at a garden center. She wouldn't have cut monkshood for her table. Besides, most people wouldn't go out in the rain. She was at the store. It'd been raining all day. She could have bought a bouquet of flowers rather than going out into the mud and rain to cut them. She'd spent enough on the food that a few extra dollars for flowers wouldn't have mattered."

Holy crap! The mud!

"When she started chopping the monkshood up, she absorbed enough to poison her. Maybe she even cut her finger and it went directly into her bloodstream. She wasn't feeling well, she might not have even been thinking straight, and she went upstairs to lie down. That's why she was on her bed fully dressed and why there was only one set of footprints. There wasn't anyone else. Those muddy, dragging footprints belonged to Sandra as she stumbled into bed. How much aconite would someone have to eat for it to be fatal?"

"Not much. A gram. She could have easily hidden that much in a well-prepared meal without Dean noticing. She had purchased a lot of fresh herbs." The skepticism was gone from his voice. "If she poisoned herself accidentally, that would explain why it seemed like she suffocated face-down. One of the side effects of aconite poisoning is paralysis. If she dropped onto her bed face first, her own weight, combined with the additional difficulty breathing that aconite causes, could have smothered her. Aconite isn't one of the substances tested for on a traditional tox screen, either." He shook his head. "But she couldn't have wrapped a plastic bag around her own head."

My throat constricted. I was pretty sure I knew how the bag had gotten there. And that it'd been an act of love rather than an act of hate, by someone who was as devoted to her as she'd been to them.

27

"If I'm not going to die from this, can we make a detour before the hospital?" I asked. "I need to talk to Sandra's sister, Nadine."

"As long as we go to the hospital afterward, and you promise to do what the doctor says."

I did an air cross of my heart.

He opened the car door for me and buckled me in so I didn't have to use my sore hands. They felt a bit better already after the flush with the garden hose.

The garden center wasn't as busy on a Sunday afternoon as it had been the other times I'd been there. Nadine was the one at the cash register, but she was staring off into space. There weren't any customers waiting.

We walked up to the table, and she jerked slightly. She rose slowly to her feet.

I'd been wondering all the way here how to get her to admit what she'd done. She'd worked so hard to hide it up to now.

My one idea for how to do it seemed cruel, but it was the lesser of two evils over wasting police resources as they hunted for a killer that didn't exist or sent an innocent person to prison. If Chief McTavish was wrong and they dismissed the charges against Dean, Ken would likely be their next person of interest thanks to his relationship with Sandra.

I tucked my hands behind my back to keep from holding them strangely and making her suspicious. "I wanted you to hear it from me first. Dean has an alibi, and the police think Ken is the one who really killed Sandra."

Nadine sank into her chair. "Have they arrested him?"

"The prosecution doesn't think they can make the charge stick because Ken shops at a different grocery store. His lawyer is saying he wouldn't have had a bag that matched the type used to suffocate Sandra, and since she kept reusable bags, he couldn't have gotten one there. It looks like he's going to get away with it."

A jumbled mess of fear, confusion, and anger rolled across her face. If I were her, I'd be weighing my options. There was a chance that if she admitted to what she'd done, the police would accuse her of killing Sandra rather than trying to frame someone else for it. She could also be charged with obstruction of justice or even perjury if the officer took a sworn affidavit from her about how she discovered Sandra's body.

She twisted her wedding ring around on her finger. I could almost see her thinking about her children and what it would do to them if she went to prison.

I was wagering a lot on how much she loved Sandra and wanted to see her killer brought to justice.

"I think I need to talk to the police about the plastic bag." Her voice wobbled. "Whoever killed Sandra didn't put it there. I did."

*D*ean's funeral, surprisingly, wasn't the emptiest one I'd attended since coming to Fair Haven. Even though Oliver tried to kill me, I'd gone to his. Russ, Mark, and I were the only ones who attended Oliver's interment besides the funeral director and the man who ran the backhoe to fill in the hole. It'd been so sad. I was glad I didn't have to relive that feeling now.

All the Cavanaughs turned out for Dean's funeral for the sake of Arielle, Cameron, and Elise. To my surprise, Ken came, as well as Nadine and Sam.

Before Nadine went to the police, I'd offered to represent her. Since the police did decide to clear Dean, it wasn't a conflict of interest anymore. I managed to get her probation. As long as she didn't commit any other crimes for the next few years, she wouldn't have to serve jail time.

I didn't tell her that I'd lied to her. Apparently, I hadn't been entirely lying even though I didn't know it at the time. Once they found out from Griffin that Dean was with him during the time of death window, they had started to consider Ken.

Nadine confessed to finding Sandra face-down in her bed. When she realized that Sandra was dead, she started to call the police. Then she got scared. She knew Dean and his ability to manipulate and lie. She wanted to do something to ensure he'd be charged with Sandra's murder the way he deserved. She was convinced he'd done it. She went out to her car, brought back duct tape and a plastic bag, and staged Sandra's body. She knew they shopped at the same grocery store.

She hadn't been thinking clearly enough to remember that Sandra used reusable bags. She'd thought about planting the duct tape as well, but she hadn't been sure whether her finger prints could be wiped off the cardboard roll the tape was on. She took it home with her.

My explanation of the evidence, along with Nadine's confession, was enough to convince the district attorney that Sandra's death was an unfortunate, self-inflicted accident.

That hadn't made telling Elise the truth about what had happened any easier. First I'd told her how much Dean wanted to do right by Arielle and Cameron, and then I had to tell her why he'd ended up in the hospital. Mark had offered to tell her for me, but it hadn't seemed right to pass it off onto him. I wanted to take responsibility for the part I'd played.

The pastor started his final words, and Elise slipped her hand into mine. Arielle wedged herself up against our legs, and in the edge of my vision, I could barely see Erik holding a sleeping Cameron in his arms.

When I'd told Elise, she'd walked out without saying anything, and I'd cried for the rest of the day despite my best intentions not to. She'd showed up at my house the next day, gave me a hug, and left without another word. Things had slowly edged back to normal, and I was the second one she called—after Erik—when Dean's brother called to tell her he passed away. The damage to his heart had been too great.

As the pastor finished, Elise laid her head on my shoulder. It reminded me of when our friendship first began, sitting by the side of the road. That time, she'd been the one to both hurt me and help me. Friendships, it turned out, weren't as easy as they seemed on TV. At least, not ones where the bonds were deep and survived the stresses of life, where the people involved showed the worst sides of themselves along with the best and made mistakes that they had to apologize for.

And those were the kinds of friendships I wanted.

"I'm glad you're staying," Elise said. "I don't want to lose anyone else."

When Mark and I finally talked about it, it'd turned out he was relieved I didn't want to move to DC. He hadn't wanted to go, either, but he didn't want to bias my preference. Being a medical examiner was more stressful at times than research, but he also found it more rewarding. And he hadn't wanted to leave his family, either. "You wouldn't have lost me even if we went to DC."

"No, but it wouldn't have been the same."

"Nope, it wouldn't have. I'm glad we're staying, too."

Now that Mark and I had decided to stay in Fair Haven and both turned down the jobs in DC, only one question remained. What in the world was I supposed to do for a career? Because a lawyer who couldn't argue a case in court wasn't much of a lawyer at all.

BONUS RECIPE: STACEY'S MAPLE SYRUP POPCORN

INGREDIENTS:

5 cups air-popped popcorn

½ cup maple syrup

½ cup nuts of your choice (optional)

sea salt

cooking spray OR 1 tablespoon butter

TOOLS:

candy thermometer

large bowl

mixing spoon

small sauce pot

cookie sheet

INSTRUCTIONS:

1. Spray a large bowl and mixing spoon well with cooking spray. (You could also butter them if you prefer.) Spray or butter the cookie sheet or cover it in parchment paper.
2. Pop your popcorn. If you don't have an air popper, find the least flavorful bag of microwave popcorn you can, and pop the amount you need.
3. Place popcorn and nuts in the large bowl.
4. In a small sauce pot, bring maple syrup to a boil over medium-high heat. Reduce the heat to medium-low. Continue to boil until the maple syrup reaches approximately 236 degrees based on the candy thermometer. It should just barely form a ball if you drop a drip into cold water.
5. While stirring with the buttered spoon, drizzle maple syrup caramel over the popcorn and nuts.
6. Spread the popcorn mixture out on the cookie sheet. Sprinkle with sea salt to taste. (If you used microwave popcorn, you'll need less salt than if you used air-popped popcorn.)
7. Allow to cool.
8. Store the leftovers (if there are any!) in an airtight container.

LETTER FROM THE AUTHOR

I hope you enjoyed Nicole's latest adventures. In every book, I'm trying to make sure that I give you something fresh and interesting, while still spending time with some of the characters we love.

In Book 8 (*Bucket List*), not only will there be a new mystery to solve (of course!), but we'll also learn whether Stacey will stay at Sugarwood and how Nicole will solve her career dilemma.

Continue on with Nicole, Mark, and the others in *Bucket List*.

If you liked *Tapped Out*, I'd also really appreciate it if you also took a minute to write a quick review. Reviews help me sell more books (which allows me to keep writing them), and they also help fellow readers know if this is a book they might enjoy.

Love,

Emily

ABOUT THE AUTHOR

Emily James grew up watching TV shows like *Matlock*, *Monk*, and *Murder She Wrote*. (It's pure coincidence that they all begin with an M.) It was no surprise to anyone when she turned into a mystery writer.

Alongside being a writer, she's also a wife, an animal lover, and a new artist. She likes coffee and painting and drinking coffee while painting. She also enjoys cooking. She tries not to do that while painting because, well, you shouldn't eat paint.

Emily and her husband share their home with a blue Great Dane, seven cats (all rescues), and a budgie (who is both the littlest and the loudest).

If you'd like to know as soon as Emily's next mystery releases, please join her newsletter list at www.smarturl.it/emilyjames.

She also loves hearing from readers.

www.authoremilyjames.com

authoremilyjames@gmail.com

Ashes of
Our Joy

THE EPIC OF KAROLAN
THE SECOND BOOK AMONG FOUR

Ari Heinze

SOLI DEO GLORIA

CONTEXT WITHIN THE EPIC OF KAROLAN

This is the second book in *The Epic of Karolan*. It describes how Ilohan and Jonathan acquitted themselves in the Norkath War and its aftermath.

The first book, **Bright Against the Storm**, told of the adventures of Jonathan the blacksmith and Sir Ilohan during the time preceding the great war between Karolan and Norkath, and of the love that was between Jonathan and Naomi the shepherdess, whom he left behind in Glen Carrah.

The third book, **Rain, Wind, and Fire**, tells of Naomi's fate in the Norkath War, and of the end of Jonathan's search for her. It tells also how a new danger arose to threaten Karolan, and what was done to guard against it.

The fourth and final book, **Darkness Gathers Round**, describes how the new danger came upon Karolan, and how it was resisted with great heroism. It concludes the story of Ilohan and Jonathan, and of others, no less significant, who were caught up in their adventures. For at the last, though darkness gathered round, their stories did not end in darkness.

To explore Karolan further, visit http://www.hopewriter.com.

Acknowledgements

Thanks to my dear wife, Jane, for supporting me in writing and publishing this work, for believing it was possible even if I didn't, and for invaluable suggestions and insights at every step of the process. Thanks also for shooting all those pictures to help me paint the cover – even when I broke the kitchen window posing with the sledgehammer.

Thanks to my parents, Dan and Judith, and my brothers, Ky and Dar, for being my first readers, and for making me believe I could write something publishable.

Thanks to Daniel Song for detailed editing suggestions for the whole series. Thanks to my brother Paul for proofreading some of the manuscript and tolerating my preoccupation with it on his vacation. Thanks to my endorsers, who took time out of busy schedules to read my book and encourage me in publishing it.

If I start naming those who shared with me the adventures I have drawn on to write my epic, this page will never be enough – but thanks to those who stood with me on icy mountains, hiked to hidden valleys, ventured into baked but splendid deserts, and dared enough heat and cold, hunger, thirst, and danger that my portrayals of these things have some taste of the reality.

Thanks to those whose love helped me dream of Ceramir, and whose courage and faithfulness helped me dream of heroes.

CEMBAR KAROLAN NORKATH

Forest

The far North is forested and unpeopled

Farmland

Bratea

Glen Carrah

Tremilin

Kitherin

Metherka

Bricheldore

Aaronkal

Nildra

Idranak

Dilgare

Felrin

Guldorak

Drantar

Church of Joyful Prayer

Drantar's Gap

Luciyr

Kyrta

Valley of Petras

Byinkal

Wykadrak

Dilfandokir

The Great Mountains

Cliffs of Doom

Ceramir

Harevain

Desert Church

Desert Gap

The Desert

Many other castles, churches, rivers, and other features exist which are not shown.

The great Desert extends beyond the edge of knowledge to the extreme South, from whence, it is said, the Zarnith once came.

The borders cannot be traced with certainty where they meet the Desert and the Mountains.

To my brothers and friends,
Companions in great adventures past and future:
Ky and Dar Heinze, Paul Greenham,
John Williams, Joel Saylor, and Ryan Wilkinson.
I trust you as Ilohan did Jonathan,
And at your need I would attempt a rescue,
Even in the prisons of tyrants and traitors.
It is my hope that instead, we will work
together in the healing of the broken world,
And see evil rolled back by the power of Christ in us.

Chapter 1

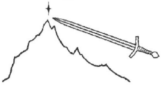

The Eagle's Return

EVEN WHILE HE WAS STILL ASLEEP HE WAS AWARE OF JOY, of singing, of brightness pouring down on him. The singing seemed to reach a crescendo and then abruptly stop as he came fully awake. King Thomas of Karolan opened his eyes and looked around. In the bright sunlight of early morning he saw the scrap of parchment, and remembered the reason for his joy. He had thought that Prince Ilohan was dead, so long was he delayed. But at last, yesterday, the eagle had come. The king took up the parchment and read again the message it had carried.

> All is well; he is safe and true and crowned.
> He starts by way of Cembar in two days,
> if you approve our choice.
> Beware of a traitor; someone knew his errand and his path.
> Hope and pray.
> Eleanor.

It was not a mere happy dream, it was true. Eleanor had not had space on the eagle-carried scrap to say what had delayed the prince, and the threat of the traitor was there, but the great fact remained. Ilohan lived, was proven true, and was returning. The great plan was reaching its fulfillment.

The king strode to the window and looked out. The autumn earth glowed beneath the freshness of the morning sky. Birds skimmed the harvest fields and wheeled around the tower wall, all singing. He knew his body was old. His heart, too, had been old for many years – but now he felt it was young again, as it sang for joy with the singing of the birds. He turned around, almost expecting to see his beloved Sarah standing by the bed to share the joy of Ilohan's success. She was not there.

"I had forgotten," he said aloud in the empty room. "She is with you, my Lord. And yet I pray that she indeed shares my joy, and sees her own faithful work here on earth reaching its goal."

He ate his breakfast with the appetite of a younger man. Servants brought him his royal robes and his newly-polished crown. He took a deep breath, feeling even the air fresher and sweeter on this morning, and went out through the great gate to the sound of trumpets.

The crowd saw the king come forth. The sun made his crimson robes glow, and sent flashes of dazzling light from his crown. He advanced toward a raised platform or pulpit that extended out from the steps before the gate, draped with hangings of cloth-of-gold, with the royal standard snapping above it in a brisk wind. Excited whispers in the crowd said that this platform, which looked grand enough to last forever, had been built only for the day and would be dismantled on the morrow. The king walked slowly, but his step was as firm and regal as it had ever been. Wave after wave of cheering echoed back from the great stone walls of Aaronkal.

Thomas stood silent for a moment at the edge of the platform, waiting for the cheering to cease. He could feel the love his people bore him, but also the desperation that had brought them here in such great numbers. They were afraid and confused, wondering about the threat of Norkath and the old rumors surrounding Prince Kindrach's death. Their desperation drained his strength, for they looked to him for salvation, not fully understanding that it cannot come from mortal kings.

"People of Karolan!" he cried, loud enough to be heard to the farthest reaches of the crowd. "Twenty years ago Kindrach your prince and his wife and son were captured at Lake Luciyr by the soldiers of Fingar. The prince was told to betray you, to pledge his crown to Fingar – or else be killed with his wife and child." Dead silence fell as Thomas paused. He could feel the crowd waiting, breathlessly.

"Prince Kindrach was faithful! He escaped and rescued the Princess Eleanor and the young Prince Niran. He died defending their retreat. Your princess escaped, and was brought here in secret, badly hurt. She went away to a distant place where she could be healed and hidden, and she left her son here that he might not share her sorrow. He lived." Again there was a total silence of strained attention.

"You never knew that Eleanor and the young prince survived. I and Queen Sarah had concealed them, and we let all assume that they were dead. We gave Prince Niran a new name, and hid his lineage even from himself. By doing this we thought to protect him from his father's fate, and to raise him in humility to understand and serve people of every rank. He lived at Aaronkal as a foundling, a ward of the throne, without royal privilege or honor. From child to page, from page to squire, and from squire to Knight of Karolan, he grew up in all ways as we hoped. Now at length the time has come to reveal his name. Fingar is a coward, a liar, and a knave. Sir Ilohan of

Aaronkal is my rightful heir, the crown prince, your future king!"

The thousands of Karolan roared their hope to the morning sky, until the castle and surrounding forests rang with it. The king could feel their exultation, their certainty that they were saved. It seemed to drain away his very life.

"Prince Ilohan is faithful and true. He will never betray your trust, never fail you as I did in my youth, before I understood... before I learned – as I failed you long ago, and years were wasted and evil sown before I won your trust again. Ilohan is as true and noble as was Kindrach his father, and he will bless you and govern well!"

Even as cheers again erupted from the crowd, King Thomas felt a terrible pain burn through him. He thought a dagger had stabbed through his heart. As his legs began to buckle beneath him, he turned to see who his assassin was. There was no one there. He looked down at his chest. There was no blood. He knew then that he was not wounded, yet he was sinking to the floor as if mortally hurt. He gathered the utmost strength of his will, and stood up straight again to face the crowd. He must not fall. He must not let them see. Yet now he must not say what he had come to say.

"Prince Ilohan has gone..." he paused to gasp for breath, yet resumed too quickly, he hoped, for any to notice something amiss, "...far away to Princess Eleanor. He will return very soon to lead you against Fingar, who... in lying greed would claim his crown. You will... be victorious! Love Ilohan well, for well he will love you!" The crowd roared once again, but then the cheers died in their throats.

King Thomas felt another searing pain lance through his chest. The bright world spun before his eyes, his body did not heed his will's command, and he crumpled down upon the platform. He lay flat for a moment, and then, gasping for breath, raised himself on one trembling hand. His vision darkened; the world continued to spin, but he still had his voice. "Steward!" he cried. "Muster the Army of all Karolan!" He gasped again, clutching at his chest. "Muster it at once, with all speed!"

A vast collective groan sounded from the crowd at the fall of the king, and then the murmur of anxious voices rose like the sound of a rising wind stirring the leaves of a forest. Two knights ran out on the platform, lifted the king between them, and carried him into Aaronkal. The steward followed. Messengers ran to and fro. Grooms brought ten fast horses from the king's stables, and heralds with trumpets came out the great gate of Aaronkal to mount them. The steward briefly reappeared to give some last instructions to the heralds. With a blast of trumpets they rushed away, carrying to every part of the realm the urgent call for the Army of All Karolan to muster at Aaronkal.

After a long, anxious interval the steward came out again and took the king's place on the platform. "People of Karolan!" he cried. "Today is a day of sorrow for us all. The king has fallen. I have spoken with the royal physician attending him..." The steward bowed his head, seemingly too grieved to speak further. At last he looked up and continued, "The royal physician says the malady is of the heart, and must bring death by sunset. Yet you are not without a leader, for I, his trusted servant, must take his place with grief until the prince returns. In keeping with the laws of Karolan, I will act for him, with all of his authority. This is my word to you: we will fight Fingar, and defeat him!

"Even now the king's messengers ride to gather the great army – the army in which many of you will fight. The prince is far away, across the mountains. There is no possibility that he will return in time to lead you against Norkath, for Fingar's army will attack within seven days. Because of this, I will lead you. I will lead you as I led you a score of years ago when we saved King Thomas from certain doom. I will lead you, and you will be victorious! Then, after we have saved the kingdom, the prince will come, and he will rule you well. He is good, faithful, and true, as King Thomas has said. He will heal you of the hurt that Kindrach's death brought upon you, and he will bring the blessings Kindrach would have brought had Fingar been less vile.

The crowd cheered, but only halfheartedly. The people felt as though they had leaned in total trust on a staff, and it had broken beneath them. They had come to hear good King Thomas tell them what was wrong and why all would be well; to have him console their worry with his strength. Now the strong man to whom they had looked for help had fallen and was dying. The hope of which he had told them would come too late. They would face the wrath of Fingar's army, and his ruthless greed, with no royal leader of their own. True, the steward had once before raised an army and led it prudently, but that army had never had to fight. Tulbur did not have the king's bright courage and fire-tested sureness of fidelity. Could there be any hope of victory for an army with only him to lead it?

Gradually the cheers gathered strength, and washed against the castle wall in tentative, trembling approval. The people felt that the steward was their last hope, however insufficient, and it would not do to offer him no sign of approval or of trust. Their king had fallen, and their prince was far away, but their faithful steward stood by them. They would stand by him also.

*   *   *

Britheldore stood at the door of the king's tower bedchamber. The sunshine was bright on the foot of his bed, and the reflected light suffused the entire room with a warm glow. The king lay still upon the bed, and his face looked more like weathered gray stone than like the visage of a living man. Yet he still breathed. The court physician knelt beside the bed, while Metherka and Idranak stood near. The physician looked up at them. "He will not speak again," he said. "Before the middle of the afternoon we shall lose him."

The room was very still and silent. The sounds of tears falling on the rich carpet could be heard as Idranak and Metherka wept. Britheldore knew their thoughts: they were mourning the king who had led them so long at such cost to himself; whose iron will had fought through his weakness so well that few had seen how hard the battle was; who had never uttered a whisper of complaint. Britheldore's own sorrow was so great that the dead weight of it seemed to stifle even his tears. He had known the king's weakness – and his strength. If that body had held together for ten days more, the spirit in it could have led the Army of all Karolan to victory. As he himself had guessed, it never would.

A shadow briefly dimmed the light that was pouring through the window, and something large sailed into the chamber. The knights started, and the physician cried out in pain as huge talons gripped his shoulder. The eerie scream of a great golden eagle split the sunlit silence of the room. King Thomas opened his eyes. The old look of stern control crept across his face, and yet to Britheldore it seemed mingled with a depth of joy that he had not seen in that countenance for many years.

"Leave us," whispered the king, "all but Britheldore alone."

Idranak and Metherka obeyed immediately. Britheldore saw that the physician wanted to remain, but he shook his head. The physician moved to depart, and the eagle released his bleeding shoulder and lighted with a great sweep of wings on the back of the king's chair. Britheldore closed the door behind the physician, and turned to meet the king's eyes – which all had thought would not open again except in death.

"Sir," whispered the king faintly to Britheldore, "take parchment and quill. Quickly. Write."

Britheldore took them from the king's table, and looked quickly back for instructions. Life was already sinking from his sovereign's eyes.

"I die. Today. Come at once. Fingar, a score and ten thousands, six days. We fall. No hope. Thomas."

Britheldore wrote down the message, and then looked back at the king to hear further commands. The old man's eyes were closing, and his gray lips looked as though they could scarcely move. The old knight bent close over the king's face to catch the breathed words. "Twine. Talon. Send. Now."

Britheldore saw the twine on the table. He tied the message securely to the eagle's talon, beside the other that was already there. Not knowing what else to do, he lifted the eagle bodily in his arms and pushed it toward the window. Skykag gave a scream of protest, flapped his mighty wings in Britheldore's face, and was gone like the wind, soaring out over the bright autumn land.

The old knight turned back to the king. His head had turned to look at something on the wall above the table, but his eyes saw nothing now, and never would again. The faithful king, who had borne the load of Karolan alone for far too long, was dead. "So be it," said Britheldore. "Now he rests, and shares in Sarah's joy."

*   *   *

The men, women and children of Karolan were weeping as they left the field in front of Aaronkal. Britheldore had told them that their king was dead, and they knew what they had lost. Thomas had ruled them for so long that most could not remember a time before his reign. They could hardly understand that his stern hand no longer held the scepter, and that his stony courage would never again lead them into a hard-fought battle.

He had been a faithful king. He had borne all the sorrow the throne had brought him, without wavering in his determination to serve and bless his people. If he had failed them once, when he was a wild young man, he never had again. He had been more faithful for the memory of that one crime. Few even in that vast crowd were stoical or indifferent enough to depart with cheerful faces, or with eyes not cast down toward the dead grass at their feet.

Britheldore turned away from the sad processions that were leaving Aaronkal for the various towns from which they had come. He made his way with slow steps back to the castle. Metherka met him on the stairs. The young knight's grief was evident, but a fire shone in his eyes. Britheldore knew that he was hearing the thunder of the messengers who were galloping to every part of Karolan to muster the army he would lead.

Britheldore put a hand upon the young knight's shoulder. "You will lead the army," he said. "You must. Tulbur will try, but you must do it." They walked together through the great gate and into the castle.

*   *   *

Ilohan and Veril walked beneath the mighty trees of Ceramir while a cool wind from the mountains stirred the branches high above them. The sky was a cloudless blue, and afternoon sunlight shafted in the mist that rose gently off the lake. Eleanor stood beside the water and watched them, as she had said she would, but there was no sorrow in her gaze.

They talked of many things: of Aaronkal and Ceramir, of the great desert and the stars that shone above it, and of the mountains meant for angels alone. They said nothing about love, or about the future, or about the fact that Ilohan was the prince. They talked of the times they remembered. Veril told Ilohan of the children she loved, and of her own childhood. She told him that as she looked back, it seemed to her that every sorrow that had touched her then had been as fleeting as a flying vulture's shadow on the desert sand, and that her joy had shone brightly, untroubled by any fear that it might ever fade. Now that she was grown, she told him, she saw more clearly, and sadness touched her soul – yet with her deepened, opened life came hope of more glorious joy, and faith to see beyond the shadows of the world into the joy of Paradise.

Ilohan thought of Thomas, of the growing weariness that had fallen upon him as the years after Sarah's death wore on. It seemed to him that Veril had never seen or imagined a weariness like that – one that could sap the joy and strength from a man's life. She had spoken of sorrows that burned like fire or wounded like nails, but not of those that seemed to drain life itself away. He wondered if anything could drain her

18

life, and he felt he would pay any price to see that nothing ever did. He thought of Sarah, and wondered if even in her death her life had dimmed. He did not think it had.

He looked at Veril, beautiful in the streaming autumn sunshine and the awakening wind from the great mountains. He told her of his own childhood, of his stern training as a page and squire, balanced by the love of Sarah and the kindness of Thomas. He told her of the joy he had felt when first he set his lance in rest and galloped across the great field in front of Aaronkal. He confessed the terror he felt whenever another knight leveled a lance at his shield, and he told her that he had never thought himself worthy of knighthood.

Then suddenly he was telling her of the creeping weariness that had come over the king, and asking her for comfort concerning it, and it did not seem strange to him that he should ask such a thing of her.

"It must have been hard to see that," she said. "And you fear it for yourself, or others for whom you care. It comes to me that he is weary only because he has lost Sarah, that while she was with him she could bring him strength. I think that if all had gone well, another could have helped him carry on, not taking her place, but only comforting and strengthening him in his loss. I cannot be sure of this."

She stood still a moment, looking up at the sunlight that streamed through the sparse autumn foliage of the trees, and then she continued, "Even if I am wrong, if this weariness was unavoidable because of the evil of the world, it is still only a small thing to the joy that shall come after. We must be true to God – that is what matters. It does not matter what happens to us. I do not even care what will happen to me, but I hope my life will bless someone. It does not seem to at present. I mean, if my life does bless anyone, I am not aware of it."

19

"You have great faith, and courage beyond my own," said Ilohan. "I am afraid of pain, as well as other things. But should you not also trust God that he will make you a blessing, whether you see it or not? Would not this ease your sorrow?"

"You have been faithful to the king," she said. "You have been given great tasks and fulfilled them. As for me, I am only Veril."

"What does that mean, Veril?" asked Ilohan. "Shall I say, 'Sarah was only Sarah,' when we both believe she sustained a king as long as she lived?"

"But Veril is a weak child," said Veril. "She loves, but she is needed for nothing, and she does no one any good."

"I have no wisdom," said Ilohan, "and I do not know what to say to comfort you. Yet it comes to me that God needs no one. We cannot give to him, but must simply acknowledge our need and delight in his generosity."

"I know that, and yet perhaps I do not know it," said Veril. "Indeed, none of us has anything we have not been given. Even if in service to God I lose my life and pour out all my blood, yet at my beginning he gave me every drop, and still I have given him nothing and owe him all. Existence itself, every loving word, every sunrise, every blossom, every star – and beyond and before all, the blood of Christ that sets me free from the fear of Hell to enjoy all – all these are from him. I can only praise and thank him, never repay him."

"Veril, do you know what we have been saying to one another?"

She looked up at him and laughter washed across her face. "Half winged with wisdom not our own, half stumbling to speak in words we do not understand," she said. "So it always is, while we walk beneath the sun." Her laughter broke forth clear and bright. "Thank God he holds us though we stumble and we do not understand."

Ilohan smiled at her, hoping she took that for assent, but he was speechless from the beauty that he saw: her laughter, the strengthening wind, and the red sunset rays kindling the barren treetops against the deep blue sky. The wind caressed her red hair, which seemed to glow despite the deep shade cast by the mountain walls. She was beautiful, and his heart was singing. Her words had been full of wisdom and comfort, and her sorrow flowed only from her shocking blindness to the blessings she brought.

In his desire to bring her joy he said, "Veril, you must always remember that you are far from useless. If you cannot see the good you bring, then you are very blind. Do not forget the words of those who see more clearly."

She bowed her head. "I only half believe them, yet at your bidding I shall try to remember them and to hope they are true. Will you climb the sheet of vines with me?"

"Willingly, my Lady."

Most of the leaves had fallen as the cooling autumn days went past, and the sheet of vines had gone from green to yellow and from yellow to bare brown and gray. They climbed it easily. Ilohan was grateful that much of his strength had returned so soon after his recovery from the plague. He could see that Veril was happy as she climbed beside him, and he delighted in her joy. When they reached the top, blue twilight was rising, darkening the sky over the eastward desert, while to the west lovely pastel shades faded into one another above the sinking sun.

They sat together on the sheet of vines and looked out over the Cloth of Joy, and the great expanse of desert beyond it. The vines swayed and flexed beneath them in the strong wind.

Ilohan turned to look at the awesome mountains, from which that wind was blowing. The edges of their peaks caught the red-gold sunset light, while behind them was the vast, cold twilight, pure and deep. His soul leaped up with exultation in their majesty. Suddenly, all that he had ever feared concerning Veril seemed utter foolishness in his mind. Why should he not be so blessed as to love deeply the first young woman who loved him? He turned toward her with a smile, searching for words to tell her what was in his heart. He did not find them.

A terrible cry lashed their ears, and Ilohan started up in terror, with Veril beside him. The cry had seemed to come from above them, borne on the cold wind. Ilohan scanned the sky in the direction of the mountains, and saw a great eagle soaring there. It passed over them, giving another fearful cry, and swept down toward the stone house with dizzying speed. "Skykag!" cried Ilohan, starting down the vines at once. "It is Skykag, and I fear his news is dire!"

Veril followed him. She knew he had been about to speak, but the words he would have said were lost forever, along with the perfect moment the eagle's cry had shattered. Her eyes filled with tears. Then she feared he would look back, so she wiped them quickly and wept no more. He was a prince, and if he forgot her she must bear it. She must let him go where he had need to go. Just as they reached the foot of the vines, Jonathan came running up. Even before she heard him speak, Veril knew from his face that Ilohan had been right about the eagle's news.

"Skykag flew straight to the house and lighted near where Princess Eleanor was standing," said Jonathan, breathless from his speed. "She asks you both to come at once. The king is dead."

Veril fell back against the vines, realizing again that everything had changed in a moment. She felt almost as if Ilohan had died too. The young man who had seemed so near to her that afternoon was gone now, cut off from her by both royalty and grief. She saw him stand stunned for a long moment, taking no notice of her, and then he and Jonathan together began running down toward the house.

She followed as fast as she could, but Ilohan and Jonathan left her behind. They vanished into the house while she was still many paces away. She reached the door at last, grasped the frame for support for a moment, and then, still panting hard, followed them into the council room. She wanted to run into Imranie's arms for comfort, but she knew her private sorrow had no importance now. She took her own seat as tranquilly as she could, and, gazing at the floor, tried to fix her mind on catching her breath. When she looked up again, she saw that both her parents were trying to comfort Eleanor and Ilohan, and she was instantly ashamed that all her own sorrow had been for herself.

Chapter 2

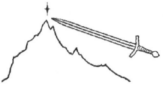

The Third Road to Karolan

"THE KING WOULD NOT WANT OUR GRIEF TO KEEP US from action," said Ilohan in the council room at Ceramir. "We must decide what to do. Did Skykag's message say anything about Fingar's invasion?"

"Skykag brought two messages," said Eleanor, "and how that can be I do not understand. The first is in King Thomas's hand. Here it is."

Ilohan took it and read aloud:

> God is good.
> Let him take the road you have named.
> Now warned, I do not fear the traitor.
> I will gather the people and tell them of their prince.
> Thomas.

"The other message," said Eleanor, "is written hastily in the hand of my own father, Sir Britheldore. Were it not for that, I could scarcely believe it. Nor, again, can I conceive why there are two messages. Skykag did come one day late, as though Thomas had confined him for a day awaiting a decision. Yet I do not think the king would cage an eagle – and even then there would be only one message. The second message was tied outside the first, with a new piece of twine and a hasty knot. There is blood on it, and because of this I think Skykag left Aaronkal hungry, and had to kill on the way for food. Here is the message."

Ilohan took it. Despite the hasty writing, the letters were clear and bold:

I die, today.
Come at once.
Fingar brings a score and ten thousands in six days.
We fall. No hope.
Thomas
I, Britheldore, wrote the king's dying words.

Ilohan looked up at Eleanor, and saw in her face the image of his own distress. "What has happened?" he asked.

"I do not know," she said.

"Thomas wrote the first message, fed Skykag, and sent him away," said Mudien. "Then, rather than coming to us, Skykag returned of his own will when the king was on his deathbed. Britheldore had to send him again, but he did not know the custom, and sent him hungry. This, I believe, is the only way to explain the two messages. God guided the eagle to return to Thomas that we might have the news."

"But alas!" cried Ilohan. "What are we to do with such news?"

Eleanor bowed her head. Mudien stood, looked at Ilohan for a moment as though he would speak to him, and then left the room in silence.

"There is hope, surely," said Jonathan. "The Army of all Karolan will gather at Aaronkal and march to the border under

the command of one of the knights. They will be ready when
the host of Norkath attacks, and they may indeed triumph. Yet
how I wish we were there – how I wish they could march
under the banner of Prince Ilohan!"

"We cannot reach Aaronkal in six days, or even twelve,"
said Ilohan. "And as for the outcome of the battle, I do not
share your confidence, Jonathan. With or without us, there is
great danger that Karolan will fall."

"That is true," said Eleanor. "The Army of all Karolan never
numbered more than thirty thousand, even in the days of
Konder when they had weeks to muster. In six days they will
be scarcely more than half of Fingar's force."

"That is not so great a disadvantage," said Jonathan.
"Surely, with all they love behind them, the men of our army
may fight with the strength of two. They may drive Fingar
back. But alas that we are so far away, and can do nothing!"

"Whether Karolan stands or falls," said Ilohan, "I cannot
think of anything for us to do but follow the Cembar road as
we have planned, and God grant we arrive in free Karolan, not
a conquered Norkath province."

"There is another course open to you," said Eleanor. "You
can wait here for seven days, and then I will send Skykag to
find out if Karolan has triumphed. Thus you may avoid
throwing your life away – for it will be death to enter the land
as prince if Fingar has conquered it."

"But what of 'Come at once,' the king's message?" asked
Jonathan. "I mean, did he not intend... but forgive me, Lady
Eleanor... I did not mean to dispute your words."

"Though the king said, 'Come at once,' he also said there
was no hope," said Imranie calmly. "That makes his saying,
'Come at once,' seem more like the unthinking cry of a
desperate man than an urgent royal command. To me, at least,

dear Prince of Karolan, it seems folly to ride hastily into a conquered land. Yet if you plan carefully instead, who knows what good you can do?"

The heavy wood door of the room opened forcefully and Mudien entered, closing it behind him with a hollow boom. "I have found what I sought," he said. "I have found the record of the secret way. Including the cliffs, it will take eight days to travel. The Cembar road takes more than twice as long."

Eleanor stood up on her crutches, with anger hot in her eyes for a moment. As suddenly, her look changed to one of shame, and she sat back down. Her face was pale when she looked up to meet Mudien's gaze. "Could the journey be accomplished in only seven days?" she asked quietly.

"I think it could; seven days to Petrag," he said, low and deadly serious.

"Then one day's gallop from Petrag to Aaronkal?"

"Yes," said Mudien.

"Still eight days in all," said Eleanor.

"Yes. The message says six," said Mudien.

"There is hope that eight is nearer true," said Eleanor.

"Yes," said Mudien. "Six days would be very short indeed for Fingar to muster a large army and then march to Aaronkal."

Ilohan listened, and fevered hope and terror burned through him. There might be a way he could keep from failing Thomas, and all Karolan – but the decision, the journey, and the war all seemed to be rushing toward him with brutal haste. He found that he had risen to his feet and was facing Mudien. "There is a path that might take us to Aaronkal before the Norkaths come?" he asked.

"Yes," said Mudien, "there is."

Ilohan felt that he could not breathe from the press of the decision and all that it entailed. "We must take it," he gasped. "We must take that way, and leave tonight." He fell back in his chair, committed. Dead silence fell in the room. Wind from off the great mountains could be heard moaning around the house and roaring in the tall trees.

Jonathan sat silent with the rest, but he could scarcely contain his joy. A secret road that took only seven days could mean only one thing: the mountains. The words that were singing through his mind were Ilohan's, from a time so far away it seemed another world: "There are places meant for angels alone, where no man will ever come."

"Why must you take that way?" asked Veril, breaking the silence at last. "You are speaking of a path across the mountains, a way of bitter cold and great peril. Why must you attempt it?"

"I do not know if I can sway the balance of the war," said Ilohan. "My coming in itself will secure neither peace nor victory. But if I can come – if I can but stand with my people, as Thomas wanted, and share their terror and their pain, I must. I am weak and foolish, but I am the prince, and this is what a prince must do."

"I understand that well," said Veril. "Alas!"

"You will do much more than simply share their pain, my son," said Eleanor. "You will bring the men of Karolan a reason to fight." She spoke these words of encouragement warmly, but Jonathan thought that afterwards her face went blank and her eyes cold: she was proud of her son's courage, but the thought of the mountain way filled her with fear.

"Yes," said Mudien. "You may indeed shift the balance of the war. Your faithfulness will not be in vain."

28

"Since the time of Dradrag, all have thought the mountains were impassible," said Ilohan. "Teach me, then, this secret way that leads across them."

"As Brogal brought the caravan you have seen," said Mudien, "many years ago another slave caravan was brought to Ceramir. Among the slaves we freed was a man of the Zarnith race. He accepted the gift of life in Ceramir, and agreed to live here in peace with all people. He relinquished the ferocity and heedlessness of the Zarnith without discarding their courage and endurance. Yet after five years in the valley, his nomad's soul felt trapped, and he left. As a parting gift, he gave to me the story of the mountain way."

"How could a Zarnith know of a way across the mountains?" asked Ilohan. "Is it not Dradrag's failure that convinces all men that they cannot be crossed?"

"The history of that time has faded into legend," said Mudien, "but even when it was new and fresh, much about what had passed was not understood. There were things even Dradrag did not know.

"Let us begin, however, with what we can know with some certainty. When Dradrag tried to cross the Mountains of Karolan, he first burned and pillaged the Cloth of Joy, and then brought his army up a mountain path behind it. They came to the Cliffs of Doom, far up in the great mountains. For thirteen days he tried to get his host up those cliffs, making them use ropes and ladders, picks and spears, and the desperate strength of their bare hands. Fierce courage spurred those warriors on – combined with the fear of Dradrag's merciless wrath. A score of thousands perished in the unrelenting attempt. When at last he accepted defeat, Dradrag ordered the ropes and ladders burned, carved his famous defiance in the rock, and went back to the desert."

"That is the story as I have always heard it," said Ilohan. "What was it that Dradrag did not know?"

"He never knew," said Mudien, "that some of his men actually reached the top of the cliffs. They were, no doubt, bold climbers of remarkable skill. The rest of the host could not follow where they had gone, and they must have lacked long ropes or other things they could have lowered to aid those below. They may have shouted down the news, but their shouts were lost in the echoing vastness, or ignored. Presently they saw the smoke of the ladders burning, and the survivors of the great host retreating from the cliffs. They knew then that they were abandoned, and that for them there could be no retreat. With terrible loss they made their way across the mountains, and at last descended into Karolan. Those few survivors passed through Karolan in secret, and managed at length to rejoin the Zarnith host in Cembar. They told the story of the mountain way that they had taken.

"Thus the story was handed down among the Zarnith, and at last reached Ceramir through the man who was healed here. Here is the parchment I made, a copy of the Zarnith's words about the path."

Ilohan took the parchment, and read the strong, even script aloud:

Stand on the top of the cliffs, and see a peak to the north.
Pass west.
Stand at the pass beneath the stars, and see terror.
Walk to the third of the mountains.
Walk in the white wildness, and know weariness.
Walk to the third of the mountains.
Stand at the foot of the third mountain, and see despair.
Climb the western flank.

Stand at the pass among the stars, and die.
Descend from the pass among the stars.
Stand at the brink of doom, and know wonder.
Cross on the bridge the Wyrkriy made.
Descend into the last valley, stand on the last mountains, and
see forbidden joy.
Descend into Karolan.

Ilohan looked up at Mudien. "It is your hand, Sir," he said, "but the words are from a Zarnith soul. They are wild and fierce and dire, even as the war song is. What do they mean to us?"

"The lines come in sets of two," said Mudien. "Each set describes one day. On the first day they saw a peak to the north, and went to the left of it. On the second day they reached a high pass, and set out for the third mountain, across a wild, icy plain. On the third day they reached the foot of the third mountain. On the fourth day they climbed up to another high pass west of the mountain. On the fifth day they descended from it, and reached an impassible rift in the rock. On the sixth day they crossed it by a bridge. On the seventh day they descended into the last mountain valley between them and Petrag, climbed the last range of mountains, and descended into Karolan. This, at least, was how the poem was understood by the Zarnith who lived here."

"What are the Wyrkriy?" asked Jonathan, "And what kind of bridge is it?"

"Wyrkriy is a Zarnith word for wild, evil spirits of the desert," said Mudien. "I think the Zarnith said the Wyrkriy made the bridge only because they did not understand how humans could have made it, or why they would. I also cannot explain these things, but from the testimony of the Zarnith man

31

who dwelt here I am confident the bridge is real. It is made of rope and planks, he told me, and spans a huge chasm."

"How can we get to the top of the Cliffs of Doom?" asked Ilohan. "We do not have thirteen days and twenty thousand men to spare."

"Brogal has been to the cliffs twice," said Mudien. "On the second time he found a crack going all the way up the face. He said that he and Rangol could climb it if there were ever need. He will show it to you."

"Ilohan," said Eleanor, looking him directly in the face. "I desire with all my heart for you to do what you believe is your duty before God. Remember this, yet consider once again. Are you sure your choice is right, sure beyond any doubt? If you are, you must carry on. But I ask you once more to consider it, before the time when there will be no turning back."

Ilohan again felt the intolerable weight of the decision, combined with the urgent need to choose without delay. He went swiftly out of the room and into the night. He stopped beneath the stars, and looked up toward the mountains. The wind was strong, and it seemed to call him toward its source. He leaned into its power, and the cold gusts buffeted him one way and then another. It roared and wailed in the great trees, and the night was alive with motion and adventure. The wind seemed to brighten the stars, to fan their twinkling white fires.

"God," he said, "you alone know the future. You know what hurt and blessing either course will bring. I do not. I only want to be faithful. Beyond that I do not even know what I desire. Please take care of me, and help me choose the course of true faithfulness and wisdom. This life you put me in is too much for me. Never leave me, or I will die without hope or comfort."

Back in the council room all awaited Ilohan's return in silence. Presently they heard the wind slam the outer door with a resounding bang. An instant later Ilohan threw open the door of the room. He stood straight and still in the doorway. The light of certainty and of adventure was in his eyes. "I will take the mountain way," he said.

"So let it be," said Eleanor. "This life was never ours to plan or make secure. As you have said, you must leave tonight."

*   *   *

"The king ordered that Metherka lead the army," said Britheldore to the assembled knights in the council chamber at Aaronkal. "We must obey."

"That was his command if he fell in battle," said Tulbur. "He has died before the war, and by the laws of Karolan I must rule in his place, with all his power, until the prince returns to claim his crown. It is my decision that I myself am the best one to lead the Army of all Karolan."

"Yet consider the words of your counselors, as King Thomas always did," said Dilgarel. "You are a wise and faithful steward, and we are glad to have you take up the king's authority, but you have never been a soldier. Once you raised an army, and raised it well, but that army never saw battle. Can you kindle a passionate courage in men as Metherka could? I know you are brave, as well as prudent, but more is needed for a great commander. Do you have that in you which men will follow to the end, fighting with stalwart skill whether they see hope of final victory or not?"

"You have said I should listen to my counselors as King Thomas did," said Tulbur. "Do you mean that truly? Might I remark, without intending any disrespect, that he listened to us well but did not seem frequently to change his own decisions because of our advice?"

"That is true," said Nildra, "but sometimes he did alter them. It was because of Britheldore's words that he chose Metherka as the commander. I advise you imitate him in this. Britheldore is a wise and seasoned soldier, and Metherka is a knight of high courage."

"And of careless words and imprudent management," said Tulbur. "His ancient castle is in disarray, and will be easy prey to Norkath if we fall. Even his affairs here at Aaronkal are disordered. The lodging that the king gave him is ill kept, and his servants are not obedient or orderly. Of all that he has, only his lance, his sword, and his horse are well cared for."

"You speak facts, Sir Steward," said Britheldore. "Truth lies behind those facts. Metherka is trustworthy, and should lead."

"He should lead his own knights, mustered from his own castle," said Tulbur. "I will lead the Army of all Karolan. Metherka's place, and the place of each of the king's knights, is back at his own castle mustering his men. I have already told the people I will lead them, and their cheers shook the fortress walls. Any who would dispute my decision will only cause discord, now when we have the greatest need for unity. Metherka is brave, but not dependable or seasoned. He is not the steady, wise warrior we need to lead our forces."

"You misjudge him," said Britheldore. "Many have. He is faithful at the core that war reveals. You see an unimportant surface. He must lead."

Metherka himself stood, very straight and very pale in the light of the candles on the dark oak table. Silence fell on the assembly. "What the steward says is true," he said in a firm, even voice. "I am not worthy to lead the Army of all Karolan. My keeping of my own affairs has shown this clearly. Farewell.

I go to Castle Metherka to muster my men." He stepped out, pulled the heavy door firmly closed behind him, and was gone.

Out in the torch-lit stables Metherka's horse was hastily saddled by servants who, at least, knew that work well. He mounted in a single swift motion and galloped away into the darkness. He lost his iron hold on his shame, and burning tears that brought no relief were blown back in the fierce wind of his going. He had made himself unworthy to do what had been his duty and his dream, and whoever might forgive him he never would forgive himself.

Back in the castle, Britheldore had risen immediately to follow Metherka, but had soon seen he could not overtake the young knight as he sprinted down passages and stairways toward the main gate. The old man stopped to catch his breath by a dark window. When the sound of galloping came to him, loud then rapidly fading into silence, he bowed his head. "Thus departs the last hope of Karolan," he said. "Yet in the end it was he who chose. I will stand with Tulbur. I must."

*   *   *

Ilohan stood beside the stone house in Ceramir, waiting in the starry darkness for the moment of final farewell and departure. Earlier, while hastily planning for the journey, he had felt joy in the prospect of adventure. Now he felt only the loss of departing from the Cloth of Joy. All people and all things that he had left to love were there, and except for Jonathan he was leaving them. He could feel no love now for the unnamed, unknown host of Karolan's people, and it seemed a grievous fate that duty should call him to throw so much away on a forlorn hope of aiding them. In Ceramir he had seen joy such as he had never known before. He had seen

35

undismayed love wielding a pure and awesome power by the blessing of God. He was leaving it all. The world beyond the Cloth of Joy was a world of love besieged, where there was not enough strength to do what must be done. Men drove themselves to the ragged edge of hope, and died, as Thomas had, for want of loving help that brought new strength.

Yet he was going there. He was leaving the Valley of the Undismayed, and going back into the bitter world. The wind was blasting from the mountains, and the horses were saddled and readied. The commotion of final preparation was all around him, and he alone, who had made the decision, seemed still and bewildered in the midst of it.

Then suddenly he found that the moment had come, and his mother stood beside him to say farewell. She gave her crutches to Imranie, and embraced him. She held him tightly, and in her embrace he could feel her unwavering love: the love of the princess who had walked on shattered feet for days on the bare chance that she might bring her child to safety. "Goodbye, beloved Ilohan," she said. "I love you, and if you die my heart will break again, yet even then I know you will only go to joy. Remember the value of your life. I commit you to God, who alone can keep you, with all my heart. You will always have my love and prayers more deeply than you know. Do not forget that. Farewell."

"Farewell, Mother. I will not forget it. I will be true to you, my father, and my people, by the help of God. I will always love you. I will always be awed by your love and your faithful endurance. I will try to be worthy of such a mother. If I die in this journey, my greatest sorrow will be in leaving you. Knowing how deep would be your grief, and how fervent will be your prayers, I even dare hope that I will live, and reign. God bless you and bring you joy!"

Ilohan saw her crown gleam in the sudden light of a torch as she took her crutches from Imranie. She walked into the lamp-lit house and was gone.

Ilohan suddenly found that he had mounted a horse, and that Brogal was before him in the saddle. Mudien was standing near explaining for a second time how their journey would begin: "In the saddlebags are supplies, rope, and two copies of the Zarnith poem. Because you and Jonathan must arrive well rested at the base of the cliffs, we will bring you a drink that will make you sleep until the dawn, even though you are on horseback. Brogal and Rangol, riding ahead of you in the saddles, will control the horses. Above the cliffs it will be colder than anything you have ever known, but do not fear; we have filled the saddlebags with furs. Now go, and the prayers of all the Cloth of Joy go with you!"

Imranie brought out the warm drinks in steaming cups. They drank quickly, and then started off through the great trees of Ceramir, whose trunks stood black against the windblown stars. They came out beneath the unobstructed dome of the sky, with the winter Ceranim brilliant above them, and the towering blackness of the mountains ahead. Ilohan did not feel sleepy in the least, as they rode swiftly through the fields toward the cliff that ended the valley. He wondered when the drinks would work.

Away across the windblown stubble on their right, Ilohan saw a white figure running. It came toward them, and Brogal stopped the horse to meet it. It was Veril; she jumped up beside them and Ilohan caught her in his arms. "I cannot bear to see you go," she said. "What thoughts of Ilohan would you have me hold within my heart while you are gone?"

"Dear Veril!" he said, "I would give a thousand kingdoms to stay with you here, and be a servant in the Cloth of Joy." His arms trembled as he held her, but not from weakness. He set her down. "Now go," he said, "or I shall not have the strength to leave! Farewell, and God be with you!"

"And with you, Prince Ilohan! Farewell." She ran back across the fields as if winged.

Brogal urged the horse onward, out of the valley and up a winding path that had been hacked out of the cliff side by some ancient, long drawn labor. Ilohan's head soon nodded. He felt Brogal tie a wide, long strip of cloth around him, and then he slept.

*   *   *

Eleanor went to bed as soon as they were gone, but she did not soon fall asleep. The darkness of the room where she was lying was a shelter for her pain, which she wished none to see. It had all happened so fast, and Ilohan was gone. The only word they had from Karolan was a short and desperate message dictated by a dying man.

Now Thomas was gone from the world, and Ilohan was gone on a terrible, mysterious journey to an uncertain end. The dreadful words of the Zarnith guide came back to her: "Stand at the pass beneath the stars, and see terror. Stand at the pass among the stars, and die." Mudien had left them out when he had interpreted the poem, but she did not believe they were meaningless. In the darkness, and her weariness, words of fear passed through her mind again and again. 'Stand at the pass among the stars, and die.' 'The legends of the miners say he reached the peak, and froze there, still holding the great sapphire in his hand.'

She turned her mind to brighter things. The miner in the old story she had told had frozen, but the knight had dug out the sapphire and returned to the woman he loved. Ilohan was a knight. "Father, protect him. When he goes up to the bitter mountains that freeze forever beneath the heartless sky, be with him. Give warmth to him, and life to him, and strength when his footsteps falter. Block the assassin's arrows, and blunt the traitor's sword. Hold back the Norkath armies, and give victory to those who fight in defense of the good lives you have given them. My son... my son is yours. Into your hands I give him." Her thoughts faded into a sleep so deep that she felt she had slipped out of her life and come to a place of more than mortal peace. She awoke refreshed in the bright morning.

To those around her, she was that day the loving servant of Ceramir that she had been for so many years. Yet she was very quiet, and was often seen standing still, gazing at the great mountains. They wondered what to say to her, and in the end were silent, waiting until she turned away of her own accord and went back to her work.

Chapter 3

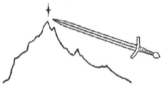

Where Dradrag Failed

JONATHAN WOKE UP AT MIDDAY IN WHAT SEEMED another world. He remembered the soft grass of Ceramir and the cool, sweet air beneath the trees. Now gravel crunched beneath a thick blanket as he moved. The air was dry and bitterly cold. As he breathed it in, it seemed to suck the moisture from his lungs. He opened his eyes to the aching brilliance of the noonday sun, and saw the Cliffs of Doom.

Straight up they rose, like the flight of an arrow gleaming in the sunlight, as high as the eye can follow or the mind conceive. Yet the cliffs were higher than that. No arrow, shot by the strongest bowman ever born, could have done more than ricochet off their lower reaches and fall back uselessly to earth. The tiny cracks in their smooth gray surface looked as though a spider might have clung to them, but nothing more. The deep, deep blue sky did not seem higher than the cliff edge.

Jonathan felt strong and richly alive, as he stood up swiftly and stretched in the brilliant sunlight. His sword was at his side, and he drew it in a single motion. He held it up against the sunlit cliffs, point straight up toward the apex of the sky. The polished blade gleamed flawless in the piercing light.

It was at that moment that Ilohan stretched and opened his eyes. His first sight on that strange waking in a new world was Jonathan's uplifted sword, raised against the staggering cliffs. "So full of life, so eager, and so strong," thought Ilohan. "My courage is a candle to his sunburst. Father, I would gladly die for him – to keep him living in that joy and courage. Yet surely I could never save him, if he had not the strength to save himself."

Jonathan lowered his sword and turned toward Ilohan. "I am glad to see you awake, Prince Ilohan," he said. "We have an impossible adventure before us – and I have dreamed of such things all my life." He ran his blade home into its scabbard with a ringing clang.

"I wonder where our guides have gone," said Ilohan, getting to his feet and looking around. "None of these cracks can be climbed."

To Ilohan's surprise, Jonathan immediately tried to climb one. The blacksmith chose a crack wide enough for his fingers, edged his feet in as well, and began inching his way up the cliff. The muscles stood out on his arms as he used all his strength to cling to the tiny edge. He got about twice his own height, but then let go and dropped heavily to the ground. He stood still for a moment, breathing hard. "No, we could never climb these cracks," he said. "They are too narrow, and the hard rock is so smooth." He threw his head back and stared silently at the soaring heights.

Ilohan heard crunching footsteps on the gravel to his right, and he turned to see Brogal and Rangol returning. They looked very tired, but undaunted. "We have found the crack," said Brogal.

"You have slept long and well," said Rangol. "That is good. You will have need of all the strength your rest has given you. Now eat something and then follow us. Hurry."

After they had eaten quickly of bread and honey from the Cloth of Joy, Rangol and Brogal led them forward with the base of the cliffs on their left. All the ground beneath their feet was covered in strange, light, grayish gravel, which ground and crunched to powder when they stepped on it. Pine trees grew beside their path, gnarled and twisted, but still green and living in the chilly air. Ilohan soon found himself out of breath, even though they were only walking. He felt again that they had traveled to another world.

He quickened his pace to walk beside Brogal. "Do you truly think that we can climb this crack you are leading us to?" he asked. "The cliffs are high beyond my imagining."

"Many deeds have been done that were unimaginable before they were performed," said Brogal. "The crack will not be easy to climb."

"But will it be possible?"

"Whether I said yes, or no, I think my answer would have no meaning," said Brogal. "These lives that God gives us are not bounded by the possible."

"I think you have more faith than I, Brogal."

"That is not yours to judge, or mine to know," said Brogal.

The cliffs had been leading them due north, but now turned at a sudden edge and bore northwest. The turn took them out of sunshine and into the deep shadow of the cliffs, where Ilohan shivered in the sunless cold. He looked up and saw that the angle in the cliff continued to its very top, where the shaded rock was silhouetted sharply against the deep blue sky. He stared for a long moment, but still could not conceive the height of the cliffs – the cliffs he had come to climb.

Not long after this Rangol said, "Here we are: we have reached the crack."

"Where?" asked Ilohan. "The cliff here seems as smooth as ever."

"There," said Brogal, pointing. "Can you not see it?"

"I see a large crack," he said, following Brogal's gaze, "but it does not reach the ground!"

"No," said Brogal, "but the start of it is no higher than a pine tree."

The crack was less than the height of a man in width, with rough sides that promised easy grip to a climber – but brutal injury to one who fell. It ran nearly straight, bending only occasionally with the abrupt, angular edges that were a common feature of the hard rock cliffs. Ilohan followed it up with his eyes until it became a mere rough black line in the far distance of the cliffs' vast height. "The crack will not be easy to climb," he whispered in awe.

"No," said Brogal, "but in the strength of God you may climb it. Do not forget this."

"No," said Ilohan, "I will not."

"Now," said Rangol, "the only thing that seems to me extremely difficult is getting up to the crack. Once you reach it, I think you will find it quite possible to climb, but getting there will be hard. I do not know how you and Jonathan will do it."

Jonathan dropped what he carried and ran to the foot of the cliff. His hard, calloused hands gripped the freezing rock. He climbed with strength and grace, swiftly yet smoothly, his fingers finding purchase even on narrow edges and flakes of stone. He found little to put his feet on, for the thick-soled leather boots that had served him well from Carrah to Ceramir were not made to stand on finger-wide ledges of broken stone.

43

Still, they had good traction, and steadied where they could not lift him.

He was several times a man's height above the ground when a flake broke off in his hand. Thoughts of the rugged rock below flew through his mind in the next instant, but his feet found a strong ledge. He continued on as before, still rejoicing in his strength, yet knowing he must reach the crack soon, lest he tire.

Ilohan, together with Brogal and Rangol, watched him climb with amazement. "He is better than I am," said Brogal, without envy. "I did not think anyone would climb that face without a rope and the loss of much time." Just then Ilohan saw Jonathan reach for a nearly invisible ledge, grip it for an instant, and then lose hold. His feet slipped off the rock below him, and he dangled from one precarious handhold. Ilohan ran forward, hoping to break his fall. Jonathan reached for the same ledge a second time, pulling himself up to it by one arm with great effort. His fingers felt rapidly along the ledge, then settled on a place to grip. He put his feet back on the wall. Ilohan could see that his arms were shaking, but he continued to climb. Soon his right hand came up over the bottom of the crack and he got a firm grip on the rough, hard edge. In an instant he had swung himself up and was sitting safely within the lowest part of the great crack.

Jonathan breathed hard and fast in the dry air, trying to catch his breath. He looked out from the cliffs, gaining from the view a better understanding of where they were. The mountain landscape of twisted pine, hard rock, and light gray gravel stretched out below him, falling rapidly away down toward Ceramir, which would have been invisibly far away in the hazy blue distance, even if it were not obscured completely behind the bulk of the mighty cliff.

He rejoiced once again in the splendor of their impossible quest. It had begun: he was climbing the cliffs where Dradrag had failed, and who could know what lay ahead? When he had regained his breath, he looked down at Ilohan, Brogal, and Rangol. "Throw me a rope!" he cried, and his voice rang and echoed in the crack on the Cliffs of Doom.

A coil spun in the air, expertly thrown by Brogal, unrolling as it came. Jonathan caught it in one sure hand, and tied it firmly to a great boulder that was wedged in the crack. Rangol tied on their bundles of supplies, and Jonathan pulled them up.

All was then ready, and Ilohan, standing at the foot of the rope, realized suddenly that the moment of parting from Rangol and Brogal had come. "I thank you from my heart for all that you have done for us," he said to them. "Bright burns the life of Ceramir – and you are part of it: wise, brave, and noble, like all the children of the Cloth of Joy. You are blessed, you and your people... blessed so much that to share your lot, a prince would gladly trade away his crown, if it were lawful."

"Farewell, Ilohan, Prince of Karolan and son of the Cloth of Joy," said Rangol. "Our prayers and love go with you, and I do not believe you leave Ceramir forever."

"Trueness to God is the only real safety," said Brogal. "In every danger he will guard you, even when all other shields have failed. So I have always found it. Now climb!"

Ilohan took a deep breath, grasped the rope in both hands, and began climbing. He found it easy to grip the rough rope without slipping, and his shoes gave good traction on the stone. The climb exhausted him, however, and he felt dizzy and insecure as he neared the top. At last he dragged himself up to sit beside Jonathan at the base of the great crack. Brogal and Rangol mounted their horses, raised their hands in a last farewell, and rode away. The two adventurers were alone on the Cliffs of Doom.

The crack stretched above them, like half a mineshaft, or a broken well. Although it was scarcely past noon, in the deep shadow of the great cliffs they felt that evening was falling fast. It was cold. By an unspoken consent they began dividing the contents of the bundles Jonathan had pulled up, and stowing them in their backpacks. They were silent as they worked, surrounded by the cold stone. "Are you ready to start?" asked Jonathan at last.

"I am," said Ilohan.

Jonathan began to chimney up the crack, with his hands and his back against one side and his feet against the other. The pack made him slightly more prone to slipping, as he could not feel the contours of the rock behind his back – but it also cushioned him from painful edges and projections. He climbed quickly for a while, then stopped to rest and wait for Ilohan on a projecting rock. Ilohan soon caught up, breathing hard. They rested together on the rock, looking down the crack and seeing what they had just climbed. They had gone no more than the height of a very tall tree, but the perspective was dizzying and the jagged rocks looked merciless. "If our feet slipped only once..." said Ilohan.

"They will not," said Jonathan. "Keep climbing."

The crack was a tiny channel in the face of the awesome cliffs. When they looked outward and down, they saw the mountainside falling away with breathtaking steepness beneath them. Jonathan wondered how Brogal and Rangol had brought the horses up that slope, and how they were taking them down. An eagle screamed above them, and they saw him fly away from the great cliffs, dive through the clear air below them, and then turn to soar out from the mountainside. He soon reached a tremendous height as the ground dropped away beneath him.

They tired quickly, until even Jonathan was panting constantly. Their climbing pace slowed to a pitiful crawl, one breathless move after another. When Ilohan looked down, it was like nothing he had ever imagined: a rough shaft through broken rock, with three sides of stone and one of dizzy air. A strong wind rushed along the cliff, and howled and wailed over the projecting rocks of the crack. A slip now would be certain death.

Despite the bitter cold, they were sweating. Ilohan felt that his lungs were dried and scorched by the harsh air that he had to breathe so fast. His arms, which had to bear the strain of every upward move, were shaking with weariness and effort. He looked up. The turns and angles in the crack kept him from seeing up it more than about the height of a tall tree, but he knew the cliff tops were much farther off than that. He did not feel that he would ever reach them.

Ilohan heard a sudden scraping sound and sharp intake of breath from Jonathan above him. He looked up, wondering if the blacksmith was about to fall, which would most likely kill them both. Instead he saw Jonathan recover himself, and shift into a secure position – where he stayed, rather than continuing to climb as Ilohan expected. "I almost fell just now," Jonathan called down. "This chimneying is safe enough for a short climb, but sooner or later one makes a mistake. We must think of a better way to climb, or at least one of us will never reach the top alive."

Ilohan felt intense relief at the mere fact that the climb must cease for a moment while they talked. He found a moderately secure resting place and stopped there, breathing hard and trying to shake life and strength back into his exhausted arms. "What else can we do?" he asked.

"We need to use the ropes to protect us," said Jonathan. "I could keep myself from harm if I fell thrice the height of a man, as long as there was a rope to catch me at the end of it. We must make sure there is."

Ilohan thought hard. He had been wet with sweat, and soon was shivering in the dry, icy air. "You should tie a length of rope around your waist, Jonathan," he said at last. "I will tie it to this boulder, and then you can climb up until you find another resting place. If you lose hold, you may fall some distance, but the rope will catch you at last. When you find another place to tie the rope, unknot it from your waist and tie it off. Then I will tie it to myself and climb past you to the next good stopping point."

"It is a good plan," said Jonathan, "but the places to rest are too far apart. I have no wish to fall the height of a tree of Ceramir before being caught by the rope."

"Can you suggest another thing?" asked Ilohan through chattering teeth.

"No," said Jonathan. "I see it must be this or nothing, and it will at least offer some protection." Ilohan tied the rope and handed it off to him, then watched as he carefully tied it around himself and began climbing. Ilohan paid out the rope to keep it from tangling, until the coil diminished and the rope at last went taut. Jonathan's voice came echoing down to him, demanding more rope. Ilohan was shivering intensely, and his hands were clumsy with cold, but somehow he managed to tie on an extension to the rope. It was now so long that he knew it would do Jonathan little good if he fell. At last the rope stopped rising, and Jonathan called down that he had found a resting place. Ilohan untied the rope from the rock and began climbing, slowly at first but then faster as his stiff muscles warmed. He was sweating, panting, and exhausted when at last he came up to where Jonathan sat resting on a boulder.

"You must not climb past me," said Jonathan. "You are too tired, and you have but recently recovered from the plague. You must let me climb first up the crack, and you yourself must follow using the rope."

"I cannot let you do that, Jonathan. We must bear equally the load of this journey."

"Do we have equal strength?" asked Jonathan. "I want neither a dead prince nor a dead friend. Let me climb."

"I am not close to death," argued Ilohan. "I must push myself further. It is what a knight should do. When I am truly weary, then, if you are not, you may always be the first to climb."

"You are truly weary, Ilohan, Prince and hope of Karolan," said Jonathan. "If you would serve as duty calls you, save your strength and live. This journey is only just begun. A time may come to push on to the edge of strength – to the death – but that time is not yet."

"You will not be persuaded you are wrong?" Ilohan had meant to speak the words cheerfully and loudly, but they came out breathless and weak. Jonathan had seen truly: he was exhausted.

"I will not be persuaded that I am wrong, because I am right," said Jonathan.

"So be it, then," said Ilohan. "I thank you, friend."

They carried on through the failing of the autumn afternoon. Ilohan lost count of how many times they repeated the cycle: Jonathan vanishing into the crack above with the rope trailing behind him; Jonathan calling back down that he had found a resting place and tied off the rope; and then Ilohan himself following, using the rope both as protection and as aid.

It was brutally hard. Ilohan's lungs were scorched and aching with the dry air, but there was no relief for them: he had to breathe hard or he could not climb. He saw that even Jonathan was tiring: he was beginning the climbs more slowly, and his strong runner's legs were trembling with the relentless effort.

Neither Ilohan nor Jonathan could avoid catching occasional dizzying glimpses of the awful expanse of air beneath them and beside them, as they scanned the rock for footholds or handholds. Sometimes Jonathan looked down on purpose, awed at the stupendous height they had climbed above the pine-studded mountainside at the cliffs' feet. The desert was lost in haze from the sheer volume of air through which he viewed it. On the mountains spread out below he could see forests, small cliffs, lakes, waterfalls, and beds of snow, all perfectly clear but staggeringly far down.

As the afternoon wore on, the deep blue of the high mountain sky grew deeper still – ominously, it seemed to Ilohan. He wondered what they would do if night found them still in the crack. Even the best resting places were uncomfortable – and so insecure that sleep, if it came, would mean falling.

They reached a place where the log of some ancient, gnarled pine had somehow become wedged in the crack. It made a good seat, and by an unspoken consent both rested there far longer than usual. At last, when even he was shivering, Jonathan tied the rope around himself and began climbing without a word.

Jonathan felt somewhat refreshed after the long rest. He climbed slowly but smoothly, and felt he could carry on through his weariness for a long time. He had climbed a good way above the log when a flake of rock that he was using to push himself upward suddenly broke under the heel of his hand. His back slipped violently down but then stopped, with his spine curved uncomfortably and his knees above the level of his head. He realized that he was very close to falling, and that it would be a bad fall: the rope was long and the wedged log it was tied to was far below. In his awkward position his feet could slip at any moment, and he could not force them back against the rock to gain better traction. He was in great danger, but he felt little fear. He would work carefully to escape, and he would succeed as always. He put a hand behind him on the rock, and tried again to lift his back. It slipped.

His feet went up above his head, and he was falling, diving head downward through the rugged crack. In an instantaneous reaction he pushed himself out of the crack and away from the cliff, to escape dreadful injury on the jagged projections of stone. Then he looked down, and it seemed to him that no eagle could ever have flown so high. He longed even for the dangerous boulders of the crack, rather than this gulf of unresisting air. Tumbling as he fell, he caught an upside-down view of the violet twilight that was already rising in the east.

Thoughts flew through his mind at lightning speed. Even while he saw crazy views and felt their terror, he worked furiously to save himself, and never stopped believing that somehow he would survive. He pulled the slack rope through his hands as fast as he could, seeking to make it come tight more quickly. If Ilohan were doing the same thing it would be better still. When the rope did come tight, he planned to let it slide with some resistance through his hands to break his fall.

The moment came sooner than he expected. The rope yanked him upright and slipped scorchingly through his calloused hands, while at the same time he began to swing in toward the cliff face. Then the slack he had gathered was all gone. The rope came tight around his waist with a terrible jolt, flinging him into the crack. He crashed painfully into an angular boulder with his hands still desperately locked around the rope. He released the rope and clawed his way onto the boulder, where he lay gasping and listening to the tremendous pounding of his heart. Presently it occurred to him that, remarkably, he was alive. He reached hesitant fingers down to feel his thigh where he had struck the boulder. It was badly bruised, but not broken or bleeding. He looked at his hands, and they were blistered, but not raw.

He got to his feet, and slowly climbed the rope back to the wedged trunk where Ilohan was waiting. The rope hurt his hands, and every step hurt his thigh, but the injuries were slight. He was alive and would heal soon. The great adventure was still his.

"Thank God! Thank God you are alive!" said Ilohan when he reached him. "I thought there was no hope. How badly are you hurt?"

"Barely at all," said Jonathan. "I can still climb, and soon will heal. But you pulled in much rope to break my fall, did you not? Otherwise I would have fallen farther and perhaps taken great harm. What has the sliding rope done to your hands?"

"I think I can still climb," said Ilohan. "I rejoice that I could thus help break your fall." He held his hands against his legs, so Jonathan could not see them.

"Let me look," said Jonathan. He turned the prince's hands over in his own. The flying rope had worn them raw, and Ilohan's clothes were bloody where he had touched them. "I am sorry," said Jonathan. "Though my slip did not kill me, this cost is high. It must burn like fire."

The injury did indeed burn like fire, but Ilohan thought it a small price to pay for his companion's life. Ilohan watched as Jonathan rummaged through their packs and found a thin, woven garment. The blacksmith cut it into strips using his sword, and soaked them in cold water. Ilohan allowed Jonathan to bind up his hands using these strips. They relieved the pain a little, but Ilohan wondered how the binding would affect his grip. The cold was intense and worsening.

"This must never happen again," said Jonathan. "I think I know how to make sure it never does."

"What do you mean?" asked Ilohan.

"I mean to wrench loose this log, and make use of it," said Jonathan.

Ilohan was still not sure what Jonathan intended to do, but he saw the blacksmith climb down a little, plant his feet firmly on projections in the rock, and grasp the log firmly in his arms. Ilohan squeezed himself against the back of the crack to give Jonathan more space. He watched Jonathan work for a few moments, positioning his hands to get the best possible grip on the log. At last a sudden heave went through the blacksmith's whole frame, and to Ilohan's astonishment the log came loose from the stone. It made a loud, groaning scrape, like the reluctant opening of some ancient door. Jonathan lowered the log down upon a wedged boulder below him. He rested a moment, panting hard.

The log had a large crack that came near to splitting it straight down the middle. Jonathan put both hands in the crack and pulled, straining with all his might, eyes closed and face uplifted with the effort. Nothing happened. "Alas!" he said. "If only I were not so tired!"

He breathed hard and tried again, this time with a violent jerk rather than steady pressure. The log gave a loud creak, and the split widened. With another intense effort, Jonathan succeeded in ripping it in two. Both pieces were sound and sturdy. The blacksmith leaned on them a moment, catching his breath, while the sweet smell of new-cut pine wafted through the crack. "Now," said Jonathan, "we will wedge these logs in notches in the rock whenever we need a resting place or a place to tie the rope. There are plenty of good places to wedge them. We will not need to use the full length of our rope any more. I will not be in danger of falling so far again, and you will have no more need to scorch your hands."

Ilohan thought Jonathan's plan was ingenious, and might save both their lives, but in his exhaustion he only nodded his assent.

Jonathan retied the knot around his waist so that two separate lengths of rope came from it. To each of these he tied one half of the split log. He left a long tail of rope hanging down below each of these half-logs, and made the length of rope between himself and each log short – no more than thrice his own height. He wedged one of the logs where it had been before, and started climbing without a word. When the rope from his waist to the wedged log below had nearly drawn tight, he sought for a good place, pulled up the free log using the other rope, and wedged it firmly in the crack.

Ilohan saw that the plan had worked well thus far, and that it was his turn to climb. He tied himself into the rope that came down from Jonathan's jammed log, and wrenched the lower log free to be pulled up later. Then he looked up along the crack, took a deep breath, and tried to begin climbing.

He could not do it. His scorched and bandaged hands could not grip the rope. Clenching his teeth against the pain, he tried again, this time chimneying up the crack itself without using the rope. This was better, but even on the rock his hands hurt intensely and he could not grip well. "I see that the price you paid to save me was indeed high," came Jonathan's voice from above him. "Now do what you can, and I will do the rest." Immediately Ilohan felt Jonathan pulling on the rope around his waist. The blacksmith did not absolutely lift him, but he took much of the weight off Ilohan's hands. Thus Ilohan easily reached the wedged log. Though he was ashamed to need such extensive aid, he knew he did need it, and spoke to Jonathan only to thank him. They sat together for a moment, resting, and then Jonathan pulled up Ilohan's log and climbed again.

The plan continued to work well, if slowly and wearily. There was no hope of reaching the top before night, but as violet twilight took the sky and then dimmed into a darkness filled with uncounted thousands of stars, Jonathan found he could still climb: by feel, and by half-seen, silhouetted glimpses. Each time he had to pull Ilohan up he wondered if he still had the strength. Finally a time came when he did not. Ilohan took off his bandages, gritted his teeth, and again climbed without aid.

Jonathan fell several times, as his weariness increased. Each time, the rope to the wedged log caught him, but he took hard knocks from projecting boulders and sometimes narrowly missed injuring Ilohan as he hurtled past him. He was bruised and aching, and desperately weary. It seemed the end of the crack would never come.

For Ilohan, the climb was torture – especially when at hard places he had to put his raw hands on the rope. He would take it then in an iron grip, despite the pain: if he did not hold on as tightly as he could, his hands might slip and scorch again. The wide notch of sky that he could see through the open crack blazed with stars and seemed like a doorway flung open to heaven. He wished sometimes that he would fall through it; that the rope would somehow fail to catch him; that this relentless pain and weariness would end. Then he remembered Eleanor, and Karolan, and Veril, and wished that no longer.

Whenever Ilohan or Jonathan looked up, hoping to see the end of the crack like a little window full of stars, they saw only the blackness of the winding rock. Finally they gave up looking. Every time Jonathan climbed he took longer to use up the short length of rope and seat the log firmly in the crack. Ilohan began to wonder each time whether his friend would make it, or if his great strength had been exhausted at last.

"God," prayed Ilohan, "it hurts so much, and we are so tired. Be with us, please, and help us. Give us the strength to carry on, and let the crack end soon."

He was climbing the rope again, and began to whisper out loud to focus his mind through the bitter weariness. "One hand. Now the other. Now the first again. Right... Left... Carry on... Never surrender... Do not slip. Do not slip... Do not slip! Another hand. Keep climbing..." Each time Ilohan put one hand over the other it seemed to him a miracle, and when he reached the log it seemed paradise had been found. Then Jonathan wearily pulled up the hanging log, tied himself to the rope, and climbed, and it was all to be done over again. It would never end, Ilohan felt. They would never get the rewards of their desperate labor. They would only move the logs a few more times, and then give up and die.

Jonathan, too, wondered if his strength would be enough. There came a moment when he stopped climbing. It seemed all he could do just to hold himself where he was. He could do that for about four heartbeats more, and then he would fall and never climb again. "No... No!" he told himself ruthlessly.

"Climb!" He would not give up. The feeling of impossibility was a lie. His strength would still be enough. He began again to chimney up the crack, and found that indeed it was possible. After a few moments he felt a hard edge at his back. He leaned his head backward, and found no rock. Puzzled, he raised himself a little higher. The rock edge pressed painfully against his spine. He leaned his head back again, and as his eyes turned upward, he caught his breath. Full half the sky was clear of rock, and filled with a splendid concourse of brilliant stars. The soft light of the winter Ceranim, the cloth of the stars, arched up in the southeast. It was brighter than he ever remembered seeing it before, and as he looked at its wondrous glow, he suddenly understood that it was indeed a great sheet of individual stars, so many and so closely packed that the wildest dreamer could not conceive the vastness of their number.

For a moment the stars had touched his heart with wonder and hope, but he had to turn from them to understand the reality of his and Ilohan's position. They had reached the top of the crack, and come to a starlit ledge. But they were not at the top of the cliff, for it towered above them still. He called down the news to Ilohan.

Back down in the crack, Ilohan heard Jonathan's words but comprehended only that at last they had come to a place where they could sleep. He climbed up the rope one last agonizing time, and crawled out on the ledge with relief too deep for words. They pulled the furs out of their packs, wrapped themselves with all that they had, and slept. No bruise or hurt made any intrusion into that sleep. It was nearly the deepest and the sweetest that either had ever known.

*   *   *

The sun rose, brilliant, piercing, and glorious. Jonathan awoke first, and his heart leaped in awe as he looked around. Snowy peaks he had never seen before stretched out below him, and the sun on their snow was like blinding white fire. The colors of the mountain dawn were rich and pure, and though his muscles cried out in pain when he moved, his heart was singing.

Ilohan awoke, and they ate a good breakfast with their faces to the brilliant sun and their feet hanging over a measureless drop. The aspect of the cliffs had changed greatly from the afternoon before. Then they had been in shadow, but now they were brightly sunlit, and the stone that had been cold and gray seemed almost white. Beautiful, pastel lichens clung to the rock. The ledge on which they sat was rough, but wide enough for easy walking. To their right it continued around the bend of the cliffs and went out of sight, but on their left it sloped up strongly, narrowed against the cliff, and disappeared.

"Brogal thought the crack went all the way up, as it appeared to do when seen from the foot of the cliffs," said Ilohan when they had finished eating. "Since it does not, it seems our hope is gone, but on this bright morning my heart will not believe it."

"Nor will mine," said Jonathan. "Shall we follow the ledge south, even though it slopes down that way, and seek for another crack?"

"Yes, let us do that," said Ilohan, "if we can walk."

They found they could, and though at first Jonathan clenched his teeth at every step, his aches soon subsided. The ledge proved easy to walk on, though always there was a tremendous drop through bright clear air one step away upon their left.

They went a long way, but the cliff face above only grew more sheer and impossible. A cold wind picked up, blowing their clothes and hair about, and buffeting them to and fro as they walked. Occasionally there were tiny patches of snow or ice frozen upon the ledge, and twice clods of snow blew off the cliff tops far above them and splintered to gleaming white fragments as they sailed outward and fell to pelt the distant ground.

The ledge grew narrower. Soon they were edging their way along, leaning in toward the rock. Looking ahead, Jonathan saw a place where the ledge seemed to vanish. He slowed and stopped as he neared the brink.

"Does the ledge end?" asked Ilohan from behind him.

Jonathan did not reply: he was too busy looking. One step ahead of him, the ledge ended in empty air. The whole cliff was offset, as sharply as if it had been cut by a knife and pushed back. Beyond the offset, the cliff continued more or less as before, but curved slowly leftward so that a huge expanse of the cliff face was in view. The ledge also continued, but the gap at the offset was too large to jump, and even a squirrel could not have crossed the smooth face.

But it was not any of this that had rendered Jonathan speechless. "There is writing," he gasped, "writing on the cliff."

"Writing on the cliff?" asked Ilohan. "What kind of writing?"

"The script is huge. Each letter is as tall as a tall man, and the whole inscription is scores of paces long. The characters are like wind twisted trees in the desert – weird, wild, and free. I cannot read, but maybe you can make something of it."

Holding himself carefully against the cliff, Jonathan crouched to let Ilohan see over him. He heard Ilohan catch his breath. *"Shronbad foovronkar thrond vronkor, staldashronbad kiergondak sradthrond vronkor,*" said Ilohan. "I have not read it, I have only remembered what I was taught. I do not know the letters of the Zarnith tongue, yet I can guess, as can you, the meaning of that great inscription: 'Man can conquer man, but no man can conquer stone.' It is no legend. It is real. He carved it at the highest point his troops could reach. They must have come up the cliff just south of here, and met the other section of the ledge."

"Yes," said Jonathan. "That section of the cliffs reminds me of the desert, somehow: its color, perhaps, or the broad curve of it. Perhaps it was that feeling that made the Zarnith choose this place. Yet I always thought the inscription was at the base of the cliff. I am surprised they got so high, even at the cost of twenty thousand lives. Dradrag had the loyalty of his host."

"What is strange is that they stopped here, having got so near," said Ilohan.

"Look up," said Jonathan. "The face is as smooth as a polished sword, without enough foothold for a mouse. It is no wonder Dradrag failed. But we shall not."

"What do you suggest we do?" asked Ilohan.

"Turn around and go the other way," said Jonathan. "What else?"

The gusting wind seemed to want to suck them out into the gulf, or buffet them off the cliff face. The sun's light was merciless, but its heat did little to alleviate the piercing cold. The sky above was blue as only a mountain sky can be, so clear and dark that Jonathan could see the Morning Star far above the sun. The cliffs were harsh, wild, and perilous, but Jonathan wished it no other way. He took one last awed look at the ancient Zarnith inscription, before he turned to follow Ilohan back along the ledge. He remembered telling Naomi, long ago, that he wanted to see where Dradrag had turned back. Now he had. He had found his adventure, and would die rather than relinquish it.

The precarious walk back to the crack seemed to take a long time, but they reached it well before midday. They went on past it, up the steep slope of the ledge, and stopped where it grew too narrow. "We cannot go far in this direction," said Jonathan. "Shall we send for Skykag and have him carry us up?"

Ilohan laughed, but not for long. He scanned the sunlit cliff face. "The top cannot be far away," he said. "Jonathan, do you see that tree, growing out of the cliff?"

"Do you mean that thing?" asked Jonathan, pointing. "It hardly looks large enough to call a tree."

"Yes, I do mean that tiny thing," said Ilohan. "But whatever you call it, it is growing out of solid rock. Do you think you could throw a rope to it?"

"I do not think so," said Jonathan, "but if even if I could, would it not break at the first tug?"

"Perhaps," said Ilohan, "but it is something we can try. If it does break, we will be no worse off than now."

Jonathan picked up a small rock and threw it as high as he could. It bounced off the cliff wall and careened out into space. They could not tell how near it came.

They tried so many things that neither Ilohan nor Jonathan kept count. They tied rocks to a rope and threw them up. They all fell short. They slung them around and threw them higher, but still the weight of the rope held them back and they did not reach the tree. Finally they unraveled one of their ropes, and made a long, thin cord from the pieces. Still the rocks fell short, or bounced away from the cliff face, or came loose from the cord and went whizzing off alarmingly in wild directions. Midday came and went, and the sun disappeared behind the cliff, leaving them in icy shadow. They put on extra furs to keep warm.

Late in the afternoon, Jonathan stood beneath the tree whirling a fist-sized rock around at the end of their cord for what seemed the thousandth time. "I am sure these are going high enough," he said. "It is only that they are bouncing off the rock. I cannot seem to throw them straight enough."

"And I cannot throw them hard enough," said Ilohan. "But soon or late, surely you will throw one perfectly straight. I will pray it happens soon."

"And I," said Jonathan, "will try as hard as I can to make the rocks fly true."

His stone was off, soaring at great speed, flying in a beautiful arc beside the cliff. "Father, let it catch the tree..." whispered Ilohan.

It was coming near. Jonathan held his breath. It went above the tree. It glanced against the cliff, but did not bounce far out. It fell, he could not tell on which side. The cord came tight with a swinging jerk. "We have it!" cried Jonathan. "It had begun to feel impossible!"

They let the rock down and used the cord to pull up a rope. The tree was so high up that they had to use every piece of rope they had, and even then, when they had a noose securely tightened around the tree, the rope did not hang all the way down to the ledge, but stopped just out of Jonathan's reach. Ilohan helped him up, and he caught it. He hung there for a moment. The tiny, rock-grown tree did not break. Jonathan bounced on the rope, tightening the noose and bringing it a little lower. Still the tree held.

"It must take us both, if we are to make it up," said Jonathan. "Climb on too."

They held onto the rope together, and jolted it as hard as they could. Still the small, valiant tree did not break off. They let go and dropped onto the ledge. "I suppose there is but one course now," said Jonathan. He shouldered his pack, took a deep breath, and started to climb.

He had always considered rope climbing easy, but he had never attempted a climb of this length. His breathing was ragged and his arms were shaking terribly when he reached the tree. With a last effort, he pulled himself up and got astride it. He breathed hard in the thin air, and shook out his weary arms.

"Look up!" came Ilohan's shout from below. "What can you see?"

Jonathan leaned his head back and looked. The edge of the cliff was only half their rope's length above, and there was a large, projecting boulder there around which he knew he could throw the rope. Even better, the cliffs above him were no longer quite vertical: they had a blessed inward slant that would enable him to walk up with the aid of the rope. The impossible climb was nearly over.

Yet above the rim of the Cliffs of Doom there loomed something that struck awed terror into his heart, and left no room for exultation. Peaks of ice, with black rock showing through only rarely, reared their unmeasured heights into an eerily dark blue sky. Their very shape seemed to spell fear, fear of a place at the bitter edge of earth, at its juncture with a frozen sky where no man could ever live. This was not even part of the world Jonathan knew. It was utterly strange, beautiful, and terrible. He asked himself what frightened him, and why. He could not answer, but neither could he quell the fear in his heart.

"What do you see?" called Ilohan again.

"If you can get here, we have made it," said Jonathan.

"Thank God!" said Ilohan. "But is anything wrong? You say we have made it up the Cliffs of Doom?"

"Yes," said Jonathan. "But whether anything is wrong I will let you judge for yourself."

Down on the ledge, Ilohan prepared to attempt the final climb. The rope hung down farther than it had for Jonathan, because the blacksmith had retied it at the tree to yield more slack – however, its end was flying in the wind, so that Ilohan had to use the cord to pull it down within his reach. He tied a loop at the end of the rope. He knew this could not really help him climb, of course, but it was a comfort to know that if he slipped, he would not be slipping toward a bare rope's end. The shadows of the Cliffs of Doom were deep and long on the sunlit mountainside far below: evening would soon come and there was no time to waste. He flexed his raw hands – and grimaced as the scabs buckled and oozed blood. But there was only one thing to do. He jumped up to grip the rope.

Then he was climbing, hand over agonized hand, sometimes making barely a handbreadth at a time, his feet finding but little purchase on the smooth cliff wall. He took his feet off the wall and hung breathlessly from his hands, hoping he was high enough to use the loop. He felt it knock against his feet. Looking down and working with focused intensity, he managed to slip one of his feet into it. He relaxed his hands, and the rope tightened around his foot and held him. Good. He had climbed his own height. He had only to do that two score and ten more times, and he would be at the tree. There was nothing more impossible. He had no splintered fragment of a chance. His hands would never make it, and already his lungs were burning again in the cold, dry air.

Suddenly he noticed that he was rising. The rock wall was slipping past him, and the ledge was already more than twice as far below as when he had stopped climbing. He knew what was happening, and also that it was the only way.

As Ilohan had understood, Jonathan was pulling the rope in hand over hand. The blacksmith was astonished at how hard he found it; astonished at his own weakness. Back in Ceramir, he was sure, he would not have had such difficulty lifting a man on a rope. Now he was panting and exhausted, with Ilohan barely a tenth of the way up the cliff. He wrapped the rope once about the tree, and held it there, resting. Then he pulled again. After pulling hand over hand a score or so of times, he stopped and rested again. The next time it was fifteen. Then ten. Then eight. Then six. Then five.

"How can I be so weak?" he wondered. "He is not one-third the way up yet. And I pant and weary so quickly." He struggled on, but before Ilohan was half way up to the tree he was resting after every pull. He could almost have laughed at himself had he not felt such anger and frustration. This was the last part of their climb – was it going to take until dark?

Hanging on the rope below, Ilohan pitied Jonathan and was ashamed, wishing he could help with the grueling labor that was lifting him. When he was two thirds of the way up, and Jonathan was working so slowly that it seemed he would never reach the tree, Ilohan suddenly had an idea. He called to Jonathan to lower the slack rope. As Ilohan had guessed, there was just enough slack to hang down in a long loop that came within his own hands' reach. Leaving alone the side of the loop that went up to Jonathan's already overtaxed hands, Ilohan grasped the side that went straight to the secure knot around the tree. Without taking his foot out of the security of its own loop, he began to pull himself up using this rope. It hurt terribly. He felt very unsafe because his hands were off the rope that held his foot, and he was now only loosely constraining it in the circle of his arms. But what mattered was that now he could help Jonathan by lifting some of his own weight. They worked together, each pushing himself to the limit of his strength, and at last they made it. Ilohan hung over the small trunk of the tree and gasped for breath, while Jonathan dangled below him on the rope and did the same.

When they had partially recovered, Jonathan pulled up the rope. The long cord, and the rock he had thrown around the tree, were still tied to it. In one easy motion he threw the rock up and over the projecting boulder at the edge of the precipice. He tightened a noose around the boulder, took the rope in his hands, and began climbing.

It should have been easy, for the cliff was no longer vertical, but his weariness made it hard. Once his feet even slipped, and he lay against the cliff clinging to the rope until he felt strong enough to stand and climb again. He kept his eyes on the rock, avoiding the sight of the terrible ice mountains.

At last, with wondering relief, he pulled himself over the lip of the Cliffs of Doom. He stood on the solid, horizontal rock, closed his eyes and drank in the marvel. He had climbed them. He had conquered stone. Then he shook himself. This was one step, and that not even finished. He turned his weary eyes back to Ilohan, who was still clinging to the tree. He felt he had no strength left to love Ilohan or aid him. Yet, though all else fail, to love at least he must cling.

He gazed into the sky, hoping to find new peace and strength. Its blue was so dark that all he felt was terror: he was reminded again that this was a place above the world, a place lost in the frozen sky. He breathed deeply, and looked down.

"Tie the rope around yourself, Ilohan," he said, "and you can simply walk up the cliff."

Jonathan's words seemed like nonsense to Ilohan, but he was too tired to argue, and he felt he must simply obey. Somehow he tied the rope, with bleeding hands clumsy from the cold. He placed his feet on the stone, leaned back on the rope, and reluctantly let go of the tree. He felt an upward tug and then at last he understood. He could walk, hands free, up the cliff face, while Jonathan pulled him in on the rope. Again he was ashamed of all that Jonathan had to do for him – but he knew it was the only way.

When at last Ilohan reached the top, the prince and the blacksmith together collapsed on the gray cliff edge. They had conquered the Cliffs of Doom, but they were too exhausted to exult.

They could not rest long in the bitter cold. Ilohan stirred first. "We must go on," he said, through chattering teeth. "The cliffs were only to take one day, and we have spent the better part of two. We must go to the pass." He raised his eyes to search for it – and was struck as Jonathan had been. The peaks stood out in savage beauty against the unearthly twilight in the sky. Ilohan found that he had unconsciously pulled himself back from them, toward the cliff edge. "Help us, God," he whispered. "We have passed out of our world, into a land of terror."

"Now," said Jonathan in a hushed voice, "is anything wrong?"

"I did not know such places could exist," said Ilohan, "yet we must carry on." He struggled to his feet.

Jonathan coiled their rope and stowed it in his pack. They set off toward the peaks of icy fear. There was nothing else to do.

Chapter 4

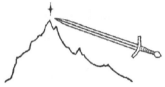

The Call to Arms

THE CALL TO ARMS SOUNDED: CLEAR, VALIANT, AND terrible. That trumpet blast had not been blown in Glen Carrah for twenty years; not since Thomas had invaded Norkath to demand of Fingar an accounting for Kindrach's death. Hannah and Barnabas rose from their work, and met each other at the cottage door. They had not guessed that it would come so soon, but it was almost a relief to have the stroke finally fall. There was no more guessing, only preparation, and their love was stronger than the storm.

Joseph and Naomi were eating supper together, huddled near the hearth because of a chill wind that seeped around the doors and windows of the cottage. The trumpet in Carrah sounded faint, carried on the wind, and they were not sure what they had heard. They raised their heads and sat still as carven statues, listening for the sound to come again. It came, unmistakable, and they jumped up from their meal. The terrible day was upon them. Joseph hugged his daughter as if he would never let her go.

"I will fight for you," he said. "I will fight for you, and they will not come and take you. Yet can I be sure? Naomi, beloved child of my heart, can I be sure..." His arms tightened around her.

"Only of my soul, Father, for that is safe forever," she said, her voice muffled against his shoulder. "God loves us, and we will meet again in brighter days. You are a hero, Father. You have been one all my life, and God now proves that you are as surely as the mountains stand. Forever I will love you, and all Hell cannot destroy our love. The storm comes, Father, but God loves us and upholds our love, and he is stronger than the storm."

"You will be safe, beloved daughter, for God himself will guard you."

"He will, and he will go with you to battle. He will stand by you and give you his strength. Remember my prayers for you every day. They will burn with all the fervor of my soul."

He released her, and they stood a little apart, too much in shock to know what they should do. The gray clouds scudded low outside the window. The cold wind buffeted and whistled round the house, and sighed in the dead grass of Glen Carrah. The fire, so small, so red and warm, seemed a symbol of all that was safe lost in a world of rising storm. Naomi knew she must help her father leave, must help him do this deed that seemed impossible to them both. She knew she must stir and act, and at last she did.

"We must pack, Father. I will gather all that you will need, and you must go borrow a pony and come back."

"Yes," he said. He had cut the word off short, as though he had intended to say more but had found he could not. He went quickly out the door, leaving Naomi alone in the darkening room. She closed the window tight against the gray, cold evening. Forcing herself to act, she lit candles all around the room. She kneaded bread, with a little salt and no yeast, to last a long time without spoiling. She put the loaves up in the chimney to bake. She gathered cheese and honey, and smoked goat's meat given them by Hannah. She set her father's shepherd's crook beside the pile, then took it away: it was no kind of thing to take to war.

She folded his leather coat, and also two wool ones for the coldest weather. She added leather boots, and more woolen garments, and then at last she wrapped it all into a bundle using the blanket from Joseph's bed. She filled all the water skins they had, and brought a generous handful of gold out of their savings to buy more. She sat and thought, then finding that too still, she got up and paced and thought. She gathered more things that he might need. She brought the fast-baking bread out of the oven just before it burnt. She went to the window and threw it open, letting the cold, fresh air strike her face.

None of it helped. She still felt sick as no illness could ever make her. There was no comfort in the world, for all her world was breaking. He could not be going. He simply could not. It violated what her heart had always known to be inviolate. Her stomach felt like it was being twisted, over and over again, tighter each time. She had known this day would come, had known it must, but the knowledge had never reached her heart nor had her soul's approval. She had not guessed that it would be this bad.

Her father, who had been father and mother to her as long as she could remember, who had loved her better and more deeply than she had seen any other father love his child, was leaving her. He must, and it hurt him more than it did her, but it broke her world in splintered pieces. He belonged to God, as she did, and in God they were safe, yet God had called him to this, to this thing that broke her heart. Or was it Fingar and his grasping evil that made this necessary? Was God merely responding to evil, or had God let the evil grow to prove and temper what was good? Evil was forever wrong, and God forever right. Yet he delayed his final victory so long! "Why, Father?" she cried, "Why, if you love us, do you let the darkness wield such power? Why, if you love us, do you call us to the things that break our hearts?"

She sank down on the floor, and looked up through the window at the scudding gray clouds. She wondered if her faith was leaving her too, now when she needed above all to cling to God. "Father, I follow, though I do not understand," she said. "My Lord, you bore the deepest of the pain that evil brings, and I will follow you forever and never hold the cost too high. You made the world, yet also suffered in it, bearing all its darkness. You know to what you call us. You know what we can and cannot bear. Be with us, Christ, and hold us close to you."

Footsteps approached the door, and she stood swiftly lest her father see her despondent. He entered quickly, took a chair and stared intently at the floor. "The king is dead," he said. Then he looked up and met her eyes. She saw his pain, and knew that her own was not hidden. He continued, speaking quickly and without emotion. "Fingar will attack in five days. The steward bids us muster at Aaronkal with all speed, taking no time to gather weapons, and riding hard. A young man named Ilohan, who was thought by all to be only a knight, is the true Prince of Karolan. Before his death, the king had word that this Prince Ilohan was safe and was returning to Aaronkal – which argues, I think, that Jonathan has been on an errand of great significance, and will also return safely – but the prince comes too late, so we must win his kingdom for him. But now, beloved daughter, please help me load the saddlebags. This agony must not continue."

"Yet it cannot stop," she thought, as she stuffed the food and clothing into the saddlebags. Soon, whether too soon or too late neither could say, the packing was over. "Buy more water skins when you can," said Naomi. "We did not have enough. Father, I loved you first, I love you now, and I will love you forever. I commit you to the care of God, and every day you are gone I will pray for you with all my heart. Nothing can separate us from his love, and there we will meet again though all the worst befall." She was crying, but she spoke on through her tears. "Oh, Father, I cannot bear to see you go, yet go you must. Farewell, and God be with you!"

"And with you, beloved child, forever! You are more to me than all, save God alone from whom our love was born. Remember how I love you. The darkest future cannot break the goodness of the past, for it lives on in Paradise. Farewell, if indeed I have the strength to go at last. Farewell! God be with you forever!"

He rode away, his hood pulled low to hide his tears, and did not turn around.

*   *   *

The falling dusk found Ilohan and Jonathan cold and weary wanderers in a world of majestic terror. They panted as if they were running, but they were only trudging along, sore and exhausted, bent beneath their packs. The rock-ice peaks around them towered into the eerie violet of the sky. Stars cut through the darkness like the diamond points of angels' spears, measurelessly high, bright without a hint of twinkling.

The great peak to the north of them had a strange shape. On its west side, the left from their perspective, it was so steep as to be almost a cliff – and it was on this side that they hoped to find the pass the Zarnith had used. On the east side the mountain rose less steeply, wholly covered in white ice. Altogether it looked asymmetrical as the broken fang of some savage beast, or as a single-edged sword stabbing up at the unearthly sky.

Jonathan was so tired that each step seemed to cost a separate effort. "Ilohan," he said, after a long time, "do you remember, long ago in Glen Carrah, what we said of these mountains?"

"I said no man would ever cross them," replied Ilohan, panting. "I said they were meant for angels alone. I think the Zarnith lied, and I spoke truth."

Jonathan looked up defiantly. "We will cross them," he said. "Do not lose hope."

"I fear," said Ilohan, "that I lost it long ago."

"No, Ilohan, that must not be," said Jonathan. "Hope must never be lost. I know we will cross these mountains, and I cling to my hope and confidence with all the strength of my mind. You must work to regain your hope, Ilohan – you must not give it up."

Ilohan's lungs felt scorched, and he tasted blood at the back of his mouth. "I will cling to faith," he said, "to God, and to a hope of deeper things than seeing Karolan again. These I will hold to; the other hope it is beyond my force of will to summon back. Still, I thank God you yet keep it."

They turned back to the mountain and trudged forward yet again. At last the ice on which they walked began to slope steeply up: The climb toward the pass had begun in earnest, and they felt their legs could no longer obey their wills' command. Ilohan fell, and did not rise. Jonathan sank down near him, and both felt they would be happy never to get up again.

"Duty... Eleanor..." said Ilohan at last.

"Hope, and victory," said Jonathan. They struggled back to their feet and carried on.

*   *   *

In the starless dusk in Glen Carrah, Barnabas shoved the last of the swords he had made for the king into his saddle bags. There were only eight, of the thirty he had planned to make by the month's end, but they were well made and he knew they would find good use. Hannah had already packed all else that was needed, and his horse stood ready on the stone road before their cottage.

Hannah brought him a hot drink, and he drank it gratefully in the cold night. He shared her desire to prolong the time before their final parting, but they both knew he must go. At last she came into his arms, and he hugged her tightly. "War can take nothing but your mortal life," she said. "Oh, Beloved, do not let it take that!"

"I will not, unless for Karolan's protection it must be. Many must die, and I am confident in the promise of Heaven. Yet for your sake and Jonathan's I would live, and I believe I shall."

"You will, Beloved! You will be victorious, and you will live."

"So let it be!" said Barnabas. "God hears your prayers, my Hannah – that I know well."

"And I will pray them! Do you think that Jonathan has helped a prince?"

"I am sure of it," said Barnabas, "and I think also that he is safe, and will miss the war."

"Thank God!" said Hannah – and then suddenly she was praying. "Oh Father, protect my Barnabas and bless him – rescue our Karolan from evil's grasp. Oh God, hold us when we cannot hold each other. We cast ourselves upon your love and grace, by which alone we live and hope!"

"Protect my Hannah, Father, and bless her," said Barnabas, taking up her prayer. "Help her also to bless others in this time of grief. Bring Jonathan safe again to Glen Carrah. Show yourself to him, and no longer let him turn away. Save Karolan, and let the lust of Fingar fail. Forgive us for our evil, make us pure, and let our true cause stand. We praise you for your love, and our praise can never be enough. In all that happens let us bring you glory."

"So let it be!" said Hannah through tears. "Now you must go. You have the whole of my heart's love."

"And you have mine! Farewell, beloved Hannah!"

"Farewell!"

He rode away into the night. Hannah stood silent at the door for a moment, and then she went back inside, wiped her eyes, gathered a cloak close around her, and set out for Joseph's cottage. There was no light in the window when she reached it.

She went in to the dark room, through the door Naomi had not latched, and found her weeping on the floor. Hannah sat down beside her and put her hands on Naomi's shoulders. The shepherdess turned and laid her head on Hannah's lap. Hannah smoothed back Naomi's lovely hair, and wiped her tears away as they kept flowing. She sat there a long time, saying nothing.

*   *   *

As Ilohan and Jonathan climbed, the small crescent moon came briefly into view above the icy peaks in the west, piercingly clear and bright in the mountain sky. But it was setting, and it soon sank down and vanished, leaving them to walk by starlight only. They slipped often on the rock-hard ice, but always rose to struggle on. Finally Jonathan, a little ahead, stopped and stood still on the immense, starlit mountainside. "We are only getting higher and colder," he said, his voice raised to be heard above the wind. "We must stop and sleep. We cannot reach the pass, if there is a pass, tonight."

"Yes," said Ilohan wearily, "But even here it is too cold to sleep. We would never wake up."

"We must find some shelter," said Jonathan.

"When did you last see shelter?" asked Ilohan.

Jonathan laughed bitterly. "The crack on the Cliffs of Doom," he said. "Yet we are not going to die here, nor will we turn back. There must be something."

Ilohan looked up at the stars, more clear and brilliant than he had ever seen them before, wonderful and distant beyond imagination. Their glory touched him with terror, for they were high and unearthly, and mercilessly unconnected with the suffering of those who crawled like ants beneath them. But this was not their fault, only their nature: to shine serene and untroubled by earthly calamity until the end of the world. And God, who had made even them, yet cared for men. "They do not know our pain," he said, "but God does – how great that wonder! He will help us here, somehow."

Ilohan followed as Jonathan trudged forward again without another word. The blacksmith was only three paces ahead, but to Ilohan that little distance seemed a heartbreaking eternity. It took his utmost effort to keep up, and try as he might he could not narrow the gap. He knew they could not stop to rest – he had told Jonathan so himself – but he felt, irrationally, that Jonathan was cruelly driving him to exhaustion. He would feel far more comfortable and in control if he were only one pace behind, and could reach out and stop Jonathan with a hand if he could go no farther.

Suddenly, while Ilohan was looking at him, Jonathan vanished. One instant he was there, trudging on, three paces ahead. The next he was gone, and there was nothing to be seen of him at all. Ilohan had thought he was far, far past being able to run. He found he was wrong, and in an instant he stood beside the place where Jonathan had been, and looked down into a deep black hole in the ice. How far down it went he could make no guess: the edge was lit by starlight only, while the interior, blacker than night, was lit by nothing at all. There was no sign of Jonathan, or of anything else, in that blackness. He stood still. His heart was pounding with fear, a feeling of shock and loss lay like a heavy stone in his stomach, and his mind was too numbed and weary to suggest any course of action.

The next moment he could not believe his eyes. A red spark appeared, then intensified to a brilliant light in the icy blackness. It burst on Ilohan's eyes, so long accustomed to the starlit darkness, almost as if the sun had suddenly appeared down in the ice. The light was warm and golden: hearth-light, home-light, in a place that seemed infinitely removed from any home of men.

The light came from a tinder-twig, burning in Jonathan's hand, while the tinderbox from which he had taken it lay open on his lap. The blacksmith was wedged by his pack in a narrow, deep crevasse. He had only fallen about thrice the height of a man. The burning twig revealed the sides of the ice, blue and strange, and intricately banded with milky color. The flame showed little of what was below Jonathan, hindered as it was by the shadow of his body, but it showed enough to give Ilohan a clear impression that if the crevasse had been only a little wider Jonathan would not have lived. The crack did not seem to have a bottom.

The twig burnt out, and utter blackness fell. Jonathan's voice came out of it. "I will throw you the rope," he said. "You must tie it to something, and I will climb out. We have found our shelter, but it is not quite ready for us."

Ilohan tied the rope around his waist, and slid himself out over the crack, until he was sitting on one edge and his feet touched the other. "Climb," he said, and Jonathan came up quickly. He seemed very pleased, and Ilohan began also to grasp why his friend thought this new threat would be their salvation.

They went carefully along the edge of the crevasse, knocking down the skin of snow that covered it with their swords. They were able by starlight to see that it was narrowing. Finally they came to a place where the edges of the crevasse were rugged with knobs and bulges of snow or ice. They hacked large pieces of this off and dropped them into the crack, until they made a floor about twice a man's height below the surface. When they were sure this floor was strong, they smoothed it with snow, and climbed down into the lifesaving shelter.

Clothed and muffled in all the furs they had, and huddled back to back with three thick blankets passing all the way around them both, they were warm at last. Even through the furs that muffled their ears, they could hear the wind howling across the mouth of the crevasse. Unable to reach them, however, it only lulled them into a dreamless sleep.

*   *   *

Hannah and Naomi sat together on the floor of the cottage, with their backs against the wall. They could have sat on the bench before the fire, but somehow both were more comfortable on the floor in the deep sorrow of that night. Perhaps they felt that only the solid earth itself could support them: the earth which bears and bears and does not break under the weight of mountains or the evil of man. Naomi had stopped crying, and the two women sat quietly, leaning gently against each other in the darkness.

"So the king is dead," said Naomi at last.

"Yes," said Hannah. "They say his last words were the call to arms. Fingar will muster his army as soon as he hears."

"So we have no king, then," said Naomi. "No one to lead us out to fight."

"I do not know who leads," said Hannah. "Yet they said Sir Ilohan of Aaronkal was the true prince, but that he journeyed beyond the mountains and could not return to Karolan before the war."

"So Jonathan has been the companion of the prince," said Naomi.

"Yes," said Hannah, "and he will not be in the war. He will be safe."

"He may not be in the war," said Naomi, "but he cannot be safe while he refuses to give himself to God. And he will want to be in the war, for he does not seek safety."

"He is right not to seek safety in this life, for it cannot be found here," said Hannah.

Naomi smiled. "Father and I, also, had to realize that," she said. "There is no true safety in this world, and if we try to achieve it, we only stifle what we hoped to shield. But how can one live, like Jonathan, who does not even hope for safety in the love of God? Father's departure plunged me in sorrow, but him I will see again. My fear for Jonathan is deeper."

"Yes, your father is safe forever," said Hannah, "while Jonathan is not – not yet, I mean. But I believe God will have him. I believe he will, with all my heart."

"I wish I was so sure!" said Naomi. "There is so much sorrow in this world, and his stubborn blindness is as hard as stone. Yet how I love him!"

"I am lonely and afraid, like you," said Hannah slowly. "But Naomi, this much I know for sure. God will bring you joy. You should follow him and trust him wholly."

"You did not say he would save Jonathan, only that he would bring me joy. I feel they are inseparable. Yet am I wrong to feel so?"

"I do not think you are," said Hannah. "It may be that God has made the two inseparable. If he has, it is because he will give you both. You must trust him and love him, and he will take care of you."

"I do trust him," said Naomi. "I do trust him... Oh God, help me trust... help me know that you are good... and please, please save Jonathan and bring him home."

They were silent a long time. The fire had dwindled to faint coals. Naomi's hand found Hannah's in the darkness, and Hannah felt her grip warm and strong. The parting with Joseph had crushed her for a time, but as Hannah had guessed, the shepherd girl possessed enormous strength.

The wind had died down a little outside, and a slight soft swishing told Hannah the first snow was falling, though likely melting when it touched the ground. "Let us light the candles!" said Naomi valiantly. They rose together to light them and stir up the fire. They hugged each other in the firelit doorway, and then Hannah went out into the night.

Naomi closed the door and looked around the room. "Thank you for her, Father," she said. "I have been brought back to hope."

Yet the house was still desperately empty, and life without her father's present love seemed as gloomy as day without light, or a land without color. She glanced at the place on the floor where she had sat and cried so long and brokenly. No. She would not crumple there again. She would do something, and then go to sleep. She swept the floor, though it needed no sweeping. Then she made a small fire in her own fireplace, blew out the candles, and lay down on her sweet hay mattress to sleep.

The warm glow of the fire and the swish of the wind and snow outside the shuttered window made the room feel safe and cozy. She lay thinking of all who had labored and sacrificed to give her what she had. Someone, long ago, had built this cottage in this lovely place. Her father had made it stronger and warmer, and had cared for her and filled her life and her home with the signs of his love. Their sheep gave milk and wool to supply her. Hannah cared for her and blessed her almost as her mother might have. Nirolad and all the ancient kings and warriors had founded and protected Karolan, so that until now it had stood firm against Norkath and all others. Even Barnabas had fought to protect Karolan, and secure for her the life that she had loved.

God watched over them all, loved them and her, and through them or without them gave her everything she had. Even Jonathan her beloved was from him, and the great flame of their love was his. The love and service of so many seemed to Naomi to roll back in great arcs of warm, golden light, surrounding her at their center as the petals of a rose surround one slender, inmost piece. Her prayer as she fell asleep was to give back some of what she had been given, and serve some as so many had served her, to take her place among the arcs of glowing light, whose source and protector was God alone.

*   *   *

It was much later when Hannah at last set out for her own cottage. She had visited nearly all the homes in Glen Carrah. In many, of course, all had already gone go bed, but in a few she had found frightened mothers, crying children, or even belated husbands frantically preparing to depart. She had done what she could for all. She had belittled no one's sorrow, knowing well the depth of her own, but she had brought hope, and the unshakable confidence of her faith in God.

Some husbands had departed for war, Hannah thought, sooner and more at ease thanks to the knowledge that she cared for the wives and children they were leaving. Children in desperate grief, and wives to whom everything looked black, had been comforted by her coming. "My own husband," she had told them, "a score of years ago went into danger, fought in a small army outnumbered by a ruthless foe, and yet returned unharmed. And the history of Karolan is full of such things." She could honestly say these things, without pretending she herself was not afraid. The days were dark. She could not point to any other time in Karolan's history where the king had died on the eve of a great war, and there had been no prince to lead the army in his place. But more than once the

Army of all Karolan had mustered in what seemed a hopeless case, and unlooked-for victory had come to them.

"There is real reason to hope – though our fears also are not groundless," she thought, as she entered her home. The cottage was dark and empty. The smell of wood shavings and leather greeted her, reminding her of her long work with Barnabas. The years had been blessed ones, and their love was all she had ever hoped it would be. Whatever happened now, she could not lose him, and she could not lose the good of what had passed. She knelt by her bed and prayed for a long time, then at last lay down.

There was too much space in the bed. She could reach all the way across it without touching Barnabas – without touching anything but cold emptiness. She lay awake a long time. Tomorrow, she thought, as she drifted toward sleep at last, she would fill the house with children. It would not be so empty then. They would love to watch her work, and if she did not get much done that mattered little, for no one would buy her goods in wartime. Her dreams were not restful, but she did not care. In them, she walked with Barnabas and helped him.

*   *   *

Joseph rode hard through the darkness and snow – which soon turned to rain, and soaked him. He knew Naomi had packed a leather cloak, but he did not reach for it. He was too miserable to do anything but keep riding. Every step of the horse carried him farther away from everything he loved on earth. Not most things, but everything. He could not believe he kept going. It was like a horrible miracle, a thing that was impossible happening before his eyes. When he had dreamed of miracles he had always thought of them as wonders from

God, greatly to be desired. Now he was in the midst of a miracle of a different sort: God's power and love were helping him do the thing above all things on earth that he did not want to do.

He was dripping with cold rain, and shivering as he rode. He could not believe that he did not turn around. Naomi was there: Naomi, Abigail's only daughter. He loved no one on earth beside her, and he knew no one on earth more loving or more faithful. She was a masterpiece from the hand of God, full of life and beauty. All her life he had protected her and cared for her, and God had given him the joy of seeing her grow to womanhood sheltered, strong, and happy. She was back there, with her grateful love for him, her bright and caring faith. He remembered all her kind words, all her deep understanding. She was there, still there, still behind him, left farther behind with every step. "Why do I go on? Why do I go on? There is no reason on earth to go on."

Yet still he went on, through the rainy mist and the chill, wet wind. The pony's feet beat a dull rhythm on the stone, and he felt colder with every step. Naomi was behind him, left to face her fear for Jonathan alone, left to face the Norkaths alone if Karolan fell – left without his guidance and his love. Who would tell her when to flee, and where was the best place to hide? Who would put flowers in her room, or build her fire while she was out in the glen? Why did he go on? She was sleeping now, but would wake when he knocked. She would greet him with her old smile, her old embrace. The stars would shine in her eyes, and she would make him something hot to drink, glad beyond words to have him back. Why did he go on? How could the pony keep walking, when a thing so strong as his desire pulled them back? Why had the road let him use it to go away from Naomi? Why did he not turn around and go back?

But if he went back, she would know that he had failed. She would rejoice, but her joy would turn to shame, shame that their strength together had not been enough. She would know forever that he had only been almost a hero. There was no reason on earth to keep going, but there was a reason in Heaven. There was a reason to keep going, and he would not turn back.

Yet still she was back there, sleeping. Still she was Naomi, his only daughter, and the only daughter of Abigail with whom his years had been so short. Still he loved no one on earth beside her. Still he thought no one more noble, true, or loving had walked on earth since her mother died. Still he knew the stars would kindle in her eyes when she saw him. Still he knew he had left her weeping at the door, and that even then she had been hiding the depth of her grief. Still he knew that few were as closely bound in love as himself and her, and that death, though not forever, was a deep curse and a gulf of separation over which Christ himself had wept. Still the feet of his pony kept moving, still the cold rain fell in his face. Still the road was being traveled, and he was going farther away from his only child.

Warm lights loomed out of the darkness to his left, and he turned toward them. It was an inn, filled with men who, like himself, were going to war. He bought three water skins from the innkeeper, and finding all the beds full, lay down on the floor near the fire to sleep. Despite his desire for rest and forgetfulness, he remained perfectly alert.

He listened to the low, earnest voices of the men who thronged the tables of the room, and the uproarious songs of some who tried to drown the war in ale. So many had left wives and children behind, so many doubted if they would ever see them again. It was not a hopeful war, this sudden conflict triggered by the king's untimely death. From the overheard speeches of the men, he learned that Tulbur the Steward was to lead the army. This was doubtful news to men already anxious and afraid. Men did not love the steward as they had loved Thomas. They might trust him, but they did not love him.

Joseph's consciousness faded at last, and his thoughts wandered without order on the edge of sleep. He drifted in and out of awareness of what was around him in the room. It was all very strange to him: the place, the crowding, the unknown voices, noise, and strong smells. Finally, still well before dawn, he gave up trying to get real sleep and arose. The saddlebag he had used as a pillow had not been rifled, and all his money was still there. His pony had been well cared for in the ample stables. Donning his leather coat at last, he mounted and continued on his way.

It was still impossible, and his weariness did little to dull his hurt. The pony kept walking. The clouds blew away, and the stars shone clear above them. The path turned and began descending in long, steep switchbacks toward the prairie land far below. Naomi was still behind him, but it was too far now, and he could not turn back. Everything he loved was gone, far away in the high foothills that he was leaving. He was going to another world, a world he did not know and did not love. He was weary, but his sorrow never tired. The pony kept walking.

Chapter 5

How Zarnith Count

THE BLANKETS WRAPPED AROUND JONATHAN WERE SOFT and kind, cradling his sore and bruised limbs. It seemed impossible to get up and dare the unearthly mountain sunrise that was pouring its piercing light into the crevasse. Every moment in the warm cocoon of furs seemed more precious than gold. Yet Jonathan did get up, clumsy in his soreness. He climbed out and stood on the rim of the crevasse. His teeth chattered instantly in the cold wind, and he blinked and rubbed his eyes, trying to convince them to stay open. He could not remember ever having felt so tired.

The crevasse in which he and Ilohan had slept was on a shoulder of the mountain: the ice around them was nearly flat for half a bowshot in all directions. Beyond that to the south, east, and west it dropped off steeply in dizzying bounds of pure white, sculpted and wind-worn into strange forms and facets. Every eastward edge caught the morning sun and shone with sparkling white fire.

Jonathan looked straight up for a moment, but the terrible mountain sky defeated him. It seemed to make him dizzy, to pull him up into its frozen depth of dark blue air and lose him at some measureless height. He turned his gaze lower with a quick motion.

Down near the horizon the sky might have paled and brightened almost to a comfortable color, but the mountains blotted it out. They towered into the morning sun: terrible, beautiful peaks of white ice and black stone. Every crag, pinnacle, and boulder stood out piercingly clear despite the vast gulfs of air through which Jonathan viewed them. He tried to understand their hugeness and their distance, as he understood the size of an anvil or a sword, but he could not. They were beyond him: great and high and far, and he could say no more than that.

To the southeast there were none, and the sky did fade to a kindly blue, and finally to a hazy white over the edge of the world, a horizon on which nothing could be seen. Jonathan felt comforted by the absence of mountains in this direction, until he understood its implication: that way lay the Cliffs of Doom. There was no rock there, only air. He sat back on the edge of the crevasse, his teeth chattering furiously. There was nothing kind in all this frozen world. Everything seemed either aloof in its majesty, or hostile in its mighty opposition to their quest. Yet still he gloried in the place, and the adventure.

Ilohan also had now awakened, and was rummaging through their packs with hands still slow and eyes half blurred with sleep. He was ravenously hungry, yet when he found the bread from Ceramir he sat perfectly still a moment, holding it in his hands. It was soft, not yet stale, having been baked only two and a half days before. This seemed a marvel to him, for the bread came from another world: the kindly world of Ceramir, left behind eons ago.

Jonathan descended into the crevasse, and they ate together. The cold blue light brightened in the icy crack, and as they ate, the two adventurers felt warmer.

"You have been up to look around already?" asked Ilohan, pronouncing the words with difficulty through lips still numbed with cold.

"Yes," said Jonathan.

"How far do we have to go? What does the pass look like?"

"I did not see it."

Ilohan felt dismayed by this: if Jonathan could see no pass, it might mean the Zarnith poem had led them wrong. Yet he found his weariness dulled even his dismay. "Do you mean the slope rises to a high ridge, in which you can see no gap?" he asked.

"I do not know," said Jonathan. "I did not look at the mountain we are climbing."

"Do you mean you looked around at everything except what we need to see?" asked Ilohan.

The crack rang with Jonathan's laughter, and Ilohan felt cheered and warmed. "Yes, I do mean that," said Jonathan. "I was too wonder-struck by all the rest. You may understand when you see it. But let us go up and look at it together."

Ilohan felt his soreness and exhaustion intensely as he climbed from the crevasse. When at last he stood on the edge, his legs shook and his breath came in gasps. He heard Jonathan panting beside him. "What is it that saps our strength?" asked Ilohan.

"I do not know," said Jonathan. "Did the sages of Aaronkal never teach you of such things?"

Ilohan raised his eyes with an effort, and looked up to the north, the direction Jonathan had missed. The great mountain filled all his vision: asymmetrical, but perfect nonetheless. Its sparkling fields of ice leaped up in steepening bounds, until the tremendous black pinnacle of the peak itself blasted through them like a vertical battering ram frozen forever in the act of punching up from the depths of the earth.

"The sages of Aaronkal never came here," said Ilohan. "They do not know..."

Another great mountain stood a little farther away, on the left where they hoped to find a pass. The notch between the two looked terribly high, adjacent to the black pinnacle itself – but Ilohan knew this was merely where the two mountains seemed to line up from their perspective. The real pass might be much lower – or not.

"I think," said Jonathan, "that the pass is just at the foot of the rock, only a little lower than it seems."

Ilohan willed himself to stand straighter, and took a deep breath. "If it is there, we must try to climb there. I had hoped it might be lower."

"Let us traverse across lower, then," said Jonathan. "It is better to climb nothing that we have no need to climb."

"I will go in front," said Ilohan, "stabbing down my sword at every step."

He set off, limping, he thought, like a wounded soldier. At every step he stabbed his sword down forcefully in front of him, hoping that if there were a hidden crevasse he would find it before falling through the skin of ice and snow to his death. Despite Jonathan's comment about traversing, Ilohan led up quite steeply. He knew they must not waste their strength trying to climb higher than they needed to, but he feared getting into a precipitous valley dropping down from the pass between the two mountains. It would be far better to come at the pass from the side, if they could, than have to climb up such a valley.

Their pace seemed pathetically slow, but still they were out of breath. The dry, icy air seemed to burn their lungs even through the woolen scarves they had knotted across their mouths. "Father, bless our lungs, and our sore legs," prayed Ilohan, half amused at the childishness of his own prayer. "Help us to keep on, and help me trust in you. I know you love us, even now, even though you have brought us here. Though you slay me, yet will I trust you." He repeated the last phrase over and over under his breath, fitting it into the rhythm of his steps, letting its meaning sink into his mind.

Suddenly his sword point sank into the ice, and he found he had fallen on his knees and was peering into a black hole. Jonathan knelt beside him. "Good," said the blacksmith. "You have found a crevasse without falling in. Since we find ourselves making a halt, shall we eat something? Are you as hungry as I am?"

"If you are very hungry, yes," said Ilohan, pulling his sword out of the ice and sitting up. They opened their packs and brought out bread, meat, and cheese.

"Cold makes men hungry," said Jonathan. "I suppose I should not be surprised, here where it is colder than in any other place I have known, to find myself hungrier than I have ever been."

"One need not study at Aaronkal to learn such things," said Ilohan. "Indeed, I expect Glen Carrah was a better teacher than all the sages in many ways."

"But in many it was not," said Jonathan. "If we had breath for talking, I would delight to hear all you could tell me of the ancient wars and the history of Karolan."

"And I would be glad to tell you all I can remember of my lessons," said Ilohan, "but, as you say, in this terrible land we cannot converse while we are walking."

They stood wearily after the meal, and cleared the ice away to expose the crevasse. It would have been easy to jump for a rested man in a kind land, but it dropped into unfathomable blackness, and in their weariness the leap was fearful. After gathering courage a moment, they both made it, and continued without looking back.

Their pace seemed a weary crawl, yet when they tried to force themselves on faster they always fell back, panting, to the same speed as before. The mountain stood above them in relentless majesty, striking awe into their hearts. They would have felt it malevolent, save that they could not feel it cared enough for their puny efforts even to oppose them.

"God made it from stone," thought Ilohan. "It has the beauty that he gave it. It is innocent and splendid. It is not living, that it could thwart us by its own will. Yet what mighty craftsmanship the mountains show! They are beyond my understanding; how much more the hand that made them! Who am I to say what is their meaning or their purpose?" His thought wandered on beautiful paths he could not express in words, but then fell back to earth with the aching weariness of his body. "Who am I to think I can cross them? But then, I do not think so. I think I was right to try, but I will die in the attempt. Though he slay me, yet will I trust him."

Jonathan knew he was stronger than Ilohan, and yet he was weary. He wondered at the prince's strength of will, to hold his pace despite his greater weariness. He was humbled by Ilohan's determination: to keep going through exhaustion when he had already relinquished hope. But Jonathan knew that his own will also was strong. He vowed to himself that there would never come a time when he saw what he must do, and did not persist in attempting it as long as he had breath. If his cause was true, he must go on, though it be through danger, dread, exhaustion, or despair – even to the death. If he did not, he would have utterly failed.

Jonathan wondered if the world of Glen Carrah, Luciyr and Ceramir still existed. Up here in the frozen sky it was easy to imagine that all he loved below had faded away into a golden mist, or that a door at the top of a stair had closed behind him, shutting him off from the kinder world forever. That world seemed vague and strange in his memory. The ice, the rock, the hard light, and the aching weariness displaced and blurred the pictures in his mind of other lands. Only the splendid, merciless world around him seemed real. The warm lake of Ceramir and the sweet-smelling wind off the autumn grass in Glen Carrah seemed only to have been lovely dreams. Like dreams, they seemed unconnected with reality, unable to bless or help him now.

Suddenly the realization struck him like lightning: Naomi was in that other world, far away beyond the terrible mountains. She must be real, or he had no reason to keep living. He forced down the feelings of unreality that had blurred his thoughts of home. They were false. There were two worlds, both real. They were breathtakingly different, so different that a man's thought could not easily pass from one to another. Yet his body could pass. He would cross these mountains and walk down into Karolan. He would come back to Naomi, even if all Fingar's host, together with the mountains, barred his way.

His heart ached for her. There was an emptiness in his soul where she should be. And yet, though he missed her terribly, he felt that she was with him somehow, caring for him, and encouraging him on. He smiled. "Thank you, Naomi," he whispered. "I feel your love, perhaps... perhaps even your prayer." He trudged on, glad of a vague picture of her that now came into his mind. He saw her kneeling in frosty grass, perhaps wearing a cloak, for once, as a special gift to Joseph. "I need not cling to memories of her in the other world," he thought. "She is with me in this one. Even the empty hurt I feel is a proof of her reality. I will come back to her." Jonathan suddenly became aware that Ilohan had stopped, and that the aspect of the mountain had changed dramatically while he was lost in thought.

"What I feared has happened," said Ilohan, "but it is not as bad as I expected."

"What do you mean?" asked Jonathan.

"We have come into a valley beneath the pass. But while I feared it might be a terrible, steep-sided notch up which we could scarcely hope to climb, it is actually broad and shallow – and up there must be the pass."

They turned and began to trudge up the valley. Ilohan had been heartened to find it so different from what he had imagined, but as they continued, his weariness became so great that he was no longer comforted by the gentle slope of the ice. The pass stubbornly refused to look any closer – if the distant depression in the skyline of which he had spoken so confidently really was a pass. Though the valley did not turn into a jagged notch such as he had feared, it did steepen. It was afternoon of their third day, and they were to have reached the pass on the second. He wondered if the Zarnith poem was any more than a fable, a wild legend concocted by Dradrag's defeated warriors on the long journey home.

But Ilohan and Jonathan did draw near the pass at last. The ice began to be less steep, and they stood straighter and walked more easily. The mountain pinnacle towered on their right, blotting out half the sky, a dagger of black stone pointed at the heart of the cold blue heavens.

"We are nearly at the pass," said Jonathan, his voice full of exultation despite his weariness. "What will we see on the other side?"

"I do not know," said Ilohan, "but it will not be a comforting sight."

"But how many have ever seen it?" asked Jonathan. "It will be like walking on a ridge of cloud, a land that perhaps we alone have seen, of all the living."

Ilohan walked on in silence. The phrase, 'walking on a ridge of cloud,' stuck in his mind. He remembered his thoughts in Ceramir, while he lay stricken with the plague and Jonathan spoke of the glories of the future that he himself believed would never come. He had thought, then, that Jonathan's words were like a lovely rainbow in a cloud, while the reality of the future was a hard black mountain beneath it. Now, in the triumph of the moment, he let his own thoughts wander on a cloud. Perhaps God would give them a miracle. Perhaps they would cross the mountains and bring a time of joy and peace to battered, tempered, lovely Karolan.

The ice steepened to a last, low ridge, and having climbed that they stood at the pass. The edges of their clothes whipped about in a cold, wild wind. The view of which they had spoken lay before them: mountains as far as their eyes could see. Great peaks of ice and rock towered on the far horizon, seen in brilliant clarity through air that knew no haze. On their left, a range of tremendous mountains went off to the northwest, curving a little to the north as it went: the wall of mountains through which the pass had brought them. Before them and below, already sunk in the blue shadow of the range on which they stood, was a plain of rough ice covered with small hills or hummocks. It was an unearthly sight, like the top of a wind-tortured storm cloud fixed forever into ice. It extended far out to the east and north, until it washed against the distant mountains that formed the splendid, jagged horizon.

The two adventurers stood there, breathing hard from the climb and saying nothing for a long time. "Stand at the pass beneath the stars, and see terror," quoted Ilohan at last. "Walk to the third of the mountains."

"It is hard to believe," said Jonathan, "that Karolan could be on the other side of that."

"Yes," said Ilohan, "It would be easier to think that beyond those great far mountains is the edge of the world: a cliff into the Abyss, or a stairway leading to the stars."

"Yes," said Jonathan. "You say it well."

There was a long silence. The heat of their climbing began to fade from them despite their fur clothes. The sun was lowering, and the wind howled. "We must solve the Zarnith riddle," said Ilohan. "We must walk to the third of the mountains."

Jonathan sat on the ice and gathered his cloak close about him. "The third by some count," he said. "Third from the west? Third from the east? Neither seems right."

"No," said Ilohan, sitting beside him, "since the mountains go on forever."

"You know more of the Zarnith than I," said Jonathan. "How would a Zarnith count mountains? What would he mean by the third mountain?"

Ilohan tried to imagine, but the cold seemed to dull his thought. What could the ancient poem have meant by the third of the mountains? There were so many mountains, so many peaks gleaming against the sky as they caught the still-white rays of the setting sun.

"It seems unlikely that the pass the Zarnith found is the only one," said Jonathan. "If we make for the lowest notch in the northern range, might we not find a pass of our own?"

"The Zarnith had to guess at the way," said Ilohan, "perhaps we could as well. But, according to Mudien's friend, only a few of the group of Zarnith who reached the cliff tops ever made it into Karolan. I do not want to share the fate of those who failed."

"Do you think they tried several ways, before they found a pass?"

"I think something like that happened," said Ilohan, "though none can guess the details of their desperate story. Do you remember their words about the pass?"

"Stand at the pass beneath the stars, and know terror?" quoted Jonathan. "No, that was this pass. The second pass was, 'Stand at the pass among the stars, and die.'"

Ilohan shivered. "I think they did die," he said. "Some of them, I mean, even among those who reached the right pass."

Jonathan did not reply, and in the silence Ilohan considered his own words. There was nothing in this terribly beautiful world that suggested mercy. If their strength failed, or they guessed wrong, it would kill them just as it had killed those Zarnith centuries before. And it seemed to Ilohan, as the sun sank lower in the west, that their strength was failing, and that try as they might they would guess wrong. The mountains were not hungry for their bones – they were too mighty to care – but nothing in this land would aid them if they stumbled. They would die without the slenderest filament of hope.

Their teeth chattered in the cold. "We must move on, or freeze," said Jonathan at last. He put his head in his hands. "Think, think, we must think... Ilohan!" he said triumphantly, "I have it."

"Tell me," said Ilohan through chattering teeth.

"You say they may have tried more than one pass. The third mountain must be the mountain of the third pass they tried."

There was a short silence. The wind howled, and the cold
sank deeper into their bones. "You may be right," said Ilohan,
"but if so, we are doomed – for how can we know which
mountain they tried third?"

Jonathan was grave for a moment, but then spoke again.
"They might have tried the deepest notch first, and one
shallower, and then another shallower. Then the third pass
would be the deepest notch save two."

Ilohan scanned the mountain range, easily finding the third
deepest notch, a narrow cleft between two tall white peaks. "I
do not think that is the way to imagine it," he said. "From here,
they could have chosen which pass to try first, but if they made
a third try after two failures, they would then have been right
at the feet of the peaks, and things would have looked very
different. I think we have not solved the riddle yet."

"There is one thing I would like to know," said Jonathan,
"and that is whether the Zarnith intended the poem to tell how
to cross the mountains, or only to record their mighty journey.
Mudien's Zarnith friend left the poem as a gift. If it is a true
gift, it must explain the way across the mountains. 'Third' must
mean something we can see from here."

"You are right," said Ilohan, "and well thought! The poem
says we should set out from this pass for the third mountain.
So if the poem is indeed a guide, that mountain must be one
that we can recognize from here."

"Yes," said Jonathan, "and I was wrong before – forgive
me."

"Too often you ask forgiveness for trifles," said Ilohan. "But
now – to solve the riddle before we freeze. How can we find
this mountain?"

"You have said that something visible about the mountain must mark it as the third. What would a Zarnith think was obvious? How does a Zarnith count?"

"I think," said Ilohan, "that to the Zarnith the greatest number was one – first, best, highest, like Dradrag, who ruled with absolute power because he was the strongest and the fiercest."

Jonathan leaped up, forgetting his weariness in triumph. "You have found it, Prince Ilohan!" he said. "The highest..."

Ilohan smiled through his cracked lips. He stood slowly beside his friend. "The highest mountain save two," he said.

"Yes," said Jonathan, and pointed.

*　　　　　*　　　　　*

The afternoon sun was warm and bright on the prairie lands, and Barnabas felt joy in the great expanses of blowing grass, still partly green since the frosts had not yet come so low. He held his old, borrowed horse to a smart trot, half wishing he had a warhorse that could gallop across the plains.

His right hand went to his sword hilt, and he felt a stern joy burning low within him. The sword was an instrument of destruction, and war was terrible, but sometimes wondrous things were tempered in its crucible. He would soon see it happen once again, and the war to which he went was just. The bands of men who fought in it would be true comrades, their comradeship good and strong even while scenes from Hell howled round them.

"Father," he prayed, "help me to depend on you, and to do only what pleases you. Protect me from evil, and bring victory to Karolan. Protect Hannah, and Jonathan; be with them and let all things be well with them. Spare my life, for Hannah's sake.

Help me to do all that I should, my duty to the full. I thank you. So let it be."

The soft breeze across the prairie was kind, almost warm, and the bright but fading twilight filled the boundless sky with gentle colors. He no longer grudged the slow pace of his horse. When night came with thousands of bright stars, he camped alone in a hollow at the edge of the woods.

*　　　　　*　　　　　*

It was dark as Joseph rode through the forest land of Karolan, and the trees obscured the stars. He was weary, and his pony was as well, trotting at a slow pace upon the half-seen road. In his exhaustion, his perception of things narrowed until he was aware only of the constant plodding of his pony – and the ache at the center of his heart. He was too weary now to find words for his sorrow, and all that passed within him was in the raw language of feelings and pictures.

Each of the images that passed through his mind was torture to see, yet at the same time desperately dear to him. He saw Abigail, laughing as she held baby Naomi close against her. He saw himself, making the cottage snug and warm for them while she looked on, happy beyond words to have a home that would be all their own. There was Naomi, still a child too young to speak, nestling against her mother when the time had nearly come for her second child to be born. That child had been a daughter too, but the birth that killed her mother took her dawning life as well.

Had he not been weary, he would have kept the pictures lovingly at bay, but tonight he had no strength against them. His tears fell hot upon the pony's neck. When her voice had been no stronger than a whisper, and he knew her body was filled with burning pain, Abigail had told him that although it seemed otherwise, she knew that death could not conquer, and that her passing from the world was not its victory. She had known, as surely as she knew he knelt beside her, that she passed not into death but life, and that she fell into the arms of God. She had clung to little Naomi, and blessed her, and then released her.

As he rode through the dark woods, Joseph could hear her whispered words, and see her beloved face, as she relinquished Naomi to him. "She will be all you have, now. But she will love you well, and grow up strong. She will be beautiful and faithful, and the life I lost will be hers, in depth of joy and hope. Love her well. I know she will love you." She had turned to Naomi, crying in Joseph's arms, smiled at her, and then looked up at Joseph. "We do not lose it, Beloved. It does not die, for God made it and blessed it. It changes, but only to be perfect. We are his, Beloved. Love lives..."

He could see it now, deep and real, striking painfully into his heart. Her eyes had closed, and then the pain that she had fought so bravely and so long was ended, and joy came to her at last. The rest was sunk in darkness, and of it he had no pictures, only the knowledge of what had passed. The weight of despair, the blankets soaked with blood he had been helpless to stop, the double grave beside a tree near the cliffs – all was faded, and instead the picture of her last bright smile stayed in his mind. She, to use her daughter's word more truthfully, had been a hero.

He was trembling with weariness and grief, and with the power of his memories. His silent tears still fell, and the pony found its own way along the dark forest road. Its hooves pounded hollow on a bridge. Joseph's head slumped over its neck, but then he roused himself and sat up straight. His stomach felt hollow, and despite the shelter of the trees he was cold. Another picture passed through his mind, one that made him laugh as well as cry. Naomi, grown the beautiful woman she now was, stood by his chair in the firelight with concern on her face. She held bread and honey in her hands, and love and care were in her voice as she said, "Father, will you not eat something?"

He looked up again, and the warm lights of a village, and more importantly those of a village inn, shone bright and welcoming through the dark forest.

Chapter 6

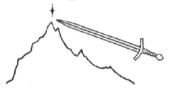

Hail of Stars

"I THINK THE TIME HAS COME TO PUSH ON NEAR THE LIMIT of our strength," said Jonathan. "If we do not, we will be too late." They had descended from the pass and trudged a little way out onto the plain, but now they were resting in the darkness, sitting on a hummock of ice.

"I agree with you," said Ilohan wearily. "Yet if we push too hard, we die."

"Do you know how much we are eating, Ilohan?" asked Jonathan. "If we do not push hard enough, we also die."

"But Eleanor put in more than enough food for two weeks' hard travel," said Ilohan.

"This travel is more than hard," said Jonathan. "We are hungry always, and if we take more than seven days our food will fail us."

"Can it be true?"

"It is."

"I think we could not live long here without food," said Ilohan.

"I think the same," said Jonathan. "And we cannot travel well without eating as we are eating now. Hunger comes and weakens us so quickly. We must press on."

"Yes," said Ilohan, his voice sounding weary and despondent through the muffler around his face. He rose to follow Jonathan across the weird, icy plain.

The sickle moon shone white and clear above the mountains to their left, and by its hard silver light they could see the third mountain immeasurably far ahead of them. It was very tall, but broad: not as steep in appearance as the mountain behind them. Very little rock showed from beneath its perfect white ice. It was flanked on either side by nearer, lesser mountains, which partly obscured it. Once Ilohan looked back at the mountain behind them, and then forward at the one to which they journeyed. It was like comparing a nearby sapling to a distant towering pine. It had not been far to climb down from the pass to the 'white wildness' on which they now walked. The third mountain, if they ever reached it, would take them up among the stars. If they came down alive it would be a staggering miracle – and though he believed in miracles, Ilohan could not believe in that.

The land they walked on was strange, like nothing from the world he knew. The shapes and colors of the ice were all its own, weird and frozen: not like rock or earth, wood, sand, or water. When he slipped on it and fell, he found it as unyielding as stone. Sometimes they passed out of the moonlight into the shadow of a great frozen hummock, broad and high as a castle, and shaped as no hill in a kinder land could ever be. Ilohan shivered in the darkness of those shadows, though he knew well that the bright crescent moon gave out no warmth.

In his weariness Ilohan's thought turned to times long past, when he had done something he thought hard or wonderful: walking all day for the first time, or scrubbing every step in the great stair at Aaronkal, or winning a sword match. Those little victories seemed insignificant now, yet he was glad to think of them. He had won them with a true heart, and if also with childish pride, that was vanquished now while the heart God had given remained. Little had been at stake then, and supper had been warm at the end regardless of the outcome, yet in some way those old challenges had prepared him for this. They had trained him to push on, taught him that what seemed impossible might not be. That was a good lesson – even if in the present case it might not prove true. He realized suddenly that he had been lost in these thoughts a long time, scarcely noticing his burning lungs and aching feet. Though awareness of his weary struggle now returned, he was glad of the respite.

The moon set behind the mountains. Its gradual departure seemed like a slow crescendo, a long drum roll ushering in true night. The stars blazed into their own, shining in countless thousands above the dark ice. The Ceranim was at its faintest time, the slender northern band of starcloth between summer's glory past and winter's yet to come. Yet even the faintest part of the Cloth of Stars was bright and wondrous in the clear mountain sky.

As they trudged on over the half-seen hummocks of stone-hard ice, Jonathan felt a strange reversal of normal experience. The night sky was now a bright reality with depth and detail, while the earth was a formless void of empty space. Bereft of earthly landmarks, he measured their journey only by the slow wheeling of the stars – until he felt that it was indeed through the bright fields of heaven that they were walking.

The stars were brighter than he had ever seen them before, even in the desert. One might try to count them, but for every bright star there were a hundred faint ones, and for every faint star a thousand fainter shone, blending softly into starcloth that would hint forever at an immeasurable, countless host. Dark as was the moonless night, the third mountain remained easy to see by its silhouette against the stars – and by this Jonathan held their course true.

A brilliant shooting star suddenly flew from high in the east, soaring across the sky to fade and vanish over the western mountains. Both adventurers noticed it, but they said nothing, too weary to think it worth the effort. Another star blazed across the sky, east to west. Then came two at once, bright and yellow, as if Varilie had taken wing. Jonathan turned back, and saw it low over the mountains behind them, still shining well and safe. They walked on.

More stars fell. Each one was so startling and ephemeral that they could scarcely hold the image of it in their minds. They had to wait for the next to be reminded what they looked like. With each star the wonder was as fresh as with the one before. It lifted their minds away from their aching bodies and the long labor of their desperate quest.

The stars fell faster now, more and more of them, all coming from a place high in the east. Both Ilohan and Jonathan felt the awed wonder that had been their first reaction now shading into fear. The stars were the last thing they had left, the last emblem of continuity with a kinder world. If the stars fell from the sky, they would be lost in a world flying out of hope and reason to a spectacular destruction. This thought was in their minds as a vague fear, at once dismissed, yet lingering in some uneasiness as the wondrous rain of stars continued.

The stars fell faster. Staring into the east, Ilohan was gripped at last with genuine terror – and yet it was a terror blended with exultation. In the Books of the Travelers, he knew, it was written that the stars would fall at the end of the world. This might be it. If it were, the end of all things was yet a glorious wonder. It showed the splendor of God, in whose hand the world, steady or shivered, rested yet. The stars fell faster, only a few heartbeats now between each one and the next.

Jonathan led on toward the third mountain, yet all his attention was now fixed on the heavens. Now and then he stumbled, got up, and carried on, still staring at the wonders in the sky. He, too, had heard of the prophecy from wandering preachers who came to Glen Carrah. Yet he felt little fear – only a wild exultation in the breathtaking hail from heaven. If the starcloth were ripping and the world falling to stupendous ruin, what a thing it was to live to see! It was an adventure beyond dreaming, to stand in a frozen land above the mountains, and see the heavens fall upon the reeling earth. The stars fell faster. They came so quickly now that one had scarcely stopped shining before another came. Ilohan and Jonathan kept walking.

The stars fell faster. There were always at least two in the sky at once now, all flying out from that point high in the east. Then there were always five at once, then more – too many to count as they flew, a storm of brilliant stars pouring from the high east into every part of the breathtaking sky. Some of the falling stars were brighter by far than any in the firmament. They shone too bright to look at as they fell, dazzling the travelers' eyes with their piercing light, and casting enormous, flying shadows on the icy plain.

Whatever the adventurers had felt before was swallowed up in pure, unearthly terror. This was too much for them, the changeless heavens rushing down to earth in a torrent, a hail, a storm of stars, some blazing brighter than a full moon. Karolan, Norkath, their quest, and even their lives fell out of their thoughts and consideration, blasted into insignificance by the falling of the stars. They stood still, side by side; they looked into the sky and gaped. Neither doubted that the magnificent ruin of all the world was at hand. Nothing they had thought so important before mattered now. They could not save Karolan, Fingar could not save Norkath, Mudien could not protect Ceramir. "Only God," said Ilohan, "has any power now."

Finding a core of peace even in the midst of his terror, Ilohan prayed aloud: "God, I thank you that even now I am yours, and may dare to call you Father. Please rescue all who love you from the ruin of the world – and save Jonathan, my friend who is beside me." He was silent then, full of awe and fear.

Jonathan looked up into the blazing star-hail, and thought of Naomi, far, far away, soon to be lost in a mighty ruin from which he could not save her. He wished she stood beside him now. There would be more glory and less terror in watching the heavens fall if he were not separated from her he loved best. Together they could stand with joy even at the end of the world, he thought.

Though Jonathan wished with all his heart that Naomi were with him, he was glad that at least Ilohan was. The Skyfall could be a lonely sight, but they would be true comrades to the last.

The stars still streaked out of the east in thousands, and Jonathan grew weary of the height of terror that he felt. He began, in his deep exhaustion, to wish that the world would end at once, and not take so long to do it. Then he noticed a very strange thing. He watched carefully to see if it were true, and confirmed that it was: Although the stars poured from the sky like a rain of silver fire, there were no fewer fixed stars than before. The stars were always falling, but they did not seem to have fallen. "Can they be going back up?" he wondered. "Yet none seem even to have moved."

"Ilohan," he said aloud, "The stars are not falling. Look up; there are as many as before, and in the same places. They have not changed."

There was a long silence. Three blazing stars fell among the thousands of smaller ones, casting flying shadows of the great mountains on the icy land. "True," said Ilohan, in a weary, shaking voice. "Yet there are no stars low in the east."

Jonathan looked, and it was true. The sky above the mountains on the east horizon was black as charcoal, without the faintest glimmer of a star, fixed or falling. Jonathan froze as still as a statue. He guessed what must be happening. No stars were rising in the east. The ones that would have had already fallen through the hole in the sky and streaked down to darkness over earth. They were falling. They were lost. The blackness rose slowly and engulfed the sky. Ilohan and Jonathan shivered in the starless night.

They sank down and lay huddled on the ice. Jonathan felt the cold seeping into him, and he knew he was drifting off to sleep, to die of cold beneath a sky without a star. But he would not give up and die, not even if the world was ending. He got all the blankets out of both packs and wrapped them around Ilohan, who was asleep, and cold. Having done this, Jonathan stood up. He was shivering, and felt that his stiffened muscles would take him no farther. But they must serve not only to carry him, but also to drag the sleeping prince, if the quest were to continue.

He tied corners of the blankets securely around his waist and began to trudge forward. Ilohan slid easily behind him over the hard ice. He hoped the tightly wrapped blankets would keep Ilohan from freezing. He thought they would, for the present, but he was sure they would both die soon. Perhaps even before the end of the world.

Strangely, though he had found it hard to remember Glen Carrah earlier, he now found his mind full of joyful images from there, even as he walked in the hopeless darkness. It seemed impossible that there had once been a time when he could see Naomi every day, when he could run over the high, sweet grass of the glen to visit her, or welcome her with joy if she came to him. Now they were a world apart, and that world was ending. The grief and loss might kill him, he thought, but somehow he could not feel them fully. The shock of the Skyfall, together with his own exhaustion, dulled his mind until the only thing he could think of was putting one foot in front of another.

A long time passed in the starless night. It occurred to him to wonder if the dim silhouette he aimed for were indeed the third mountain, identified so long ago in a world that was not ending. He wondered if the dawn would ever come, or if the sun had perished in the hail of stars. He was weary – endlessly, achingly weary, and he did not know why he should go on, uncertain of his direction while the whole world was plunging into nothingness.

*   *   *

Naomi and Hannah stood on frosty grass watching the last of the falling stars. Children sat at their feet, huddled in blankets and clinging to them for comfort. Naomi had been sleeping in Hannah's cottage, helping her with the children. Cries of wonder and terror from other villagers had awakened them near the beginning, and they had watched it all.

At the peak of the star-hail, it had been all both women could do to keep the children from hysterics. They themselves had clung to one another, cried and prayed in fear and awe.

Now they and the children were calmer, the stars were falling more seldom, and they could see clearly that all the fixed stars were still in their appointed places.

"So," said Naomi, "God wills there to be another day. Thanks and glory be his!"

"So let it be!" said Hannah. "Let us take the children in and go to sleep."

The roof shut out the terrible glory of the sky, and the indoor darkness seemed calm and safe. Hannah and two children shared the big bed, while Naomi, at her own insistence, slept near it on the floor. As Naomi felt herself drifting toward sleep, she shook herself awake once more to speak, wanting Hannah's answer before bright morning dimmed their wonder. "Hannah," she said sleepily, "does such a thing have a meaning? Does a hail of stars mean disaster for Karolan, or for something?"

"I do not know," came Hannah's voice in the darkness. "I have never heard of such a hail of stars. If it is a sign, I tremble what great thing it must mean. What we know for certain makes the future look dark enough. Yet the future belongs to God."

"I think it is only a wonder in the heavens, like the stars themselves," said Naomi. "I do not think it has a meaning for events upon the earth."

"I think it has meaning for something," said Hannah, "but I feel the same as you: it means something about events in the heavens, not on the earth. Yet I hope it strikes fear into Fingar's heart."

"As do I!" said Naomi. "May it scare him into peace! Yet I wonder," she said slowly, "I wonder what it has scared others into – or what it was meant to do."

"Father," prayed Hannah, "we have seen one of your heavenly wonders tonight, a wonder with great power to stir people to fear and awe. Let its effect be all for good, and may it frighten those who are evil. Protect the ones we love, and rescue them from death."

There was a silence in the sheltered darkness. "I thank you for your prayer, and for your faith which upholds mine," said Naomi to Hannah. There was no answer, for Hannah was asleep. Soon Naomi slept also. The unfallen stars of heaven shone calm and bright above their dreamless rest.

*   *   *

The ice beneath Jonathan's feet was dry with intense cold – never slippery with wetness as lowland ice could be. Nevertheless in places it was smooth and slick as polished marble – and in one such place he slipped and fell hard. He lay there, panting and wondering why he should ever get up. Ilohan, still wrapped in blankets, lay behind him. He had pulled him over the ice for an eternity of hopeless night. Jonathan wondered if Ilohan was dead, or if the blankets had kept him warm enough.

He knew that if he himself lay still, without the blankets, he would die in the bitter cold. Yet going on was so hard and painful, now, and there was no use in it: he would certainly die soon whether he slept or walked. He rolled over and looked into the black sky. Was he staring into an everlasting night, spared by some strange accident to be alive and awake after the destruction of the sun? The night seemed unreasonably long, but other nights had seemed so to him until at last the sun had brought the morning. He did not know why he still lived when the stars had fallen. He did not know why he should get up.

But he had made a vow. He was almost too tired to remember its content, but he knew he had vowed to keep going as long as life remained in him. If he had lost everything except the bare call to keep on, to that at least he must cling with all the force of his iron will: it was the last thing he had in the dying, killing world. He must go on. He must get up.

But he was weary. He could barely shiver any more, despite the cold. Strange, nonsensical images passed before his closed eyes. His thought drifted from his control, not from cold as in the black lake, but from pure exhaustion. He tried to put forth all his strength. "I must get up. I must get up. Get up!"

He struggled up to a kneeling position on the ice. It seemed impossible to go on, but he knew it was not. He put his right foot on the ice, so he was kneeling on his left knee only. Every movement took an act of will. He stood in one motion and took a step. He stumbled and fell back on the ice. He felt a weary anger at his weakness. He knew the strength to go on was still in him, if he could but call it out. All he had to do was try again, more carefully and slowly, and soon he would be walking on again, dragging Ilohan behind him.

Dragging him for what? To live now, and die a little later? And he was so heavy... Jonathan's mind wandered again, and his will did not call it back. He saw strange places, and labored at strange tasks. The weary dreams brought peace, but also a feeling that all that had value was now lost to him. Something heavy touched his leg, and he came to agonizing remembrance of where he was.

"Jonathan!" There was terror in the voice. "Jonathan, wake up! Can you hear me?"

He groaned. "Yes, Ilohan. I failed you..."

"No, you did not. You have saved my life. Have you dragged me? Do not answer; I can see you have. Get into these blankets."

He felt Ilohan trying to wrap the blankets around him, but the young knight could not manage his weight. "No. You are not strong enough," said Jonathan.

"I must have strength, for you have spent yours for me. Now help me with these blankets."

Jonathan did help him: his will was too weary to resist. The last thing he remembered before falling asleep was a dim grayness all around.

Having finished wrapping blankets around Jonathan, Ilohan stood up to see what the world was like after the Skyfall. He saw the mountains around them lit with a cold gray dawn, very faint, as though light itself were frozen. Here was a light that did not dazzle: one thing to look at that held no terror. Soft, gray dawn. Dawn after the end of the world. Dawn without the sun? No, dawn through clouds. Clouds... Clouds that would, blowing in from the east in darkness, look like the utter blackness of the void holding sway where the stars had fallen.

Ilohan raised his face to the cold, third mountain far ahead, then to the sky above. Despite their situation, triumph was ringing in his heart: the triumph of one to whom the very heavens are restored, when he had thought they were lost forever. "They have not fallen!" he cried, his voice ringing through the eerie hills of ice. "Praise God! They have not fallen! And now I ask... I ask, oh God, that we also may not fall!"

Then he was walking on, pulling Jonathan behind him. His rest had given him new strength, and the blacksmith slid heavily but smoothly over the ice. The gray dawn brightened slowly, and the third mountain stood out clearly far ahead.

Jonathan had not lost their way in the dark. Ilohan was cold, and tired, but he was neither frozen nor exhausted, and as he kept on across the wild, white ice, he almost began to hope.

*   *   *

Tulbur stood upon the battlements of Aaronkal with a few knights about him. A cool, wet wind, heavy with the threat of rain, blew in their faces. The sky was gray and overcast.

"So, the stars fell last night," said Tulbur. "The sun appears to have risen, and the world is still solid beneath our feet. The prophecy has not been fulfilled, yet you ask me to be afraid?" There was a mocking tone in his voice.

"The Books of the Travelers say that at the end of the world, the stars will fall from the sky," said Sir Idranak. "It was not the stars of the heavens that fell last night, for at the end they were still shining. But things like stars fell, in great numbers. Not the oldest of our people has seen such a thing, nor is it written in our histories. Do you not think this a mighty sign, worthy of study and concern?"

"It is a curiosity to those who study the heavens," said Tulbur, "not to us who plan the policies of earth."

"You did not see these stars, Sir Steward," said Sir Nildra, "If you had, you would not so lightly dismiss them. Have you seen a hailstorm?"

"Once, far up in the valley of Petrag in autumn, I was hit by a few small pieces," said Tulbur.

"That is not what I mean by a hailstorm," said Nildra, "You have never seen a real one. But have you ever held a torch when snow was falling heavily?"

Tulbur smiled strangely, as if he was remembering something far more significant to him than a mere snowfall.

115

"Yes," he said. "The snow melted when it struck the torch, yet the torch did not go out."

"Did you not see the snow flakes, score on score and thousand on thousand, glistening in the light of your torch, like stars against the black night as they fell?" asked Nildra.

"Do they fall like that?" asked Tulbur. "I did not look at them. I saw King Konder, riding on his great horse with Prince Thomas on another beside him, while I stood in the icy slush holding a torch."

"You are not wise to brush off our warning, Sir Steward," said Idranak. "Imagine the stars of the heavens, and stars brighter than any in the heavens, falling like snowflakes lit by a torch, falling from the sky in scores and thousands, while the people cry, wail, run, pray, or faint beneath them. That is not something to be ignored. And the stars came from the east, like the armies of Norkath."

"But the torch still shone," said Tulbur dreamily, staring off into the rainy sky. "The torch still shone, and the snow was powerless to extinguish it. It fell away to nothing in the heat. So with the falling stars. The earth remains, and still wise men shall rule it. Will you breakfast with me?" The knights were silenced. They followed Tulbur down to breakfast. During the meal the steward made plans for a grand address to calm the people, to assure them that the stars meant nothing.

*   *   *

Far away on a well trodden path in Karolan, Joseph the shepherd rode on toward Aaronkal. He had paid little heed to the star-storm. The cataclysm in his own life was greater to him than anything short of the destruction of the very earth beneath his feet. He had left Naomi, and gone to war, and if the stars fell he cared little, so long as they destroyed not the earth where she lived. He had not slept much, starting out as soon as the cries about the star-storm woke him. His weariness dulled his capacity for worry and wonder, if it did not dull his pain.

Far behind him Barnabas also rode, musing what it might have meant. He had seen early that the stars of the firmament were not dropping, and though his heart had thrilled with terror, it had also lifted with awe in the heavenly wonder. Seen through the branches of trees, with the smells and sounds of a peaceful forest all around, the star-storm had not wielded the same overwhelming terror that it had in open fields – or upon the unearthly heights of the mountains. Barnabas had prayed calmly through the storm, for those whom it would terrify, for the protection of those he loved, and for Karolan's rescue.

Chapter 7

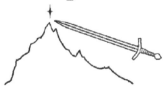

Failure at the World's End

ILOHAN'S PACE WAS ONLY A SLOW WALK, BUT considering the circumstances he was grateful to be moving at all. He dared not stop to rest and eat, but he snatched a bite now and then from a loaf of bread in his hand. Jonathan, wrapped in blankets, slid along the ice behind him.

The third mountain still seemed impossibly high and distant, but it loomed noticeably larger than the previous day. The smooth gray cloud cover remained, softening the glory and terror of the mountain world a little by its diffuse light. Nevertheless, when Ilohan paused to gather ice chips for their water-skins, the lonely terror of the landscape struck him with force. A feeling that it was preposterous and unnatural for him even to be there assailed him. He was a man, in a place of ice and stone where men could not live – an awesome place meant for angels alone. But it had been his duty to come here, to try to help Karolan at any cost. At least, he had thought it was his duty.

He shivered as he chipped at the ice with his sword: the warmth of his walking was deserting him. He looked all around, seeing in every direction the terrible mountain peaks, majestic and aloof. Did God intend him to be here? The very sight of those mountains seemed to call it into question. "Father," he said, "I have been sure you meant me to make this attempt. If I have been wrong, forgive me. If I have been right, sustain me. Do with me as you will. Yet save Jonathan, I pray, and let him wed Naomi in a world at peace."

He knelt wearily to pick up the ice chips and put them in the skins, to melt slowly with the heat of his body. A glorious wave of certainty washed over him. He had been led to come here, and had obeyed. The thoughts that told him otherwise were lies. This place might be the home and realm of mightier beings, but he, now, was meant to try to cross it. He had little hope of success, but he had confidence that he was right to try. That was enough.

Jonathan stirred, pulled blankets aside, and sat up. "You have dragged me," he said. "Your strength was greater than I guessed, and I have been a fool. I have betrayed your trust."

"You have proven thrice worthy of it, my friend," said Ilohan, continuing wearily to gather ice. "What ails you, that you say you have betrayed me?"

"I have betrayed you, and myself, and all who thought I would be true. I gave up, before my strength had failed. I did not keep on. I lay down on the ice and gave us both up for dead. There was nothing left to me but going on, and I did not go on. Now it seems the world has not ended, but I have lost everything. I have lost my honor."

Ilohan straightened and stared at Jonathan. "How can you say that?" he asked. "You pulled me up the Cliffs of Doom. It was I who fell asleep beneath the star-storm, I who surrendered to awe and fear. You stirred yourself to go on, and saved me from freezing. At last your strength failed – you collapsed and slept. But you had done enough. I was rested: I awoke and carried on. You have done me no harm, and great good."

"It was only by your chance awaking that my error did not kill us," said Jonathan. "My strength had not failed – it was there, if only I had called it out by force of will. And I did not. I did not even rouse myself to try to wake you. No words you say will change the evil I have done."

"Jonathan, you speak like a fool! Any other man would have given up long before. It was only natural that your strength should fail at last. You say it did not fail – but what, then, do you mean by its failing?"

"I mean death," said Jonathan. "As long as I have life, I must not abandon my duty. I have, and have lost everything."

"Would it have been better for me if you had kept walking until you died? Then I would have lost my friend, and you could not help me with the rest of this hard journey."

"Whatever followed does not justify my choice. I should at least have tried to wake you."

Ilohan paused in gathering the ice chips, and put a loaf of bread into the blacksmith's hands. "Eat, and do not despair," he said. "I need time to think."

He thought, and shivered, while he filled the last of their water skins. "Jonathan," he said at last, "do you know what it means to be forgiven?"

"That God does not hold your wrong against you?" asked Jonathan.

"Yes. And to be true to him, you must also cease to hold it against yourself. Now, if indeed you have wronged me, I forgive you. And you must accept that your guilt is gone, and our friendship unbroken. If you do not, you are not being true to me."

"There is no God," said Jonathan, "and I do not think I believe in forgiveness either. The mountains and the cliffs do not forgive: one error, and we die. Is forgiveness in the nature of the world?"

"Yes," said Ilohan. "Do your father and mother remember against you every hurt that you have ever caused them? Does Naomi?"

"No."

"Then let it be, and carry on, my friend. This adventure is too harsh already. Do not let needless sorrow make it harsher. We have no strength to spare for such things."

"So be it," said Jonathan. "I will carry on now, at least, and not worsen my crime."

He stood, rolled up the blankets, and put them in his pack. They trudged forward together. Jonathan came to understand that it was the clouds advancing in the night that had made it seem the stars were disappearing. The storm of flying stars, though a great wonder, had not meant the world was ending. Jonathan also considered what Ilohan had said. He still felt that he had lost his honor – that he had lost everything. Yet perhaps he could be forgiven; perhaps the word 'forgiveness' had real meaning. His crime began to loom less large in his mind, and gradually a resolution came to him. He would never do such a thing again. He would rather die, if there was no other way, than give up and thereby fail a friend. His one failure would be buried in faithfulness, and would matter little. He could still live, and would, and he would never fail again.

They trudged on together, cold, sore, and weary, until the day began to darken to a cloudy dusk. The third mountain loomed ahead, majestic and forbidding, but still some distance away. It faded slowly into the darkening sky, until it was only a faint black outline. Jonathan asked Ilohan to wrap himself in blankets and be dragged, but he refused, saying he would not be able to sleep, and should keep walking.

Despite their deep weariness they found they could make better speed than on their first day in the white wildness. Ilohan's feet burned and ached, simultaneously sore and numb. Still he kept tossing one out in front of the other, and still they carried him on at a good pace. The two adventurers often saved each other from stumbling, or pulled one another onward in turn. Ilohan knew that without Jonathan beside him he would have given up and died. Jonathan knew that if he had been dragging Ilohan, he would have had to wake him.

The night seemed to last forever. Both adventurers hovered near a delirium of pure exhaustion. The fleeting, mocking visions that had troubled Jonathan before came back to him even while he walked, and fighting them drained his energy. Ilohan also fought to turn his thoughts from evil and irrational paths. The strange wars were hard and long. Always there was the harder, longer reality of the impossible quest hovering behind all dreams and delusions. Still they trudged onward.

The desire to lie down and sleep was intense, overwhelming. No fear of death was strong enough to defeat it. Ilohan felt that it was by the power of God alone that he did not yield, but kept walking. He wondered what it was that kept Jonathan from giving up. He longed to accept his old offer – to lie down on the blankets and be dragged – but he knew Jonathan was too weary to pull him now.

The night was starless, and even to their dark-accustomed eyes the mountain appeared only as the merest outline against the sky. The whole world seemed empty: a void of shapeless cloud, of harsh and lightless land. Only their own bodies seemed real: the unrelenting soreness, the familiar friction of their clothes, the constant motion of their legs. Still they urged each other on, and somehow did not give up.

Ilohan prayed desperately for help, too weary to form coherent sentences. He thought of Eleanor, and the life and beauty of Ceramir, now left so far behind them. He thought of Veril, and longed for just one look at her face. He thought of Thomas and Kindrach, their faithfulness and heroism. He thought of soft blue skies and trees blown in the wind, of sunshine on warm grass and rivers gurgling as they flowed. He kept walking.

Jonathan turned his mind from the endless sequence of aching steps to think of valiant fights, and of the heroic battle he hoped to have a part in at the journey's end. The war song of Karolan passed through his mind again and again, falling in with the rhythm of his walking, slightly changed to fit the situation:

Against the host of Dradrag
Our fathers stood alone.
Their valor was unneeded;
But we shall conquer stone.

And though now soon in battle
Our banner must be flown,
Stands Karolan forever;
And two shall conquer stone.

Against love, joy, and freedom
The gauntlet has been thrown.
Fight on, fight on together;
And we shall conquer stone.

From the one who weeds the barley
To the king upon his throne,
We walk in honest freedom
And two shall conquer stone

So you who come in conquest
Of a land never your own.
Tremble before our banners;
For we can conquer stone

The words cheered him. He enjoyed thus boldly defying both Norkath and the mountains. Yet still each step took effort, and his aching muscles rebelled against the continual order to keep on. He thought of his father's strength and faithfulness, of his skill, and all that he had taught him. He wondered if they might fight together, side by side against the might of Norkath, wielding their swords at last in deadly earnest. He knew he would soon recover from his weariness, if only they could get through the mountains. Would Ilohan recover so easily? The prince's great goal of bringing hope by his presence would be much hampered if he were sick or weak. "My own strength should be spent for his," thought Jonathan, "yet it has not been: I have failed him. And though I hold true now, will I in truth have strength enough?"

Ilohan stumbled, and Jonathan pulled him up. "Can you go on?" he asked.

"I must," gasped Ilohan, and struggled onward.

Ilohan stumbled often after that, and Jonathan had to help him along without receiving much help in return. The prince was simply too exhausted to keep walking. Jonathan went carefully and slowly, knowing how discouraging it was to collapse on the ice and have to struggle up again to carry on.

Ilohan leaned on him heavily, but Jonathan still marveled at the prince's strength of will, at the fact that he was keeping on at all.

"Your strength has always been less than my own," said Jonathan. "The strength of your body, I mean. But your will is like iron."

"It is upheld by God," said Ilohan. "I understand King Thomas better now, I think. But I am sorry that once again you must bear my weight."

They walked on in silence for a while, both breathing hard. Like a prisoner on trial, Jonathan felt a judgment gradually building against him in his mind: duty was condemning him to pain. He welcomed it. "Ilohan," he said. "You must let me pull you. You cannot carry on, and we cannot both sleep at once. We would freeze."

"No, even you are too exhausted," panted Ilohan.

"You mistrust me where I failed before," said Jonathan. "That is just and prudent. However, if you do not sleep and let me drag you, you will force yourself onward until you die. The hope of Karolan will die with you. You must trust me in this, though I am not worthy."

"I do not mistrust you," said Ilohan. "I do not mistrust you at all."

"Then do as I say. I can pull you."

"You will not kill yourself?" asked Ilohan, panting hard as he struggled to keep walking. "You are exhausted too."

"I will not drive myself to death, I swear it. If I must, I will wake you."

"Very well then," said Ilohan. "I thank you, true friend."

Ilohan lay gratefully on the blankets, and Jonathan wrapped them tightly around him. He spent precious moments in the cold tying ropes that would allow him to pull Ilohan more easily. Despite numb fingers trembling with weariness, he finished this at last. He set off across the ice. His toes, as well as his fingers, had been numb so long he scarcely remembered what it was like to feel them. The sky above held no hint of a star.

The knowledge that he was helping Ilohan when help was greatly needed gave him strength. Even when he had only been helping Ilohan walk, he had felt stronger in the knowledge that the burden was coming to rest on him alone. Yet the night seemed endless.

He was cold. Cold seemed slowly to be overcoming the heat of his walking; slowly sinking into him to weaken and to kill. He tried to walk faster, but his sore legs would not keep up the pace, and his lungs felt scorched by the harsh, dry air. He pulled bread out of his pack and ate it slowly. It was frozen, but when it thawed in his mouth it tasted good, reminding him of sunshine on windblown wheat, and of his mother baking far away in Glen Carrah. The food, and the thoughts, brought warmth.

He realized that he could not run: he was too tired and stiff. The thought bothered him intensely. He had always been fast, and rejoiced in running. And was it now impossible? Of course. Long ages ago in this starless night, he had already been almost too weary to carry on. It was a wonder that he could pull Ilohan at a walk. Of course he could not run. It was no cause for dismay: if he ever reached a place where he could sleep in warmth, he soon would run again.

Yet he could not shake off the annoying thought, and he was too tired to fight it. He was not content to reason that if he survived the mountains he would soon be able to run again. He, Jonathan of Glen Carrah, should always be able to run. That he could not was intolerable.

He tried again to turn his mind from this. He looked at the black sky, and gazed long and hard ahead to make out the faint outline of the third mountain. It towered very high in his sight now. Hopeful dreams ran wild, and told him that the ice was sloping upward, that he was already climbing the mountain's feet. His set himself to find if this were true or false, and after a long moment of concentrated attention he decided there was no reason to believe it. The eerie land of ice had far too many sudden dips and hummocks; he could discern no general slope in the deep darkness.

Suddenly he found himself running. He scarcely remembered making a conscious choice to try, but somehow he had tried. He almost laughed as he ran. He was stiff and sore and slow, hardly lifting his feet as he stumbled along, pulled backward by Ilohan's dragging weight. It was a miserable parody of his smooth, leaping stride in Glen Carrah, but he was running! It was not impossible: the utmost effort of his will, spurred on by his intense desire to prove himself not crippled, was enough. He stopped soon, gasping and panting as hard as he ever had in his life. The fire in his lungs was terrible. He threw a scarf across his mouth, spat into it and put his hands over it, trying anything to warm or moisten the harsh air he had to breathe.

The panting died down until he was breathing no faster than had been usual with him on this plain of ice above the world. He coughed a few times, but the burning of his lungs soon subsided. Then he noticed that his legs no longer ached. It was like a miracle, and he felt as if he were reborn with fresh new limbs to replace the old and sore ones. He was still weak and weary, but the new-found comfort greatly cheered him.

He walked on into the freezing darkness, and his soreness gradually came back. His weariness was dull and deep. It threatened to close over him like cold, black water. He tried everything he could think of, every trick of mind and will, to stay awake. He fixed his mind on Naomi, and his heart cried out for her and for his home. Yet thoughts of her were too much like lovely dreams. His mind wandered, and his vivid memories seemed to beckon him to step effortlessly into a dream world, and not fight on to reach her in the world that was real.

He fixed his attention on the crunching of his feet on ice, trying to listen carefully to each step. What did they sound like? Not like a sword on a sharpening stone, not like the frosty grass of Carrah beneath his feet. Not like footsteps on gravel, or sandy rock. He gave up. Like so much in this incomparable, harsh and majestic land, the sound of his weary footsteps was like nothing else he knew. And he would like to lie down on that ice, and sleep. And though he would never consent to that, soon it would be out of his control. He would sleep on his feet, and fall on the ice unwillingly to freeze and die.

"No!" he said aloud, his voice sounding harsh and weary. "No! Anything else." He thought desperately what else he might do to keep awake. He consciously turned his mind to think about his pain, the aching soreness of his body. This proved a dreadful sort of success. Thinking about his hurt increased it, and pain lifted him away from sleep. He walked on, in misery. He clenched his teeth, that he might not moan with every step.

This wretched method of staying awake carried him on a long way, but like all weapons against weariness it failed at last. The thought came to him that he must run again, that only that would keep him from sleeping on his feet. He fought the idea, remembering the pain that running had cost him before. It seemed impossible that he could command himself to do it.

He trudged on, fighting the inward battle with his thought and with the weariness that dragged him down toward sleep. Finally he was sure that he must try to run, and with an agonized wonder he realized that he would. He picked up his feet as he had before and lunged forward. He ran three steps, then his feet slid from beneath him and he fell hard.

The nightmare that had proven false before was true now. He could not run. He raised himself painfully on his elbows and looked ahead. He could see nothing but blackness. The fall had knocked the breath out of his lungs, and he lay gasping on the ice for some time. Still he could see nothing ahead of him, not the slightest trace of the third mountain, or of any light from anywhere. "A star... Only one star..." he thought, suddenly wishing he could pray. But it was no use to say words to a God who was not; only Jonathan could save Jonathan now. But Jonathan was weary and sore and bruised, and lay on the brutal ice unable even to breathe. Perhaps he could save no one. He longed desperately for some help from somewhere.

His breathing came a little easier. He turned his head listlessly toward the east, and gazed intently into the darkness. The faint outline of the mountain wall appeared, half seen, very slightly blacker than the black void of the sky. He felt chilled, soon to be frozen, almost too tired to move. Then he saw a point of light above the mountains. He blinked wearily and shook his head, sure it was a dream, but it did not vanish. It brightened to a brilliant, yellow-white star, so bright it cast his shadow dim and sharp upon the ice. "The star..." he whispered. It was the Morning Star, seen through a break in the clouds. It was the emblem of hope: hope that dawn will come.

He found that he was standing on his feet again. He could not see the third mountain ahead, only blackness, but as long as the Morning Star shone on his right he knew that he was going north, toward the mountain. He felt that he had to lift his feet higher than he should at each step. He wondered if this had been true for a long time, but he was too tired reason it out.

The Morning Star soon faded, covered again by clouds. Now he could see nothing. He trudged on, too tired to make a decision what to do. Suddenly, he felt that there was a solid object ahead of him – whether he had seen a vague glimpse of it in the darkness or sensed it in some other way he did not know. He moved forward cautiously, and bumped his chin against a rough edge. He touched it with his gloved hand. It was hard and unyielding, and seemed to grip the glove as ice would not. He took off his glove, and hit the object with his numb, bare hand. It was as cold as ice, but in some indefinable way it did not seem like ice.

Somehow he became certain it was rock. He put his glove back on, and ducked down to go underneath the edge. His feet slid out in front of him. His mind had just formed the thought, "crevasse!" when he struck something solid ahead. Ilohan, wrapped in blankets, slid against him. The prince was still asleep, or dead. The air was still and the place seemed sheltered. They had slid down several paces. Jonathan felt around, and decided they must be in a sort of slot between the overhanging rock above and the ice below. He was lying where he had slid, resting against the back or bottom of the slanting slot. There was hardly enough distance between rock and ice to crawl.

Fighting one last battle against sleep, he unwrapped the blankets from Ilohan, and used them and the packs to make a warm, tight shelter surrounding himself and Ilohan at the back of the slot. He pulled the blankets over them. No wind could reach them, and the air soon became warm with their breathing. Surrendering to weariness at last, he fell asleep as one falls off a mighty cliff. Flying down through the clouds of dreams and delusions, he sank into a dreamless darkness and oblivion that he needed more than anything else on earth.

*   *   *

Jonathan awoke to see dim light shining through the cocoon of blankets that surrounded him and Ilohan. He was not truly warm, but he could feel his hands and feet. The ferocious cold outside could not penetrate the defenses he had found and made: the sheltered slot between rock and ice, the rampart of their packs, the wrapped blankets and furs that surrounded them. Jonathan felt comfortable – and realized suddenly that he had almost believed he would never be comfortable again. It had been hard to remember, while trudging over the bitter ice, that comfort even existed. It was good to be reminded. He drifted back to sleep, and awoke again in darkness.

He was more alert this time, and though he was still intensely delighted with the mere fact of comfort, he knew he must soon leave it. Ilohan shifted beside him, and then the prince's voice came through the darkness: "You have proven faithful, my friend. Where are we?"

"We are somewhere on the way to the third mountain," said Jonathan. "We may be quite close to it, but I do not know. We have slept a long time. Do you feel able to set out again?"

"Yes, of course," said Ilohan. "I am able to set out, to begin another march. But to finish, to come to the end of this journey... that is what seems impossible. This third mountain must be so high..."

"Try still to hope," said Jonathan. "I do not say my own hope never wavers, for it is founded on my strength and my will, which have both failed once already on this journey. Yet I do believe we will reach Karolan – and I will see you crowned as king, my friend."

"Perhaps," said Ilohan. "Brogal said something like that at the cliffs – that just because we cannot imagine a thing does not make it impossible. If we keep trying, the impossible might happen, with the blessing of God. But death is all I can imagine, and I am sorry that my choice to come here has imperiled your life also."

"You will not die, Prince Ilohan, and neither will I. If you take no comfort in my hope, think of the prayers that you believe God hears. What is Lady Eleanor doing at this moment? Or even Veril?"

There was a long silence. Then Ilohan sighed. "They are praying. But still I do not know."

"Then do you think Karolan will fall to Norkath? Can you believe your God would permit it?"

"I belong to my God," said Ilohan, "but he does not belong to me. I do not understand him. He lets many terrible things happen in this world, but at the end of the world I believe it will be seen that he worked good through all of them, and that evil injured only itself."

"That does not make sense. Do you think Karolan will fall, or not? Are you willing to leave off assuming you will die, or not?"

"God can save Karolan without me – or let her fall and yet watch over his people in her. But yet I pray..." he paused for a long time, and when he began again Jonathan was surprised to hear tears in his voice, "I pray that God will at least save your Naomi, and bring you back to her. But let us cease to speak of this. I cannot force my heart to hope, but I will carry on as steadily as if I had hope – to the last."

Jonathan shifted in his blanket. The little space around them had grown wonderfully warm. Jonathan slid his hand out into the cold, and brought in frozen bread from one of the packs. "We can eat while we talk," he said.

But for a long time they ate in silence. They had to gnaw at the frozen loaves to get off small bites at first, but at last the bread thawed in their hands, and they devoured it.

At last Jonathan spoke again. "Though my hope is strong, I have often thought on this journey of Eleanor's words: 'Those days shattered her. They broke her, spirit, mind, and body, as she had not known she could be broken.' I have wondered if I – or you – could be broken thus. I have thought such a thing impossible, and still I wonder, but not without fear."

"Do you remember Eleanor's vow to try with all she had to save her life, and mine?" asked Ilohan. "I think the time has come to make a similar vow ourselves, a promise to uphold us and force us on. For we climb now toward the highest pass, and into bitter cold that will kill us if we rest."

"Is not such a vow made implicitly with our every step?" asked Jonathan. "And even if it were not, I did make a vow in words as we climbed to the pass above the Cliffs of Doom. I broke it once, but never will again – though I will speak the words aloud for you, if it would help you trust me."

"You have never failed me, Jonathan. I trust you absolutely."

"What did you mean, then? Need we any other vow?"

"Father," prayed Ilohan, "I ask you to give me strength, and keep me true. Do not let me fail in this mission, or relinquish the life you gave me, until the utmost of my self is spent for you. May I try to the very last to save Jonathan's life, to save my own, and to reach the people of Karolan to bring them hope. Father, I scarcely dare to ask this, so undeserving am I beside my mother, but I ask that neither I nor Jonathan will be shattered as she was. I ask that Jonathan will come safe into Karolan, to wed Naomi in a land at peace. As for me, do with me as you will. I can say no more, for my own hopes and desires fly wild as fallen leaves, before the winds of this life you have given me."

"I promise," said Jonathan, "that if your life, or mine, is lost it will be after I have done my utmost, using every strength I have, to save it. I promise that if I die it will be because I had no strength left to live, and that if you die it will be because I had no strength left to save you. Yet I am sure that we will live, and go to fight in the war that rescues Karolan. So let it be. My promise has been made."

"And my prayer spoken. Let us go. We will not sleep again before the pass."

They crawled shivering into the moonlight and the bitter wind. They destroyed the lovely shelter Jonathan had made, rolling up the blankets and shouldering the packs. Before them stood the third mountain in terrible majesty. They were at its feet: the ice around them was already sloping upward. They threw back their heads to look at its peak, a moonlit point of stone far up among the brilliant stars. To their left the half-moon was sinking over the western mountains.

"The peak after the Cliffs of Doom was a small rock above the plain of ice," said Jonathan. "This is a mountain."

"Stand at the foot of the third mountain, and see despair," said Ilohan. "How can we ever climb it? Yet we will try."

As they set out together up the icy slope, Ilohan thought he heard a phrase whispered on the howling wind. He looked at Jonathan questioningly, but said nothing. Yet when he gazed again at the awesome mountain, his heart leaped with some of Jonathan's own adventure-joy, carried by the half-heard words: "And two shall conquer stone."

They walked in silence, breathing hard, up an ever-steepening sheet of ice. The plain fell away below them. They felt dizzy with the unimagined height: they were climbing from a world above the clouds to one among the stars. Soon they were using their swords as walking sticks, to stab into the ice and help them up the mountainside. The wind grew stronger and colder with every upward step. Snow blown up from the icy slope stung them like frozen sand.

The moon set and left them alone with the stars. Ilohan felt that the refreshment of his long rest was fading fast. He thought of the promise he and Jonathan had made, and of what it might cost them to carry on to the very end of their strength. Yet he felt little fear. The plague had taught him much about pain. One could bear it, trusting in God, one moment at a time. One could believe even while it burned that life was a blessing and that God was doing his good work. Ilohan was not disciplined or faithful enough always to do these things, but merely knowing they were possible brought him strength. He was glad of Jonathan's companionship. The third mountain showed in vast, black silhouette against the brilliant beauty of the stars, and they tried to bear westward, toward the unseen pass.

As time went on they breathed faster and climbed slower. Ilohan wondered if the pass lay so high that men could not stand there and live. Would their breath come harder and harder until they had to pant merely to stay still – until they died of cold? But he turned his mind from these speculations to the mere task of keeping on.

The howling wind blew these words to Jonathan, whispered into its power: "Though he slay me, yet will I trust him." Jonathan looked intently at Ilohan, sure he must have spoken them. The prince was climbing steadily on, his eyes lifted to the stars just above the mountain peak. Jonathan smiled. Though God was not real or powerful, Ilohan's faith was both, he thought. He would always respect those who had faith in God, even while he considered them foolish, founding their lives on a lying dream. He gazed for himself at the stars blazing above the hard blackness of the peak. He also had faith – a faith with power – and his faith was true. He had faltered once, but he never would again.

The night slipped on: long, long ages of windswept darkness, while the stars wheeled silently by the mighty peak ahead. The air kept growing harder to breathe, but somehow they were no longer getting slower: they had settled into a dull rhythm in which they held the same weary pace hour after hour. At last the Morning Star rose brilliantly on their right: a sudden, unlooked-for wonder. The clear, blue dawn flooded the east soon after it.

The two adventurers paused a moment, looking at the dawn, and then pressed onward lest they freeze. The light revealed a world of bewildering beauty higher and more unearthly than anything they had seen before. Far, far below them was the vast icy plain that they had crossed. In the dawn twilight it looked blue rather than white. The hills and hummocks that had been huge and eerie when they walked among them were invisible now, and the plain seemed almost smooth. At its edges the mountains towered, immensely far away in every direction. They appeared small, but no one looking at them could have doubted that they were great beyond imagining. They were piercingly clear despite their distance: wild pinnacles of stone and ice against the morning sky. Ahead there was only the one great peak they climbed – except that now, high up in the west, a new mountain had come into view. Only a sliver of it was visible above the mighty flank of their own mountain, but it was the first indication of what they sought: the pass must go between that new mountain and the one on which they stood. It seemed impossibly high and distant, lost in a fairyland of sunlit ice and dark blue sky.

"Everything is so far away," said Jonathan. "We are alone on a tower of ice, climbing up above the frozen sky."

"It is so beautiful," panted Ilohan hoarsely. "Jonathan," his voice was clearer now, and louder, "it is a place of splendid beauty... This place that is killing us..."

"Yes," said Jonathan. "Few ever see it." He paused a moment, gaining breath to continue. "Yet we have, and shall live." He would speak thus, he thought, in defiance of the mountain, as long as he had breath. They turned to the slope and struggled on again, always tending westward.

Their breath became so short that it was nearly impossible to eat. If they stopped to rest, they might get down small bites between their panting breaths – but they could not stand still long without freezing. They could not eat while climbing, so desperately did they need each breath. Finally Jonathan tried biting off small morsels and swallowing them in one breathless gulp. This worked for Ilohan as well. Thus they slowly assuaged their fierce hunger, and struggled on toward the distant pass – the pass where, according to the Zarnith poem, they might stand among the stars, and die.

Chapter 8

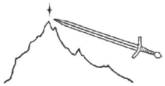

Pass Among the Stars

BARNABAS RODE INTO AARONKAL IN THE BRIGHT morning. The autumn sun was warmer here, the sky a paler blue, than at his home in Glen Carrah. He thought of kind, soft autumn days with Hannah, as he came around the last grove of old oaks and into view of the great castle.

Those thoughts soon left his mind. Thousands of men, and hundreds of horses and tents, covered the wide field before the castle. Many banners waved above the army, bright in the morning sun. Each one bore the beautiful symbol of Karolan: the Stone, Sword, and Star. The blacksmith's heart leaped at the sight, for he remembered the splendid courage of the men who had fought beside him, beneath those banners, many years before.

But he suddenly realized that something was wrong with this army. The men did not lack courage, but they lacked something. They lacked hope, hearty camaraderie, the sense of being one body under one leader, ready to dare and die together. They were not sure of one another, or of fighting bravely. And Barnabas knew that what they lacked was essential.

But then he doubted. Could he know so much merely by looking at a great army from a short distance? Could he guess thus the thoughts and concerns of so many hearts? Or had his misgiving no more substance than the shadow of a cloud? He did not know. He rode on, slowly, singing the anthem of Karolan in a low voice.

He was cheered by the sight of the guards, standing smartly, spears upright, on either side of the road in front of him. They saluted as he neared, and he acknowledged their welcome. Yet suddenly, just before he passed them, the spears tilted forward across the way. "Halt!" said one of the guards. "Do you come in obedience to the king's command?"

"I do," said Barnabas. "I come to defend my home, and the realm of my king."

"You have taken time to gather weapons, however, contrary to the order of King Thomas. Or is that not a sword at your side, and near a dozen more hilts within that bag? The penalty for such disobedience is imprisonment until the army marches out to fight."

"I am a blacksmith, a maker of swords. The king ordered these. I did not gather them with loss of time, I merely snatched them up and brought them to arm true men who fight for home and kingdom. I have been loyal to my king in this, as in all things before it."

The guards crossed their spears over the road. "The order held no exception for swordsmiths. No man was to bring a weapon, for the armories of Aaronkal are enough for all. You are guilty of disobedience and presumption."

Barnabas turned his horse side on to the guards, wondering what to do. He wanted to demand that they hear reason, and so escape the humiliation of imprisonment. Yet he was confused, and did not know how far the foolishness might extend. "Will you unjustly disgrace a loyal soldier of Karolan?" he asked.

"We will punish the disobedient and arrogant," said the guard.

"I have been neither. Is there no man of honest justice to whom I can appeal?"

"None but the steward, and he is too busy to hear such petty matters."

Barnabas was on the point of saying, "The king I fought for would have heard me," but he closed his mouth. He would not argue more: that would only dishonor him, since the guards had already settled the matter against him and would not listen. "I will go with you then," he said. "The war will prove my loyalty."

He dismounted, and the blankness of his face did not reveal his inward fight with anger and with shame. He followed the guard to his prison, which was a small room made of logs, situated a short distance from the south wall of the castle. Before they reached it Joseph ran up to them. His face showed clearly, to his friend Barnabas at least, his grief at leaving Naomi, and his brave struggle to bear it.

"Guard," said Joseph, "what has this man done, that you lead him to prison?"

"He has gathered swords and brought them here, in violation of the king's command," replied the guard, without slowing down.

"There is no more loyal warrior in the realm," said Joseph, "nor any braver or more honest. If you imprison him, you do a very foolish thing, and hurt the cause of Karolan. I am a truthful man, though not a brave one, and all I tell you is true. If it had not been for this man, I myself would have stayed in Glen Carrah, and never come here to fight for Karolan."

"The disloyal will be punished," said the guard.

"True loyalty is not blind slavery," said Joseph.

The guard made no answer, but, as they had reached the prison, he flung Barnabas inside and closed the door. Joseph thought that the blacksmith could have caught the guard in the very act of pushing him into the prison, and thrown him onto the roof. Yet there was Barnabas, standing quietly inside the log-frame jail, while the guard marched back to his duties.

Barnabas inspected the structure carefully. "Quite sturdy," he said quietly. "It may even be that I could not break it. But Hannah would do better work."

"Barnabas, my friend," said Joseph, going up to the log bars, "has the world gone mad?"

Barnabas looked seriously at Joseph. "I do not know," he said. "Something is far amiss here, I think. Yet, though the injustice of this is great, it is a small thing. If I am freed to fight, and not mistreated, all may yet be well."

"It is horrible that you are disgraced thus," said Joseph.

Barnabas saw the pain in his face. "Do not concern yourself for me, true friend," he said. "I will not be cast down by any disgrace that I have not deserved. Now go; do not stay here and be seen deploring my fate."

"Do you ask me to go?"

"I do; in love for you I ask it."

"Farewell, then," said Joseph. "I go unwillingly. May justice triumph soon."

He walked away, and Barnabas sat down against the prison wall. The unjust disgrace stung him more than he had let Joseph see. The truthful boasts that he had never spoken, except once to Hannah, passed through his mind. "I carried a wounded man on the retreat from Guldorak," he thought. "I fought side by side with the king in our rear guard at Dilgarel.

And now I come to this." He shook his head and stood up again. "I must not be cast down," he said. "I told Joseph I would not be."

Meanwhile, Joseph had returned to his place in the great army. He lay still there, on a blanket near his horse. The days since he had left Naomi had scarcely seemed real. All his feelings and thoughts were overwhelmed and dulled by the single, relentless ache in his heart. He had been faithful. So far. But had he any power now to serve still further? What good had he done if, in leaving his home, he had expended all the strength he had to serve or fight?

He closed his eyes, and the sunshine was warm. His ears were near the ground, and he could hear the motion of many horses: near and far, fast and slow, small and large. A measure of comfort and of peace came to him as he lay there, amid the sunshine and the footsteps of the horses.

*   *   *

The sun arced up into the sky over Jonathan and Ilohan, blazing down without warmth and reflecting dazzlingly off the ice. The earth was too bright, the blue-black sky too dark. Squinting weary eyes against the sun and wind, the adventurers climbed onward, still tending toward the west where they must find a pass, or die. The ice grew steeper. It came to Jonathan's weary mind that the pass must go over a ridge or steep saddle connecting the two mountains, and that the slope up to it would be nearly a cliff. The sun passed its peak and sank down toward the west.

Scenes of stupendous beauty blazed around them and beneath them, but they were dully focused on the next step, and the next, in an endless sequence. They began to see rock coming through the ice, and they were occasionally forced to clamber over an outcrop of stone. The dark colors of the rock were a relief to their eyes after the painful brightness of the snow. Nothing could be a relief to their exhausted limbs, except the sleep they must not have. The slope grew steeper, and they climbed wearily on, now using both hands and feet. Each movement required a conscious act of will.

The sun set behind the western mountains, and the dimming of the light was good. Yet with the twilight came deeper cold, until they wondered if they would freeze while climbing. Jonathan thought back to the time, down on the plain, when he had proven he could run. It seemed to him that then he had been a child. The moon, a bright gibbous now, showed them where to place their hands and feet.

Everything in Ilohan's mind sank beneath the ceaseless struggle to keep on. He ceased to think of Karolan, the pass, or the mountains, and his whole world became one aching body and the next foothold or handhold in the moonlit stone. He struggled not to lose even that awareness. He knew Jonathan climbed beside him, and the vague awareness of his presence was a blessing. In the war with pain and weariness he had forgotten why they climbed, but he had not forgotten that they must keep on. They would keep on together to the last. Their vow, his prayer, still stood. God would hold to him even if he could not hold to God.

Jonathan, too, could scarcely think of anything except the rocky slope he was climbing, and the ways he must force his aching body still to move. Yet now and then he looked over at the high, bright moon, slowly moving westward with the stars. It was not an encouraging sight, but he kept on looking. He had seen the moon so often before, and nothing else within his vision was familiar. It was harder and brighter here, but not so different from the moon of Glen Carrah, which now Naomi might be watching.

Ilohan hardly knew why he kept on, or by what will his limbs kept moving. He felt his own will far too weak and weary to push him on through such pain and deep exhaustion. It had to be God, he thought: he lived and breathed, and kept climbing only because of God. Weary as he was, he felt a sense of wonder at the thought. "By the grace of God alone," he whispered. Then he looked down in sudden surprise at his hands. He was looking down, straight down – not forward. His gloved hands were resting on level ice. They had reached the top of the slope at last.

Ilohan looked ahead. The horizon was only a few paces in front of him. Jonathan's voice called, "Keep on! We have reached the pass!" Then somehow he found he was on his feet, staggering toward the horizon beside his friend. The majestic peak of the third mountain soared into the moonlight on their right. The other mountain, lower but still tremendous, towered on their left. The moonlit snowfield that lay between them and the horizon grew larger as they tried to stagger across it. Ilohan wondered if they would ever reach a point where they could look down into Karolan, or whether they would fall down and die here, almost within sight of home.

The horizon was twenty paces away, a rounded ridge of moonlit snow. Ilohan kept on: one, two, three paces, each one an agony in his soreness and exhaustion. Then suddenly the horizon was immeasurably distant, and the brilliant stars dropped into haze somewhere, immensely far away, over an invisible dark land. That land was Karolan. With Jonathan he struggled slowly up to the edge. An ice slope fell away steeply toward the moonlit mountain land far, far below. They collapsed together on the ice, and lay there, gasping in the harsh, cold air. The stars shone piercingly clear all around.

"We are near the peak," whispered Jonathan hoarsely between breaths. "Not much still above us."

"Yet still so high..." gasped Ilohan. "Stand at the pass... Stand among the stars and..."

"And live," whispered Jonathan defiantly, though even he wondered how they could, "for two have conquered stone."

"No... Not yet... But still must try..."

Jonathan sat up, realizing dimly that they were very close to freezing, though they had been there only a moment. His own mind recited the true version of the Zarnith line that described their position, as he tried to open his pack: "Stand at the pass among the stars, and die." Despite the moon in the west, the stars were bright almost all the way down to the horizon. It seemed there were stars even below them, brilliant with the fearful clearness of the air. The dark, impossibly distant north horizon might be Karolan, but it appeared only as blackness. They were still in a frozen world amid the terrible glory of the stars. And they were close to death. Very, very close.

A blanket flapped in the wind and rustled harshly on the ice as Jonathan pulled it from the pack. He sat on it and wrapped it around him. The wind seemed to pass through it unhindered. He thought of Eleanor's miner, frozen on the peak of Vykadrak, frozen above the world in a place of stupendous glory like this one. He almost would not mind dying here, if he could without breaking his vow: if his strength was truly gone. It was a place of wonder that few had ever seen. And he did not think he had the strength to stand.

His gaze fixed on the north horizon. That hazy, distant horizon. That other world, unseen, and only guessed at. "Naomi. Glen Carrah. Life, love, joy, peace. To die here... No!

Not yet!" He was on his knees, tearing blankets out of their packs. He fought the wind to lay them all together, and with a terrible effort rolled Ilohan onto them. He sat on the blankets beside him, and pulled the cloth around them. He lay there, panting desperately. Still the wind came through. He could not walk. They were freezing. "Glen Carrah. Mother... Father... The forge. The grass. The sweet, soft snow in winter. That snow... Mother... Sledding high up in the glen... Sledding..."

The outer blanket, the one he had laid against the snow, was smooth, slick leather. It would slide. With both hands, and all the strength he could muster, he pushed back against the snow. They slid toward the brink, and tipped downward. Jonathan pulled the blankets as tight as he could around himself and around Ilohan's unconscious form.

They slid down the steep slope, gathering speed. Soon they were flying faster than a galloping horse. The tremendous wind of their going blasted in Jonathan's face. He squinted into the gale, looking out for rocks that could kill them in one terrible instant. He saw none. He found he could steer a little by shifting his weight in the blankets. There was no way he could stop. He was so tired... Yet he must not sleep. The moon was low over the mountains to the west. If it set they would be hurtling along completely blind.

It felt to him like a wild dream. He had only a little control, and he was so tired he thought he might fall asleep at any moment. He saw a huge rock outcrop far ahead, but by leaning as far as he could to one side, he was just able to avoid it. They struck a place of bumpy ice that pummeled them terribly as they flew across it. For a long time the great mountain's flank was smooth, with only shallow ridges where rock never peeped through the snow. They sailed over these ridges, or flew down long shallow valleys between them. The character of the mountain changed as they got lower, but still all was covered in ice and snow. They rushed through great frozen valleys, over snow as soft as silk and ice as hard as rock. They flew over breathless horizons and banked against steep ridges covered in snow.

They were sailing down a deep, wide valley of moonlit snow, when Jonathan suddenly realized that they were slowing down: the slope was getting shallower. He wondered if they would stop altogether, for he knew that unlike a real sled, the soft blankets would not keep sliding unless the slope was fairly steep. Then he saw a horizon ahead, and knew the slope must steepen dramatically there. He thought of trying to stop them, but he was too weary. They slid over the brink.

It was not a cliff, but it was the steepest slope they had come to yet. They sped up until Jonathan wondered why they did not leave the mountainside and fly. He squinted desperately ahead, trying to tell what they were hurtling toward. He did not see any rocks in their path, but there seemed to be a broad line of black at the foot of the slope. He stared hard, forcing his weary, wind whipped eyes to see what was there in the moonlight. Suddenly he realized. It was a great chasm, a tremendous crack in the ground. The slope became a little shallower just before the crack, but that would not be nearly enough to stop them. There was only one thing to do. He clung to the thought of Naomi, and the knowledge of his vow, and with what seemed surely the last effort of his will, he did it.

He released his grip on one side of the blankets, and put all his strength and weight into a mighty tug on the other side. The blankets ripped away from beneath him and Ilohan, and they tumbled free on the steep snow. For a moment the world seemed only a whirlwind of flying whiteness, hard impacts, and spinning stars. Then Jonathan was lying still on his back on the slope, looking up at the mountain stars. The moon was just slipping behind stone peaks in the west. The blankets were still clenched in his hands: he had not forgotten it would be death to lose them. He rolled over and sat up slowly. There was a dark bundle on the snow about thirty paces away: Ilohan. Jonathan crawled slowly over to him. The journey seemed to take ages.

But he was not hurt, as far as Jonathan could tell – only unconscious, as he had been ever since the pass. Jonathan would have tried to rouse him, tried to make sure he truly was unharmed, but life was quickly becoming a waking dream for him. In moments he would be too tired to think at all. He dug a shallow depression in the snow, wrapped all the blankets around them both, and was instantly asleep.

Jonathan awoke, cold but not frozen, to see the morning star shining bright above the mountains to the east. He crawled, pulling Ilohan after him, until they reached an outcrop of rock nearer to the chasm. A great black boulder leaned against it on the eastern side, making a natural shelter from the wind. Jonathan barricaded it with their packs and swaddled himself and Ilohan in blankets just as he had done before. As he drifted off to sleep there, Jonathan wondered wearily why they had not frozen earlier, sleeping as they had on the open mountainside. The answer came to him. They had slid down so far that they had reached a warmer land: still bitterly cold, but not cold enough to reach through their furs and blankets and kill them while they slept. He smiled in the darkness. They had conquered stone. They would make it into Karolan.

*   *   *

148

Ilohan awoke. Dim light filtered through the blankets around him. He felt cold, tired, and very hungry, but otherwise unhurt. Too weary to think about much beyond his hunger, he pulled aside the blankets over his head, reached into his pack for bread, and then re-formed their shelter as best he could. He ate hungrily for some time, took a long drink of barely-melted ice from a water skin, and fell back asleep.

Sometime later hunger woke Jonathan. He considered hazily whether they should get up and continue on, but the extreme weariness he felt decided him against it. He too ate and drank, and went back to sleep.

At dusk they both woke up together. "You tumbled hard on the snow," said Jonathan when he realized Ilohan was awake. "Are you hurt? Can you move your hands and feet?"

"Yes," said Ilohan, "I am unhurt, but very hungry."

They ate again together. Jonathan was shocked at how tired he still felt. Despite this, he said, "We must go now. No one can tell how soon Fingar will attack."

Ilohan was silent for a long time, and Jonathan could tell he was thinking hard, perhaps praying. At last he took a deep breath, and spoke. "I cannot go on yet. If in truth we have a hope of reaching Karolan, we must come there with some strength left. I will have none, if we go now. I do not say this lightly."

"We have not far to go," said Jonathan. "We are at the edge of the chasm Mudien spoke of, but one day's journey from Petrag. Knowing that, do you still say we should not go yet?" Ilohan gave no answer, until Jonathan turned and saw that he was asleep. "I did not understand his weariness," he thought. He lay down himself, and soon slept also.

*   *   *

Metherka lay by the fire outside his tent at Aaronkal. A man on horseback came slowly up to the fire and dismounted. Metherka looked up, but did not otherwise move. "What news?" he asked.

"Little," said the messenger. "The moat is being filled as you ordered. The portcullis is beyond repair, and no smith can be found to remake it. We are making a gate of oak logs, and filling every vessel in the keep with water. We have also a large supply of food, and some arrows. The men are lining the battlements with large rocks."

"I thank you," said Metherka. "Return to Castle Metherka, and bring me word again at evening tomorrow – unless we are attacked before that. Tell the men to wall off the gate with stone, if that can be. Logs will burn despite your water if there is a siege."

"It shall be done, Sir," said the messenger. He mounted the horse, and rode off into the night. Metherka lay still, staring at the ever moving flames of the fire. He spoke, alone, his lips barely moving. "Easy prey to Norkath..."

He heard slow footsteps on the grass beside him, and looked up. Britheldore stood there. He wore gauntlets, and his sword was at his side. Metherka sat up, and would have risen, but the older knight motioned him down and took a seat beside him, leaning against a pile of firewood. They stared at the fire in silence for a long moment.

"I was wrong," said Metherka at last. "I was wrong to let him have it so easily."

Britheldore said nothing. Metherka went on. "It is true that I am careless and lazy. I have not ordered my affairs as befits a Knight of Karolan. But I could have made our soldiers love me."

"As they never will the steward." Britheldore's voice was gruff and slow in the firelit darkness.

"No. They will never love him. Their heads are hung like dogs already beaten."

"Do not despair," said Britheldore.

"You think there is hope, then?" asked Metherka.

"No. Not of victory. But do not despair of yourself."

"When I dashed the last hope of Karolan? What is there to do but despair? I have made nothing but mistakes all my life, and this last one cost an endless price."

"All sins cost that. But despair also is evil. Do what is best now."

"That is hard."

"You must do it."

"I am fortifying my castle."

"That is good," said Britheldore, "but who can be spared as a garrison?"

"Five soldiers, two butlers, and a scullery maid."

Britheldore laughed, a strong, gruff sound that rolled off into the night, that seemed to carry the old knight's crusty courage. He laid a strong, gloved hand on Metherka's shoulder. "Do not despair," he said again. "Even now we know not what may come." He stood up slowly, saluted Metherka, and strode off into the darkness. His first few steps were slow, but after that there was little sign of stiffness in his gait.

Chapter 9

The Miners of Petrag

ILOHAN AWOKE FROM DREAMLESS SLEEP IN EARLY DAWN. "I can move today," he said, "so today we must go down."

"Good, you are awake," said Jonathan. "I have been lying here thinking for some time. Let us hurry: perhaps we can reach Karolan today."

Ilohan rose slowly, pulling the blanket above them aside. The third mountain, lit by cold twilight, towered before him. Seen from the other side. He was struck dumb with wonder.

"What happened?" he finally asked. "What did you do?"

"I wrapped us in blankets, and pushed us off the edge of the pass," said Jonathan. "We slid down two day's journey in a part of a night."

"Thank God," said Ilohan. He fell down on his knees. "We will make Karolan. Thank God. And thank you, faithful friend, who dared so much when my strength was too little and I slept."

"It is only what any true friend must do."

"And I would thank any true friend. But friends as faithful as you are seldom to be found, even in all the great tales of the world." They packed up their blankets, ate another meal of bread and cheese, and stood up to continue on their way – but their way, of course, was blocked.

The view from their shelter looked east, and the great crack stretched out as far as their eyes could see in that direction: a staggering black rift in a land of snow. "Where is the bridge of the Zarnith poem?" asked Jonathan. "I see no sign of it."

"Nor I," said Ilohan, wearily. "Perhaps if we climb this outcrop of rock we may see it."

The view when they had climbed up was breathtaking, and not only in the direction of the crack. Behind them, the staggering rampart of the mountains blotted out the sky: an impassible wall of black stone and white snow – over which, nonetheless, they had passed. Ahead of them, beyond the chasm, there was more ice and snow, with a range of rocky hills poking through like broken teeth. But of course it was the crack itself that held their gaze. It yawned at the foot of the outcrop on which they stood: incredibly wide, sheer-sided as the Cliffs of Doom, dropping off into darkness.

Presently Jonathan stepped back from the windblown brink. He did not do this from fear of falling so much as from a stranger motive. He tried to name it, but could hardly do so. It seemed a mix between the hypnotic attraction of the immeasurable black gulf, the fear that he would leap into it – and the weirder, less earthly fear of what might come out of it. Though a frail bridge did span the crack, starting almost at their feet, Jonathan could not think of crossing it yet. As the Zarnith poem had said, he and Ilohan stood at the brink of doom, and knew wonder.

"It is like a gulf dropping into the Abyss of night," said Ilohan, "from which things both forgotten and condemned might crawl." He paused. "Yet they cannot. I know that they cannot."

"I feel the same," said Jonathan, "though I could not find the words. But you are right: they cannot. Our feelings in this mean nothing. No place in the world is evil but for men who make it so, and no men have lived here. And there is the bridge, which we must cross."

"Yes," said Ilohan.

They had not seen it from their resting place only because the outcrop had blocked their view. Its thick ropes swept down and then up in huge curves, anchored by massive rocks on the farther side. Smaller cross-ropes held them together, and planks made a walkway broad enough for two to go abreast. Great skill had crafted the bridge in centuries past – but now it was fearful. Frayed cross-ropes dangled in the wind. Broken planks hung at odd angles, and gaps in the walkway opened on black void.

"No men have lived here," said Ilohan. "But they must have come here – unless indeed the Wyrkriy built the bridge."

"Surely that is only a legend of the Zarnith, as Mudien thought," said Jonathan.

"I do not believe it either," said Ilohan, "though when I look at this bridge, in this place, I confess it seems nothing but probable."

"You mean this looks like the kind of bridge demons would make?" asked Jonathan.

"Yes," said Ilohan. "It looks like a bridge made by the Wyrkriy, intended for mortals' doom, not their aid. But this is only foolishness. Demons are in the world, as told in the Books of the Travelers, but they are not like the Wyrkriy, and they do not build bridges. Though the bridge looks dreadful, I think it is only a bridge, not a curse."

Ilohan and Jonathan descended wordlessly to the place where the bridge was anchored to two great boulders the size of houses. Four ropes spanning the whole crack formed its main structure: two higher, like handrails, and two lower, undergirding the plank walkway. Thick as a strong man's arm, the ropes seemed likely to hold even though they were frayed and worn.

Jonathan took a deep breath and set out across the bridge, his hands on the two higher ropes. The planks were thick wood, black with age. They seemed sturdy under his feet. Through the gaps left by missing planks he could see the sides of the chasm in the morning twilight, narrowing down to an unseen bottom. Though he knew he could die on those rocks, he was comforted by the sight. They were not the Abyss. He tried not to look farther out, where in the depths the rock walls still faded into utter blackness. Since he trusted the planks, he found it easy to step or jump over the gaps, his hands still riding over the ropes, just in case.

"The planks are sound," he called back to Ilohan. "I am sure we can cross."

Ilohan still stood on the rock, his hands at the start of the handrails, frozen. The unearthly fear of the Abyss had left him, but he was consumed with pure vertigo. He could not walk across that bridge. He wondered why not. He had climbed the Cliffs of Doom. How was this bridge worse?

"I am sure it will hold both of us," said Jonathan.

Ilohan could not go out on it. It was impossible. But Jonathan – and duty – called him forward. What could he do? "This must not be," he thought fiercely. "I cannot be held back thus. Father," he prayed, "what shall I do?"

His trembling eased, for he had an answer. He put his right foot on the first plank. "I trust," he said. "I trust. I must. I will." His hands shook, but he walked steadily, without a tremor. He tried to think only of the planks, of moving his feet from one to another. The effort helped, though he could not avoid seeing the gulf below him through gaps where the planks were broken or missing. The upper part of the chasm walls showed clearly: patterned with jagged outcrops and ledges, beautiful with the subtly changing colors of the rock. But as the sheer walls dropped off into the depths, they vanished into impenetrable, inky darkness. They sloped a little toward each other as they went down, but Ilohan could see no hint of their meeting. The chasm seemed bottomless. As he got farther out, he felt the bridge rock and sway in an icy wind that blew along the rift and wailed over the long ropes. Again and again he whispered, "I trust. I trust. I trust..."

Then he was on the far side, kneeling on the broken rock, trembling and thanking God, while Jonathan stood still beside him. They had made it. The Wyrkriy-bridge was passed. Finally Ilohan stood up. "I think we will reach Karolan," he said.

"It is a wonder," said Jonathan.

"Yet you scarcely ever doubted it," said Ilohan.

"I think it is a wonder still," said Jonathan. "It seems as if we ought to shout and sing."

"I do not feel like shouting," said Ilohan.

"Nor do I. There is still too much... Still too much ahead, unknown. We may have come to a conquered land."

"Let us go and see," said Ilohan. He set out toward the north, toward Karolan, and Jonathan followed.

"So he is indeed to be a prince," thought Jonathan. "We have triumphed. Perhaps we will soon be conquered, but we are victors now, and though he still cannot believe it, Ilohan is the Prince of Karolan. Prince, and worthy of it. He goes swiftly, though he is weary, and in his face there is no hint of fear." Jonathan remembered the moment in Ceramir when Ilohan and Eleanor had stood together, and he had known that, if necessary, he would die to save the prince's life. That was still true – it would always be true. He loved Ilohan as his friend, and as his prince, and he would love him as long as he lived.

They walked over the ice and down into a valley where a few stunted pines grew among piles of splintered stone and drifts of snow. Jonathan stared at the trees, feeling that he had been starving for the sight of green, and that his ravenous eyes were now devouring them. He breathed great breaths of cold air, slightly scented with pine, and it seemed to bring new life to his heart and limbs. The harsh, bitter air of the high mountains was left behind. He guessed that Ilohan felt the same way, for the prince was holding a pace that would have killed them both up in the mountains. Though his feet were sore, he delighted to fling them forward in a rapid stride, devouring the stony land, leaving farther and farther behind the mountains that had almost killed them.

They climbed the stony ridge beyond the valley, and began descending again through a forest of pines. The dark green branches, waving, sighing and creaking in the cold wind, spoke of the world below, the world of earth and growing things and the life and homes of men. Ilohan stumbled, and Jonathan was surprised, for the ground was even and the prince had not seemed exhausted. He stumbled again and fell to his knees, and then suddenly Jonathan understood.

"Lord God, I praise you for your mercy," said Ilohan, lifting his hands in worship. "I praise you for bringing us through the mountains. I praise you for the sweetness of this land, beyond my memory, and beyond all deserving. Truly you have made a home for man. Great is your mercy! Now I ask yet further: may this land still be free, and may the courage you give me and my people keep it so." Ilohan rose.

"I thank you, also," he said to Jonathan. "You are my friend and equal, and the preserver of my life. If Karolan is saved, your name will go down as long as records are kept as one of the heroes of the realm."

"As will yours," said Jonathan, and he drew his sword and saluted.

The swift march went on, through air that grew ever softer and less cold, and woods that grew higher and thicker. Presently they crossed a stone road, and while Ilohan went hurrying past it, Jonathan stood a moment in its center and called to him. "Prince Ilohan, surely this is the road to Luciyr, just above Petrag! We have come full circle!"

"So we have," said Ilohan, laughing and looking around at the tall pines, "and I remember thinking before that the forest was sparse here in the high foothills. What now shall we think of the lowland woods?"

"I do not know, but let us hurry to find out," said Jonathan.

They pressed on through the pinewoods, which were not yet thick enough to hinder them, and at last joined a small forest path that led, as near as they could tell, northeast toward Petrag. The trees as they descended did indeed seem astonishingly thick and high to them, comforting and rich with life. It was evening when they came out suddenly through a gap in the forest, and the great stone valley of Petrag lay before them. They had come to Karolan, and Aaronkal lay only a day's fast ride ahead.

The cloudy twilight was falling softly on the hard stone when they reached the valley floor after a steep descent. The crude path that they were following wended its way over the uneven stone, tending ever north and down, toward Aaronkal, but also angling across the valley from the west side, where they had descended, toward the east. As they went, Jonathan thought of all the ways he had imagined they might arrive in Karolan. He had feared they might come in as Eleanor had, almost dead with pain and exhaustion, to be found and rescued by a farmer or a soldier. He had imagined them coming upon an army of either friends or foes. He had dreaded seeing the smoke of burning towns. But all these visions had been wrong: they came quietly and wearily into Petrag in the cloudy twilight of a late autumn day. There was no one to greet them, and the land seemed empty and at peace.

"We must get horses," said Ilohan, "fast ones, to ride to Aaronkal tonight – or tomorrow, if the moonlight will not serve for a swift journey. Castle Byinkal is near, and there may still be horses in its stables."

"I counsel you to take up your crown, Prince Ilohan," said Jonathan.

Ilohan moved with a slowness that was more than merely weariness as he took off his pack and knelt beside it. "It is very strange..." he said. "You are right, but I can hardly believe... my crown..." He dug through blankets and stale food to the very bottom of the pack, and reverently lifted out something wrapped in a heavy cloth.

He unwrapped the cloth, and brought the crown out into the light. Yet then he stared, not at the crown, but at the cloth. It was the banner of Karolan: the Stone, Sword, and Star. Where the star of Karolan appeared on the great banner, diamonds set in gold were worked into the cloth. "A royal banner!" said Jonathan. "I have never seen one, but my father spoke – just once – of how the diamonds would flash in the sun, and men would cry out, 'The star! The star!' and fight with new courage."

"Yes," said Ilohan quietly. "It is a royal banner. The wisdom of Eleanor – and Thomas – guides us still. But as we have no staff, we cannot raise this standard yet."

Prince Ilohan folded the banner and put it away, but placed the crown upon his head. The gold and jewels were dull beneath the cloudy sky, and he who wore them was weary, yet still what Auria had seen in him so long before was intensified: Ilohan of Karolan had the bearing of a prince. He had passed through pain without breaking faith. He had faced terror, and carried on in spite of it, trusting God. Ceramir, too, had left its blessing upon him: he still had many fears, but he was not dismayed. He and Jonathan continued down the stony path toward Byinkal.

The sun broke through the overcast far down in the west behind the walls of the Valley of Petrag, lighting the undersides of the clouds with a rosy glow, warm and kind as nothing in the mountain world had been. The jewels of Ilohan's crown gleamed softly, and Castle Byinkal loomed forth out of the stony twilight in front of them.

Jonathan looked up at it, and the vision seemed to strike down into his heart. It stood like a symbol of all indomitable courage and heroism, a tall fortress on a rocky crag, weathered, battlemented, impregnable. He had seen castles only twice before, in childhood, for there had been none on the high road to Luciyr. Now all the stories he had ever heard of epic battles in the great history of Karolan rushed through his memory like a mighty wind. All doubt vanished from his mind: Fingar would die. Karolan would stand.

To Ilohan, raised in Aaronkal from infancy, there was little awe in Byinkal. Its major fault was that it could not be used to seal off enemy access to the mines. Except for that it was a good fortress, built on a bedrock outcrop, with short but sheer cliffs leading up to it on three sides. It had no moat, but there was a steep rock gorge before it, crossed only by a narrow drawbridge. The drawbridge was down now, and he could see two human figures standing side by side upon it. They turned to each other and passionately embraced.

That action seemed suddenly to give meaning to the whole picture, so that Ilohan saw it for the first time: On the high drawbridge before a castle, in a mighty land of stone, two lovers embraced while the last red glow of sunset enfolded them. The vision seemed flawless, a sacred thing he must not interrupt. But he must approach, must speak and act, for the man and woman, the castle, and the whole land were in peril.

The lovers stayed in each other's arms as Ilohan and Jonathan walked to the bridge. Soon Ilohan could see that the man was tall, brown haired and strong, and the young woman's hair gleamed golden in the light. They looked up suddenly and parted at the sound of footsteps, then stood together, holding hands. Her beauty was very great.

"I grieve that we disturbed you, friends," said Ilohan, "but we have come a long way, and we need aid and news."

The man and woman stood absolutely still for a moment, and then knelt down on the bridge. "Pardon our discourtesy, Your Majesty," said the man. "We could not believe at first, but indeed you have come beyond hope!"

"Rise, friends," said Ilohan, "and tell me from whom I received so good a greeting. I have come to fight beside my people, and I pray I do not come too late."

"I am Yalron the miner, and this woman, newly my wife, is Therinil. By command of the steward and of Joseph the master of Petrag, I have been spared from the muster at Aaronkal. However, we are wholly at Your Majesty's command."

"I thank you," said Ilohan, "and I confirm the order by which the steward spared you. But tell me, what news is there of Fingar."

"His invasion is hourly expected," said Yalron. "It may have come already, but I doubt it: we have had no word, and there has been no sign of burning in the northeast."

"May I ask a question, Your Majesty?" asked Therinil.

"Yes indeed," said Ilohan smiling, "you can speak freely: your love and joy and loyalty are better than all the great manners of Aaronkal."

"I thank you," said Therinil, "and I ask how you have come here. The steward said you could not come before the war."

"For love of his people, the prince dared the great mountains," said Jonathan. "We have crossed them on foot where Dradrag failed. Last night we slept upon their icy feet. At dawn we crossed a dreadful chasm on a hanging bridge of four great ropes, and have walked swiftly all day to come here."

"It is true," said Ilohan. "When the kingdom is in peril, a prince should lead the army, if by any means he can – not straggle in to claim the throne after the battle is already won, or vanish into exile after it is lost. We attempted the mountains, and by the blessing of God we have crossed them, though indeed they are terrible. Death has been near us, and we are weary. But weary or not we must reach Aaronkal in haste, and therefore we need horses."

Yalron turned to look at the castle. "There may be horses there," he said, "but I think not: I think it is deserted. Five days ago many wagons came from Aaronkal, and all that they carried was brought into the castle. The men who brought it said the steward feared it would be necessary for the Army of All Karolan to retreat into Petrag, and so he filled Byinkal with the supplies and weapons they might need if the war went so ill. But they left no garrison."

"Yet we have horses at the mines," said Therinil. "They are bred in the high prairies west of Petrag, and they are fast and never stumble."

"I have no time to go back to the mines, unless it is the only way," said Ilohan.

"Your Majesty knows best," said Therinil, "but it is not far. I do not know where else you will find horses, and at the mines we would delight to give Your Majesty all the best we have."

"Your Majesty will not, surely, ride to Aaronkal tonight?" asked Yalron. "Thick clouds will shut out the moon, and the path is treacherous."

Ilohan stood silent a moment, staring absently at Yalron and Therinil. He noticed that Yalron had a strange expression on his face, and seemed to be counting on his fingers. "There is another reason, also, for Your Majesty to come to the mines and speak to Master Joseph," said Yalron presently. "I cannot say more here openly."

"Though I have wished to force on without rest before, I do not advise that now, Prince Ilohan," said Jonathan. "You know more of horses than I, but is it not possible that you could reach Aaronkal as early by leaving tomorrow and riding hard, as by leaving tonight to go slowly through the darkness? And the men of the Army of all Karolan must not think you exhausted when you stand before them."

"Every moment is precious, but I am indeed weary," said Ilohan. He was so weary that he knew the ride to Aaronkal would be a nightmare, and then he would have to speak words of courage and wisdom to the assembled thousands of Karolan. It seemed impossible. He felt he could collapse there on the drawbridge and sleep for days. He knew that seemingly impossible things could be, in reality, duties that must and could be done – but he prayed that this might not be such a duty, that the decision he was rapidly coming to might not be wrong. "I will come to the mines," he said. "But we must depart in the darkness before dawn."

Yalron and Therinil led them back toward the mountains. Ilohan and Jonathan looked in wonder at the huge, overhung cliff face that formed the back of the Valley of Petrag, and at the many dark holes that went into it: the mines of Karolan, from which came abundant riches of gold and iron. Some were far up in the cliff, reached by dizzying ladders. But what amazed the travelers more was the row of lighted windows in the cliff base, far to the right. They looked like the windows of a huge castle, but there was no building there: the windows were cut directly into the living rock.

Their guides brought them to a doorway that led into a large, pillared room, hewn from the rock and filled with tables. A fire burned on a wide hearth, and strong-looking men sat talking around some of the tables. Ilohan had only an instant to notice this, before Yalron said, "Behold, Prince Ilohan of Karolan, come beyond hope over the great mountains!" and after a brief, stunned silence, the room erupted with cheers.

Ilohan sat down with Jonathan in the midst of the commotion, a little dazed and very weary. Silver plates appeared before them, heaped with hot beef and pudding with gravy. They ate ravenously. The food was good, though simple, and after the mountain crossing it seemed an incomparable feast. When Ilohan had emptied his plate, a timid, awestruck young man appeared to refill it, and he found himself devouring almost all of the second large helping as well. At last he became aware that the room had filled with people, both men and women, and a gray-bearded man had stood to speak on a block of stone before the hearth. He was tall and straight, and he had a huge pickaxe which he sometimes leaned on and sometimes carelessly lifted in one strong hand.

"Men and women of Petrag," he said, "our prince has, by some wonder of courage and strength, crossed the mountains to come to Karolan in the time of her greatest need." There was more cheering, and Ilohan felt equal parts unbelieving, overjoyed, and embarrassed. The old man went on as soon as he could make himself heard. "We will, of course, provide the prince with the fastest horse in Petrag, and everything else we have that could help him. Yet it comes to me that we can do more than that. He is the prince, and thus can overrule the steward's order. If he wills, I say that every man of strength in Petrag shall take his horse and his axe, and ride with the prince to Aaronkal when morning comes."

There was another great burst of cheering, but some men were silent. Ilohan sat still for a moment, gathering his thoughts and his determination to do whatever he must do. He stood. "Men and women of Petrag," he said, "I thank you for your hospitality and your loyalty. And I thank you more than I can say for your willingness to ride with me to Aaronkal. I call a council, now, to consider what shall be done. I ask that whoever is a leader among you, or especially concerned by what is happening, join in this council to decide what we must do."

The room was silent. Ilohan's words had somehow conveyed the uncertainty and danger that still threatened Karolan, and sobered them all. The old man went quietly through the room, speaking to some of the men. He led the ones he had chosen out of the room, Ilohan and Jonathan following. They went through a dimly torch-lit underground passage and into a rough round cavern. The rock walls had been hewn so as to make a natural bench that encircled the room, offering ample seating for the old man, the five miners he had selected, and Ilohan and Jonathan.

"First," said Ilohan, "who are my counselors?"

"Joseph, master of Petrag," said the old man.

"Yalron, master rock-breaker," said Yalron.

"Sarag, gold miner."

"Verkal, iron miner."

"Petragal, hewer of passages."

"Dran, refiner of gold."

"All do everything as occasion requires," said Master Joseph, "but each has a task at which he is an expert."

"What was the steward's order?" asked Ilohan.

"That all the miners stay behind to guard the mines," said Joseph. "I would have questioned the messenger more strongly, save that ten of us were but newly married on the day he came, five days ago, and I grieved at the thought of their marching out to so desperate a war."

"Alas," said Ilohan, "I grieve too, for all who march out to this war. But I do not understand the steward's order. If Karolan falls, so will Petrag."

"Not easily," said Master Joseph, "but certainly it would after a long and bitter fight."

"Then surely the steward was mistaken," said Ilohan. "Surely it is best for us all to march to battle – save only the newly married, whom I, like Master Joseph, would excuse."

"I fear there can be no true exceptions in so desperate a war," said Yalron, "though I am among them."

"I, too, am among those newly married," said Petragal, "yet I think that justice and honor require me to go forth, and not let another take my place in defending her I love."

"I will not forbid a loyal man from going where his courage calls him," said Ilohan, "but before you choose finally to fight, remember that I wished to forbid it, and would have, had I not prized your freedom too highly."

"Our time is very short," said Jonathan. "The prince must sleep, and afterward ride to Aaronkal like the wind. Already eight days have passed, and Fingar was to attack in six."

"May I ask who you are, companion of the prince?" asked Joseph.

"I am Jonathan son of Barnabas, a blacksmith from Glen Carrah."

"He is trustworthy to the core," said Ilohan, "and has saved my life more times than I can say. He speaks the truth. Our choice is dire, and must be made quickly."

"Fingar may already be at the border," said Dran.

"Then why should the prince go to Aaronkal?" asked Yalron. "The army may already have marched out to meet Fingar."

"Yet if they have," said Ilohan, "I will not know where to find them."

"Scouts could be sent to the border," said Joseph. "On finding the army, they could ride back to Aaronkal and bring you word. Our horses are swift and do not easily stumble."

No one spoke for a long moment. The candles burned straight in the still, cool air of the cavern. Ilohan prayed silently and fervently for wisdom, overwhelmed by what he had to do. At last he spoke slowly, and all listened in silence. "I must lead the Army of all Karolan, if I can. If the army is not at Aaronkal, there will at least be those there who can tell me where it has gone. I will ride to Aaronkal. Since there is great need of haste, I will take your fastest horse, and go alone, departing before daybreak. To Jonathan I entrust all who wish to follow me: he must lead them to Aaronkal and hence to join the Army of all Karolan."

"It is the prince we wished to follow," said Petragal, "yet I, for one, will follow Jonathan of Carrah at His Majesty's command."

"But not willingly to Aaronkal," said Dran. "Your Majesty, here we are with fast horses, willing to serve you in any way, and shall we simply ride to Aaronkal? Will you not rather send us as scouts to the border, as Master Joseph said? We might find the steward and the Army of all Karolan – or the enemy – and ride like the wind to bring you news of them. But I beg you, do not merely bid us tag along to Aaronkal, last to muster to the great army."

"As scouts you will be in great peril," said Ilohan. "I would spare you this."

"Your Majesty's kindness makes me glad," said Joseph, "but my people do not want to be spared. Does Your Majesty not think scouts would be useful?"

Ilohan was silent again for a long while. "We know very little of what is passing," he said at last. "The steward may be at Aaronkal, or he may have led the army out to the border. He may have sent out scouts and raiding parties – as Fingar also may have done. We must learn of these things as swiftly as may be. Therefore if I send you out as scouts, you will indeed serve me – but the danger is great."

"If we encounter a Norkath raiding party, we must simply fly," said Dran. "We will have no weapons but pickaxes – but our horses will leave theirs in the dust. Our chief danger, with that of all Karolan, will come later, when we join the great army and battle begins in earnest."

"By then, I hope, you will at least have swords from the armories at Aaronkal," said Ilohan. "If you wish to go as scouts, I will send you. I commend your loyalty and courage."

"We need not wait to arm ourselves at Aaronkal," said Yalron. "Many weapons have been stored in Byinkal, and the castle is open."

"So it is decided," said Ilohan. "All who wish it among the men of Petrag shall ride to the border as scouts, armed with whatever weapons can be found at Byinkal. At the first sight of our army, or of Fingar's, you will dispatch messengers to me at Aaronkal, as swiftly as may be. Only one thing remains: choosing the leader of the scouts. I would have Jonathan lead them."

"As Petragal has said, it is Your Majesty we wish to follow," said Yalron. "Yet I think I speak for all in saying that if by following another we may serve you best, we will."

"Jonathan is my truest friend, whom I trust more than any other," said Ilohan. "He is bold, swift of thought, and swift to choose and act. You may follow him as you would follow me, and know I will approve of what he orders."

"Such praise is too much for me," said Jonathan. "But Prince Ilohan, though I too will obey you gladly, I confess I wished to ride to Aaronkal with you. Will you go alone, all unprotected?"

"It is thus that I can go most swiftly," said Ilohan. "And if I met Fingar or a Norkath raiding party, you could only die with me. So my choices are made. Now we must sleep."

"Your Majesty," said Joseph, "there is something I wish to show you before you sleep. Will you follow me, alone?"

"Is it of great importance that I see this before the war?" asked Ilohan.

"It is," said Joseph. He lifted a great stone slab that leant against the side of the cavern, revealing a small passage leading into darkness. Lighting a torch at one of the candles, he beckoned Ilohan to follow him.

Jonathan's hand went to his sword hilt. "Master Joseph, can you give us surety that this is not a trap?" he asked.

"If it were, we could hardly escape from it now," said Ilohan. "But the miners are trustworthy, and you are wrong to doubt them."

"I am sorry," said Jonathan.

"You are forgiven," said Joseph, "and it is good that the prince has so zealous a protector. He is in no danger from us, and any who would harm him are." Joseph bent down and squeezed into the passage. Ilohan followed him, and soon their light was lost in the darkness.

Jonathan turned to the other men. "Forgive my distrust," he said. "The strangeness of the action made me forget your obvious loyalty.

"We forgive you," said Yalron. "The miners are not strangers to times when distrust was wise and needful. Let me show you to a place for rest."

Yalron led him to a room with a large fire of coals, and small windows opening to the cloudy night, so that the air, though warm, was also fresh. He lay down by the fire, wrapped in a single blanket, and drifted toward sleep. But even as he slipped into dreams, he knew that Yalron and Therinil stood just beyond the windows, talking as they gazed out into the darkness over Karolan.

"I cannot acknowledge the rightness of this choice," said Therinil.

"And I cannot turn back from it," said Yalron. "Yet I can tell you that I love you more than I ever have before, and that leaving you will break my heart. I may soon return."

"Or never," said Therinil.

"Would you have me leave other men to fight for you?"

Therinil embraced him. "How I love you! I cannot let you go, and I will not hold you back. Your heart will not break alone. Oh, let it soon be mended! Yet I fear that will not be."

"As do I," said Yalron. "But know that, whole or broken, my heart is always yours."

"I thank you, Beloved," said Therinil. "Now let us speak of other things, and have one more night together – the sixth! How few they have been!"

"Yet more precious than the rarest diamonds of the earth, dear Therinil. Let us walk to Byinkal again." They went away, and Jonathan sank into dreamless sleep.

*   *   *

If Master Joseph had desired to trap the prince, he could have done so easily. He led Ilohan through a labyrinth of passages, and several times lifted aside a great stone that seemed, until he moved it, but a part of the rock wall. Finally one of these disclosed the hidden doorway of a room, and Joseph held up the torch to reveal its contents.

The room was small and perfectly square, hewn expertly from the native rock. Stacks of metal ingots filled the floor, rising as high as Ilohan's shoulder. They gleamed redly in the torchlight, and Ilohan, seeing them with his weary eyes, was not sure what metal it was. He reached forward and took hold of a bar, then strained to lift it. And he knew. It was solid gold.

Joseph was speaking to him, and he listened with an effort, trying to take the words into his weary mind. "Ten score and seven years it has been since Garthan the Vulture took Marie, daughter of Master Deran of Petrag, over the dead bodies of her father and brothers," said Joseph. "The Vulture dragged her to Aaronkal for his pleasure, and she was never seen again. When next Garthan sent a messenger to Petrag to collect payment of the mine-taxes, the messenger was shot with seventeen arrows and fell dead upon the stone. Garthan the Vulture then sent a band of soldiers against Petrag, but they found it impregnable and well-supplied, until one by one they fell to arrows from within.

"Corzogad, son of Garthan, was a good man who hated the Vulture's deeds. When Corzogad took the throne of Karolan, it was the will of the people of Petrag to pay the royal tax again.

All this matched what Ilohan had learned from the sages at Aaronkal. Of all the evil kings in Karolan's history, Garthan had been the worst: proud, lustful, clever, and cruel. He had made Aaronkal a place to be shunned. In his time the men of Petrag had boldly refused to pay the royal tax on their gold. King Corzogad, Garthan's successor, had hated his father's memory and tried to heal the harm he had caused.

"King Corzogad," continued Joseph, "believing that wealth had enabled his father's evil, refused the miners' offer. He decreed that Petrag need no longer pay any taxes to the king, forever. Yet we of Petrag did not forget the older commands, that the fourth part of all gold mined at Petrag is the king's by right. Our fathers swore an oath to abide by the order of Corzogad only until the seventh of his worthy successors took the throne. Through the ages between then and now, we have carefully set aside the king's portion as before. You are the seventh successor of Corzogad. You have proven worthy. All this is yours." There was a long silence, as Ilohan stood speechless, looking at the incalculable wealth before him.

"You may have heard the legend of this treasure," said Master Joseph. "To keep it safe against this day, we have denied it. But the legend was true. It is yours."

Ilohan suddenly forgot where he stood, and in his thoughts he was back on the Luciyr Road, before the mountains, before the plague, even before Eleanor. He had wanted then, passionately wanted, to find all who were sick or poor or hurting in the land, and bring them what help he could. He had wanted to see the joyful release that Tharral, Mer, and Jenn had known shining from a thousand careworn faces. In the untold riches that room contained, he saw a hope of fulfilling his old dream. He might be king, and he might have all this.

Then, as he reeled with the power of his thoughts, and reached out his hand to steady himself against the straight stone wall, he remembered the ten men, newly married, who would ride out to fight for him tomorrow. In his weariness his thoughts were strong and strange, and those ten men seemed to stand before him, with Jonathan and Naomi, Eleanor and Veril. "You cannot hold back our pain," they told him. "You cannot protect us from what we must do, and what we have had to do. It was our choice, and we had to make it. You are powerless."

They seemed a symbol of all whom he could never help, who for a thousand varied reasons would cut themselves off from his aid. They would make choices, both evil and good, that set them beyond the reach of his compassion. Even all the gold of Petrag, or the world, would not bring them back within it. There would be so many he could never help. Even if the war was won.

He hardly knew what nonsense he spoke to Master Joseph, and the walk back through the passages seemed like a waking dream. A phrase passed over and over through his weary mind, too tired to do anything but stupidly repeat it. It seemed to match itself to the rhythm of his walking, or his heartbeat: "The free cannot always be rescued, the free cannot always be rescued, the free cannot always be rescued..." He knew, with deep sorrow, that it was true. Yet... Yet sometimes they could be rescued, and he could try to... He could try to... But all he had to do now was sleep. He lay down beside Jonathan, and fell into oblivion.

Chapter 10

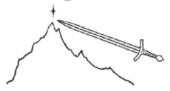

The Traitor and the Prince

A SENSE OF URGENCY CALLED ILOHAN OUT OF HIS dreamless sleep just before dawn. He rose with an effort, feeling that sleep still enwrapped him like a warm blanket, slowing his movements and dulling his senses. That blanket fell away rapidly as he remembered the wonder and terror of his position. He was the prince, coming to bring hope to a people at war, and lead them. Yet he was weak and weary, and might have come too late. He looked up to see Yalron leading out his horse, a majestic, black animal that moved like a shadow in the pre-dawn darkness.

"I thank you," said Ilohan. "You are loyal and generous far beyond your duty."

"Yet not beyond the calling of our hearts," said Yalron. "God go with you, Prince."

"I trust that he will," said Ilohan.

Something flapped above Ilohan, dark against the stars. "Your royal standard now has a staff, Your Majesty," said Jonathan, handing it to him. "Hold it high as you ride, that all the people may see it."

"I thank you, faithful friend, and more than faithful friend. You need use no royal titles to one you dragged across a frozen wasteland above the world."

"Ilohan, then," said Jonathan earnestly, "I wish you would not ride alone. Remember that there is treachery afoot."

"At Ceramir you said yourself that if the traitors strike again they will come with overwhelming force," said Ilohan. "Do not seek to protect me when no safety can be found. But what traitor will watch my road today? All will think I cannot be in Karolan. Or have you forgotten that when we crossed the great mountains, we did what was impossible?"

"Even so, I wish I were going with you."

"I could wish that too," said Ilohan. "I have no friend like you in all the world. But for this very reason I want you at the head of the scouts of Petrag, on whom my safety and that of all Karolan may hang. And maybe we will stand together again in the end, you and I."

"This parting puts a deep foreboding in my heart, but I yield to your reasons, and your will," said Jonathan. "Look out for archers, for if you see them far away you may evade them. The love of a brother goes with you. Would the God you trust were real, that he might guard you!"

"He is and will, best of friends. Farewell!"

"Farewell!"

A hint of gray dawn was already in the sky. Ilohan strapped the banner to his saddle and spurred his horse forward. Its hooves struck clattering thunder from the stony path. The royal standard snapped in the wind of his going, and the Morning Star blazed furiously in the east, just above the rock walls of the Valley of Petrag. The stars faded as the twilight arose blue and clear. The hard rock valley widened around him. The great horse of Petrag never stumbled, though the path was treacherous with sudden drops and flanked by jagged boulders.

That was an unforgettable dawn. It seemed to Ilohan to be the beginning of a new world, a world he had believed would never be. The rock ramparts of Petrag showed dark against a sky that brightened with every moment. The zenith took on a lovely autumnal blue, sweet and soft after the terrible skies Ilohan had seen in the high mountains. Rosy light crept down the western wall of the valley, until the sun burst over the eastward hills like a trumpet blast and fell full upon him as he rode. His horse's mane glowed richly as it tossed and blew in the wind of their going.

In bright mid-morning Ilohan rode out through the mouth of Petrag, where the great stone ramparts ended suddenly in high cliffs, and the land opened into a wide wilderness of gravel and hardy grass. As he galloped down through this, he could see the beginnings of a sweet land of meadows, woods, and farms not far ahead. He anxiously scanned the blue sky for the smoke of plunder and burning, but it was clean.

He rode at a thundering gallop down the stone path through the woods, lowering his banner that it might not strike overhanging branches, exulting in the strength of his horse. He came to higher trees and deeper forest, where the shade was cool and he could see clear brooks flowing. He could not hear them over the thunder of his horse's hooves.

Presently he rode out into a space of farms and meadows. Here harvested fields predominated, separated by copses and fencerows of trees. And here it first happened: something for which he was completely unprepared. It was not what he had feared: the clamor of soldiers, the screams of peasants, the little farmhouses collapsing in flames. Women and children of Karolan indeed came running out from their homes, in fear at the sound of galloping hooves – but then they saw his banner and his crown. Instead of screaming in terror, they filled the air with their cheers.

He could not name the feelings in his heart when he heard them. They shouted and danced, and wept, and fell to their knees in the fields. He was overwhelmed by the depth of their wonder and their joy. "The prince, the prince!" they cried, calling to one another as though they had not all seen. "The prince has come!"

Young mothers took their children in their arms and ran up to the road to see him. Girls milking cows or feeding chickens dropped their work and ran, as fast as they could, across the stubble fields to get a better look. Ilohan saw them all, and knew that he was truly bringing them hope. And yet, as he heard their cheers and saw their tears of joy, he wondered whether it was right that they should greet him with such unrestrained exultation. He was but a man, a stumbling Knight of Karolan, no better than they – not an angel bringing awesome miracles of rescue and protection. And yet they cried, and cheered, and clapped, as though he were an immortal hero who could destroy the army of Norkath with one sweep of a flaming sword. "Save these people, and teach them wisdom, oh God," he said quietly as he rode. "Do not let their hope be disappointed, but let them know that indeed it is only you who save."

Yet he knew it was right that they should have joy, and he knew the mountain journey had been worth all its cost. He held high the banner of the Stone, Sword, and Star, and waved it to his people as he passed, and the crown of Ilohan son of Kindrach, Prince of Karolan, flashed in the morning sun.

*　　　　　　*　　　　　　*

An arrow whistled shrilly through the cold air in Petrag. It shone against the sky as it reached the peak of its flight, and then arced down to land with a sharp clatter on the distant rocks. "So," said Jonathan, who had shot it, "are we all armed?"

"We are!" called many voices. Jonathan looked behind him. More than ten score of miners, mounted on their great, black horses, stood about on the stony ground, ready to ride. All held great longbows, and quivers filled with arrows. They had found them wrapped in canvas within the deserted castle of Byinkal that morning: weapons that Tulbur had stocked there, lest the Army of All Karolan be driven back into the valley of stone. But they had found no swords.

"Men of Petrag," called Jonathan, "it is not for my great strength and wisdom that I stand as your leader today. If we chose our leaders by these, one greater than I might well be found among you, and willingly would I follow him. But I have been longer in the counsel of the prince, and so he has chosen me. I will listen to any man who counsels me. With whatever wisdom, strength, and honor I have, I will strive to lead you well. Will you follow me?"

There was a roar of assent. "I thank you!" said Jonathan. "With all I have I will seek to be worthy of your trust. Behold! The day is bright, but we go into danger and darkness. True hearts of Karolan, we ride into the storm together! On then, for love, home, prince, and kingdom. Ride!"

Ilohan's lone horse had been loud enough in the echoing valley, but now Jonathan felt that he was riding on a storm. Deafening thunder of hoof-beats rang from the rocks, until he wondered if the soldiers of Norkath would break ranks and fly at the very sound. But then his joy was dimmed, for they had no spears or swords. A cavalry charge with bows and pickaxes was more a matter for laughter than for fear.

The sun blazed in the cloudless sky as they thundered down the great stone valley. Sometimes their cavalcade seemed to fill the valley from side to side, and sometimes they had to slow as the horsemen at the edges guided their mounts carefully over the rugged ground. Jonathan felt strong, and the soft cool air was like honey he could breathe, compared to the air of the frozen mountains that had cut like a knife.

As they rode, Jonathan kept a vigilant watch for danger ahead, but his thoughts were elsewhere. It seemed many years since he had left Glen Carrah. He had had adventures more wonderful and terrible than any he had dreamed of while he dwelt there at peace. He looked back on his youthful dreams in Glen Carrah, comparing them with the reality he now knew. The dreams had left out the pain, the endless, relentless struggle to climb mountains or cross deserts. They had left out the desperate fear of fights, and the moments when death seemed as close as the next breath, inevitable as falling night. Yet he had dreamed truly when he had imagined the exultant joy, the sense of being tried and proven, that accompanied great and hard adventures. Those things were every bit as real as the horrors his old dreams had lacked.

Was the wonder and joy worth the horror? He did not know. It would never truly be his to choose, for whenever he had a choice, wonder and dread alike would be shrouded in the future. Honor, not some balanced estimate of pain and joy, must decide him. But would the glory outweigh the terror, if from some omniscient viewpoint they could both be measured? Was adventure worth its cost? He almost laughed at the thoughts. Was life worth its cost? Was love? It was never a man's right to try such questions. He must live, must love, must take all the adventures to which honor and justice led him. He, Jonathan, loved life and would live it. He would dare all its horror, and love all its wonder. He would never turn back, and never wish he had.

He looked to the left, at the rock wall that bounded Petrag on the west, and suddenly his thoughts took a new direction. The great gray cliff seemed like a curse. Beyond it, only two days' ride, was Glen Carrah. Beyond that stony wall was Naomi, and he was not going to her. He could see her now, though the rugged sunlit rock was before his eyes. The grass would be dry, and dusty-gold, tossing in a cool wind from the mountains. Naomi might be running there, her brown hair glowing in the sun, her lovely form flying over the windblown grain with grace and strength, vibrantly alive. She might run to him, and he would hold her to his heart forever. Suddenly all his hopes of glory and adventure in the coming war were nothing compared to one great desire, the desire to hold her in his arms again, to tell his love, and know no danger threatened her.

The world seemed dark and terrible, and Naomi dwelt in it loving and unafraid, yet desperately vulnerable to the coming storm. Suddenly Jonathan remembered a thing he had said long ago, when Naomi had asked him if he could be content without the adventures he dreamed of: "With you to love me? Naomi, do not imagine that any of this compares with my love for you. I will be content, and more than content – joyful beyond measure, in your love, and in living with you in Glen Carrah, if none of this happens." He would have been content. The memory that he had said so was the best comfort he had, while the adventure he had desired kept him far from her, and the storm bore down upon them both. He had said he loved her more than adventure, and she might remember that, whatever came.

A strange sight punched through the veil of his thoughts and brought him suddenly back to the present. "Halt!" he shouted, and reined in his horse. Far off to the right, near the cliff wall, were several large sheets of rough canvas like what had covered the bows and arrows at the castle of Byinkal. Piles of rocks weighted the sheets and half buried them, and the gray color of the fabric itself concealed it. It had caught Jonathan's gaze nonetheless: the canvas was not stone, and eyes that had scanned the stones of a journey as long and wild as Jonathan's could not be easily deceived.

"Something is buried beneath the rocks there," he said. "Is it more weapons? If so, Tulbur's preparations for retreat are beyond all reason." He dismounted and called several men to help him. The miners easily swept the rocks away, and Jonathan pulled off the first sheet in one strong motion. The stiff fabric folded awkwardly in the air, like a tent without poles, and Jonathan looked down at what it had unveiled. For a long moment he stood as still and silent as if he had been turned to stone. In the shallow pit below him the sun glanced off the bright blades of innumerable long, straight swords.

At last Jonathan bent and lifted a sword. He swung it into the air in a slow, almost reverent arc. "Here are the shining swords of Karolan," he called. "Here are our terrible tools of war: the blades that wise King Thomas gathered to defend his people and his realm. The steward has hidden them like a fool, for there were none to spare. But here his folly serves us well. Men of Petrag, arm yourselves!"

*   *   *

Ilohan galloped into the oak wood south of Aaronkal, leaving the last cheering peasants behind. The silence and cool shadow of the wood blew past him, and even the scent of its earth and leaves was a familiar friend. He rode past the chapel where he had kept his vigil long ago. The forest path's opening onto the field of Aaronkal appeared before him as an arch filled with brilliant sunlight. He rode through it, and the encampment of the Army of all Karolan lay before him.

He had heard for most of his life the accounts of old battles, and he had talked without understanding about a score of thousands. Now he saw it, the great Army of all Karolan in the afternoon sun. It was overwhelming. Men covered the land into the far distance of the great field, more men than he had ever seen or truly imagined. Thousand on thousand on thousand; sitting, standing, talking, eating, or sleeping. And each one a life, each one a son or husband or father, each one a man with blood and bone, strength and weakness, courage and fear. War was more terrible than he had thought it. If two such armies marched against each other, it would be as though the stars of heaven fought and cast each other down. Whichever side triumphed, good without measure would be destroyed, and pain beyond counting inflicted.

Then the first men saw him, and leaped to their feet in wondering joy. The news, and the joy, spread across the field like swift fire. For the prince had come, the prince of Karolan's hope. No more must the men of the great army look to Tulbur, who could not inspire them or win their love. A prince of the line of Thomas, wearing the lost crown of Kindrach, sat on his great horse at the edge of the woods, and the star in his banner flashed the dazzling sun.

"The prince! The prince! Beyond all hope, he comes!" The sound of shouts and cheering rolled and thundered until the ground shook and Ilohan could feel the very soles of his shoes ringing with it. He walked the great, weary horse slowly forward, holding the royal standard high. Still cheering, the men parted to make a narrow corridor before him.

As the prince approached Aaronkal, the sound of Karolan's joy echoed from the castle walls and rang in the oak woods like thunder. The sun reflected blindingly from the gold of his crown, and the rubies glowed as if each stone held captive a ruddy flame. "The prince has come!" the men shouted again and again. The steward had said it was impossible, but nonetheless he had come. Was anything impossible for the rightful heir to Karolan's throne? He would lead them to war and victory, as the steward never could. All darkness, uncertainty, and doubt were swept away at his coming. They would follow him at any cost, but they knew now that they would follow him to victory. Fingar would never stand against them, for they would be fighting for their prince: for a future worth the winning.

Their cheers overwhelmed Ilohan, suddenly the center of exultant hope for a score of thousands. He could not imagine himself to be as significant as they thought him, and he was frightened by the trust they placed in him. He tried hard to think what it was best to do. Still the mighty cheers rang on, drowning their own echoes, seeming to shake even the clouds that sailed above. Ilohan rode toward the steps of Aaronkal, and the soldiers still parted before him, making an open corridor that led up to the great gate, which was closed. Still the cheers rang on. "God, help me!" he prayed silently, hoping that no one would be dismayed to see how weak and bewildered he truly was.

The horse from Petrag easily climbed the wide stone steps, and on the broad, open dais above them Ilohan wheeled to face the crowd. He lowered the banner for silence, and a score of thousands obeyed the command. "Men of Karolan!" he cried, as loud as he could. "I am Ilohan, son of Kindrach, son of Thomas, Prince of Karolan. I am not great in strength or wisdom, nor am I sinless. Yet it is my heart's desire to lead you well, and always to be faithful to your trust. I look to God to give me strength. I trust him to grant me wisdom, that I may lead you rightly and help you truly. I pledge to you that I will love and lead you faithfully, whatever that shall mean and whatever that shall cost. I will pray for you, and God will hear me. I will always seek to bless and serve you. I expect your loyalty in return."

"And shall have it! And shall have it forever!" cried the men of Karolan, as the prince raised his banner. The cries soon gathered again into a storm of cheers. Yet the storm was not so strong now as at the prince's first arrival. Some in the great army thought God a falsehood, and doubted whether a man could be wise who founded his life so firmly on him. Some, too, were silent because Prince Ilohan's sober words had re-opened their eyes to the war ahead, and they knew Karolan might turn to ashes on the very day its hope was blooming. Moved, perhaps, by such thoughts of the reality of war, and of the need to temper exultation with wisdom, some began to take up the war song of Karolan. The song gathered more voices until the whole army was singing. The ancient song rang out across the woods and plains with the full force of twenty thousand voices: a song of hope and of stern valor, a pledge to stand together and defy all would-be conquerors to the last:

Against the host of Dradrag
Our fathers stood alone.
Their valor was unneeded;

No man can conquer stone.

And though today in battle
Our banner must be flown,
Stands Karolan forever;
No man can conquer stone.

Against love, joy, and freedom
The gauntlet has been thrown:
Fight on, fight on together;
No man can conquer stone.

From the one who weeds the barley
To the king upon his throne,
We walk in honest freedom
No man can conquer stone.

So you who come in conquest
Of a land never your own,
Tremble before our banners;
You shall not conquer stone!

Ilohan looked out over the great army. Their mood was less exultant now, but they were still filled with the hope he had brought them. So many seemingly impossible things had happened that he wondered if indeed Fingar of Norkath might be stopped at his own border, and sent back utterly defeated by this army, the Army of all Karolan. "Father," he prayed, "so let it be!"

The foot soldiers were standing, silently waiting, when he raised his head. The banners and spears of the knights gleamed brightly in the westering sun. Ilohan raised his own banner high. "No man can conquer stone!" he cried. "I go now to hold a council of war. I will return soon to lead you out to battle, and by the blessing of God, we will triumph!"

They cheered for one last time, and Ilohan wheeled his horse around and rode up to the great gate of Aaronkal. He raised the banner to knock upon the gate, but before he could do so there was a blast of trumpets from the battlements, and a herald cried, "Sir Tulbur, Steward of Karolan, welcomes Sir Ilohan, Crown Prince of Karolan, to his rightful place as Lord of Aaronkal!"

There was another trumpet blast, and the gates swung open, moved by three pages each, in perfect symmetry. Tulbur the Steward came forth, dressed in his finest robes, with a gold chain around his neck and six guards behind him. He knelt before Ilohan on the stone pavement. Ilohan dismounted. He was stiff and weary, but he knew a score of thousands watched. He would not look weak or exhausted, for God would give the strength he needed, and he must not discourage his men. He walked slowly toward Tulbur, holding his head high.

Metherka had come running up, but he stopped and stood still to watch the steward and the prince. The steward was perfectly dressed, clean, magnificent, confident and at peace. Ilohan was dusty, travel worn and weary. Only his bright crown and the immaculate banner that he carried looked worthy of a prince. Yet Metherka had no doubt that Ilohan loved Karolan, and could rule it well, while Tulbur, for all his cleverness and wisdom, lacked something indefinable that the people would always need.

"Rise, Sir Steward," said Ilohan. "I thank you for your royal welcome." He paused, thinking carefully what he should say next. He was too tired to think easily. He said what was most important, without prelude or embellishment. "Where is Fingar? How long have we until the invasion?"

Tulbur stood, bowed to the prince, and answered with great ceremony. "The latest report from our principal spies, which was received at sunrise this morning, informs us that His Majesty Fingar of Norkath is still at Guldorak and cannot march for another day, perhaps even longer. He could arrive at the border of our land late in the evening of the day he marches, or more likely in the early morning of the day following. Therefore we have some days, two at least, to deliberate in safety. We can even consider the advisability of invading Norkath, and engaging Fingar's army before he marches. There are many other matters on which Your Majesty must render judgment. Yet I have something more pressing to report immediately."

The torrent of flowery words washed over Ilohan, and he felt it painfully difficult to grasp the meaning of each and form them into a coherent whole. He wished the steward would not speak so formally. Yet he had learned the answers to his questions, and rejoiced to hear them. They had time. "I thank you, Sir Steward," he said briskly. "Please make your report."

"We have captured a Norkath spy, in the woods to the west of Aaronkal," said Tulbur. "We have him in the eighth cell of the dungeons now, and I hope he may reveal many things that will be useful in our council of war. Since Your Majesty is here, I will leave to Your Majesty the choice of how we attempt to obtain information from him. I counsel Your Majesty to come down at once, for his words may be of utmost importance to our plans."

"It was well done, to capture a spy," said Prince Ilohan. "As you suggest, I will come down at once to question him."

Metherka turned away. He would speak to the prince later, in the council of war. He was shocked that he had somehow missed the news of the captured spy. He supposed that he had been more despondent, more wrapped up in his own thoughts, than he had realized. But no – more likely Tulbur had kept the capture secret, hoping another spy would fall into the same trap. Such cautious prudence was to be expected of the steward.

Ilohan followed Tulbur through the great gate of Aaronkal. He was very weary, and having heard that there was no immediate danger, he wanted nothing more than to sleep long and deeply. Yet the council of war must come first, and before that, the interrogation of the spy. There might be time before Fingar invaded, but there was no time to waste.

They entered the throne room, and Ilohan felt an almost unbearable surge of loss. The throne was empty, and the light of the windows above it fell in empty beams upon the floor. A thousand times he had seen the commanding figure of King Thomas on that throne, or watched the shafts of sunlight from the high windows glancing on his crown as he spoke with counselors or paced in meditation. The memories were so vivid he could almost see him still: Thomas, the only father he had ever known, his white hair and beard glowing in the light, his rich crimson robe like the essence of royalty. He could still hear his kind, strong voice. He remembered their parting at the beginning of his quest, and his eyes filled with tears.

He blinked them back. Tulbur led him through a side door and along a torch-lit passage that Ilohan knew very well. One of the heavy oaken doors that lined it opened on the stair that led up to his own tower room. He knew the very pattern of the stones upon the floor. A quiet joy stirred within him: the joy of homecoming after a long journey. It faded quickly. Those who once had made this place his home were dead. There was no comfort or security here for him now. He was the master, the one to whom others would look for aid and comfort. He was no longer Ilohan the squire, ward of Sarah and Thomas. He was Prince Ilohan of Karolan. Aaronkal might be his palace, but it would not again be his home.

"Where can I go and find the shelter that I once knew here?" he thought. "Ceramir? Yes, but even there I had bitter choices to make, and no one in whose authority I could truly rest." Despondent thoughts wandered through his weary mind. "To this hurt, too, God will provide a healing," he told himself at last. "Home does not concern me now: all that concerns me is doing what is right. I may well need no home but heaven soon."

Then he willed himself to think again of what he must do. They were going to see a captured Norkath spy. Already the steward, holding a lighted torch snatched from the wall, was leading the way down a spiraling, subterranean stairway. The air was cool, stale, and damp. He wondered how they should question the spy. The thought that came to him made him weary. Yet another heavy choice to make...

"I command that the spy shall not be tortured," said Prince Ilohan.

"Then we can expect little help from him," said Tulbur.

"That does not matter. I will not have him tortured."

"You are like Kindrach and like Thomas," said Tulbur. "Always they valued chivalry more than prudence, and this cost them much. Yet still the people loved them, as they love you."

They came to a heavy door at the bottom of the stairway. Tulbur turned a key and the door opened smoothly, though with a groan of rusty hinges. They passed into a grimy, cavelike passage beyond, and Ilohan suppressed a shudder. The air was heavy with damp and dreary smells, and torches had left great, black smoke stains that were never scrubbed upon the mildewed walls. This place might sometimes be needed in the reign of a good king, but it was the evil kings of Karolan who had left their mark here dire and heavy. Here they had done things Ilohan turned from thinking of.

The place was well lit by torches, but they could not dispel the feeling of darkness. Living men seemed out of place here: life and health in hostile territory, where death and sickness had more often reigned. Near the end of the passage stood the jailer, with several guards, before the iron-grill door of one of the cells. They looked like displaced phantoms in the torchlight, where a real ghost would have seemed fitting and at home. The jailer fumbled with his keys before the cell, then spoke in a low voice to his men, and suddenly Ilohan knew that something was desperately wrong.

The men were reaching for their swords. He turned, and Tulbur was retreating behind the guards who had followed him, a look of merciless exultation in his face. Jonathan's uneasiness and his warnings passed through Ilohan's mind in a flash: too late. He was betrayed. In an instant they would be upon him. He drew his sword in a motion quick as thought. The jailer and his men came at him from one side, and Tulbur's guards from the other. His thoughts, that had been slow and weary, now flew like wild lighting. This could not be. Too many had sacrificed too much that he might live as prince. The traitor must not conquer. Hot desperation surged through him; terror mounting on terror.

"No!" he shouted. "Will no man help his prince?" He backed into a niche in the rough wall, and somewhere in the whirlwind of his thoughts there flew a lightning fragment of a prayer. Then they were upon him, and he fought. The memory of the cliff above Luciyr passed through his mind, and the thought of the glade near Ceramir. There was no Rangol here, and no escape. But there was no wondering if life were worth the winning, no wavering of his desperate strength. He fought until the men who tried to close in around him drew back in awe. He turned their blades against the walls, the torches, or each other. Twice a cold blade of Karolan iron shattered before his sword, the sword that had been Kindrach's. He fought beyond his strength, in utter desperation. The extremity of his need winged his thought and sharpened his eyes, so that he saw all that his enemies did and foiled them.

The sounds of the terrible fight rang and echoed wildly in the stone passage. Sparks flew like tiny lighting bolts from the clashing swords. The torches flickered in the winds of quickly moving men, and two of them were knocked from the walls and extinguished.

One man, who had been with the jailer, stood back and did not join in the fight. It was Benther. As the weeks had passed that taught him more about his father's treachery, he had still declined to make a choice. And so he had been swept away in Tulbur's scheming, too weak to stand against his father's will. He had listened to the steward's plots, and even let the poisoned dreams of power and pleasure enter his mind. And it had come to this. His father had ordered him to help kill his friend and prince. And he had thought he would be willing to. He had forgotten who Ilohan was, and how he used to love him. He saw the prince hard pressed, hopelessly outnumbered as they forced him back against the wall. And suddenly he made the choice he should have made so long before. It was too late to save the prince, but not too late to die with him. "I am with you, Ilohan!" he cried, and plunged into the fight.

The men on that side of Ilohan turned to face their new foe. One of them went down beneath Benther's blade. The knight fought along the wall toward his prince. Ilohan rejoiced to see him, but his own strength was failing. His endurance had a limit, even when driven by utmost desperation – and that limit swiftly approached. One sword was almost parried, but not quite, and he felt a burning pain in his thigh. It seemed to sap his strength still faster, but he fought on, and did not stumble or falter.

His breath came fast and hard in the stale, damp air. He could see the sweating, scowling faces of the men who fought him, and the dance of their swords flashing in the torchlight. His arms felt strange, as though burning with a fire that consumed strength, burning more hotly with every passing moment. Still he blocked his enemies' cuts and turned aside their thrusts. He saw Benther driving the men up the passage. If only his old friend reached him, they could fight side by side. Just outside the gates were a score of thousands who would fight for him if they knew his plight. He parried a blade with a clang and a flash of sparks. It slashed into a torch above his head and put it out. It was the third torch to be extinguished, and it plunged the dungeon into a weird, fiery twilight. Ilohan found it hard to see, yet he must see clearly to parry all the blows. The dank passage was stifling with the heat of sweating, fighting men.

Ilohan saw Benther's sword forced straight up and pinned against the stone wall. He met Benther's eyes, and read in them what the knight had no breath to say, "My prince, my friend, I am sorry." A gloved fist struck Benther in the face, even as he tried desperately to free his sword, and he crumpled upon the floor.

"God help us!" said Ilohan in a lightning gasp. The men grinned in triumph at the desperate prayer. Ilohan's arms felt too weary even to hold his sword. He thought once more of the loyal thousands so short a distance away. Could they hear him? Might some stray servant pause beside the dungeon doors? He tried one last desperate call. "I am betrayed!" he cried, so loud that fear showed in the faces of the men who fought him. "Will no man help his prince?"

The words echoed deafeningly in the dungeons, but no answer came. Somehow Ilohan found the strength for another mighty blow. Two swords flew back before its force, and one man was wounded badly across the stomach. Some drew back, dismayed by the strength the prince still had. But one sword of Karolan iron flashed the torchlight in a mighty arc. It struck the blade of Kindrach just above the hilt, and smashed it out of Ilohan's burning hands.

The men surged forward, but did not kill him. Their sword points paused just in front of him, trembling with the weariness and vicious triumph of those who held them. Ilohan stood there, panting hard, struggling to remain standing and not sink down onto the floor. All the strength of his desperation had left him. Like his captors, he trembled with weariness, while burning sweat dripped off him to the floor. He felt an impotent anger at the injustice of the world, that the whole of his strength had not been enough to win his righteous cause. Still he could scarcely believe this staggering disaster was real, and no angel had come to set it right.

Tulbur the traitor came down the dungeon passage, and stood before the prince. "Excellent," he said, "tie him hand and foot."

Ilohan had little strength to resist, and many swords threatened instant death if he did. He felt hopelessness and anger, but little fear. The knots forced him to kneel upon the rough floor, and even when he was securely tied the men did not leave off guarding him with their swords. Tulbur stood straight before him, and took his crown gently off his head. Ilohan looked up at him, longing to say something defiant, but the words would not come. The traitor's triumph was too complete.

"You were the hope of all Karolan," said Tulbur. "The magnitude of what has been sacrificed to set you on the throne is beyond your comprehension. And today it is all lost because you were too weak.

"Today, Kindrach's death is in vain. Eleanor's sorrow is in vain. The dream of Thomas's whole life, and many years of Sarah's patient love and labor: all are as though they had never been. Today, all Karolan is doomed, because you were not strong, and did not fight the fight of a true knight. Even though my foolish, double minded son threw in his lot with you, still you failed. You cannot even imagine what your failure has destroyed. Your mind cannot conceive what Kindrach, Eleanor, Thomas, Sarah, Britheldore, and many others suffered, lost or gave so that you could have the throne of Karolan today. All this, this unimaginable offering, is thrown away today because you have not fought as Thomas, or as Kindrach. All that their valor won, and more, is lost because your valor was too little. You have called yourself a prince. Look up at me now, prince! You are a feeble, trembling little worm, trapped in a dingy burrow like all others of your kind.

"Do you wonder why I have thought to catch that worm? It is not against you that I quarrel; you are too insignificant for that. It is against those whose hope you represent that I have a grudge. This is vengeance. I have brewed it long and patiently, and now it breaks forth and nothing shall restrain it.

Ilohan was too weary to fight with either body or mind. He was beaten down and cowed by the barrage of words, and dazed by his hopeless defeat. The crown of the Prince of Karolan gleamed on the traitor's head – the crown on which Eleanor had written her blessing. Tulbur sat regally back against a protruding rock to explain himself.

"You know that many kings of Karolan were evil men, but if you think along the list of names you know so well, you will find one that stands out black and strong: Garthan, Garthan the Vulture. His lust knew no bounds. He wished to lead a life of endless license, and being a prudent man as well as a vile one, he found a way to do so. With gold he wrested from the people of Karolan, he hired mercenaries to oppress them. When his band was strong, he took whatever he wanted. No woman of beauty in the land was safe from his lust. Often he took them deviously, by night or by surprise, so that no man could be sure it was the king's servants and not lawless bandits. The things he did in this very dungeon, to any man or woman who resisted his will, do not bear speaking of. Your tender ears, worm, would shrivel at the very words, and my chaste mouth would smoke to say them."

Somehow Ilohan could still compare this dispassionately with the history that he knew, just as he had back in Petrag with Master Joseph. Garthan the Vulture had been so evil that Ilohan felt it was dangerous to think of him. He had twisted wisdom and mated it with cruelty. His wickedness had marred all that it touched, and poisoned Karolan. The very knowledge that he had lived so long, and had not been struck down by God's lightning, could be a wound in a man's mind: a wound that made him doubt if judgment always falls on evil, or if he himself might follow Garthan, and never have to look up from a ruined life to face the wrath of God. Yet why would Tulbur now condemn the atrocities Garthan had committed in this dungeon? Was he blind to the horrible irony of his words? Ilohan wondered idly what Tulbur would do to him, but it mattered little, for already all was lost. Tulbur went on.

"Corzogad, son of Garthan, was a good man. He lived haunted by his father's evil. He swore that no man of uncontrolled lust would ever again rule Karolan. He made a law that every Prince of Karolan must pass a test before being crowned: a beautiful woman must offer herself to him for fornication, and he must refuse her. This test is called the Joseph Test, for the Books of the Travelers tell us of a man named Joseph who was proven faithful in such a case; many in Karolan still are named for him. Any man who does not pass the Joseph test loses the right to Karolan's crown.

"My father was Prince Grandor – the younger brother of King Konder, father of Thomas. Therefore I am the late king's cousin, the nephew of his father. Thomas failed the Joseph Test when we were young together. The guards that watched him scarcely saved the woman from his lust. He failed most miserably and deeply, proving that he had not mastered himself. With his failure, my father should have had his crown, and when my father died in his own brother's wars, the crown should have come to me. I, not Thomas, should have been Crown Prince of Karolan. Yet Konder reinstated his son Thomas, and it was Thomas, not I, who took the throne on Konder's death. I have bided my time, wise and patient not for years but for decades. Now at last I have my vengeance – and my crown. Prudence dictates that I will not challenge Fingar. I have buried the swords of the Army of all Karolan in Petrag, and as Norkath's regent I shall rule. You and all the hopes that gathered round you shall rot to dust.

Ilohan looked up at him, thinking of the times before when it had seemed there was no hope for the dreams of Eleanor, Thomas, and Sarah. Each time an act of heroism had saved the dream. Until this time, when it had been his turn to give that act, alone. He had failed. And yet he could not have succeeded. All his strength had been too little. He was the first for whom this had been true. He was the weak one.

And yet Tulbur was evil, and did not admit it. He exalted himself over Thomas as though he himself had done no wrong. Forgiveness was real, and Thomas had received it.

Ilohan spoke, in a dull, flat voice out of his exhaustion. "Tulbur, may your name be paired with Garthan's in the history of Karolan, henceforth and forever. I strip you of your knighthood by my royal authority. You are Tulbur the Unknighted, disgraced by truth and condemned by judgment."

"Proud words from a worm," said Tulbur. "Let him be taken underground, to his proper home."

Ilohan shuddered at what the words might mean. The servants of Tulbur lifted him roughly and carried him to a large cell, the one the jailer had been opening before the trap was sprung. They flung him into a rectangular pit that was cut into the floor of the cell near one wall. He clenched his teeth against the pain of the fall, then turned awkwardly in his bonds to look round. The pit was less than half his height in depth and in width; in length it was just over the height of a man, like a coffin. Tulbur's servants stood over him with their sword points hovering just above his body. The traitor himself held up a torch, giving red, unsteady light to the grim cell.

Ilohan's mind unwillingly named the place where he was cast: the forget-me-not. No torture in the world seemed worse than the one he knew awaited him: death by thirst.

Through his fear, as through a cascade of fire, Ilohan heard Tulbur say, "Cut his bonds. He is ours now, and a worm should be free to squirm." He felt a cold sword cutting the rope that bound his hands, and he struggled to rise as he was freed. But there were swords to spare, pressing against his chest. A shadow loomed above him, the swords were swiftly withdrawn, and there came a deafening crash. The forget-me-not was plunged in darkness.

At Tulbur's command, a thick iron slab had been dropped down across the narrow death-cell. Ilohan could hear the scraping of the bars that would lock it down – as if its weight alone were not enough to trap him forever. Small holes bored in the slab glowed like evil red eyes in the light of Tulbur's torch. But all else was darkness. Perhaps Ilohan could have held back his fear, searching in the depths of his soul for some weapon against it, but he did not. This was darkness, no light of hope or peace or comfort. Fear overwhelmed him. No defense was proof against it, and it swept him away. It washed over him in dizzying waves, until he felt its power would destroy his body. He screamed, and screamed again. He knew the screams disgraced him, yet the darkness was taking him and he could not hold them back. Everything seemed shapeless, void and horrible. The shameful screams did not seem to be his own, though they rang loud and dreadful in his ears.

Tulbur's laugh came dimly through the iron. "Make the door of this cell as if it never was," said the muffled voice of the traitor. "Then even if we fall, none shall find him. Four days, perhaps five, until thirst ends the line of Thomas in agony and despair. I will think of you with pleasure, worm. Farewell." The red eyes disappeared and total darkness came. Ilohan screamed once more, and then clapped his hand over his mouth. He fell back onto the bottom of the narrow death-cell, sweating and breathing hard.

"Think," he told himself aloud, in a trembling voice. "This is not the chapel, you can think if you but try hard enough." He tried to think of other things, but his mind reverted over and over again to the chapel. He could feel the Darkness reaching for him, struggling to suck him back into the void, this time forever. "This is not the chapel," he told himself again and again. Yet all that the chapel had seemed to be, this was. This was hopelessness, not only for him but for everyone he loved. He was cut off and impotent, lost in a place of despair in a world he could not understand. Tulbur was utterly ascendant, the trusted steward proven now a fiend. Karolan, Jonathan, Naomi: all were doomed without hope, and he could not even die in their defense. Eleanor would lose him, as would Veril, and he knew too much to think he understood how deeply they would feel his loss. The dream, as Tulbur had said, had perished – the dream that had cost more than he could imagine.

And then there was his own life. He had thought he trusted God, and looked forward to Heaven with faith and longing. Yet he could not conceive of Heaven, and death by thirst, simplest and most dreadful of tortures, stared him in the face. What life could there be for him beyond the life of his mortal body? He was so tired, so doomed, so far from hope. He was on the point of shedding mournful tears, when the hot force of fear took him again. Life was good and wonderful and known – death was a veiled horror, with cruel claws half seen beneath the darkness of its cloak. Overwhelming terror gripped him again. He had no point of reference here in his living grave. The unseen stone on which he lay seemed to be spinning, falling, carrying him down into some dreadful abyss. Hot fear dispersed his thoughts; panic tightened around his stomach like a giant's fist.

He seemed to sink through this fear, and his mind turned unbidden to other things. He remembered Sarah's embrace, and sunlight on warm grass. He remembered summer swims in clean millponds, looking up at blue skies and white clouds. He remembered the trees of Ceramir, tossing in the wind and sun. Then he moved his hand, felt the stone, and was back in the forget-me-not, gripped in the black claws of despair. Fear came upon him again with dreadful force. This was real, this was all he had, this was what his life would be for the short days of agony until it ended. This was real. Had he felt the Darkness of the chapel reaching out for him again? No, for it had him. It did not need to reach for him now. In the chapel it had been only pretence, only a warning: now it was real. The Darkness had conquered. He screamed.

He was trembling, sweating, and breathing hard with the power of his fear and despair. Yet again his mind turned to other thoughts, sweet and strong. He felt Eleanor's arms around him, and looked up again at Jonathan's adventure-joy. He saw Veril's face as he bid farewell to her, and heard the thousands of Karolan cheering for joy. Cheering in vain. His thoughts dissolved once more, and again he knew nothing but the despair of the forget-me-not. The unseen rock and iron once more seemed to spin around him, carrying him spiraling down into void and Darkness. This was real. They had lost.

Chapter 11

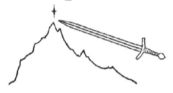

If Prayer is Real

JONATHAN AND THE ARMY OF PETRAG GALLOPED LIKE thunder over the wild foothills east and north of the miners' valley, racing toward a small castle on the Norkath border south of Aaronkal. Jonathan had consulted with Master Joseph, who knew the geography of eastern Karolan well, and they had concluded that if they struck the border at that point and then followed it northward, they would cross every route that Fingar could practically use for his invasion.

The wind was cold, but the foothills had a calm autumnal loveliness: tall golden grass, thick clumps of barren bushes garnished with holly, and here and there a stand of trees beside a stream. In one sheltered hollow Jonathan saw to his surprise that a few battered flowers still hung their drooping heads beside a marshy pond. They had a somber, poignant beauty as the light of the setting sun caught them, and they swayed in the wind off the mountains.

As the army neared the border, they came to lower, gentler hills with more trees. The woods slowed their progress. Jonathan looked intently ahead, trying to find clearings, meadows, or at least places where the trees were sparser. He realized with dismay that they had no hope of reaching the border before nightfall, and the going would be slower after dark.

A stand of poplars caught his eye in the falling twilight; they were like white spears stacked against the evening sky. Suddenly he reined in his horse. "Halt!" he cried. He wheeled to face the miners. "Men of Petrag," he said, "we have axes, bows, and swords, but we lack one thing that would make our charge a terror. We have no spears. Now, each one of you, cut down a poplar and fashion a rough spear. Work quickly, for we have no time to spare."

Many of the men stirred at once, guiding their horses toward the poplar wood. But Dran, one of the leading men of Petrag, said, "Stay! Will not the soft wood shatter before the force of our riding? And we have no shields."

"Make them a man's height longer than a Norkath's lance of oak," said Jonathan. "I will show you the length. Though they shatter, yet they will break the man who breaks them, and our lack of shields will mean nothing if no lance can ever touch us."

"But the weight will strain the horses," said Dran.

"Bah!" said Yalron with good humor. "It will be no more to them than a reed upon their shoulders. Let us do as Jonathan has said!"

*   *   *

They made camp late that night, in a forest glade near the border. They ate cold food from Petrag, and lit no fire. Jonathan ordered five guards posted at the edges of the camp, to be changed four times during the night. He ordered that every man lie down quickly and be silent, that all might sleep the faster and awake refreshed. Yet he did not obey his own command.

He walked quietly about the camp in the light of the gibbous moon. The men lay wrapped in blankets: dark, elongated bundles on the moonlit grass of the meadow. The horses stood quietly, or gently munched the dead grass. Many had blankets thrown over them, to guard their health after the day's hard ride. The long poplar spears seemed to glow in the bright moonlight, where they lay scattered at haphazard angles on the ground.

Jonathan shivered suddenly, and gathered his wool cloak from Ceramir close about him. What they were doing seemed for a moment utterly absurd. How could they hope, with spears of green poplar, to charge the Norkath army? Would their charge not break and falter, as the splintered spears fell from their hands and the lances of Norkath skewered their bodies? And why had he wasted precious time arming his men with spears? Ilohan had sent them as scouts, to report back to Aaronkal as soon as the Norkaths were sighted. They were not to engage Fingar in battle. But what then? They would arrive at Aaronkal with the Norkath army close behind them. The Army of all Karolan would prepare to meet the enemy, and...

He did not know what would happen next. He did not want to meet his death in a futile but heroic charge. He did not want to meet his death anywhere, any time. Poplar lances... And yet he would not order the miners out of the battle, nor would he turn back from the fighting himself. As honor and loyalty called him, he would fight. And since he and his men rode swift horses of Petrag, it would be foolish not to use them. If they must fight on horseback, they must also have lances. Poplar was better than nothing. His action, thus far, had not been foolish.

He made his way slowly back to his horse, and rolled himself up in a blanket. He drifted toward sleep, still feeling uneasy. He could not imagine a thing that he must not only do, but lead other men in doing. He could imagine the preparation for the charge, but the charge itself, with poplar lances leveled... His mind was still wrestling with the problem when he finally fell asleep. His last thought was a memory of his army in full gallop. He could hardly believe that any force on earth could stop them, short of a high stone wall. It seemed they must sweep men and horses, swords and spears before them like leaves before a gale.

When he awoke, the moon had set and the morning star was burning its white fire in a twilit sky. He roused the men nearest him, and sent them through the camp to wake the others swiftly and quietly. Soon the whole camp was filled with a sense of urgency, strangely combined with a silence that was half furtive and half reverent. They ate quickly, packed their blankets and weapons, and rode away well before sunrise.

The morning came, cool and fresh, with a bite of autumn chill in the air, and a sweet smell of leaves and wood smoke carried on the breeze. The grass beneath the horses' feet was lush with dew, while mist hovered over meadowlands in sheets, and made soft white pools in forest dells. They started out much slower than the thunderous pace of yesterday, but gradually as the horses warmed and the morning seemed to call them on, they sped up until the ground shook beneath their flying hooves, and every man's heart leaped for the moment's joy.

They seemed once again to Jonathan to be invincible, and though the lances burdened the horses more than might be wished, he did not regret their presence. It was not as scouts alone that the miners of Petrag rode, nor was it as scouts alone that Jonathan of Carrah led them.

*   *   *

Far away in Harevan, Auria rose to see the sun shining brightly on the autumn trees outside her window. She dressed quickly and went into the kitchen. White sunlight was streaming through the windows, leaving the rest of the room in shadow. Eleanor was already awake, kneeling in prayer beside the table. A square of light from a window fell full upon her, so that her simple white clothes seemed to shine against the darkness behind her.

Auria was sorry that her mistress had awakened before her, for she would have liked to fling those windows wide herself, and do other small things that Eleanor had now done for her. Many things remained in which she could serve Eleanor and show her love, and the little tasks called out to her. Yet for a long moment she only stood, and looked, and wondered.

It seemed to her that the sun and the morning had woven around Lady Eleanor a beauty that showed her as she truly was. If the world were less broken, and the glory and power of goodness less veiled, Eleanor might look all the time as she did now. The light of heaven might always strike so upon her patient, prayerful figure. She might always look purified and tempered, with a halo of white light gently reaching into the darkness around her. The light was not her own. She knew that, and was not proud. In her love there was no arrogance, no grasping certainty of understanding. She blessed, and wondered at the deepness of the blessing. She rejoiced in it as humbly as those to whom she gave it.

Auria knew that today, as for many days past, Eleanor prayed for Ilohan. She had no doubt that Eleanor's prayers were heard by God and answered. Ilohan must be riding to war now, on a great white horse, his victory as certain as the sunrise. Auria was sure of it.

She remained looking at Eleanor for far longer than she could usually be still. It was not often that she saw those she loved looking as they ought to look, but when she did, she drank in the sight and remembered it forever.

Finally Eleanor looked up and saw her. The moment was broken. Birdsong banished stillness, and there was deep anxiety in Eleanor's face.

"I will serve bread and honey for your breakfast, my Lady," said Auria contritely. "I am sorry that I awoke so late."

"I was glad to let you sleep, for once," said Eleanor, smiling at her. "Yet now that you are awake, I want you to go to Ceramir without delay. Take up that bread, to eat it as you walk."

"I will go at once," said Auria, obeying her. "What am I to do there?"

"Ask your father and mother, and Veril your sister, to pray for Ilohan more intensely – for him, and for Karolan. My heart is deeply troubled, and I am afraid."

"I go," said Auria. "May God ease your fears and prove them groundless."

Auria was gone before her mistress could reply, walking quickly up the path to Ceramir in the bright morning.

*   *   *

Darkness. Dull weariness lifting like a veil, sure to reveal something horrible, yet lifting inexorably. Pain, relentless thirst, dark agony of hopelessness yet unremembered. Layers of sleep and confusion lifting one by one, until all shelter from reality is lost.

Ilohan awoke. He felt sick and weak, and despair was like lead in his empty stomach. The cycles of terror and darkness that had filled the time before his sleep seemed to march toward him inevitably, sure to sweep him into their maelstrom again now that he was awake. Yet now, in his weakness and his thirst, he could not fight at all.

There must be something more than this, he thought, some faint hope that he might yet live. Or else, there must at least be hope of some good thing happening outside this narrow cell where he would die. There must still be something he could do, some act that had meaning, that might bless those for whom he cared.

No. There was nothing. He was dead: Tulbur had killed him. Though his heart still beat, he was dead to all that he had loved, all that he had hoped to guard or bless. Even a blind worm could do more good.

And yet he was Ilohan! He had lived. His life had been beautiful and good, and had brought him joy and pain that mattered, that were real. This could not be reality; this could not be life – this darkness, this scraping of grimy stone against his arms, this stifling stale air, this hopeless hole.

But he knew, as the panic and darkness rose like a black tide, that it was real. This was his life, this was how it would end, and there was no hope of rescue.

The scream of absolute despair, of living death, rose within him as the Darkness dragged him down. He would go mad. The Darkness had him, and would have him. The Darkness of the chapel had been but a foretaste of this; now he knew it to the full. It had destroyed him, but would torment him still.

No... No! Scream on scream, despair upon despair, cycling, spiraling, depth on depth, agony on agony. No rescue... No rescue... Abandoned. But... But.

"God help me!" he whispered. Then he cried out, "God help me!" in an agonized scream that rang dreadfully in the black cell of iron and stone. He could not speak, he could only scream, through cracked lips, from a mouth parched with thirst. "God, come to me and help me!" He remembered faintly that the Darkness – or what he had thought then was the Darkness – in the chapel had lifted.

How had it lifted? When had it begun to lift? When he had been given back the ability to pray.

"Father," he said hoarsely, "Father, give me the power to pray."

He waited, absolutely still and silent. His wounded thigh throbbed. He thought of Jonathan and of the thousands of Karolan soldiers who would be slaughtered or enslaved through Tulbur's treachery. He thought about prayer.

"I have never truly believed in prayer," he whispered in a hoarse, awed voice.

He did not mean his prayers had had no faith in them. He had believed that God loved and heard him. Yet he realized that his faith had been weak. Without examining them, he had believed many things that were foolish if it was actually true that God, almighty and loving, heard the prayers of men. He had believed he must have some part in answering his own prayers. He had thought it useless to pray for things he could not see or know. He had not prayed in the expectation of wonders. He had not thought of prayer as action, as a work of love and blessing in itself. He had thought of it as words, almost as words spoken in the wind, a fairy blessing that might do good. He had not thought of it as what he now saw it must be in fact: a brilliant act of faith that could break mountains in thunder and turn the courses of the stars. Such must even his feeble prayers be, if the Lord of All heard, and loved him.

"Father," he croaked again, "give me faith, and the power to pray."

He was thirsty, and there was no escape from the little cell of iron and stone in which he lay. There was no light, and he would die here. Yet prayer was real, and he would pray. He slowly turned his panic-wearied thoughts to other things. "Jonathan... Father, please protect him... Give him wisdom. Use him to rescue many of my people. Many? No. All of my people. Bless him, bless his strength and his sword. Father, I dare ask you to rescue all of Karolan through Jonathan. But if you will not do that, if my failure must reach so deep, and Karolan must fall, please rescue Jonathan himself, and Naomi his beloved."

Ilohan stopped. Little seemed to have changed. He did not feel that his prayer was heard. One phrase had stuck in his mind: "My failure." He considered it. "My failure... Tulbur, at least, would have me think of it that way. Lord God, help me understand. What have I done? What did Thomas do? Is there a great fault from which I must turn, and for which I must ask your forgiveness? Or have I been true? Lord, help me. I would not cover my sin..."

Ilohan waited. If prayer was real; if God indeed was almighty and willing to hear and act, he would respond. So Ilohan waited for his answer. He wondered what might happen. Would guilt strike him like an arrow, showing him where he had been wrong? He had certainly been foolish to trust Tulbur. Was that his great sin? His thoughts trailed off into nothing, and he waited in the darkness.

The stone was rough and grimy behind his back. He knew he could raise his hand and touch the cold iron just above him, but he lay still on the stone instead. He knew too well already where every wall and corner of this tiny death trap lay. The air was stale. Panic reached for him again, like a great black dog a long way off, but coming nearer on flying feet.

Yet it did not reach him. The dark arrows of guilt also did not come. He lay still against the stone, and the unconscious tension in which he had long held his body faded away. Peace came to him, a strange visitor in the cell of death and torment. He felt no pride, and no guilt. "I have forgiven you. Thomas also I have forgiven. I love you. I have led you, and will lead you. You have followed me, and will follow me. I am with you." The words passed into his heart like an explanation of the impossible peace he felt. There was no audible voice, but he could not doubt that God had truly spoken to him, even though he scarcely dared to frame the thought. He was awestruck, humbled, frightened – yet conscious of overwhelming comfort poured into his soul.

"Those people, Father, the men of Karolan who have mustered before Aaronkal. Rescue them by your power, I pray. Provide a great miracle to free them from Tulbur's trap and save them from his treachery." Ilohan's prayers took wing, and carried him far from the thought of the narrow death cell in which his body was confined. "All those who cheered for me when I rode to Aaronkal, Father. Teach them wisdom, to put their hope in you alone. Do not fail them. Do not let them fall into the hands of Fingar or Tulbur. Send your angels to defend them, and may all the enemies turn back before them." Hope was all around him like a golden light, and he knew as never before that God heard his prayers, and loved him with an everlasting love. The power to pray did not fall from him, and he did not cease to pray, upheld by faith and joy.

*   *   *

The hills where the men of Petrag rode were soft and rolling, cloaked with brown grass that sparkled with dew in the midmorning sun. It was a kindly land, far down from the mountains' stony feet. To miners from the barren valley of Petrag, it was sweet, beautiful, and strange. Though woods stood here and there in the valleys, for the most part the land was open, and they rode swiftly through it with ease.

Many times they passed a castle on a hill, with cottages and harvested fields clustered around it: they were following Karolan's border, and the ancient kings had fortified it well. Jonathan had not been in this region before, but Master Joseph had, and he guided them. They skirted the castles at a distance, half afraid that a loud trumpet would sound and soldiers issue forth to challenge them. Occasionally a farmer in an outlying field saw them and fled in terror, but they heard no challenges and saw no sentries.

"The border is guarded poorly," said Jonathan to Joseph as they rode side by side.

"That is true," said the old miner. "Nonetheless I would that we had a standard, that we might be known as Karolans."

"I wish the same," said Jonathan. "There may be spies within the woods, who report our coming though they do not challenge us."

"There are," said Joseph, "unless the steward is a fool. But if they come to Aaronkal, the prince will hear their report and know that all is well."

"How far are we to the south of Dilgarel?"

212

"Not far, for the horses of Petrag. Dilgarel is the first castle on the plains. Before midday we will reach the last of the hills, where we may stand and look down over the flatland with its farms. We may see Dilgarel then, if the air is clear enough."

Jonathan smiled, and spurred his horse down the slope of a high, treeless hill. The last dew was fading away in the sunshine, but the wind rushing in his face was crisp and cold. The air was full of the thunder of the great horses. Beyond them, the land still seemed at peace. There was no black smoke of pillage in the sky, no sound of distant trumpets in the air.

Yet Jonathan thrilled with thoughts of adventure, and a little fear. The plains ahead, which they would reach by midday, had seen uncounted battles between Norkath and Karolan. For every castle on that border, there was a tale of heroism that could be told. Their walls had echoed to the thunder of desperate charges and shuddered before the might of catapults and battering rams. The air had rung with valiant trumpet calls and with the shouts of men whose love and loyalty were stronger than their fear. Such shouts would sound again, thought Jonathan of Glen Carrah, before the sun set red and lovely over Karolan in the west.

*   *   *

"Where is the prince, and where are the swords?" demanded Metherka in a thunderous voice. The servant of Tulbur who heard him looked a little frightened, and backed one step into the postern gate of Aaronkal, but then stood his ground.

"The swords are being tested and sharpened in the armories," he said. "The prince is still weary from his desperate journey across the mountains, and must rest until evening. He bids all men know that he is well, and that he will call a council at sunset."

"But, man," said Metherka, "the Norkaths may attack by sunset. Are we to have no swords when they come? May I not talk to the steward?"

"What would you say that cannot as well be said to me? The steward is very busy, overseeing those who care for the prince in his weakness, and those who sharpen the swords."

"I would ask what certainty he has that we will not be attacked until tomorrow," said Metherka.

"We have many spies, and they report that Fingar cannot leave Guldorak until sunrise tomorrow, or later."

"And are they infallible?" asked Metherka. "Man, does your master not know that spies can err?"

"Our men have not. They have certainty that the army of Norkath cannot reach the border today. As for the swords, many were ill-made, and require sharpening. Others are to be discarded, for we have some to spare. It is needful for us to find all that are weak, before we give them to the men."

"That is most certainly a lie!" said Metherka. "I know that Thomas did not gather twenty thousand swords. I know that his servants tested them before they paid the gold that bought them. The blades are sound and sharp, and we need every sword the smiths have ever made."

"Patience, fiery knight. What I have said is true, and you must believe it."

"I do not believe it, you discourteous knave! Tell your master that if he does not bring out five thousand swords at least before the shadow of Aaronkal strikes the oaks, I will throw ladders up against the walls and lead three score soldiers in to get them."

The servant stepped back again, alarmed. "You would assail the castle of your prince?"

"Let the steward come out and speak to me if he would not have it so," thundered Metherka. "Or better still, admit me and let me speak to the prince. The knavery that comes from your lips is no invention of Ilohan of Karolan. It bears the stamp of Tulbur the Steward as surely as you, his hireling, bear it yourself."

"Have a care, Sir Metherka," said the servant. "Do you forget that there are archers in Aaronkal? The adventure of the ladders may cost you dear, should you attempt it."

"Be still," said a gruff voice. "It is enough to fight Norkath."

Metherka turned to face Britheldore, who had walked up behind him during the conversation. "I mean to do no wrong," said Metherka, "but I fear that all is not well."

"It is not," said Britheldore. The servant turned, a frantic expression on his face. He slammed the postern gate and pushed across the lock.

"What do you advise?" asked Metherka, but before Britheldore could answer, the postern gate swung open again and the servant stood briskly at attention beside it. Tulbur came out, dressed in majestic finery as before.

"I offer you my greatest regret for my hireling's discourtesy," said Tulbur. "I will never be so ungrateful or unwise as to refuse speech with two noble knights who are doubtful of the prudence of my actions."

"What do you know of Fingar?" asked Britheldore.

"My spies report that last night he camped at Guldorak with all his army, even the cavalry. This morning they saw no preparations to break camp. The cavalry cannot reach Aaronkal until midnight tonight at the earliest. The main bulk of the army is not to be expected until after midday tomorrow."

"But the cavalry could reach our border at sunset!" said Metherka angrily. "They could rape and pillage any town in eastern Karolan, and we cannot prevent it. Why are we not at the border?"

"Be still," said Britheldore.

"A town is a sore loss," said Tulbur, "but we will give it up if we must, rather than abandon our position of power. Aaronkal is the place of prudence and strategy, until we know where the bulk of Fingar's army marches."

"How is the prince?" asked Britheldore.

"He is weak, after his long and difficult journey. He has, you must realize, crossed the mountains of Karolan, which all since Dradrag have believed to be impossible. He is not ill, and has spoken now and then to me and to the physicians who care for him. He will rise at sunset tonight, and you and all the other knights will be summoned to his council of war. Until then he rests in bed."

"How many are our swords?" asked Britheldore.

"Eighteen thousand made by the smiths of Karolan in recent years. Six thousand stored in the great armories of Aaronkal in ages gone by. Many have rusted, and my pages and servants are sharpening and cleaning them."

"You will give them to us," said Britheldore. "How soon?"

"I will produce five thousand swords when the shadow of Aaronkal touches the oaks. The rest will be prepared by sunset. It is a great work."

"Swear that you speak truth," commanded Britheldore.

"I swear by my crest of the Whipping Willow, and by the Stone, Sword, and Star. I swear on my honor as a knight that I have spoken truth, and will do as I have said so long as it lies within my power."

"May it be so," said Britheldore. "Farewell."

"The tongue of Sir Britheldore was never known for over-courtesy," said Tulbur. "I thank you for this interview, then, if you will not thank me. Farewell until tonight."

He nodded to them and withdrew. The servant bowed and gently closed the door. Metherka heard the soft scrape and thud as the gate was locked, but if Britheldore's ears were keen enough, he made no sign. Instead, Metherka found the older knight looking keenly into his face. He was instantly ashamed of his hotheaded words. But Britheldore offered no rebuke.

"You are a true knight," said the old man. "You asked my counsel. I give it: Arm yourself and all your men. Bid them eat and drink for strength, but keep them ready." With those words he was gone, back down the steps to disappear in the great army. But Metherka stood still on the steps of Aaronkal. "You are a true knight." From many it would have been but a meaningless courtesy. From Britheldore it was high praise. Metherka did not agree with the statement: he was hotheaded and careless, and had caused much harm. Yet, with Britheldore's accolade still in his ears, he went to follow the old knight's terse advice. He was not a true knight now, but perhaps there was still time...

Chapter 12

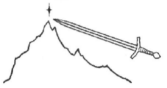

The Shepherd at War

"THE PLAINS!" CALLED JONATHAN, AS THEY CRESTED THE last hill and looked out over the great expanse of fertile lowland. "Halt, and look!"

A line of broken stone pillars marked the border. It ran far, far across the plains until it disappeared into the hazy distance. On either side of it were farms, meadows, and scattered clumps of forest. Red and yellow remnants of autumn finery graced the gray woods in places, while the harvested fields lay brown and empty. The wind over the crest of the hill was strong, fresh, and cold.

Jonathan sat like a statue on his motionless horse, absorbed in looking. The hill on which they stood was in Norkath, as far as he could tell; they had been following the border since early morning, now on one side, now on the other. The long, smooth grass slope seemed to call him, but still he tarried, searching intently for any hint of dust or smoke, or moving men. His eyes followed the line of broken stone sentinels far out into the distance, toward a tiny gray outline near the blurred horizon that he thought must be Castle Dilgarel. He looked left from it, into Karolan, and something caught his eye.

218

THE SHEPHERD AT WAR

"Look!" he cried. "Far away, west and north beyond Dilgarel!"

A young miner rode up beside him. "I see the glint of sun on polished iron, and here and there a spot of red," he said. "A vast army, or my eyes see false!"

"They do not," said Jonathan, after a long look. "Your sight seems keener than my own, which is high praise, yet what you have seen I also see." Others around them murmured agreement. A silence followed: a deep, clean, hilltop silence. The land below seemed a lovely picture; the thing at which they all stared more a wonder than a threat. It was almost lost in the distant haze, and looked merely like an irregular field of gray bushes. But the field was moving. Here and there they saw a flash, and knew it could only be the sun glancing on a weapon. Despite the great distance they could also see tiny specks of muted color, always red. The silence broke.

"The banners are red," said Jonathan, "not Karolan..."

"A fist of iron clenched before a wall of fire!" said Yalron, at his side. "The emblem of Norkath is red enough! Let us ride to Aaronkal on the wings of the wind." With the eager words the last of the hilltop silence was dispelled, and all knew that the vision was real, its message terrible. Even the horses seemed to shy with tension and excitement, ready, like the men, to dare tremendous things for Karolan.

"There is a ruined border castle not far behind us and below," said Jonathan, turning to Master Joseph. "There is a road from it leading west. Do you know if it leads to Aaronkal?"

The old miner looked back to see it. "Most likely," he said, "but I am not certain."

"Then we must guess and hope," said Jonathan. "Men of Petrag!" he called. "That army we have seen looks insignificant as a band of fairies. But it will take on flesh and blood, and greed and anger. The swords we have seen flash like distant diamonds will be hot for our blood and the blood of our countrymen. Yet we will fly to Aaronkal ahead of them, and when they come they will meet courage like a mighty fire. Men of Petrag, we will vanquish them! Ride now for Aaronkal! Ride like the wind!"

They wheeled west and south, and thundered down the hill with such speed that the cold wind of their going brought tears to Jonathan's eyes. They swept past the pile of ruined stone that had once been a castle, and crowded onto the old stone road, slowing their horses a little to avoid accidents. Still the sound of their going seemed to shake the earth. Jonathan knew that no speed could be too fast for their errand. Far ahead, unchallenged as yet, rode Fingar – and Ilohan must be warned in time.

At midday the horses were strained and sweating, but they still held up their heads. They entered a thick forest, through which the old road yet made a good, clear path. Sunshine filtered through the barren branches, and cast bright patterns on the carpet of autumn leaves. Nature still brimmed with beauty, while the riders thundered through it intent on violence and war. The sun flashed dizzyingly in their eyes as they passed through the mingled light and shade. The living glory of the wood flew by them, seen only in brief, stolen glances.

Yet in those glances Jonathan rejoiced. The war he fought was to defend the beauty of the world, not break it. The beauty did not frown on them; it cheered them on. It was wild, untamed, autumn on the edge of winter, yet all undismayed. Keen winds were singing through the branches. Jonathan could hear the living forest bend and blow, even over the thunder of their hooves.

He thought of this season in Carrah, of gray-gold grass dead from many frosts and stiffly frozen with another. That grass would sparkle in the sun, and crunch beneath the feet of those who walked on it. Soon the lovely snow would fall, and the Carratril would run dark below a sheet of ice. Then that too would be covered, and from the cottage to the mountains the pure white snow would cloak the world. He thought of his footsteps running beside Naomi's across the snow; of warm hearth-light afterward; and of hot food and drink beside the fire together.

Suddenly, even as Jonathan galloped at the head of his army, he felt that he was no more than a child, a child of Glen Carrah. He had never seen Aaronkal, had never fought in a pitched battle. Who was he to lead two hundred men, many older than himself, into war? He was not enough. But it was too late to think such things. He had to do this. He could not turn back, could not abandon his charge to another man. He was not ready, but his course was set.

Was any man ready, or did all feel the same? Jonathan did not know, but he guessed that each in his own way felt unprepared. War and death were terrible and strange, beyond the world men loved or understood. None could ever be ready for them. True men would face them nonetheless.

They rode out of the forest and into farmland again. The thunder of their hooves was loud on the hard stone road, and they had no standard to tell on which side they would fight. Women screamed and ran to find and hide their children as the army passed. Old men who had not gone to war looked up, and then turned away, despairing, at the sight of the cavalry from the east.

Jonathan drew his sword as he rode, and raised it high above his head. "For Karolan!" he cried, loud enough to be heard above the noise of their galloping. "For Karolan we ride! Long live Prince Ilohan!"

Then fearful mothers who had gathered children close against their skirts looked up with incredulous hope in their eyes. The army of Petrag thundered past, and did not wait or turn aside. Jonathan did not often spend his breath to declare their loyalty, but when he did, two hundred voices echoed his, and always they could see the bystanders were calmed and heartened. Nevertheless, three times an arrow whistled shrilly past them – shot, Jonathan guessed, by a man who had not heard their cries. These arrows worried Jonathan, though they had done no harm. He began to sing the war song of Karolan, and the men of Petrag took it up behind him, loud and strong above the thunder of their ride. Then there were no more arrows, and rather than screaming or flying, the people of Karolan looked up – half scared, yet with hope also in their faces as they wondered what it might mean.

*   *   *

Joseph, the shepherd of Carrah, lay on his blanket in the midst of the army. His pony stood still beside him, tethered, waiting far more patiently than the men. Unease gripped the whole great concourse, and the tension in the air was palpable.

Joseph's thoughts ran in two strands, each tangled round the other. One was of the waiting tenseness of the great army, and the swords they still had not been given. He had spoken about the swords with Barnabas, who was still in jail. The blacksmith had objected to Tulbur's count, which had become widely known among the men. "Scarcely more than ten thousand swords have been made in recent times," Barnabas had said, "and thousands more are left in the cottages of Karolan thanks to the foolish order not to gather them. Such is my count, and I have spoken with many sword-buyers of the king through many years. I do not lightly contradict the steward."

Joseph wondered what it could mean. He knew Barnabas would never accuse a man of lying without good reason – and there could be no doubt that his words had been an accusation. But if the steward's count was false, why was he lying?

Joseph felt sick. He had come here, and had left Naomi. The men had feared much, and hoped little, and the steward had not won their love. The prince had come, but seemed to have faded away into darkness. Now the rumor among the men said that Fingar would enter Karolan tomorrow. They had expected it age-long days before. And still they were not given swords.

The shepherd from Carrah could feel the worry and discontent of the thousands of men around him. He longed to calm them, as he could calm his sheep when they scattered in dismay at the first thunder-crash of an approaching storm. Yet when his sheep were frightened he was not. He could protect them, and lead them back to the fold that was their safety and their home. Today he was among the fearful, powerless to help. He was a sheep himself, one of the weakest of the flock.

The other train of thought was like a shaft of gold shining brightly in his mind. He dreamed, beyond the darkness of anxiety and war, of a future that, despite all, might yet come. He dreamed of coming back to Glen Carrah and seeing his daughter run out of the house to greet him. He dreamed of knowing that the eastern storm was past forever, the shadow gone, her golden life secure. He dreamed that he would be again a gentle shepherd in a kindly land. That which was

223

fearful, dark, and unknown he banished from the dream, even as he prayed God might banish it from reality.

Before the freezing of the Carratril he might be back, to watch with Naomi the white snowfalls blanketing the glen. He knew his love for her was holy now – sprung from God, the source of holy love, and guarded by him from all that was wrong in Joseph's own heart. He knew his love would never do Naomi harm; its power was for good alone. With fearless joy he entrusted her into the hands of God, and knew that he would keep her. In the selflessness and surrender of his love, peace and freedom came to Joseph despite the restless worry that surrounded him.

Awakening from these thoughts almost as if from a blessed dream, Joseph again took note of his immediate surroundings. He looked up into the clear blue sky, swept with strong wind. The sun was low, in the west behind Aaronkal. He guessed that the shadow had nearly reached the oaks. His ear was to the ground, and he could hear the creaking of windblown trees and the anxious patter of footsteps near and far. The peace and joy that he had felt began to fade away. He was a gentle shepherd of Carrah, lost in a rising storm of war.

Thunder. Faint as a whisper, half heard in the distance, yet deep and strong: the noise of a great storm. The low rumble was coming to him through the ground. The sky was cloudless. His mind was full of thoughts that flew like lightning. Then one stood out, a dire and brilliant inspiration, and drowned them all. Joseph the shepherd knew the truth, and stood.

He looked swiftly around, understanding all in a blinding instant of vision. Aaronkal stood black against the brilliant west. Its banners snapped in the breeze, and archers lined its battlements with arrows on the string. He alone of all the great army seemed to know what it meant: their doom was thundering toward them. And he who had sought to hide his daughter knew also a place of strength where they might fly. He knew even instants were precious, yet he balked at the awesome call he felt. "I am a gentle shepherd of Carrah," he whispered in his mind.

"Then shepherd men, for once in all your days," came an answering thought, from honor and conscience – or from God.

"The cost... The hopelessness..." whimpers flew like lightning through his mind, as he stood frozen on the field beside his pony.

"The price the good shepherd will always pay," came the answer, and the call.

"Naomi..."

"Love her now as you have always loved her." And then the choice was made, and all the wondering had passed in only a fraction of a heartbeat. Joseph leaped upon his pony, and stood above the host of Karolan. He could see the archers on the battlements bending their bows, but the men around him were like frightened sheep, desperately in need of a shepherd. He would warn them. Though it would cost his life, though he would not see Naomi again on earth, yet he would warn and guide them. He would be for once a shepherd of men.

"Men of Karolan, we are betrayed!" he cried. His voice rang out with a strength and authority such as he had never heard before. "To Petrag!" he cried. "Fly to Petrag! The steward has betrayed you. Norkath is upon you!" The arrows came, gray birds of evil flying through the shade. He did not even turn to see them. "Fly!" he cried, in a voice like trumpets and thunder. "Fly to Petrag!"

The arrows struck. In the unbelievable instant his only thought was, "Father, save!" He coughed on blood. He gestured one last time toward the mountains, and croaked, "Betrayed... Petrag..." Then he toppled from his horse.

Chaos reigned in the camp of Karolan. Arrows slashed down from the sky, shot by the archers who stood like mocking devils on the battlements of Aaronkal, slaying whom they chose. Men struggled to arm themselves with something, anything, and mount their horses to fly toward Petrag. Metherka, fully armed and mounted, strove to gather the Knights of Karolan around him through the press of wildly moving men. The thunder of approaching horses was loud now, but no one could tell from whence it came. Men looked around in panic, expecting at any moment to see the Norkath cavalry gallop into sight.

*   *   *

The anger of Barnabas burned hot as a furnace. From the prison that unjustly held him he had seen his friend and neighbor fall. His blazing wrath was selfless, and as strong as iron. "Lord God, help and guide me," he prayed, in one split instant as he raised his hand to strike the wall.

He felt anger, love, and the blessing of God fall upon him like fire. He was stronger than the prison wall. The oak beams cracked and bowed before his fearsome blows. He struck, forced, wrenched, and twisted, fighting to get out with more strength than he had ever used before. He broke out beams as thick as a man's arm with his bare hands. He wrenched them from the sockets and nails that held them and sent their fragments springing and whistling through the air. Even in the midst of his fury, with his hands bloody from the force he was using, still he was a craftsman. Still he struck and wrenched with skill as well as strength, aiming to shatter his evil prison as swiftly as could be. Three guards stood around the cell, axes raised, afraid but ready.

A wall gave way and fell outward with a crash of splintering wood. One of the guards fell crushed beneath it. Barnabas leaped out with a great oak bar in his hands. The second guard dropped his axe and ran. The last guard rushed at Barnabas, his axe held high. Barnabas parried the blow and then returned it. Both axe and man were broken, cast ruinously to the ground before the blacksmith's fury. Barnabas was free. Panting hard, heedless of arrows, cries, and running men, he raced with all his strength to the place where he had seen Joseph fall.

*　　　　　*　　　　　*

The cavalry of Norkath came like thunder from the north, and swept around the unarmed host of Karolan. They came in two great columns of knights, one to the west behind Aaronkal, and one to the east beside the oaks. They rode in perfect order, their lances aimed a little inward toward the men they were trapping like fish caught in a seine. When the columns met in the south the Army of All Karolan would be surrounded.

Heeding Joseph's warning, the men of Karolan did their best to escape by running, riding, or stumbling south toward Petrag – but they had seen their shepherd fall, and they knew their cause was hopeless. The horsemen of Fingar were coming on too fast.

With the cold wind in his face, and thoughts flying through his heart like leaves in an autumn gale, Jonathan of Glen Carrah came riding from the forest. He saw the blue sky, and the dark castle, and the bright flags waving. He heard the cries of dismay, and saw the Knights of Norkath riding. Their armor gleamed, and their spears were tipped with steel. Above them the banner of the Fist of Iron snapped in the wind and glowed red in the setting sun.

In vain Jonathan looked for bright swords among the Karolans, and for valiant men marching in ranks, or charging with reckless bravery. Then with wild joy and hot fear in his heart together, he looked at the men of Petrag, close behind him. He raised his lance. "Men of Petrag!" he roared. "To break the trap! For home and love! For honor, hope, and justice! For Karolan, and Ilohan her prince! Charge!"

There seemed to be magic in that cry, to spur tired men and weary horses on with deadly speed. The western column of Norkath had turned eastward to close the trap, and against it Jonathan guided the thunder of their charge. The ground shook. Jonathan's heart pounded, and his blood seemed to sing with the glory and the terror of the moment.

The Norkaths came on ten abreast, ordered rank on ordered rank, with visors down and shields raised, with perfect discipline born of long training. The Karolans rode ragged and disordered, without shield or armor, with only poplar lances to lower against the foe. Yet they rode with blazing fury, their hearts aflame with loyalty and courage. They rode as if no law could organize them, nor fear dismay them, nor foe resist them.

"Naomi," said Jonathan softly beneath the roar that filled his ears, "I will come back to you. I will not die. I will find you." He lowered his enormous lance for the impact. He looked at the shining armor of the Norkath knights. "Throw them down!" he roared back to his men. "Break their charge!"

He could see the froth in the Norkath horses' nostrils, and the veins bulging on their chests. He could see the jewels on the sword hilts of the knights. There were perhaps three heartbeats more. The white wood of his lance was rough, and there was a deep notch that easily fit his hand. He held it with a grip of iron. What he had done in ordering this charge seemed mad to him. It seemed the impact must be hard enough to kill both men and horses in the first terrific shock. Yet it would break the Norkath charge, and keep the trap from closing. One heart beat more, perhaps his last. No, it would not be! For Naomi, it would not!

The crash came. Wild, unbelievable, too fast for thought or sight: blinding, deafening confusion, men doing things they would not remember, and seeing things they could not forget. Jonathan saw his lance unhorse an armored knight and throw him brutally back against the legs of the horses behind. But the lance too was knocked downward. At the last instant he steered it toward the chest of a Norkath charger; there was no time to aim higher. He saw it bash bloodily into the horse's breast, but then the lance itself broke with a deafening crack. The butt end went up like the arm of a catapult, tore him from the saddle and hurled him into the air. He drew his sword as he fell and landed unharmed on the back of a terrified, dying horse. From then on the fight was pure chaos. He fought with all his strength, parrying and attacking in all directions, trying to slay both horses and men among the Norkaths. The charge had become a tempest, an avalanche of men and horses and blood and splintered bone, shot through with screams of terror and of pain. Jonathan fought still, and was not wounded. Into every blow went all his strength of mind and body, force of arm and lightning thought. He broke lances, felled horses, cut through man and armor, always turned to face the nearest foe. The knights of Norkath were all around him, and those who could bent all their force to kill him. Still he fought on, uninjured, while the mighty charge of Petrag broke and splintered against the foundering column of Norkath cavalry.

*   *   *

"Still time to be a true knight..." Metherka whispered. In his hand he held a single banner of Karolan, and the knights, thanks in part to Britheldore's hints and warnings, were at last all armed and gathered close behind him. His heart sang, for death could not hurt him, and to lead the Knights of Karolan had always been his dream. His laziness and others' ridicule had drained his joy and marred his life, but now he was free of them forever. Fear of death or cowardice might assail him, but they were futile against his blazing courage. His only sorrow was that others would die with him on this day of courage without hope. Yet they too were knights, and they too would be heroes.

Their joy must come from his, like a flame that leaps from torch to torch. They needed no hope of ultimate victory, only the certainty their cause was right. "We cannot live, and so we shall die well!" he cried. "Onward, Knights of Karolan! Shatter the trap, teach Fingar courage, and Tulbur honor! To die your leader is blessing beyond my deserving. Charge!"

The banner flew back in the wind. The unarmed foot soldiers of Karolan scattered before them. The wall of the Norkath knights closed strong and hard ahead of them. The Knights of Karolan lowered their lances in the hopeless charge. Metherka had won their love and kindled their loyalty to flame. There was joy in many faces as the red sun flashed from their bright armor, and they knew their courage was forever proved.

Britheldore too rode in the desperate charge, and looked at Metherka, far ahead. The young knight wore no helmet, and his brown-gold hair blew back in the wind and shimmered in the sun. "I wish I had seen Eleanor again," said Britheldore. "Yet it is good to see the young lion set free."

The Knights of Karolan rushed onward in flawless ranks. They came to break the trap as it was closing, to smash the eastern column of Norkath, even as it turned west to strike the men of Petrag from behind. While Jonathan's charge had crashed and broken against the Norkaths like a battering ram, halting their column but killing relatively few, Metherka's charge cut through the cavalry of Fingar like a spear. The Knights of Karolan came like the wind, and the Norkaths fell before them. Still the charge of Karolan was not broken, and the knights thundered past stumbling horse and fallen man, deep into the ranks of Norkath that they shattered. Then one by one they fell, unhorsed and skewered where they lay, or overwhelmed with downward blows even as they fought furiously on foot.

Metherka alone carried all the way through the ranks of the enemy, and emerged still mounted, with lance and shield-arm broken, but triumph in his face. With less than ten score Knights of Karolan he had charged a Norkath column over a thousand strong, and shattered it. The remnant of the column was now struggling to reform with but a tithe of its riders still on horseback. The sun setting behind the mountains turned the brown grass before Metherka into gold. Its warm light shone all around him, clear and bright and free. He wheeled his winded horse, leveled his broken spear, and charged the Norkath remnant, alone. So great was the fear the Norkaths bore him that the first man he met speared not Metherka but the horse he rode. As the great animal foundered beneath him, Metherka tore from his saddle the pole that held the banner. He threw it like a spear, far out into the free land beyond the Norkath ranks. "You shall not conquer stone!" he cried, as it stuck in the ground and trembled there, outside the farthest reach of Fingar's trap.

The Knight of Metherka leaped free of his falling horse, struck a one-handed sword blow against the armor of a mounted enemy, and then went down beneath the fell stroke of a Norkath axe. So died the man Thomas distrusted, Tulbur ridiculed, and Britheldore loved. The Norkaths raised a shout of victory, but it was hollow. Man for man, the Knights of Karolan had crushed them.

*   *   *

Jonathan struck a Norkath horseman a mighty sword blow to the shoulder, cutting through armor, flesh, and bone, and hurling the man dreadfully wounded from his saddle. Jonathan leaped up to take his place, and, for an instant unassailed, looked around him. The charge of the miners was over, its power spent, but many of them still lived and kept their saddles, fighting around him with swords and axes and all the strength they had. In the immediate vicinity of Jonathan the miners were ascendant. The ground was littered with broken men, and horses dying in their blood. Jonathan was stunned to realize that, for this brief moment, he was safe. He looked farther afield.

Metherka's splendid charge had destroyed one jaw of Fingar's trap. The miners' charge had blocked the other jaw, and through the gap the men of Karolan were running, hope and valor kindled in Metherka's wake. Yet the gap would soon be closed. An endless host of foot soldiers was already coming up behind the cavalry of Norkath, and the horsemen from the rear of the west column, who had not faced the fury of the miners' charge, were galloping up to do all that they could.

Soon they would close the trap forever, and butcher the fleeing Karolans, who had no swords.

Jonathan knew where they could get swords. He raised his own blade, red with blood and notched with the blows of weapons he had shattered. "To Petrag, men!" he cried. "To Petrag, and no man shall conquer stone!"

He rode out from the wreckage of the broken charge, to where the grass was clean and brown save where his horse left hoof prints red with Norkath blood. He took the banner that Metherka had thrown, and lifted it high against the evening sky. "Onward to Petrag!" he cried again, "And all who still have sword and horse, ride with me and cover the retreat!"

Perhaps five score miners rallied around him and turned back to face the charge of the remaining Norkath cavalry from the western column. The charge came, but far beyond them, far too soon for them to hinder it or to block it. The horsemen from rear of the west column came flying east, cut a savage swath of blood across the fleeing Karolans, and closed the trap. Five thousand soldiers from the Army of all Karolan were free, and thrice as many lost behind a wall of spears.

*   *   *

Free flying from the closing of the cruel trap's jaws, a single horseman came riding, with a wounded comrade held before him on the saddle. He did not join the fleeing men of Karolan, nor Jonathan's cavalry as they stood still, dismayed. He sought the oakwoods, and rode through them until he found a sweet, cool stream that glided gently over mossy roots. He dismounted, and laid his wounded friend gently down upon the bank. He was Barnabas, who in his fury had struck down one of Tulbur's guards and taken his horse. The friend was

Joseph, whom he had caught up into the saddle with one motion of gentle might when he had reached him.

The stream flowed deep and clear. The last sunlight of the failing day caught the tops of the oaks, illuminating their dark wood and deep red leaves. Only the moss upon which Joseph lay was green. The wind, so strong earlier in the day, was soft and gentle in the creek hollow, and in the oak branches above. Joseph opened his eyes, and they were clear.

"So you are free," he whispered.

Barnabas wept. "So you are a hero, friend," he said. "Would that I could take your place! The steward's treachery has cost a fearful price."

Joseph closed his eyes. His breath came with a wheeze, past the blood that was filling his lungs. "It is not I who pay it," he whispered. He brought his left hand to his mouth, and touched the ring upon it to his lips. He removed the ring with a patient effort, and laid it on the moss. "Abigail's," he said. "It was the symbol of her love, my faithfulness. Both are God's forever, and I need no symbols now. Give it to Naomi. She will be your daughter now. Love her and defend her. Tell her I love her. Tell her I am sorry to leave her."

"I can never be to her what you were, dear friend," said Barnabas through his tears. "Yet you need not fear I will not love her. If I live, I will be her father."

Red blood stained the green moss. "I could not stop the blood," whispered Joseph. "Abigail... Abigail. So this is what you passed through. The letting go is very hard. Oh Lord, my God, are you there, waiting?"

Barnabas gripped his hand. The gold ring lying on the moss shone dull in the soft forest twilight. "Oh Lord," whispered Joseph, "forgive my doubt. I know that you are waiting... And Abigail is yours, and you love her. I will see her. How can that be? Yet I will see you, deeper wonder far, beyond thought or dream. How can it be... Yet I trust myself to you! I know that you have loved us, and we are yours, forever. Yours, forever... Free and bright, forever, all things are well, as they were meant to be. Oh Lord our God, how greatly you have loved us. How we love you, and love is... always yours..."

There was a long stillness in the forest, and even the wind seemed to Barnabas to make no sound. The creek flowed with the merest whisper of a ripple. Then a distant trumpet call came, carried on the wind. Barnabas took the ring, and stood up. "Be with the living also, Lord, as you are with the dead who pass through death to life. Be with me in the storm to which I go, and be with those I love."

Barnabas gently took up the corpse that lay beside the stream, and carried it back into the woods, to where a now dry rivulet had once carved a deep, earthen canyon among the trees. He climbed into it, and laid the corpse gently on the bottom. He buried it deep with the bright forest leaves. "Farewell, dear friend," he said, looking not down but upward. "The night draws dark upon the ones you left behind, but thanks to you Karolan has a hope."

He ran light-footed through the forest, and swung into his saddle with one swift motion. The tears were still wet on his face, but his voice rang through the trees. "To Petrag, and may hope shine bright forever! Father, be with us, for from earth we have no aid. Onward!"

Chapter 13

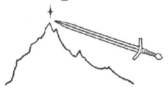

To Petrag and the Swords

FLAMES GLOWED BEHIND THEM AS DARKNESS FELL: THE flames of Karolan, burning. Few save those from Petrag had emerged with horses from the deadly trap at Aaronkal. They fled, unarmed, unmounted, at a forced march through the falling twilight. And only one man brought them hope.

Back and forth among the host rode Jonathan, upon a lame horse captured from a Norkath knight. He held a torch in his right hand, and the banner of Karolan fluttered from a shaft firmly tied to his saddle. That lonely banner, shimmering in the red torchlight, heartened many in the fleeing, unarmed army. Yet his words shone brighter than his torch and kindled a flame of courage in their hearts. They listened, and remembered that they were men, and Karolans – that they were the Army of all Karolan, still hoping to give Fingar battle.

"Onward!" called Jonathan as he rode. "Onward to Petrag. At Petrag there are swords by thousands. In Petrag we will stand, and we will triumph. They will fight us there – they must – and the rape of Karolan will cease as long as we can stand against them. We are the ones they will come to kill, in Petrag where the gold mines are."

The army was great still, though it was only a quarter of the army that had been. Nevertheless, Jonathan rode back and forth ceaselessly, neglecting no part of the great host, calling out his words of courage and hope to all. It seemed to the men that his strength could never falter, and his courage would never dim.

It did not seem so to Jonathan himself. His heart was heavy with many troubles. The land was being pillaged, and he was not with Naomi to defend her. If the words he shouted to the men were true, Fingar would march straight to Petrag, leaving western Karolan unmolested, so she might be safe – at least as long as they could hold out in the valley of stone. Yet his father – no, he could not think of him, for the grief struck too deep and his mind must be free for other things. Most of the men had not brought food from Aaronkal in their rush to escape. He did not know the land between Aaronkal and Petrag. Master Joseph, who knew it better, had fallen in the charge. Though the flames behind them proved that at least some Norkaths were tarrying to pillage and burn, Jonathan feared that the remnant of Fingar's cavalry might at any moment overtake them and attack.

He paused a moment, on the right flank of the army, holding the torch high while the men marched past. Far off in the darkness he heard a single horse galloping. "Who goes there? Speak, in the name of Prince Ilohan!" he cried.

"Barnabas, loyal blacksmith from Carrah," came the reply.

"Father!" cried Jonathan, the word rising with irresistible joy to his lips. "Father! I feared you perished in the trap."

Barnabas rode out of the darkness, into the circle of red light cast by Jonathan's torch. "Jonathan?" he asked uncertainly, and then, "Jonathan! How is it with you?"

Jonathan was silent for a moment, looking at his father, overwhelmed by what he felt. It seemed a lifetime of events had passed since he had heard his father's voice or seen his face. Now he saw again the man who had cared for him all his childhood, who had always been worthy of his love and respect – the man who had taught him courage, strength, and honor, and prepared him well for the dire adventures that had come to him. He remembered his father's patient reproof of his childish errors. He remembered how his love was shown – on bright days when all was well in Carrah and they had sword matches or hunted together in joy and freedom, and also in harder times when Barnabas had to work all day and into the night, to provide for them and keep the pledges he had made. Jonathan remembered that his father had never complained, and had hardly raised his voice in anger, in all the days he could remember.

Now Jonathan knew that he himself was a man, his father's son but no longer a child. And he knew that he had not disgraced his father, but had acted in justice and honor that would bring him joy. Now they could stand side by side with no shadow between them, and fight with all their strength even if Norkath came a score of thousands strong.

"I am unhurt, Father, and I rejoice beyond words to see you free and well," said Jonathan at last. "Yet the whole host looks to me as their leader, and I do not know the land, and they have no swords. The Norkaths are burning Karolan behind us, and we cannot turn and rescue our people. We must flee to Petrag, where there are swords."

Barnabas turned his horse and rode up beside his son. For a moment Jonathan shifted the torch to his left hand, and reached out toward his father with his right. They shook hands, and their eyes met in the torchlight. "It is a bitter joy to stand with you in so desperate a war, my son," said Barnabas. "It is a joy nonetheless." He paused, and smiled. "Thousands look to you to lead them. It is no light honor that you have won. Do not by faltering cause all of them to falter. If there are swords in Petrag we may triumph yet."

"Karolan is burning behind us... What of those we leave to Fingar's mercy?" asked Jonathan. He expected no good answer, but he spoke aloud the thought he could not bear.

Joy faded from his father's face until it looked like stone. "We must not think of what we cannot help, when the road lies clear before us," said Barnabas. "Tomorrow, if we live, we may look to Karolan's healing. Today, her rescue."

Jonathan looked at him, and his father read the question in his face: the measure of Hannah and Naomi's peril. "They are far away," said Barnabas. "The storm may not reach them, if we face it here with courage. If we fall, God still stands, and he will guard them."

"We will not fall," said Jonathan.

*   *   *

"Lord, you know that I am dying. I do not want to die. There was so much I hoped to do..." So ran Ilohan's prayer, in the forget-me-not at Aaronkal. His thirst was terrible. He felt desperately sick, and his mouth was dry as dust. He did not move, for he had no wish to remind himself how narrow were the confines of his tomb. The air he breathed was stale and musty. He had no idea how time had flowed since he was captured. No events marked its passing here, and the torture of thirst twisted whatever sense of it he might have retained. He did not know how long he had been dying here.

"Father, please let me pray again, and let me die while praying. I was held up by prayer so long, as though I had great wings to fly above my pain. Please take me up again... I hardly know what to pray for, now. Everything good seems so impossible. I know that you can still accomplish good, even for Karolan, but I cannot imagine how... I would like Jonathan not to be killed. I would like Naomi to live... And Eleanor... I would like Eleanor never to hear the news that I am dead. And yet I ask long life for her, and joy. That is impossible. But then you have done the impossible. Even for me – or, at least, in my life... Lord, I would like Tulbur to fail, and Fingar to be defeated. I ask for the lives of my people. Do not let them be slaughtered. Do not let the traitor and the evil king have the victory. Defeat them, throw them down, let them fall before faithful men who love you... Or before Jonathan who does not... Oh Lord, do not let that always be true. Bring Jonathan to love you. Preserve his life, I pray. Give him wisdom. He was the commander of the only army of Karolan... A bitter laugh, the army of Karolan, but twelve-score miners strong. Yet he must have met Fingar by now. Father, though this is impossible too, let him still be the commander of the army of Karolan. Give him and his men all that they need to fight well, and do not let them fall... Yet they must have fallen already. Yet nothing is impossible. Glory to God, I am on the wings again..."

*   *   *

Jonathan's desperate retreat continued. The fires of Karolan sent lurid light into the northward sky. Many of the men felt that back at Aaronkal, Jonathan had appeared from nowhere – an angel of war with the Stone, Sword, and Star in his hand.

Most did not even know his name, yet he had their loyalty almost as if he had been the prince himself. He was all they had.

Jonathan himself felt more hopeful now that his father, with much better knowledge of the land, was beside him. He was heartened also by the fact that so far there was no sign of cavalry pursuit – though he tried not to imagine what this inevitably meant: Fingar's army was being given free rein to pillage, at least here in eastern Karolan. Jonathan had sent Yalron ahead on a swift horse, to ask the women of Petrag to prepare all the food they could, and bring it down to the sword pits to feed the army. Yet it would be a lean and hungry night and morning, for he knew they could not reach Petrag until the next afternoon. Until then the men would have to eat whatever they had, which was little.

Jonathan and Barnabas talked much, as they rode together. Of Ilohan they said little, for they could do nothing. Barnabas said he might yet be alive, but Jonathan thought that hope as false as his father's faith in God. They agreed that Tulbur and Fingar must soon come against them with all their force. Fingar would want the mines, and Tulbur would counsel prudently as always – in this case, to vanquish first and pillage later. Karolan was not safely conquered while five thousand of its defenders roamed free, with swords – and Tulbur must know they could get swords in Petrag.

"Tulbur sent all the swords of Aaronkal to Petrag, to disarm us?" asked Jonathan incredulously when they spoke of this.

"It seems likely, since you say there are many swords there," said Barnabas. "He may have ensured that there were none in Aaronkal, so that even if Metherka led us to sack the castle, we would not find our swords."

After a long silence Jonathan spoke in a strained voice. "I could tear him to pieces. Let Tulbur beware now of Jonathan! No darker treachery than his has ever mocked the beauty of the world."

Barnabas was silent, remembering the arrows in Joseph's chest. He, too, could shut his eyes and feel his imagination drawn with terrible force toward an evil dream, a dream where his hands closed with iron power around the steward's throat, crushing his bones and killing him with a force as cautious and as irresistible as the steward's own well-planned treachery. Yet he forced that dream away to a place from whence it would never return. The reckoning was God's to make, not his. His son's anger frightened him a little. "Beware of revenge, Jonathan," he said. "True valor does not seek it."

"Let Tulbur beware of Jonathan," said Jonathan again. "I love justice, and justice demands his life." There was a long silence. Barnabas made no reply, though he thought hard to find one. Finally Jonathan said, "Whatever comes, it is unlikely I will ever murder him. If I see him it will be in battle, and then I will kill him as one warrior kills another, though such a death is too good for him."

"So let it be," said Barnabas. "He does deserve death. It is yourself that you would hurt by seeking for revenge." They rode side by side in silence a little longer, and then Jonathan rode away to encourage the men in another part of the army.

He pushed the men on as fast as they could go, to reach Petrag before the cavalry of Norkath came to annihilate them. They had no light but the gibbous moon and a few scattered torches. They marched over farmers' fields, and past silent houses. No man knew what to say to the women and children who woke in those houses, and ran out to see them, or fled to hide from them. They marched by in frantic silence. How could they speak to those they must abandon? Many a man felt himself cruel, a monster, for leaving them to the Norkaths' mercy. Yet they could not stop for them.

A few times in the dreadful night a man came upon his own house, and ran in to seek his own family. Fewer times still he found them, brought them out into the fleeing army, and with heroic effort helped them keep up the pace. Men set their wives and youngest children on weary ponies, took older children on their shoulders, and pressed on to the limit of their strength. Bitter exhaustion came to all who carried children in that swift retreat, and yet the men who labored thus were envied. Most had no way to protect the ones they loved.

They marched through forests that shut out the moon, where unseen branches clawed at them, especially the horsemen. In meadows and farmlands they could go faster, but the long, swift march taxed all their strength. The wind began moaning in the trees and driving great, tattered banks of cloud across the sky. When these obscured the moon, many stumbled and their pace was slowed. Some found their hearts lifted by the dramatic sky, spangled with stars but blacked out here and there with moon-gilded shreds of inky cloud – but to many, the wild heavens simply looked eerie and far away.

At last they left the forests and farmlands behind, and began climbing up rocky meadows toward the great mountains, toward Petrag and their forlorn hope. The sky was wild above them, and the wind blew cold and unhindered across the land. Whenever they looked back, they saw many fires burning, below in the darkness, in lost Karolan. Strong men shed tears as they turned again to the cruel mountains, to the stone valley that was all they had left.

There was still no sign of pursuing cavalry, and many men were stumbling with weariness. Remembering his journey with

Ilohan, Jonathan decided that if the men did not rest soon, they would not fight with all their strength in the morning. The clouds were taking the sky, and there seemed good hope that any Norkath pursuit would be stymied by the moonless darkness. He rode to the front of the army, and stopped his horse.

"Men of Karolan!" he called, holding his torch high, "I am Jonathan of Glen Carrah, loyal friend of Prince Ilohan, and warrior of Karolan. I claim no right to lead you, save that I have been a leader to you thus far. I ask you now, will you still follow me? Or will another step forth to take my place?"

There was a confused mass of weary shouts, but they were nearly all of confirmation. "Then," said Jonathan, "I tell you again that we have hope. Not far ahead are swords to arm you all, and the Valley of Petrag can be well defended. Yet tomorrow, if we are to save Karolan, we must fight with all the strength we have. We must sleep to preserve that strength. I command each of you to lie down where you stand, eat anything you have to eat, and then sleep. Share your blankets if you must. Let no man be left to die of cold. I will set a watch, to wake us ere the dawn."

The words seemed weak to Jonathan, and he did not know if they would be obeyed. Yet they were. He went through the camp on foot, listening to the rustle of blankets being laid on the ground, saddle bags being opened, and men lying down. Some might be too cold to sleep, he knew, but many had warm clothes, and would rest well. He saw men helping one another on this bitter night, and it made his heart glad. Few went without a morsel to eat, and none without a part of a blanket or cloak to bring him warmth. Some grumbled that the cavalry of Norkath would come to kill them all. Many of these Jonathan chose as guards. When he had done all that he thought was needed, he sought out his father, and they slept warmly beneath a blanket from the saddlebags of the horse that he had captured.

Even in the midst of their danger and loss, many of the men slept well. Some were simply too weary for any terror to keep them wakeful. Some in the darkness of despair abandoned both hope and fear, gladly accepting the forgetfulness of sleep. Trust aided some to sleep, to let their lives slip from their own keeping into that of another. Some drifted to sleep by putting their trust in Jonathan; others, by giving it to God.

*   *   *

Dawn came, cold and cloudy, with no fires, no food, and no men who had had their fill of sleep. Jonathan's horse had died in the night. When he went to the front of the army, he rode the horse that Barnabas had captured at Aaronkal. He knew the men were cold, hungry, and discouraged, and he must stir them up to continue the swift retreat and then turn to fight with blazing courage. Yet he also was hungry, cold, and weary. He began to speak, putting as much warmth in his voice as he could.

"Men of Karolan," he cried, "today we must save our land! Rise up and march! Not far ahead is the food from Petrag that will bring us strength, and the bright swords that will bring us triumph. Onward! For all you love, and all you hope to save!"

Slowly the weary men got to their feet, gathered their blankets or cloaks around them, and began to march. As motion brought warmth to weary muscles, the army moved faster. Jonathan rode back and forth as he had before, calling out his encouragement, hope, and iron determination to carry on. When some complained that he tried to force too fast a pace, he gave the horse he rode to a man with a pregnant wife and four young children, and went on foot. No one murmured then, for shame, for Jonathan still ran throughout the army, bringing what encouragement he could to every part, pushing himself far harder than he pushed any other man.

Yalron galloped down from Petrag late in the morning, to say that the women had brought a great quantity of food down from the mines, and that it was all at the sword pits. Jonathan leaped onto a jagged gray boulder and shouted the news in a voice that all the men could hear. They sent up a great cheer, and carried on, encouraged.

Still they marched with sore feet over rugged stone, while the cold gray day wore on. Many felt they would never reach the sword pits – never be fed and armed to turn and fight at last. Young children who had been snatched from their beds to join their fathers' flight shivered in the cold. Women and children who had no horses pressed on with all their courage, but neared collapse. Men who had left their families behind in conquered Karolan tried not to think of what might be happening to them. They would have given anything to share the fate of those whose wives and children stumbled on beside them.

One great rift opened in the clouds, and far ahead a sunbeam poured down warm and bright upon the gray rocks of Petrag. Men looked up with joy at the sight, for they had almost forgotten that the sun could shine so glorious and so warm. The clouds closed, and the light faded, but some still kept their eyes fixed on the place where it had been, as if the light had left some holy blessing on the cold stone. They reached the place where it had fallen, and marched wearily on; there was nothing there.

At last their way was blocked by a low, jagged cliff, perhaps twice the height of a man. To Jonathan, who had crossed the mountains, it seemed hardly a greater obstacle than a stair step. Yet he knew that to many behind him it would be a disheartening barrier, and he was glad to see that though the cliff spanned the valley, a large pile of rocks on its left side made a crude ramp up to the top.

A few of the boulders that made up this rock pile tilted as Jonathan stepped on them, and he remembered riding past the same place two days before, with the rocks shifting and clattering alarmingly as the horses of Petrag went over them. His heart leaped, for he remembered another thing: the sword pits had been just above this place. He bounded up the rocks and saw that indeed the sword pits lay before him. To his right, surrounded by bags, pots, bundles, and horses, the women of Petrag were waiting to welcome the army with cautious joy. The quantity of food they had brought was beyond his highest hope.

Jonathan ran forward to offer hasty thanks and explanation to the women, and then he leaped up on a large boulder to address the army. Men were still climbing the rock pile as he spoke, but his voice was loud enough for all to hear. "Men of Karolan!" he called. "At last our hope is rekindled, and we need no longer fly from our foe! We have reached the swords. The women of Petrag, who deserve great thanks and praise, have brought enough food for us all. Yet, soldiers of Karolan, arm yourselves before you eat! I command each one of you to take a sword, and then to eat your fill." He jumped down from the rock and ripped away the rough-woven canvas that covered the nearest sword-pit. The polished blades shone, even in the diffuse light of the overcast sky.

The men of Karolan crowded forward to take them, and their hope rose like a flood. Some cried for joy as they lifted the bright blades. Their dignity had been restored to them. At last they had no need to fly: they were armed to stand and fight, to rescue those they loved.

But Jonathan walked slowly uphill, away from the confusion of men getting swords and food. He looked up the valley to where it melted into gray mountains and gray clouds. He thought of Ilohan, and suddenly he was too weary even to feel great pain. He felt only a dull, heavy sorrow, as though he had lost a great treasure, and could not yet realize it was gone. He remembered his father's words about not thinking of things they could not help. Yes, numbness was good, now. He must not feel too much, or he would not be able to do what he must.

A surprising sight brought his thoughts back to immediate reality. He smiled a little, as he felt strength within himself to do whatever he must: to live and act with or without the feeling of hope. What had startled him was the sight of two ponies, coming slowly down the rock valley toward him. A man rode alone on one, while a woman and a girl together rode the other. The hair of the man and the woman was gray, but the girl was young. Jonathan ran up the valley to meet them, wondering if they also were from the mines. When he reached them he stopped and looked up, first with vague recognition, and then with shocked surprise.

"Tharral!" he cried, and then stopped, at a loss for more words.

"We are well, thanks to your kind help, and that of the prince," said Tharral. "I judged that I was too strong to stay at home, when the prince who saved my life needed an army."

Jonathan looked questioningly at Mer and Jenn, on the other pony. Mer said, "Once we would not leave him. We will not leave him still. Where Tharral goes, Mer will go, and where Tharral dies, Mer will die. I promised him this long ago, and my love only grows truer with the years."

Jenn looked up at her mother with love and trust. "And I would not be sent away," she said. "There is no one else I love, no one to whom I would go." Mer held her daughter close, and Jonathan turned away his face, that they might not see his tears.

He blinked them away and looked up again. "Your loyalty and love are great," he said gravely. "I commend your faithfulness, and I would with all my heart I had better tidings to give you. Yet the steward has betrayed us, and the prince has fallen into his hands, and all Karolan save Petrag only is undefended before Fingar's greed. The army you see before you is all that is left of the Army of all Karolan. We hope that Fingar will seek the mines, in his insatiable lust for gold, and here in this rock valley our small force may defy his greater one with some hope. I lead our army, by the choice of the men, and I beg you with all my heart to obey the command that I would give you."

"What is that command?" asked Tharral.

"To ride back immediately, by the way you have come, to your cottage. To gather there all the food and water you can, and set out on the Luciyr road. South and east of Luciyr you will find a mountain pass that will bring you into the desert. Take that way, and travel west along the mountains to a place called Ceramir. There you will be safe. I beg you, obey me. Do not kill your love in this desperate place."

"Would you have me kill my loyalty, then?" asked Tharral. "Are there not other men in the army who love their wives and children, and are loved by them?"

"To what are you loyal?" asked Jonathan. "To your own thoughts of duty, or to me, the prince's companion, whom he chose to lead the men of Petrag?"

"I ask that you give me time to speak to Mer and Jenn of this, and come to a decision."

Jonathan suppressed a growing anger, born of frustration. He did not want Tharral to come to a decision whether to obey his command. He wanted to be obeyed at once: he felt it would be a terrible injustice if Tharral fought and were killed. Yet Jonathan knew his anger also was unjust. "You may have a little time," he said. "Yet remember that if you obey me, it will mean rescue not only for you but also for Mer and for Jenn."

With that he turned and ran back to the army. He plunged into its midst. He saw many things that heartened him, and some that almost brought tears of gladness to his eyes. The women of Petrag, young and old alike, moved through the army bringing good food to hungry men. The very smell of it seemed to banish weariness and kindle courage. Men sat on rocks, naked swords across their knees, and cradled bowls of steaming stew in their hands as though they were treasures of measureless worth. Children who could barely hold up their heads for hunger sat on their mothers' laps and ate warm stew or hearty, buttered bread. Jonathan was astonished to see that besides abundant food and blankets, the women of Petrag had also brought hundreds of bows and quivers stuffed with arrows from Byinkal.

Though all these sights pleased Jonathan, he passed them by, preoccupied, bent on another objective. It was not easy, but he accomplished it at last. He found eight of the ten men from Petrag who were newly married. The others had died in the charge at Aaronkal. Jonathan ordered all of them to find their wives among the women, and meet with him a little distance away from the main body of the army.

"Each of you rode in our great charge at Aaronkal, and helped buy Karolan the little hope she now has," said Jonathan when they were gathered. "Your courage is proved, and your duty done. But these brave women of Petrag have been your wives for seven days only. I do not choose that they shall henceforth be widows. I command you now to go: fly together up the southeast road to Luciyr, and hence west to Ceramir. There you and your love may flourish, whether here we stand or fall. I hope to send three others with you, who will help you find the way."

In the shocked silence that followed, Yalron felt as though he were being torn apart. His love for Therinil his wife urged him to go. Jonathan's command was to go. Yet he felt another call – one with incredible power but at the same time great weakness – that said he must stay, that Jonathan had no right to give the command he had given.

Yet Yalron looked into Therinil's eyes and said, "I will go." He saw joy flood her face, and he rejoiced, for one fleeting moment. Then he saw that in the midst of her blazing joy there was a shadow of shame, like one hard rock in a field of sunlit grain. The vision struck him to the core. A mocking voice in his heart, not the same as the call he had rejected, said, "Those who neglect duty can never again have unashamed joy. You do not know what you have lost." The other seven miners followed Yalron's example: they chose to go to Ceramir. Jonathan led them quickly to the place where Tharral, Mer, and Jenn stood talking earnestly to one another.

Tharral was speaking to Mer as they arrived. "For your sake, and Jenn's, I would go," he said. "I would like to see you both free and at peace in a place of joy and healing. I have more than one duty..."

"I want you to obey, Thar, to lead us to safety," said Mer. "Surely nothing in this world is so precious that God cannot call us to give it up, but I do not feel his call to stay and die here. I feel that he would not have us broken, that we have another purpose yet to serve."

"Perhaps more than one purpose, Beloved," said Tharral. Then he looked down at Jenn, "Child, I want you to have life," he said, with love strong and warm in his voice. "We will go to Ceramir!" But he turned then to Jonathan and said, "Beware what you command, dear friend from Glen Carrah. There are things no man, however great, may rightly demand of another. Yet in this I yield to you. We will go."

Jonathan ran back to his army with a feeling of peace and triumph. It soon vanished, however: he had won only a small victory, for those he had sent to safety were a paltry few compared to thousands who would never see the dawn. He surveyed the host of Karolan with grim determination. They must win, he thought; their courage and strength must prove enough, their hope must not die. Yet he knew he could not command the outcome. Staggering, unjust calamities had occurred before. They might fall. Suddenly he realized how hungry he was. He took a bowl of stew from one of the women with many thanks, and climbed a boulder at the edge of the cliff to eat it and keep watch.

It tasted intensely good to him. He understood now why the men had held their bowls with such reverent care: the stew brought life, in feeling and in truth. When he reached the last spoonfuls he paused a little, not wanting to forget the taste of this warm meal in the cold stone valley. Then suddenly he leaped to his feet, and the precious remainder of the stew spilled on the jagged rock. Far down the valley, the Norkath cavalry had at last come into view. He made rough plans in a brief moment; there was no time for more.

"Men of Karolan, the enemy is upon us!" he cried. "Every good archer, take a bow. Find cover from which to shoot, above the cliff. The rest, take your swords, and lie down among the rocks. Women and children, go to the mines! Men of Petrag, follow me!"

Jonathan leaped down the cliff to stand on the rough valley floor below it. The men of Petrag followed him, perhaps seven score in all, survivors of the charge at Aaronkal. They stood straight up, without cover, without the little cliff's protection, in plain sight to the men of Norkath. Jonathan looked to his right and saw his father there. He was glad. They would stand together.

Jonathan turned to scan the low cliff. A few of his archers were exposed to view. "Archers, hide yourselves!" he cried. "Do not shoot until I give the call! If you can, clamber up the valley walls on this side of the cliff. But do not cut off your retreat, and do not show yourselves!"

The last scrambling and confusion ceased as the archers of Karolan found their places. The vanguard of Norkath was still a considerable distance away. The wail of cold wind from the mountains seemed only to intensify the silence. It was a silence full of fear, tight as a string about to snap. After months or years of growing dread; after all the tumult of more recent days, the storm at last was breaking. Karolan awaited Fingar's onset in the valley of Nirolad's ancient courage.

Jonathan looked up as the last moments passed before battle. He could see no bright spot in the southwest to indicate the sun behind the clouds. He felt that it was not long past midday, but by the gray sky it might have been evening. The clouds rushed along from the northeast, borne on the icy power of high autumn winds, torn and swirled into a great, wild, random tapestry. It was beautiful, he thought. So much was beautiful, and transient as a wind-torn cloud or the farms of Karolan burnt to ashes in a night. So much was beautiful and fragile in a world of endless danger; so much was already lost. Yet on this day of battle, there was some still that might be saved.

He trembled with the power of his thought. There was some that might be saved... He would save it. He would forge this band of brave men into an army of heroes, with strength and will beyond the mightiest legends of the past. The Norkath army would turn back in dismay before their anger. Fingar had come to break the beautiful, to shatter lives that had been lived with joy. The men of Karolan stood against him to fight for that fragile, lovely goodness. They would dash him in pieces and destroy him. They would send his host away in shattered fragments, as a waterfall is shattered and diverted when it falls upon a solid stone: the water flows feebly away, and the stone remains.

The host of Norkath came, banners rippling in the wind. Their horses were weary and lamed by the rocks, and their stumbling cavalry was only just ahead of the foot soldiers. Yet even the most fearful imaginations had scarcely exaggerated the greatness of that host. To Jonathan it seemed like a living flood as it came on, filling the whole valley. The curses of the cavalry, the clink of armor, and the tramp of thousands of feet could already be heard above the wailing wind.

Suddenly Jonathan spotted Fingar himself, wearing a splendid green robe over his shining armor, riding near the center of the army. The blacksmith froze, fascinated with the sight of Karolan's old enemy, actually there, advancing toward him with an army unequaled since the days of Dradrag. The old king looked arrogant and confident. Jonathan could almost see him laugh as he ordered his forces forward to crush the tiny Karolan resistance that he saw.

The Norkath cavalry rallied as best they could, and gave a limping charge toward Jonathan's small army. "Stand!" cried Jonathan as they drew closer. "Stand!" The lances were lowered; the armor clattered, and the iron-shod hooves sparked on the stone. Finally, only a moment before the impact, Jonathan cried, "Petrag, charge! Kill the horses!"

The men of Petrag ran forward into the midst of the Norkath cavalry. It looked foolish, a throwing away of lives, but laughter soon died on the Norkath lips. Lances were meant for combat of rider against rider, and for a charge at full speed, but now as their lame horses stumbled over the uneven ground, the riders of Norkath realized that the stones of Petrag rendered all their training useless. The Karolan swordsmen evaded their lances with desperate ingenuity, and began slaying every horse they could. The dying animals bucked and plunged, often dashing their riders to the ground while the Karolans jumped aside.

Some of the Norkaths rose again, however, or leaped from the saddle even as their horses died. They fought fiercely, guarded by their armor from all but the mightiest blows of the swordsmen of Petrag. Norkath knights from the rear of the charge abandoned their lances and rode forward to rain down sword blows on the men of Karolan.

Jonathan and Barnabas stood side by side, and fought with strength that made even the armored knights turn pale. Their well-chosen swords withstood fearful blows without shattering, and no armor was proof against their strokes. Jonathan fought with burning intensity and ferocious joy.

Barnabas beside him was no less deadly, but his face was set like stone.

In an instant of respite Jonathan swiftly scanned the valley. The cavalry of Norkath surrounded his little army of miners. Beyond the horses, filling the whole of the great valley, the countless foot soldiers of Fingar were sweeping up like a flood. They would soon be surrounded and utterly cut off from the cliffs.

"Petrag, to the cliff!" he cried. Then, as the miners turned to fight their way toward the doubtful safety of the low cliff, he gave another call, and the whole valley rang with its echoes: "Archers, shoot!" The thousands of Norkath, who had swept so confidently around the band of miners, now looked up in terror to see the arrows as they came.

A thousand arrows, beautiful in the white arc of their flight, leapt up from as many archers that until then had been invisibly concealed behind boulders and crannies of the stone. The arrows' shrill wail of death rose above the crying wind, and they slashed down among the Norkaths. Fingar's troops were as shocked as if the cliff walls themselves had assailed them. The Karolan bowmen shot as fast as they could draw arrows. The air was filled with beautiful, flying death, and with the screams of panicked and dying men. Even the armored knights were not safe from the strong marksmen just behind them on the cliff, and they fell back in shock and disarray.

The men of Petrag fought their way back through the disordered cavalry. With Jonathan and Barnabas still unhurt at their head, they reached the low cliff and scrambled swiftly up, those above reaching down to help those below. Soon they stood together at the cliff edge: triumphant, and, for the moment, unthreatened. Their numbers were sadly reduced. Yet they had stood alone against the overwhelming host of

Norkath, and they had been the bait of a trap in which their enemies were fully caught.

Jonathan stood beside his father, looking out over the host of Norkath while the arrows of Karolan hailed down upon it. His sword was red with Norkath blood, and the hands that held it shook from the desperate exertion of the fight. Far away he could see Fingar, well out of arrow range, trying fiercely to regain command of his terrified army. The air of cool, arrogant laughter that had been his while his cavalry charged the men of Petrag had vanished, displaced by red-hot fury. He would have been angrier still if he could have heard the words Jonathan addressed to him, in a low voice only Barnabas could hear: "Always make sure your enemy's mistake was an accident, before you attack."

The ghost of a smile lit Barnabas' stony face for one fleeting instant. Then Jonathan roared, "Lie down! Behind the rocks!" A moment after his order was obeyed, hundreds of Norkath arrows clattered and broke against the stones. Fingar's authority had prevailed, and Norkath was fighting back. Few of the arrows found living men, but still the moments that followed were terrible. The boulders above the low cliff offered only uncertain protection, and the Norkath arrows fell by thousands. With all the rest of his army, Jonathan huddled behind the rocks and hoped. The whistle of the arrows flying and the fast, hard clatter of them hitting the stone seemed to fill the air with fear. Beneath these sounds came the screams and heartrending groans of wounded men. The wailing wind had fallen silent: there was no voice of nature raised to cry against the sounds of war.

Jonathan looked out from behind his rock, and saw the standard of Karolan lying where he had dropped it on the stone. He ran out among the flying arrows to recover it, and miraculously returned unhurt. He raised the Stone, Sword, and Star high above his boulder. Immediately it became a prime mark for Norkath archers. The arrows that ripped the cloth or knocked splinters from the wooden shaft did no man harm, however, and Jonathan thought the injuries of Norkath arrows only made the standard of Karolan more proud.

At last the archery of Norkath ceased. Fingar had angrily concluded it was ineffective – but he had other weapons. At his command the vast infantry of Norkath advanced on the low cliff in ordered, slow array, heedless of the Karolan arrows that still slew many as they came. "Archers to the cliff!" cried Jonathan. "Karolan, arise!"

Chapter 14

Unconquerable Stone

AT JONATHAN'S COMMAND, THE THOUSANDS OF Karolan's army seemed to appear from nowhere among the stones. The archery of both sides ceased, as the Karolan bowmen hurried back to the cliff to avoid being cut off. The whole valley echoed to the ringing tramp of the soldiers of Norkath. Fear seemed to rise like a sickening vapor in the cold, windless air. Many men of Karolan shot frantic or despairing glances south, up the valley, the way they might still run, and get away, if only they deserted their hopeless cause. Surely it must be hopeless; surely in only a few moments the army of Karolan would be overwhelmed and utterly destroyed.

Jonathan stood at the edge of the cliff, facing his army, "Men of Karolan!" he cried, with a sweeping gesture at the north behind him, far away beyond the host of Fingar. "Men of Karolan, there below you, in the hands of the enemy, are your farms, your homes, your children, your mothers, and your wives. There, at the mercy of Norkath, is all that has been your life. There, in flames, in chains, or dead, are your country, your prince, and your hope. Men of Karolan, nothing is left of you but the rock on which you stand! Fight then as men of stone, which no man can ever conquer! Fight as you have never dreamed you could, as Fingar in his deepest nightmares never feared. If we halt Fingar here, we will win back our lives! We will stand, and at the price of the blood of all Norkath Fingar shall not gain this cliff. Will you stand with me?"

The words were like bright, hot fire against the gray gloom of the day and the cold fear that gripped men's hearts. Gloom and fear alike seemed to wither before the flame of Jonathan's courage. There was a tremendous cheer. Then Jonathan cried, "Long live the army of Karolan! No man can conquer stone!" Across the whole width of the Valley of Petrag, the men of Karolan advanced to the brink of the low cliff, swords at the ready. Flinging themselves easily up the uneven stone, the soldiers of Norkath swept on to the attack.

Fingar's warriors met a fury the like of which they had never known. The warriors at the top of that low cliff were not fighting to defend all that they loved, but to win it back. They knew the enemies who fell beneath their desperate swords were those who had burned their homes and captured or killed their wives and children in the night before. They had seen no mercy from Norkath, and expected none. They fought with a terrible strength that astonished even themselves: the strength men do not know they have until such a time.

Jonathan fought as fiercely and as desperately as any. His single strokes could behead strong men or sever warriors' arms even as they were raised to strike him. Yet even in his fury he felt the horror of the things he saw, and the things he did. He found no better word for it than Hell: the place of boundless horror without end; of loss and torment beyond human understanding. Hell was unreal, he knew, no more than a lying nightmare in the minds of those who also believed the fantasy of Heaven. Yet now, in the midst of this battle, the nightmare lived and darkened lovely earth, stripped of none of its horrors save its endlessness alone.

And it was hard to remember it must end. One end, victory, seemed further off than the end of the world. The other, death, was a horror from which Jonathan's mind turned. When he was dying, he would think of death. Now, he would only fight. None of the horror and fear that roared around him shook his determination to stand. He knew why this war must be fought and this hell endured, and why he was right to kill the living, breathing men who struggled up the slope to fall in agony beneath his blade. He never doubted the rightness of his cause. He never considered any course but the one that lay straight before him – to fight until the end.

Far on Jonathan's left fought his father Barnabas. There was no joy or fire in his eyes, though they never blurred or lost their keenness. Barnabas fought with terrible strength and calm caution. Many who faced him thought him a ruthless, unfeeling killer. His face as he fought would be set like stone: grim, implacable. Yet again and again when a Norkath soldier got his death blow at last, and looked up with burning hatred into the face of the warrior who had killed him, he saw only a deep, strong pity, and eyes glistening with tears beneath the cloudy sky. It was the face of one who grieved for all that might have been good but was destroyed forever in the Hell of war; of one who fought with all his strength, but did not forget that those he killed were men – men who might have lived, and loved, had Fingar's choices and their own been different.

Even as Jonathan fought with wild intensity, he tried to keep some knowledge of how the wider battle was progressing. He saw the men of Karolan hard pressed on the far right, where the ramp of fallen rock made the cliff easy to climb. He knew that if the Norkaths gained the cliff edge and pushed left, all was lost. He worked his way to the right, still fiercely assaulting any Norkath who struggled up the cliff near him. Fierce, hand-to-hand fighting was raging at the top of the ramp when he reached it. It was very different from the fighting elsewhere on the cliff, where the Karolans could rain down blows on the Norkaths as they climbed. Here there was a terrible equality, and the Norkaths' overwhelming numbers could be used to dire effect.

Jonathan paused a moment at the side of the ramp, where a small, precious backwater of peace had formed in the fierce battle. The Norkaths were not attacking there simply because the cliff was steep, while only a few paces away was the ramp. Jonathan took a deep breath, shouted, "For Glen Carrah!" and plunged into the battle raging at the top of the ramp.

The first two enemies he encountered fell swiftly, surprised to be assaulted from the side. A strong warrior of Norkath who was just coming up the ramp noticed his success, and pushed forward to attack him.

Jonathan met him, and for a long moment the two seemed alone in the midst of the fierce battle. Jonathan could see his enemy's face as he fought him, and thoughts flew swiftly through his mind. The face was the face of a man, a man who at another time might have wished him good morning or bought a bag of nails. They might have passed each other on any road and exchanged a friendly greeting. Instead they were trying to kill one another with swords. The terrible unreason of it came home to Jonathan as it had not done in any of his previous fights.

In the turmoil of his thoughts, overwhelmed by all that he had seen and done, Jonathan wondered when the other man would simply realize that fighting was foolish, and leave off. It did not happen. The Norkath pressed him hard, and Jonathan knew that one of them would die. Suddenly his anger blazed. He was not angry chiefly at his foe, but at the thing, whatever it was, that brought men to this place, the place where they strive to kill each other and will not stop. He fought the murderous injustice of it: that a man who, like him, lived and knew some joy in living, was really and steadfastly trying to kill him. Jonathan fought harder, pressing his attack, and suddenly his sword flashed forward and sank into the other man's chest. The Norkath fell backward hard, writhing and groaning as his lifeblood rushed out upon the stone. Jonathan turned away and kept fighting.

He felt sick and weak. The horror around him was relentless. He felt that men could not stand such horror, that it must break them or twist them. He felt he would never recover, even if he lived, from what he had done and seen this dreadful day. Surely the fighting would ravage the men – put gentleness and compassion out of their reach forever – or else hurt their hearts so deeply that they fell down unwounded, and died rather than see more.

He was fighting a very powerful man now, parrying stroke after stroke with fierce impacts that sometimes struck sparks from his sword. He struck a mighty blow of his own, and with a crash his sword shattered in his hand. His enemy roared in triumph and brought his sword down in a terrible overhead stroke. Jonathan had only time to realize he was doomed, nothing more. But as the lethal blow fell another sword sang over his head and struck the Norkath blade away. Jonathan staggered backward, away from the fiercest part of the fight, and saw the man who had saved him. He was not especially tall, but he seemed to wield his sword with the strength of three. The Norkath was parrying everywhere, ringing, bone-jarring blows. He was absolutely on the defensive. A few of his countrymen tried to help him as they came near in the wild fight, but his Karolan assailant blocked their swords also, with perfect aim and terrible force. Finally the Norkath's sturdy blade shattered before a staggering blow, and the next stroke beheaded him even as he tried to draw his dagger. The man who had killed him turned around, and Jonathan saw that it was Barnabas.

"I thank you, Father," cried Jonathan.

"Find a sword, my son," said Barnabas, "and bring your soldiers hope."

Jonathan ran back through the ragged ranks of Karolan to the sword pits. As he ran he saw scattered here and there the bows and quivers of the archers, dropped in haste as they ran to defend the cliff in hand-to-hand combat. The gray sky was darkening with the failing day. Jonathan took a new sword in his hand, and placed another in his empty sheath as a spare. But he did not immediately rejoin the battle. He ran along behind the Karolan lines and selected several small groups of men for different tasks. A few he told to gather swords from the sword pits and distribute them so the Karolans could replace broken swords more quickly. Others Jonathan sent all the way to the mines, to bring back wood and oil for fires. But most he sent to gather the fallen bows and arrows, and put them once again to use. Then at last he turned again into the battle.

"For Karolan! For Glen Carrah!" he roared as he ran to the top of the ramp. "Fight on, men! No man can conquer stone!" The Norkaths fell back in terror at his onset, and the men of Karolan rallied. Yet the fight went on, brutal and wild. A great press of Norkaths was always coming up the ramp, keeping their feet and fighting all the way. Jonathan often fought multiple assailants at once. Sometimes in three strokes he parried three different blades, and he was often helped by other warriors of Karolan who fought at his side. He still felt overwhelmed, sickened and made weak by horror, but in truth he was strong. Sometimes, swinging his sword for a moment with a kind of furious joy, he knew it.

Along most of the cliff things were not quite as bad as at the ramp, yet all up and down the battle line men were wounded and dying. Away from the ramp, few Norkath climbers survived to reach the top of the cliff, and none who reached it lasted long. The Karolans rained down blows upon them, or drove them back and threw them down upon the swords of others just beginning to climb. But the Norkaths were still dangerous even as they faltered and fell. Many a soldier of Karolan was wounded or killed by their flailing swords. Every moment many on both sides fell, and their wounds were terrible. The screams of men for whom pain had swallowed shame and self-control rent the air, striking terror in the hearts of those that heard them. But even worse was the sight of men who had not yet had time to scream, when torn and broken flesh had only just gushed blood and did not yet feel pain, when unbelieving hands reached out to finger broken jaws or severed legs. There was no more painful vision in all that desperate, dreadful battle than this: the moment when a man learns that his life is shattered, that even if by a miracle he lives, his body has been broken and will never heal.

Jonathan left the fight for a moment, backing carefully through the ranks to give the men around him time to close the gap. As soon as he was behind the line of battle, he ran over the rocks looking for the men whom he had ordered to gather bows. He found them gathered in an anxious group, about five score strong, near a great boulder behind the battle line. "Why are you not shooting?" he asked.

"How can we, without hitting our own?" asked one of the men. "And will Fingar not bring ten bowmen against Karolan, for every one of us you send to shoot them?"

"He cannot," said Jonathan. "We are above them. From the cliff edge, or a boulder behind it, you can see the whole of the enemy. They cannot see any more than our front line, fiercely fighting at the cliff edge. Do you not understand? You can shoot at them without fear of hitting your countrymen. They cannot do the same: they would hit their own soldiers in the back. So go to the boulders and crevices, every one of you: aim well, and kill a Norkath with every shot! Go! Let many defend the right, for we falter at the ramp. Quickly!"

The bowmen scattered, and Jonathan ran once again to the top of the ramp. The situation there was dire. The Karolans had been forced back several paces from the top of the ramp, and there was grave danger that they would break altogether. If the Norkaths could break the line at the ramp, they would come pouring through the breach, attack the remainder of the Karolan army from both sides, and soon win the victory.

Jonathan ran toward the faltering battle line. "Forward, Karolan!" he cried, "Send them back on their own swords! Onward! No man can conquer stone!"

He roared, "For Glen Carrah!" and plunged into the fight like a whirlwind. His flashing sword was like a wall of iron. No matter where the Norkaths thrust or slashed, it was there to meet and block their blades. The men of Karolan followed him, pushing the Norkaths back toward the ramp. Though the Karolans were weary, and many were wounded, their ragged line moved forward until the Norkaths were fighting just above the ramp. Many brave men, who had loved peaceful farms now lost in the captured plain below, fell at the head of the ramp and died there on the cold, hard stone. Still those who remained fought on. Still Jonathan was unhurt, and held his ground at the center of the ramp.

Then at last the archers began to shoot. It had taken them time to find the high, protected places that they needed, but now their arrows slashed down among the Norkaths: short, deadly flights of iron-tipped shafts. The attackers faltered and looked around in terror. The defenders cheered and pushed forward. All along the battle line the Karolans found new hope and the Norkaths faltered in dismay. Hidden in boulders just above the cliff, the bowmen of Karolan shot their enemies at terribly short range. The arrows advanced too quick for sight, and struck with deadly force.

For the first time in the long, horrible battle, Jonathan could almost imagine a Karolan victory. But the Norkaths rallied and pressed forward again, and the desperate fight went on. The arrows continued to fall, slaying many, but Fingar could stand the loss. He continued to urge his soldiers on into the teeth of Karolan's defense.

*　　　　　*　　　　　*

Ilohan licked his cracked lips, and his swollen tongue felt like sandpaper. He was dizzy with thirst. His whole body cried out for water, but impenetrable stone and iron walled him off from it. As Tulbur had desired, he would die here in this living grave. The pain seemed to blot out everything else, even the hopelessness and terror of his position. He could not reach beyond the suffering of the moment anymore, could not think about the time of his death, surely approaching; or about the injustice that had put him here; or about the iron and stone that imprisoned him. There was only pain.

Trying to turn his mind from it, he reached up his hand to touch the iron slab above him. His fingers reached it before his arm was straight, so small was the cell – or tomb – in which he lay. But he could barely feel the iron. His dry hand was numb, and his arm trembled with the effort of reaching upward. He let it fall, and rolled over, resting his head facedown upon his arms. "Oh God," he said, "thank you that I can pray."

For he could still pray. That was the only thing he had besides pain: prayer. In the darkness of the death-cell his prayer could still bloom like a flower of heaven, shedding light and warmth in his heart that he could not comprehend. As he lay on the cold, grimy stone, he knew that his Lord was with him. "I am with you always," Christ had said. Ilohan knew now, far more fully than he ever had before, what he had meant. He knew that he was with him, then and there, lifting him above the pain and showing him love with power from beyond the world. He prayed, and tears of gratitude brought life and wetness to his parched eyes. He could still pray, though so much that seemed easier was now beyond his strength.

"Lord, let Eleanor find joy and peace in you as long as she lives. Please comfort her when she hears news of my fate.

"Oh God, I pray that Jonathan is still alive. I pray that Glen Carrah is still free, and that you will protect Naomi. I pray that evil will not triumph in these days, but that you will defeat the lust and greed of Fingar and his soldiers. Father, you have blessed Karolan in the years that are gone, and there are many among us who have worshiped you in thanks and wonder, who have desired to live obediently the lives you gave us. Protect the women of Karolan, Lord, by your power. Save them from rape and slavery, the fates they must suffer at the hand of

Fingar's soldiers but for your rescue. Rescue them, Father, though all reason cries out that their rescue is beyond hope.

"Save the men of Karolan. Let them still be alive, though it seems they must surely have been ambushed and slaughtered by the Norkath armies and the traitors among their countrymen. Please give them swords, and other weapons – and skill against which their enemies cannot stand. Give them help, so they may save their wives and children. If some must die, then let them die as heroes, not as murdered captives. Let them die, trusting in you, and laying down their lives in defense of those they love. And, Father, win the cause for which they died. Do not let Karolan be pillaged, raped, and burned. Temper us, but do not break us. Be with us. Help us turn to you, and not away; help us trust in you through the darkness, and see light and healing come at last.

"Father, you know that I am dying. I do not ask to see the things for which I pray. But I pray that Jonathan will see them, and Naomi. I pray that Karolan will be a nation that belongs to you, a land where you are worshiped, and where people live in the joy and freedom that come from obedience to you. Do not let us be conquered. Do not let Fingar swallow us up.

*   *   *

Tulbur stood on the battlements of Aaronkal and looked eastward over the great field. A light breeze from the north was blowing, and it had cleared the sky of clouds. The light of the setting sun fell red upon the gold crown in his hands. He read the inscription inside the circlet. "As your days, so shall your strength be."

He was the victor, he knew. His long awaited vengeance had come at last. Care and caution could always defeat heroic chivalry in the end. He had played Thomas in chess and lost, but he had played him in real life and won. Thomas the immoral was at last defeated: Thomas, who had failed the Joseph Test, who had shown himself unworthy of the crown and yet received it. Tulbur put the crown of the Prince of Karolan back on his head. The right to wear it was his alone. Thomas had no successors. If the blessing written on the crown applied to anyone, it applied to him.

Yet he rejected it. He, not God, was the overseer of his own strength. His strength had always been equal to his days not because God had blessed him, but because he had been wise. He had worked hard to learn prudence and make himself strong. He had guarded himself from the future. He had chosen his own days, to suit his own strength. Usually his strength had been more than enough. It had never been too little. When at last he was ready to make his final move, to capture the crown and realm he had so long been owed, he had made that move with strength to spare, with all precautions taken.

There had been some accidents, yes. He had not expected Ilohan to come through the mountains before the war, but that had only given him the satisfaction of a fitting revenge. He had waited age-long years to get the crown he now held, and Ilohan, the brat who should have died so many times, who had hindered his plans in so many ways, would wait age-long days of suffering to die. The fact that his treachery was seen too soon had been a greater upset. Fully five thousand, he guessed, of the men of Karolan had broken free of the trap. Worse still, they had gone toward Petrag, where the swords were... But the swords were hidden, and the men had no leader. Fingar had a score and eight thousands of soldiers armed with swords, and more than a thousand each of cavalry and archers.

The Karolans who escaped would soon be dead – unless Fingar had followed his advice and offered them terms of surrender.

Tulbur looked down again at the great field below him. Three thousand Norkath foot soldiers guarded the captured Karolans. They were bound hand and foot, and had not been given food since they were taken. Tulbur congratulated himself on the sight. There, Fingar had followed his advice. Fingar had wanted to kill them all. It had seemed safest to him, and had appealed to his liking for things that were brutally and irrevocably successful. Tulbur had looked the master of Norkath coldly in the eyes, and said, "Your Majesty, if you begin butchering them they will have nothing to lose." He had prevailed. The men were only captured, to be enslaved, pardoned, or killed later on at leisure. They had made no resistance.

Now Tulbur turned back to the west, which was glowing gold in memory of the departed sun. He made for the stair that would take him down to his chamber, to his supper, and to the servants that worshiped his wisdom. Perhaps he would dispatch some message to King Fingar, who already feared him. But something about that sunset seemed to get through his eyes, into his cold, calculating, deceptive mind. He was not quite immune to its flawless, selfless beauty. He took off the crown and read the words again, and noticed that the script was beautiful, done freely by a swift but careful hand. It crossed his mind to wonder whose, and he guessed the answer. A lightning memory passed through his mind, and he seemed to hear the voice of the young, beautiful Princess Eleanor praying for her infant son long ago on a day of hope and sunshine. A shiver passed through his body, and then he coldly set the crown back on his head and started down the stair.

Chapter 15

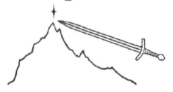

Ramp, Bonfire, Barricade

IN THE GLOAMING IN PETRAG THE TERRIBLE FIGHT continued. Fingar had stationed archers behind his foot soldiers, and ordered them to shoot at the battle line of Karolan. The arrows killed as many Norkath soldiers as Karolans, but Fingar could spare many and the weary defenders of Karolan could spare none. Jonathan was still unhurt, but even he was weary. His cries of encouragement were as strong as ever, and the valiant soldiers of Karolan still answered him with cheers, but hope was faltering in all their hearts.

A sudden trumpet blast sounded from among the Norkath ranks, and a voice cried, "White flag! White flag! Receive Fingar's messenger!"

The men of both sides wavered, doubtful as to what they should do. "Let all men cease fighting!" called Jonathan. Men of Karolan and Norkath both obeyed him. "I will receive the messenger," he said, and stepped forward from the line of Karolan.

A knight of Norkath, fully armored and carrying a large white flag, rode toward him on a powerful horse. "Keep your positions, Karolan!" cried Jonathan. "Watch for treachery!"

The knight stopped only a few paces short of the cliff. He raised his visor, but Jonathan could see his face only indistinctly through the gathering dusk. The silence on the battlefield grew eerie. The wind could be heard moaning gently over the hard stones. The knight spoke at last, and his voice rang clear and loud.

"You need fear no treachery," he said. "I have come only to offer terms of surrender."

"Offer them," said Jonathan shortly, still standing warily on the cliff.

"If you and all those with you will immediately and finally lay down your arms, His Glorious Majesty King Fingar of Norkath will spare your lives. The only condition is that you must swear allegiance to His Glorious Majesty, and all of his subordinates, and obey any commands they may give you."

"What of our families, our farms, and our homes?" asked Jonathan.

"They are at the disposal of His Glorious Majesty and his subordinates. You may bring to him whatever petitions you will."

"Tell Fingar that he does not understand men, since he has all his life been a dog. His accursed terms we, the defenders of Karolan, finally and irrevocably reject."

"Your ranks are ragged," said the knight calmly. "Your strength is faltering. Your doom is certain. How long will you fight?"

"Men of Karolan!" cried Jonathan. "They claim they own our families, our homes, and our lives. They would give us our lives, but for what? To be their audience for the rape of Karolan, and later on their slaves. If we are men, if we would rescue those we love or die in the attempt, we must still fight. How long? How long will we fight?"

The question hung in the air, and for a long moment no man dared answer it. Then one old soldier, sorely wounded in one arm, stood and cried out, "Until the dawn!"

Jonathan smiled in the cold, falling dusk. "Thus shall we answer!" he cried in a voice that rang across the valley. "How long will true men fight? Until the dawn!" The men of Karolan gave a cheer, warm and strong. Some laughed grimly at the impossible idea that they would last until dawn, but none doubted they would try. Their own courage, and Jonathan's, had forged them into an army such as he had hoped for. They would fight with all their strength down to the last man. But they were wholly unprepared for what happened next.

The knight of Norkath called, "By order of His Glorious Majesty, all troops of Norkath shall withdraw to make camp. There will be warm fire and good food. The Karolans will be all the easier to kill after they have had a cold night of starving."

The valley was filled with the tramp and clatter of thousands of footfalls, and, like a flood that has reached its height receding, the great army of Norkath left the cliff and ramp, and began to make camp just out of bowshot down the valley.

Jonathan stood still, frozen with weary amazement, for a long moment, and then he stirred himself and spoke. "Men of Karolan, keep your swords ready and your eyes open. But now, go and eat whatever is left of all that the women of Petrag brought us. Let those from the ramp guard eat first, while the others stand watch, and then let the rest eat."

The gray twilight darkened as they ate. The food from Petrag was cold now, but still good, and there was enough for every man to get almost a good meal. When they had all finished, nothing was left. They remained sitting on the cold, rough rocks, as still as if the falling of night had turned them into stone. With the cessation of the desperate fight, all life seemed to have gone out of the exhausted men, even as the last light faded from the sky. They were so weary that mere stillness seemed a paradise, and they did not know how they could ever find the strength to rise.

Then one man clenched his teeth, and stood. He looked into the east and saw a soft pattern of cold silver light shining through the clouds above the valley wall. The moon was rising, and the clouds were not so thick as to block all its light. He walked slowly away from the cliff edge, toward the mines, until he found the great piles of firewood that men had brought from Petrag just before the falling of the night. He was astonished at the amount. He saw a man resting, half lying and half sitting, on one of the piles.

The man who had come from the cliff edge laid a hand on his shoulder and said, "Were you among the ones who brought this wood?"

"Yes," came a weary, low voice in answer.

"How is it that so much was brought? It is far beyond all that could have been expected."

"Petrag has hard winters. We keep great store of wood. This is all of it." The same low, despondent voice.

"And all this was freely given? All that would have kept the people of the mines warm through the winter?"

The man on the wood pile turned his head for the first time. "If we do not win today," he said, "this firewood will not be ours to use in the winter that comes. We gave our all. Will anyone bring hope that it is enough?"

The man who had been questioning him knelt down and found a leather pouch containing flint and tinder at the base of the woodpile. A spark flew, shining blue-white like a star in the darkness. The tinder kindled with fragile flame, and the man held a pine-branch above it. Bright yellow flames licked hungrily at the sappy wood. As the crude torch blazed ever brighter, the man leaped up on a boulder and lifted it high. Weary faces looked up to see it burning warm and bright against the cold darkness of the world. Then they stood, with a few groans but no curses or complaints. They had seen who it was that held the torch.

"Men of Karolan," called Jonathan, "tonight we shall save Karolan." In his weariness each clear syllable cost him effort, but he did not sound defeated or dismayed. "Now is the time when heroes are truly proven," he called. "We stand at the end of our strength. We look into darkness, and even our hope falters. But we will not merely stand. We will work, we will hope, and we will win. Tonight, while Fingar lounges in his tent, we will make this cliff a fortress he shall never conquer. We will give our all, for in the storm that is upon us, nothing less can be enough."

In the cold darkness men who valued sleep more than life and stillness more than gold stood up to work, to do whatever Jonathan told them to, to fight, as they had promised, until the dawn.

*　　　　　*　　　　　*

"The terms of surrender which Your Glorious Majesty so graciously offered were refused in a most insulting manner." The light of fires and lanterns outside shone through the green and gold cloth of Fingar's tent, and cast a strange but pleasant light on the king and the other two men who were inside. The knight who had just spoken stood before Fingar's throne, awaiting further questioning with some anxiety.

"Who refused them?" Fingar's voice was cold, but something in the tone revealed his anger. It was a dangerous sound.

"The commander of the Karolan army," said the knight

"Who is this commander?"

"We know nothing of him, Your Glorious Majesty, save that he is not a knight."

"Then you are a fool. How can a peasant command five thousand men? What is unusual about him?"

"Only his strength, Your Glorious Majesty. He is as strong as a lion. Our men cannot stand before him. When he charges among them, crying, 'For Glen Carrah,' or, 'No man can conquer stone,' they fall back in fear. A score of times he has been in mortal danger, but each time, even as we rejoiced that he at last was conquered, he has escaped without hurt. At his battle cries our soldiers tremble, but the brigands of Karolan take courage and fight the harder."

"What did he say when he refused our gracious offer?"

"I fear to repeat it, lest it offend Your Glorious Majesty."

"Failing to answer our questions is not the way to avoid offending us. Speak, dog."

The knight felt a fleeting delight in the irony that Fingar should at that particular moment choose to address him thus – but the delight was swallowed up in fear. He took a deep breath, and said, "The commander of the army of Karolan bade me tell Your Glorious Majesty that you do not understand men, since all your life Your Glorious Majesty has been a dog. He went on to say that Your Glorious Majesty's terms of surrender, which he labeled accursed, are finally and irrevocably rejected by the defenders of Karolan."

Rather than standing up in a rage, as the knight expected, Fingar bowed his head and gripped the arms of his chair. "So I do not understand," he muttered. "Kindrach also said... but will his echoes never cease to haunt me?"

"Did Your Glorious Majesty command anything?" asked the knight.

"No!" roared Fingar, standing up now in the anticipated rage. "And it is your good fortune that we do not instantly command your execution for impertinence. Now go! Leave us!"

The knight bowed and then hurried toward the tent's entrance, awkward in his haste. His sovereign's voice, calm now but imperious, called him back even as he parted the curtains to leave.

"Stop!" demanded Fingar. "Return. Yet one more thing we would ask you."

The knight humbly returned and bowed his head.

"Tell us again what are the battle cries of the Karolan commander," said Fingar.

"Sometimes he says, 'for Glen Carrah,'" the knight began, "and at other –"

"Stop!" interrupted Fingar. "That is all we wished to hear. Go now, and summon Sir Cygnak to us."

The knight was very relieved to depart from his master's tent.

Fingar turned to his son, a tall young man who had sat grim and silent beside him until now. Prince Andokar was slouched forward in his chair, his head resting on his right hand. He did not notice his father's motion.

"So they have refused my terms of surrender," said Fingar. Andokar sat up quickly at the words, and turned to meet Fingar's gaze.

"Father, they are honorable men," he said. "Your terms were not ones they could accept. Had you altered the terms as I advised, it might have been otherwise."

"Why offer good terms to men we can crush like ants?" asked Fingar

"Perhaps because ants have stings, or perhaps because charity is a virtue. But what you have done is done."

"Charity is a virtue for maidens in peacetime," said Fingar.

Andokar held his peace.

"Kindrach saved his wife," said Fingar. "He chose to fight for her life, not for his, and he won. The death of such a man brings little pleasure. But this commander of the army of Karolan will lose more than his life."

"This, then, is why you have sent for Cygnak?" asked Andokar.

"Yes," said Fingar. "He is known as one of my most satisfactory commanders."

"He is known as the cruelest and most licentious," said Andokar.

"Excellent qualities for such a time as this," said Fingar.

"Father," said Andokar, "do you love me, your eldest son and heir? I have never shown myself unworthy of your love."

"Of course I love my sons," said Fingar. "What father does not? Though I have sometimes wished it, you need not fear that I will ever disown you."

"If you love me, if the words you have just spoken have any meaning, then I beg you, confirm them by granting me my wish."

"What is it, my dear son?"

"Do not do the thing that you have spoken of. Send Cygnak on a different mission."

Fingar gripped his chair. "Not that," he said. "I would have done anything for you but that. Now go. Leave me. But do not forget that I love you."

Andokar stood tall in the luxurious tent. His head nearly touched the tassels hanging from the cloth ceiling. He strode swiftly to the door, and then turned back and met his father's troubled gaze. "You have never loved me, Father," said the Prince of Norkath. Then he vanished into the night.

*   *   *

"Ella, why are you crying?" Eleanor looked up to see a little girl standing near her, beside the fire. She had been praying in one of the big rooms of the stone house in Ceramir, having traveled there with Auria the day before.

"You should be asleep, little fern," said Eleanor gently to the girl. "There is no deep sorrow touching you."

"I know," said the girl. "Everyone has said my mother will not die, and I believe it – but still I could not sleep. I came in here, and you were kneeling by the fire and crying. It makes me unhappy to see you so sad, and I want to know why. Is there a deep sorrow touching you? Is it because you cannot run and dance?"

Eleanor sat down upon the hearth, and gathered the little girl into her arms. "I thank you for caring about me," she said, "and since you have asked, I will tell you what is wrong. But you must remember that it is far away and cannot touch you, and though it may make you sad you must not be afraid."

"I will not be afraid, Ella," said the girl, snuggling down in Eleanor's arms.

"Across the mountains something very terrible is happening," said Eleanor. "There are two kings, each with a huge army, more men then I could count even if I counted all day long. One king is greedy, and wants the cottages and the farms in the other king's land. He wants to come in and kill the other king and all the men in his army. He wants to take all the cottages and farms. He wants to push little girls like you, and their mothers and brothers, out to starve in the cold – or else to make them slaves."

The child interrupted, "But cannot the little girls' fathers stop the bad king from doing that?"

"Their fathers are the men in the army, little fern," said Eleanor. "The bad king wants to kill them all, and then they will not be able to protect their wives and children and their houses."

"And you were crying because you feel sorry for all the people?"

"Yes, little fern, and because the good king is my son," said Eleanor.

The little girl thought for a long time. The low fire cracked softly now and then in the silence. "Were you praying to God, Ella? Was that why you were kneeling by the fire?"

Eleanor smiled down at her. "Yes, I was praying," she said.

"Then I am sure the good king will win," said the girl. "The bad king will be squished like a spider, and all the people will stay in their warm cottages. My father says God always listens to your prayers, Ella. I will ask him too, though, before I go to bed, so if he wants to hear it from both of us he can." She slid gently off Eleanor's lap and knelt beside her on the hearth.

"Lord God," said the child, "please do not let the bad king win. Do not let him kill the good king, Ella's son, or the fathers of all the little girls and boys. Instead, please to crush him like a spider, and let the fathers and mothers and children stay in their own warm cottages, with the good king on the white horse ruling over them. Now I am finished, Ella."

Eleanor smiled at her. "I thank you for helping me pray," she said. "Can you sleep now, little fern?"

"I think so," said the girl. "I will go back to my bed."

Eleanor stayed kneeling by the fire, and the girl stood, half reluctantly, and went slowly to the door of the room. Once there she turned back. "Did you say your son was a king, Ella? Are you a queen?"

"Yes, little fern," said Eleanor, with laughter in her voice, "but that is not important. Please to keep from telling anyone."

The little girl opened her eyes wide in awe, and put a finger to her lips. But she turned back once more, and Eleanor saw only her head peeking around the door. "Are you sure my mother will be well soon? And I will have a new brother or sister?"

Eleanor smiled. She had already heard that the birth had gone well, and the girl she called little fern had a happy mother and a tiny new sister. Eleanor told her. The child's head disappeared, and the woman who fervently hoped she was queen mother of Karolan heard small footsteps going off to bed. She took her crutches and stood, to go to her own bed. Then suddenly she knelt again and gave thanks to God, from the depths of her heart, for the love and prayers of children.

*　　　　　*　　　　　*

Jonathan stood in the midst of the army of Karolan, above the cliff. Every man who was not wounded, and many men who were, had worked with iron determination at the impossible task he had set them. They had succeeded. The backbreaking work had seemed to last for ages – aching, exhausted ages of sweat and cold, numbness and pain, and clanking rock. But it was finished now. The ramp that had so nearly brought their doom in the afternoon was utterly gone.

They had carried all of its rocks, even the very largest, up to the top of the cliff, and had piled them there in a long barricade about three paces back from the cliff edge. There were six great piles of firewood, towering above and just behind the barricade, and spaced evenly along it. They had poured oil, also brought from Petrag, over each pile, so that the wood would go up in flames in a moment once it was lighted. The fortress was finished. The men were longing to sleep, and Jonathan knew it.

He gathered them together quietly, for fear of the watchmen of Norkath. "Men of Karolan," he said, only just loudly enough to be heard, "we have done what seemed to all of us impossible, and we have pushed on beyond what seemed the limit of our strength. Yet, alas, we must not stop here. There, below us, our enemies are sleeping. We must bring them, sleepy, disordered, and angry, against this fortress for which they will not be prepared. I need ten score archers to make fire-arrows, and shoot them into the tents of Norkath. The rest must arm themselves with swords or bows and await the attack. I will hold the torch that lights the arrows. Who will shoot them?"

There was no answer. The night was dark and cold. The moonlight shone dull silver through the black clouds high in the west. It was a feeble light, and there was no other. The men were weary in every bone and muscle, so weary that fears and imaginings of death were dulled, and the wakeful envied the slain. The silence grew long.

One man, wounded in his foot, stood up and said, "I will draw a bow for Karolan again." It was Barnabas. He hobbled forward to reach the oily rags that Jonathan had made from tattered blankets, and began to make his fire arrows. Unwounded men came forward then in awe and shame, until Jonathan had more volunteers than he had asked for. He ordered the rest to supervise the arming of the men who remained, and to be ready to light the great bonfires at his order.

It was a strange commotion, that bustle of utterly exhausted men in the darkness. They wrapped oiled rags over arrow points, and lifted long-relinquished weapons. When they spoke at all it was in low voices, like those of men hushed and awed by the grandeur of a mountain or a starry sky. Yet what awed them was their own endurance. They felt that their strength had ended long before, yet something still pushed them on. As Jonathan had said, they had come to a time when heroes could be proven: they stood in awe of a heroism that was their own, and yet not their own, for it moved them with power that did not come from within them.

When at last all was ready, the archers clambered down the cliff, unaided now by any ramp, and walked quietly about half way to the Norkath camp. They could make out the shapes of the tents by the veiled moonlight and by the coals of Norkath's campfires. "Arrows on the string," called Jonathan in a voice as low and weary as that of any one of his men. "Shoot as soon as they have firmly taken fire." He knelt down to light the torch he carried. It flared brightly in the darkness. Then he walked swiftly down the line, lighting each arrow as he came. It took only a moment for the oil to burst into strong flame, and soon the arrows were flying through the darkness like shooting stars.

Loud cries and screams arose from the Norkath camp, and red flames blossomed there. When Jonathan reached the end of the line of archers, he bade them place another arrow on the string, and he again passed down the line lighting the arrows. The tents that had not been hit in the first barrage stood out black and obvious now in the light of those that were in flames. The aim of the weary Karolans was deadly. Dry tents kindled like pine boughs, and the camp of Norkath filled with panicked men. Some of the Karolan arrows struck living soldiers, and their screams were terrible.

The Karolans shot a third volley of fire arrows, then ceased as wild arrows from the Norkath camp fell around them: they had no wish to reveal their position with fire. Still Jonathan did not immediately tell them to retreat; instead he had them shoot dark arrows at the silhouettes of running men. The black shape of Fingar himself appeared against the flames, clad in complete armor on a tall horse. The arrows of Karolan rang and clattered against him to no effect. The archers with Jonathan heard Fingar's imperious orders, and saw iron discipline descend upon the Norkath troops.

"Archers, to the cliffs!" cried Jonathan, in a voice that rang with some of its old strength. The Karolans turned and ran, with blindly shot Norkath arrows clattering around them and the vanguard of Fingar's foot soldiers not far behind.

Barnabas tried to run with his wounded foot, but fell behind. Norkath arrows rained down around him. He struggled onward with all his strength, but at last a flying arrow found his thigh. He fell and could not rise. The rock was hard. He was doubly wounded and desperately weary. "Father, save my wife, and save my son," he prayed. "Comfort them. Forgive me all my wrong, and love me forever. I have given all I had to give. Thank you that I have had it." He pulled himself along the ground, determined not to give up before he died.

Jonathan turned, and saw the fallen man. His thoughts wavered for an instant, and then he was running over the rocks, heedless of the Norkath arrows, to rescue his fellow soldier. As he reached him, he saw who it was.

"Father!" his horrified cry tore the air. Forgetting that he was weary, forgetting everything except that his father was wounded and in great danger, he bent down and lifted Barnabas on his shoulders. The arrows fell thickly all around them, and the Norkath soldiers shouted for blood.

"Leave me, my son," said Barnabas, "you will only die too."

"So be it if I cannot save you," roared Jonathan, and he ran for the cliff with his father's entire weight on his shoulders. His feet pounded the rock with bone-jarring force, but still he put forth all his strength and ran.

Fingar saw it, guessed that he was seeing the terribly strong commander of Karolan's army, and roared, "Kill them, fools!" to his archers in a voice like thunder. But Jonathan ran with the strength of absolute desperation, jumping the rough rocks as though they were good stairs. He quickly disappeared into the darkness beyond the light of the burning tents, and the arrows of Norkath cracked and splintered harmlessly against the stone.

Jonathan reached the cliff and climbed it in one moment of supreme strain. He knelt down and laid his father in a sheltered place behind the barricade, then returned to the cliff edge and looked back. The army was almost upon them. "Arise, Karolan!" he cried. "Light the fires! Archers, aim and shoot!"

The bonfires kindled with a roar, and the entire army of Norkath was flooded with their ruddy light. The Karolans, however, were in the shadow of their barricade. They were absolutely invisible to their enemies, in the wide swath of blackness above the cliff edge. Arrows hailed from that swath, down into the advancing host of Norkath, until the men of Fingar felt that they were being shot by ghosts.

The Norkath soldiers scrambled up the cliff as before, but there was no ramp, and there was no unguarded place. The soldiers of Karolan were weary, but they were not cold, and they were not hungry, and they were desperate. The fight was more hellish than ever before, in that terrible place of black shadow and red flame. The Karolans held the cliff, fighting with furious anger and hopeless courage. No Norkath lived for long on the bloody stone of the cliff edge. They were killed by scores and hundreds, thrown down upon the swords of their comrades, but still they came.

They came with the fear of Fingar driving from behind, and lust, greed, and anger calling from before. They came with thousands behind them, and though five of them fell for every Karolan they killed, there were always five more to try the climb again. The night was filled with screams and groans, and the clashing of swords, and orders shouted by desperate men. The rocks ran with blood, eerily bright red in the firelight. Stalwart men in the defense of Karolan broke down and cried because they had given their all, and saw nothing but death without hope before them. Yet they did not give up fighting.

Fingar's anger mounted at the terrible losses among his troops, and at the fact that they still had not taken the low cliff. He drove them on with thunderous threats, with wild promises of wealth and land and slaves. He sent wave after wave of strong warriors, and wave after wave faltered and was lost.

Many of the men of Karolan slipped into a haze of battle, blood, and horror. They thought no longer of anything except the next moment, the next sword thrust, the next parry. Would the horrors that they saw haunt them all their lives, keeping them from loving, or rejoicing in beauty again? Probably. They did not care. Their lives would not be long. Would the next sword thrust of the enemy mortally wound them at last? Perhaps. Would they live on, and fight many more enemies in this long night lifted from Hell? Perhaps. They cared little. Few knew which fate they would prefer.

The rock beneath them was slippery with their blood. Fallen comrades groaned and died behind them. The bonfires blazed like the fires of Hell, and the redly lit troops of Norkath in their anger, greed, and fear seemed like legions of devils. Men of Karolan hoped for a miracle, but it did not come. The only miracle was that they still fought on: an agonizing wonder. Why fight when hope is lost? They did not know why they kept fighting, but they knew they would not stop until they died.

Jonathan fought in the center of the cliff, and he was as weary as the rest. Whenever his sword paused in a tiny lull, it trembled with the weariness of his arms. Yet still he swung with terrifying force, and still he stood unwounded. Now and then he cried out encouragement to the men who fought around him. Now and then, in the midst of the horror of that night, visions of Naomi would flash fleetingly, mockingly, through his weary mind. He would never hold her in his arms again, he knew. Even if Fingar yielded to his terrible losses and surrendered, Jonathan knew that the horrors of this battle had broken and twisted him, so that his love would be forever marred. He would not again laugh, and he would not again be gentle, happy, or free.

The archers of Karolan, who were desperately needed in the defense, became so weary that their arms trembled when they bent their bows. They could no longer shoot accurately. One of them remembered seeing crossbows, which, once loaded, require no strength to aim, among the weapons brought from Byinkal. He found them again, but could not find the crank-handles needed to load them. While running along the barricade searching for them, he stumbled over the prostrate form of Barnabas.

The man who had stumbled lay where he fell, though he was unhurt. Barnabas of Glen Carrah reached out his hand and gently took the crossbow he had been carrying. He drew a deep breath, closed his eyes, and loaded it fully without the crank. He handed it back to the archer, and said, "Carry me to a better place, and by the help of God I will load and you can shoot."

The man looked down at his crossbow in awe, and then back to Barnabas. He set down his weapon, and with a weary effort and a groan lifted the blacksmith up to a sheltered niche within the barricade. Then he ran off to find other archers: if the blacksmith could load crossbows with his bare hands, he should not load for just a single man.

Soon a score and ten archers had gathered round Barnabas. They took a position in the black shadow of the barricade that gave them a clear shot into the Norkath troops. Barnabas loaded their crossbows, and they shot with deadly aim. Because there were more crossbows than men, Barnabas could keep some loaded ones always near him. An archer would bring him an empty bow, take away one already loaded, and go off to seek a clear shot while Barnabas loaded the bow he had left.

The crossbows took no strength to shoot: the archers could bide their time, aim well, and kill a Norkath with each bolt. Many a soldier of Karolan saw death one heartbeat away that hellish night, and then heard an arrow whistle past to strike the man who would have killed him. Few guessed they owed their rescue as much to a wounded blacksmith as to the archer who had shot the crossbow bolt.

Oblivious to all this, Jonathan fought on. For him, as for most others, hope had vanished but steadfastness remained. He would not give up. Yet he was weary. Once, when he looked up for a fleeting instant at the eastern cliff, he thought that a place far up on its black face was glowing red, like heated iron. He shook his head to clear it, and turned back to the fight. He felt it was a wonder that his army had held on so long. For ages of this desperate night, he had felt that at any moment a portion of the cliff might be captured, and they might be driven back and overwhelmed.

*   *   *

The light of prayer, and prayer alone, shone in the darkness of the forget-me-not. Ilohan was dying of thirst, but he thought of that not at all. The act of praying consumed all that he had and was. "Father," he said, "preserve those whose cause is just, and crush the evil that would crush them. If any are standing now in Karolan, dismayed or hopeless, hunted or afraid, please be with them, and guard and rescue them. Do not let them die without hope. Come to them and comfort them, and give them the strength they need.

"God, you gave many men of the land of which I was prince families whom they loved and cared for. Now evil threatens those, and true men must stand to resist it, if they can. So sudden and so dire was Tulbur's treachery, it seems that all must have perished or been captured without even a chance to fight. Yet I dare to hope some men may yet be standing, men who escaped and gathered swords Tulbur did not lock away in the armories of Aaronkal. If men are standing thus – and Lord,

I see, I know they are – do not let them fail. Do not let them fail! Oh, God, do not let men die knowing that those they love have not been rescued. If they give their lives in defense of their loved ones, and the land of their birth, do not let that defense fail.

"Father, I thank you that you have come to me here, and have brought hope that goes so far beyond the stone walls of this cell that is to be my grave. Bring such hope, hope beyond knowledge and understanding, to any who need it now, and do not let them hope in vain. Though Tulbur's treachery has sealed their doom, bring them a miracle: escape beyond hope.

"Father, I know that you are enthroned above the world, and that you have all power, to do all things that you desire. I know that you will make things of blinding beauty, of goodness beyond the reach of all the evil of this world. Darkness and disaster have overtaken my land and my life – but even darkness and disaster can be your chisels as you sculpt us into the fullness of who we were meant to be. I know there is no evil so powerful that it can defeat you, or so vile that you cannot turn it on itself, and from the wreckage bring forth good.

"Yet, Father, I beg you now to show your power in defense of those who love you – and even in defense of those who have not given you their allegiance, but who nevertheless have lived peaceably in the land, wishing harm to none. Thwart now the deeds of evil men, of Tulbur, and Fingar, and all who fight with lust and greed in Fingar's cause. Thwart their evil – even in mercy to them, that their guilt may not increase. Surely every evil act kills something good, and though you can redeem and rescue, it were better for all the world that the evil had not been done. This world holds pain, horror, and darkness that are beyond my understanding even now. I know that to redeem the world, you took immeasurable pain upon yourself. I know that evil tortures and destroys, and that the ways you foil its work and make it break itself, if those words even say well what you do, are beyond my understanding. Perhaps I understand nothing, and all my words are only folly.

"If that is true, forgive me. Yet one thing remains, which swallows all the rest, in which there is no fear and no confusion. Father, I trust in you. I give myself wholly to you, and I thank you with all my heart that you will take me.

Ilohan's prayer lost words, though perhaps it did not truly end. He had no awareness of the dank, small death-cell that enclosed his body. He felt as if he were being carried, by someone strong and worthy of his trust. A little like Jonathan, he thought, but not quite... and he did not remember that Jonathan had ever carried him. He turned to the man, but could not see his face. He did not need to. "Lord," he said to him, "I have a good friend, Jonathan of Glen Carrah. Please do not let him die in this war, and do not let him escape from you. I thank you." Then he was silent.

Chapter 16

Dawn and Dust

IN PETRAG, MEN OF KAROLAN STOKED THE BONFIRES with wood that had been kept in reserve, giving the archers the light they needed to keep up the desperate defense. Barnabas continued to load crossbows for the men around him. The now-roaring fires cast a bright but eerily changeful red light on the troops of Norkath as they came, and bolt after bolt flew from the great crossbows to fell the strongest as they climbed the cliff.

Barnabas lay back against the rock, his hands bloody now from the cuts of the strong, thin bowstrings. He was weary, and knew he could not trust his thoughts. Yet when it seemed to him that the defense could last but a little longer, he found small cause to doubt the feeling. The defiance Jonathan had shouted in the evening would soon ring hollow: dawn would find no warriors left to fight for the doomed cause of Karolan. Long before that, he would become too weary to continue loading bows.

But Barnabas had not turned away from God. What he had told Hannah long ago was true: war could take from him nothing but his mortal life. He trusted God now, and would trust him always. "Father," he prayed, as he closed his eyes and put forth all his strength to bend a bow, "please do something good in this evil place. If we all perish, many who love you and have lived in obedience to you will be at the mercy of evil men. Many who wanted to live in gratefulness and peace have perished or been captured even now. Strengthen my arms, Lord. Put fear in the hearts of our enemies, and do not let them utterly destroy us. Bring something good out of this, Father. Do not let these men all die here on this barren rock – these men whom you have tempered in this desperate furnace, and refined in courage and loyalty and honor. Have you not another purpose?"

The blacksmith loaded three more bows. The fires roared, the wounded screamed, and the weary fought on through the nightmare that was real. Barnabas looked up into the blackness of the sky. Red sparks from the fires flew past, like evil, inconstant stars. There was no hint of Heaven there. He could just make out the silhouette of the eastern cliffs, against the slightly less dense darkness of the starless sky. His eyes rested on the outline for a moment, even while his hands reached out to load a bow. He loaded five bows, each one a desperate effort of his weary arms, and then he looked back above the eastern cliffs, compelled by hope that a thing he had glimpsed there might be real.

It was: a tiny star, cool, high, and free, one lone light from Heaven shining down upon the night of Hell. It brightened as the clouds receded, blown back by cold clear air off the mountains. It seemed to kindle with a clear white fire, shining more brightly than any star of heaven can, save one alone. It was the Morning Star, the herald of the dawn.

Barnabas grasped a great rock of the barricade, and pulled himself up to stand upon his bleeding legs. "The star!" he cried, in a ringing voice such as had not been heard in that valley through long ages of the horrible night. "Above the eastern cliffs. Look, Karolan! The Morning Star!"

All along the battle line men stole fleeting glances to the east. Jonathan felt stabbed to the heart by the piercing beauty of the star. It brought tears to his weary eyes, and suddenly he knew that he could still love Naomi, and that no horror in the world could break his love. He had believed that he was broken, rendered incapable of love and of delight, but this was a lie. Cold, bright anger grew within him at the night that had made him believe such a lie, that had persuaded him thus to abandon the center of his faith. He drove the Norkaths back before him in his anger, and they faltered and fell down the cliff in confusion, astonished at their weary foe's sudden increase in strength.

In the instant of respite that followed, Jonathan cried, "Men of Karolan, the Star has risen. How long will we fight?"

The Norkath soldiers had long been thinking that the next moment must bring their victory. They turned back in wonder and dismay at the great shout that rose up from their foes, "Until the dawn!"

But still they came. Still the decimated troops of Fingar stormed the cliff. Still the weary men of Karolan held them off, with strength born of desperation alone. And the blue light of morning crept into the sky.

*   *   *

"You were right, beloved Therinil. We had to stay. Do not reproach yourself, whatever follows. You were right, and you have saved me from a great crime." Yalron held her in his arms and said these things to her as they stood together on the eastern wall of Petrag, high above the battle.

As they had passed that place the day before, seeking the Luciyr road in obedience to Jonathan's command, Therinil had dismounted, fallen down, and wept. "We cannot go," she had cried. "My heart is breaking, for we cannot go. We would be wrong, we would be wrong to go."

Yalron had heard her, and agreed. He had dismounted and knelt beside her, and his own tears had mingled with hers upon the stone. They had felt the condemnation they were under: they loved at a time when the world was crumbling, and the life they had hoped to live together lay in the path of the storm. To fly, and thereby save it would violate the uncompromising loyalty that was its strong foundation. To stay threatened the wreck of all their hopes.

They had stood together and walked to the edge of the great cliff that was the eastern wall of Petrag. They had looked down upon the desperate fight far, far below, and had known with certainty that they could not go to safety while men fought and died there for the rescue of their land. And then Yalron, the master rock-breaker, had looked down at the gray stone and seen a deep crack two handbreadths in width.

The miners had examined the crack, and Yalron's thoughts had been confirmed. A huge slab of rock had broken free of the cliff. It could fall at any time. The army of Fingar was directly below it. Every man and woman there, from Tharral to Jenn, had chosen to stay, whatever the risk, and do all that they could to push it off. That had been a day and night ago. It still stood.

Yalron's hands as he embraced Therinil were blistered and bloody. Her face and his were smudged with ash. Jonathan had not hallucinated when he thought the rock on the eastern cliff was glowing in the night. The miners had lit a great fire far down in the crack, to weaken the rock by flame. They had broken the boulders and projecting crags that still held the rock slab in place. They had pried at it, using small pine trees for levers. Still it stood. The crack that had been two handbreadths wide was now too big to cross without a jump, and still the mighty slab of rock did not tilt forward and fall, as they had so long hoped it would.

Therinil held Yalron tightly. "The men down there are dying," she said. "Will the rock ever fall?"

"I do not know, Beloved," said Yalron, "but it may not. I would have you set out for Luciyr now, for if Jonathan falls the Norkaths will soon overrun the land. If we fail, there will be nothing for me to do but fly, and I will follow you."

"You want me to leave you, and no longer try to help you here?" Her voice was weary.

"Beloved, you are at the end of your strength. I would not have you stay here in such danger, though it will grieve me very much to let you go."

"Yalron, how I love you! I want to do what you desire me to. Yet could I be worthy to be called your wife, if I left you here, now, to fly to safety?"

"I would not have you do a thing that you consider wrong, Beloved," said Yalron, "but I would keep you from danger. If we are seen, this place will become a mark for Norkath archers. Fingar may even send a band of soldiers against us, and there are paths to climb the cliffs. Do you see any great good you can do by remaining here?"

"Yalron, my husband, ask the same question of yourself. Must you stay? Alas! I know you answered that question long ago. But did not I as well?"

Yalron released her. "I do not know," he said. "But as long as there is any hope of success, I will stay here and try to show

Fingar that no man can conquer stone. There is still a chance we may push down the slab."

Therinil gathered the dark cloak that she wore about her, and pulled the hood down low over her face. It hid her golden hair. She looked poor and weary, far older than her years. "How much danger will I find, dressed so?" she asked. "I will go down to the army of Karolan, and be a nurse for wounded men behind the shelter of the barricade. If our army is overrun, I will nurse the wounded of victorious Norkath too, and thus secure their goodwill. Then I will slip away under cover of darkness. You must look for me tonight on the Luciyr road, and we will fly together."

Yalron embraced her once again, and held her tight. "How I love you, Therinil. You must keep well back from the barricade, for near it the peril will be very great whether Norkath triumphs or we at last push down the rock. But if you tend the wounded far behind the battle line, I think your danger will be less than if you linger here – though you will not be safe. You will be like an angel to the men you help. If we triumph, I will find you in the valley; if not, as you have said, the Luciyr road. Watch for arrows, Beloved, and whatever happens let no Norkath see your beauty."

"Farewell, Yalron, prince of my heart," she said. "Do not die here! You also watch for arrows. Farewell!"

She turned away and walked steadily back from the cliff to mount her horse. She did not go alone. For after more tearful farewells, each of the miners' wives followed her. Once more her courage and faithfulness had led them all.

Mer's eyes met Tharral's in the cool blue twilight of the dawn. He wanted her to go with them, but he saw that she would not. "Together, forever, Tharral," she whispered. He smiled at her. She had always been faithful, and though he feared for her, he rested on her faithfulness and love. She was as trustworthy as the dawn, which will come every day as long as the sun shall last.

*   *   *

The morning light was cold. In the eyes of men who had worked and fought through the darkness of the firelit night, the stone landscape and the terrible battle ground stood out with mocking clarity. They saw the pale faces of their comrades, and their clothes stained with blood, ash, and dust. They saw the vast numbers of the dead, maimed and distorted, strewn upon the stone beneath the cliff. In the soft, cool light, the plethora of detail seemed to crowd against their eyes. They saw too much, too many things they had no need to know, and the distractions made it harder to maintain the desperate focus they needed to keep on fighting.

The hope that the Morning Star had brought to Karolan was short-lived, for the battle raged still, and the light favored the Norkaths. To many soldiers of Karolan it seemed a devastating injustice that they should still have to fight, after holding the cliff for so long, and going on through such merciless exhaustion. Yet the Norkaths still attacked. Though Fingar's great army had been decimated, though the Norkath dead were piled high all along the base of the cliff, still thousands thronged the valley and stormed the bloody stone.

At the back of the army of Norkath, Fingar and Andokar held a brief council with a few of their knights. Fingar was coldly angry. "What are our losses?" he asked one of the knights.

"Easier, perhaps, Father, to ask what remains," said Andokar.

"Answer the question I asked, dog," said Fingar, addressing the knight.

"We marched here a score and seven thousands strong, Your Glorious Majesty," said the knight. "We have no more than nine thousands now, perhaps fewer."

"And we have lost how many?" said Fingar sharply.

"The difference, Your Glorious Majesty. Nearly a score of thousands."

"It is an insane war," said Andokar. "It is folly to fight when the losses are so high."

"If you were not my son I would call you a coward," said Fingar. "It is folly to turn back when the fight has been so long. Yet I would not lose more men if it can be avoided. You!" he turned to the knight, "Go and offer terms of surrender to the Karolans."

"What are the terms, Your Glorious Majesty?"

Andokar looked intently at his father, who ignored him. "The same as before," said Fingar sternly. "Remind them that the dawn has come. Go!"

The knight clattered up through the army of Norkath, the foot soldiers standing aside to let him through. He blew a long trumpet blast, raised his white flag, and called in a loud voice for the fighting to stop.

Jonathan saw the Norkaths cease fighting and warily step back. The men of Karolan were only too glad for the blessed cessation of the hellish fight. "Karolan, hold your positions!" said Jonathan. "Stand! Do not sit to rest!" His voice rang thinly in the morning air. In the depths of his weariness, he felt that the words were not his own, that they were spoken by another man of stronger will.

"I offer terms of surrender from His Glorious Majesty, King Fingar of Norkath," said the knight.

"Are they at all changed from those which we have heard already?" asked Jonathan.

"They are the same," said the knight, "the same gracious terms."

"The dog has already received our answer," said Jonathan. "Does he – fickle as he is – think that justice and honor can change in a night, like the shifting wind?"

"You said that you would fight until the dawn," said the knight. He raised his voice and turned to take in the whole of the Karolan army on the cliff. "The dawn has come. You are weary and bleeding. Your strength is at an end. Your comrades are dead at your feet. You cannot even raise your swords. Stop fighting, as you have said you would, and keep your lives."

There was a long silence, eerie in the twilit valley full of death. When Jonathan spoke it was as though he were breaking the silence of a thousand years. "We said that we would fight until the dawn," he said, the strength of his voice rising with the words. "Though none expected it, we have! We never said we would not fight beyond the dawn. The dawn has come, and still we will fight. Men of Karolan!" he cried. "How long will we fight?"

There was no answer. The men stood silent: demoralized, exhausted, hopeless. Some had even sat down on the bloody rocks, in weary disobedience of Jonathan's cruel order. The silence hung unbroken in the morning air, save for the soft whispering of a light wind. To Jonathan each moment seemed to drain his strength. He called again, desperation showing in his voice despite himself. "Men of Karolan! We yet live and breathe. How long will we fight?" Silence. No answer came.

*　　　　　　*　　　　　　*

"I know that would push it out," said Yalron. "We have broken everything that held it back, save the gravel below it on the northern edge. It hangs by a thread. Pry out the southern corner, and it will lean forward and fall."

The other miners, and Tharral, stood on the rock around Yalron in their torn and soot-smeared clothes. They nodded their agreement.

"Of course you are right," said Dran, "but how does that help us? Where could we stand to pry out the southern corner?"

Yalron led Dran to the edge of the cliff. He pointed to a ledge of rock well below the cliff edge, perhaps four paces from the edge of the slab. It was a precarious place, looking more like an eagle's aerie than a place for men. A wrong step in any direction would lead to a gulf of cool, clear air, followed by certain death on the valley floor – or on the swords of the Norkath soldiers that thronged there.

"That is where we will stand," said Yalron, "and there," he turned around, and pointed at a straight, tall pine not far from the cliff edge, "is the lever we will use."

"You are mad, Yalron," said Dran. "Your schemes are like catching lightning bolts or throwing rocks at the moon. Yet – " he smiled, "I will work beside you."

Verkal the gold miner came running along the cliff edge to join them. His face was grave. "All is lost," he said. "We may as well go and die with them. Look! I myself have listened well, and could hear Jonathan say, 'How long will we fight?' There was no answer. They are lost. They have no more strength to fight, and they will not even speak."

Yalron knelt on the cliff edge, heedless of the rough, jagged stone. He looked down at the army far below, and saw that Verkal was right. The Karolans sat still and dejected on the rocks of the low cliff. The knight with the white flag sat regally upon his great horse, waiting for their reply. The Norkath troops still filled the valley, waiting for the command to resume fighting. The knight rotated the white flag slowly in his hands, lowering it until the pole was horizontal and the flag hung down, rippling softly in the breeze. Then he dropped it on the bloody rocks at his horse's feet.

The miners on the cliff top could not hear the orders given to the Norkath troops. They could only see the result. The disorderly groups formed into ranks. The weak and wounded were carried away. Swords glistened in every man's hand. The Karolans still did not move.

Fingar rode up through the ranks of his army, stopping when he reached its center. The standard bearer at his side lifted the banner of the Fist of Iron. Even the miners heard the order that Fingar shouted, as the banner was thrown forward and unfurled in the wind of its motion: "Charge!"

*   *   *

Somehow the soldiers of Karolan stood up to meet that charge, and somehow they fought. Stiff muscles sprained and tore with the renewed exertion. Men wondered what curse had kept them alive to fight so long. The battle line of Karolan faltered in every place. The defenders stumbled on the bloody rocks, and swords were smashed from their weary hands. The Norkaths roared with triumph as they gained the cliff edge in many places.

In the center, where Jonathan was, the battle line was broken entirely, and several scores of Norkath soldiers poured onto the cliff top. Jonathan was forced back against the barricade, fighting with all the strength he had left. He was fighting three men at once, overwhelmed, with no one near to help. Yet still he fought with all the force of his hot anger and his iron will, and he did not give up. He saw everything, and his enemies found no weakness in his defense. Their frustrated hatred mounted, the fury of their blows increased, and still he stood, one man, forced back against the barricade, but still alive. Then the sword shattered in his hand.

He crumpled to the ground to escape the blow that had broken his weapon, but he knew the next stroke would kill him. Jonathan saw that it was a sturdy Norkath axe man who would give it. The man rushed forward eagerly, proud that he would be the one to kill the mighty commander of Karolan. Jonathan was still aware of everything: of the disappointment the other two men felt at not being able to give the deathblow, of how the wooden shaft would feel in the axe man's hands, and of the jolt it would give as the iron blade crushed his own skull. He knew exactly how his death would feel to the man who killed him.

The axe-stroke came with speed and dreadful force, and with a deafening crack it struck a rock in the barricade just above Jonathan's head. The axe man had been weary and over-eager. Jonathan knew the terrible, jarring rebound that his enemy felt, and knew that his numbed hands had lost their grip. He reached up in one lightning instant, seized the axe haft in a grip of iron, and wrenched it from the Norkath's hands. In the same motion he swung it with tremendous force, roaring with anger, effort, and desperate weariness. All three attackers fell broken before him. It was his own hands, in the end, that felt the jolts of the axe haft, each of which meant the ruin of a man.

Jonathan came away from the barricade with the axe flying. "For Karolan!" he roared. "For Glen Carrah! Stand up and fight!" And men stood up and fought. Inspired by that cry, from the center they had thought was lost and the commander they had known was dead, they found new strength and hoped against all reason. They drove the Norkaths step by step back off the cliff. Everywhere along the line Karolan rallied. It seemed an impossible miracle to all, not least to those whose strength achieved it. The defenders of Petrag regained the cliff.

Jonathan stood at the cliff edge and fought. His blood was so hot within him that his exhaustion did not seem to matter. He had a sword again, the weapon that he knew, and in his hands it was like a wall of flashing iron above the cliff. The fight was strange: a dream, yet deeply real; Hell, yet beneath a clear blue dawn. It seemed to him that Naomi sang behind him, safe and free, trusting wholly that he would save her. He fought as if she truly were there, and began to wonder if he would indeed win her rescue.

All around Jonathan the Karolan defense weakened. He was lost in his dream and his desperate weariness. He had thoughts only for the motions of his enemies. He did not see that the army he led was faltering again, and that this would be the last time. It would have mattered nothing if he had seen. There was nothing to be done. Every wonder that can spring from the will, love, and courage of men had already come to them. This time there was nothing left, no reserve, no strength of iron determination or staggering bravery to which they could turn. They were only men, and too few were left to hold the cliff. The army of Karolan had reached the last edge of its strength.

*   *   *

Fingar and Andokar stood together near the western wall of the valley, well out of arrow range of the battle. The king had a bodyguard of several hundred men, and the prince commanded five score master archers. Neither group had seen much fighting, but Fingar, impatient, fuming at the incredible repulses and devastating losses of his army, judged it time to lead his own bodyguard into battle. He wanted Andokar to do the same with his archers.

"Son," said Fingar with controlled outrage, "why will you not fight with me?"

"The victory is yours whether I fight or no," said Andokar. "I have no stomach for killing men as much better than myself as the Karolan defenders are. If you needed me, I would fight for you. You do not. You have ignored everything I have said through the whole of this miserable war, and your bloody victory is certain."

"Son, you speak like a fool. You will be telling me next that the defenders of Karolan are better men than I am. What do you say to that? They will be defeated. We will triumph. They must die, and you will help me kill them."

Andokar looked up at the rock walls of the great valley, strong and clean against the lovely brightness of the morning sky. He drank in the beauty like a man dying of thirst. The sun had not yet risen, but the east was brilliant yellow-white. Tall pine trees stood dark and majestic on the cliff tops, far removed from the hellish battlefield below. "Father, even now I will not speak evil of you when it serves no end," he said at last. "But I will not fight for you in this. You must go alone to seal your triumph. Punish me however you will."

Fingar whirled his green cloak around in a rage. "Stay, then, fool. When I die an old man Norkath has a puppy for her king; you will never even be a dog." He walked swiftly to his great black horse and mounted it in one quick motion. He did not notice that his son's gaze had frozen on one point of the eastern cliffs.

"Father!" called Andokar with desperate urgency, "Father, call a retreat! The stone will fall!"

"Yes," called Fingar behind him as he rode away to lead his bodyguard into battle, "the Stone, Sword, and Star will fall. Do not fear for me!"

Andokar stood frozen for a moment, watching tiny figures far up on the great cliff trying to pry a huge slab of rock away from the wall. The slab was moving. Andokar could see it. He did not know what to do. Then loyalty and love for his father came over him in a great wave. Did it matter that his father was an evil man? Should his son sit by and let him die? No! He had refused to fight to seal his father's victory, but he would fight like a lion to save his life.

"Archers of Andokar!" he cried, "Rally to your prince! Disaster has come on Norkath, and only we can save her. Follow me!"

He led them up the west side of the valley, desperately seeking a high outcrop of rock that would give them a clear shot at the handful of men who threatened the whole army of Norkath with immediate destruction.

*   *   *

"What is Ceramir? I would like to have gone there." Jenn lay on the rock with her head against her mother's lap. They sat together not far from the cliff edge, just out of sight of the battle below. Both were very weary.

Mer smiled sadly down at her daughter. "I wish you would not say 'would have' as if you never will. The name Ceramir means Cloth of Joy, and I know little more. But I guess much. Did you see the light in Jonathan's face when he spoke of it?"

Jenn shifted on the hard stone, looking up at her mother's face and at the brightness of the morning sky above them. "Yes, I saw it. But, Mother, do you not feel that we will never go there? This is a day for love, but not for hope."

Mer held her daughter close against her. "This is a day for love and faith, Jenn. I feel what you feel, but feelings can lie. No one can say what will happen before the night, save God alone, who loves us."

"I wish we were with Father. We could push on the tree."

"We are very near him, Jenn, and on the outcrop where they are working we would only hamper them. The work takes great strength, and there is scarcely room across the rock for all the men. The tree trunk that is their lever can bounce, and crush those not strong enough to control it. Father might hurt himself, trying to protect us, if we were there."

"You will never leave him, will you, Mother?"

"No," said Mer, "I never will."

"You will always be together," said Jenn, "and I will never leave you. There is no one else I love in all the world."

Mer was silent, her heart full of mingled joy and foreboding. She looked around at the cliff top scene: rugged rock and towering pines, lit by the cool, clean light of dawn. She was strong now, the ravages of plague and hunger passed. Despite her gray hair, she felt young, and despite her weariness she felt happy. Jenn, her beloved daughter, was warm and real in her arms, no longer sick, starving, or weak. Her love for Tharral was pure and strong, blessed, she was certain, by God.

Jenn stiffened suddenly in her arms. "Mother, what are those?" She spoke very quickly, with a note of terror in her voice, and sat up, staring fixedly in the direction of the cliff edge. Mer followed her gaze, and instantly was on her feet. Arrows were flying up over the cliff, gleaming against the blue sky. They fell far short of herself and Jenn, but she knew they were not the intended target.

"I must go to him," said Mer, calmly, to her own wonder, in that terrible moment. "Jenn, you must stay here. I command you, for love of me, stay here."

Jenn said nothing, but she looked up and met Mer's gaze. Her eyes were aflame with love and resolution. "You intend to follow me, do you not?" asked Mer. "You do not intend to obey me."

"No," said Jenn simply. "I love you too much."

Mer was crying now. "Jenn, you must not go! Please do not go!"

Jenn stood and hugged her mother desperately. "I am sorry, Mother. But I will not stay while you go to the arrows. I must follow you. I will not be left! I must go!"

Suddenly Mer was calm. She gently pushed Jenn away. "I love you, Jenn," she said, "so much that my heart is breaking. Never forget that I love you." With those words, Mer reached down and ripped the hem of her dress through on a rough rock. Her fingers were skilled and strong in her great need. She tore the strong, homespun cloth all the way around, until the hem came free in her hands, a narrow, long strip of doubled cloth.

There was a small pine tree just behind them. Jenn was surprised and confused, and could not resist her mother. Mer dragged her to the tree and tied her hands securely behind her. The cloth strip was as good as rope, and Mer's knots were strong and tight. Jenn could not get free. Mer hugged her close one last time. They were both crying. "I am sorry, Jenn," said Mer. "I am more sorry than I can say. I love you with my whole heart, and I want to win for you a new life in a world at peace. I am going. God will heal all our hearts. May he be with you, Daughter. Farewell."

Jenn tugged desperately at the rope around her arms. "Mother!" she screamed. "Mother! I love you! Do not die. Mother, come back! But I know you will not turn – you will go. God guard you! Farewell, Mother!"

*   *   *

Tharral and the miners had been overjoyed at first because Yalron's plan to lever out the slab seemed to be succeeding. Now they grimly struggled on, knowing they were racing with death. The range and force of the Norkath arrows astonished them: they flew from across the valley, soared to the vast height of the valley walls, and still retained deadly speed. The stone slab leaned slowly forward in response to the miners' utmost, sweating, straining effort, but still it did not overbalance and fall.

The arrows were horrible, like deadly flies that filled the air. One after another the men of Karolan were hit. A few fell, but most, though wounded, kept pushing on. With every shred of their remaining strength, they forced the huge, rough pine-trunk outward. The little company of weary men had a defiant, dogged courage, careless of life and of pain. They did not cry out when they were hit, but only grimaced or grunted. They spared no breath for words. There were no heroic songs or hopeless denunciations of the Norkath foe. They put forth all their strength, despite arrows that tore their muscles and blood that gushed out on the jagged rock at their feet. And the slab was moving.

It suddenly gave more easily, and ground forward a full pace with majestic slowness. The miners looked on with grim joy, but then to their horror the slab eased to a halt. They struggled back up to push the lever again, but this time they had to come to the very edge of the outcrop. They were brutally exposed to the Norkath archery. Terror seemed to have urged the bowmen down below to their utmost strength, and the arrows came fast and deadly accurate.

Yalron fell, an arrow through his heart, and died on the bloody stone with words of love for Therinil upon his lips. Dran fell, struggled back up again to push once more, took another arrow, and fell again. Verkal fell. The lever still crept forward, but few had any hope the slab would fall. One pace more, and the lever would swing out over empty space before them, and they would be able to push no longer. Miner after miner took his last arrow and fell back on the stone. Each man who fell died quickly; none would give up his place at the log until he had used the last of his failing strength.

Finally there were two miners, and Tharral, and the slab did not fall. Then there was one miner, and Tharral. Then Tharral felt a brutal, piercing impact in his chest. It was not at all as he had thought it would feel, but he knew that he was dying. Blood spurted from the wound with his heartbeats and poured down upon the stone. His strength fell from him, and he collapsed in a pool of red. The last miner pushed on for only a moment before he too sank down mortally wounded upon the jagged stone. He pulled himself to the edge, struggled to his knees, and toppled outward into space, hoping to kill one Norkath more as a futile gesture on this day of Karolan's disaster.

Then Mer reached the outcrop. She was calm and sure, though she knew her life was shattered. She ran to the edge of the stone, put both hands upon the trunk, and pushed with all her strength. She could feel it moving, but slowly. She tried to push harder. Her strength faltered, but she breathed hard, and kept pushing. Then the archers, who had thought they were victorious, saw her, and their arrows leaped up swift and deadly. She saw them, and kept pushing, and the huge log moved beneath her hands. Then the arrows struck her. She pushed herself backward onto the outcrop, knelt, and then slipped sideways to lie upon the rock as blood splashed down from her wounds.

She had fallen beside Tharral, and he opened his eyes at the motion. "Mer…" he whispered. "You came."

The terrible pain she had felt was rapidly fading, replaced by a numb, choking feeling that she was broken beyond all healing. With an effort she reached out her left hand – her right was pinned under her – and touched his. "I am sorry, Thar," she whispered. "And we failed…"

"Do not be sorry… Beloved… love never fails…"

The sun had caught the cliff top now, and the sky was brilliant blue. All the world was bathed in clear morning light. Their hands touched in a pool of their blood. It was bright red, soaking their sleeves, staining them its own rich, terrible color. It was their life, which they had given, running together. There was a loud grinding sound in Mer's ears, and the stone was not steady beneath her.

"It falls," whispered Tharral suddenly, opening his eyes again.

Mer smiled, and said, "So… And together we fall…"

The rock on which they lay tilted, and Mer slid on the bloody stone, ending in Tharral's arms.

"Together… into the arms of God," he said. Her face was fading before his vision even as he spoke. For an instant he saw her eyes lit with the joy of Heaven-hope, and then he saw nothing more in the broken world. The slab on which they lay tilted vertical, and their bodies fell together.

*   *   *

Fingar had swiftly re-ordered his weary army as he led his bodyguard into battle. He had wanted to form all his troops into an organized, invincible phalanx, to run up the cliff and end Karolan forever. Now the host of Norkath advanced at a run, and Fingar, surrounded by his bodyguard, smiled. It was all exactly as he had willed it should be. At last the Karolan army and its absurd peasant-commander would be crushed like the annoying insects they were.

Jonathan watched them come. The sword sagged down in his weary hands, and there was a sad, grim smile on his face. He held his thoughts gently away from the life he would lose. All around him men stood like him, too tired to shout, too steadfast to run, awaiting their death. Fingar's army came on, strong across the whole valley, shouting in triumph. Karolan waited, hopeless, dogged, too weary even to think.

Then Jonathan felt the ground tremble, and sensed a shadow falling from the eastern cliff. He looked up, and terror struck him even through his exhaustion. Some part of his mind took in the reality: a giant slab had split off from the cliff and was falling. But to all the rest of his being the rushing shadow meant the end of the world: the sky, the hills were falling, crashing in unimagined ruin. He heard himself shouting words he had never planned or chosen to say: "Back, Karolan! Fly! We are lost!"

Some of the warriors of Karolan heard Jonathan's cry as a final admission of defeat: they had lost, and they were lost –

there was no longer even courage. Others had looked up themselves, and understood. For whichever cause, most abandoned the cliff and followed Jonathan as he climbed the barricade in desperate haste and sprinted up the valley. A few, the bravest of the brave, disobeyed him, defied the stone, and held their positions on the little cliff.

The mighty slab of rock swung out, broke free of the cliff wall, and fell without tumbling or tilting. Andokar, having led his archers high up on the western side of the valley, knew they would likely survive. As for the rest, he had failed them. He saw his father dive beneath a horse in a futile attempt to save his life, and then the Prince of Norkath covered his face with his hands.

Though Jonathan ran with all his strength, he was not even four paces past the barricade when the crash came, so loud it seemed to destroy the world. A blast of wind threw him down upon the stone. The solid earth jumped like a startled child, and the sound seemed to tear his head apart. Flying rocks filled the air, crashing and shattering on the stone around him. Then silence fell like the silence at the end of the world.

He lay still for a long moment, his head bleeding where it had struck the stone. He raised his head and looked around. He noticed that his sword was still in his hands. He tried to let go of it, but he could not. He had fought so hard and long, gripping that sword so tightly, that now his fingers were locked around the hilt. He jammed his blade between two rocks, and worked his hands open with painful effort. Pain burned them like fire as the skin, which had been stuck to the hilt by coagulated blood, pulled free of the rough leather. He looked at them a moment, his hard blacksmith's hands, covered now with raw and bleeding blisters. Such was the cost of a day and night of desperate sword-strokes, fighting every moment for life and land.

He got to his feet. The air was full of hanging dust. The sun roofed the valley with airy gold, as the highest dust caught the light that poured over the eastern cliff. The long, deadly battle was over, and in the dead silence of the morning valley it seemed to Jonathan that he was the only one left alive.

The crash had taken only an instant, but it had changed everything. Jonathan hardly felt that this was this same life he had been living those few moments ago, before the rock fell. He was weary, deeply weary, almost too tired to think. But it was spring in his heart, for though he could not fathom all that might follow, he was sure that Karolan was saved, and saved forever. Fingar and his army, with all their greed, had perished. Even if but one man remained of the army of Karolan, yet Karolan had triumphed.

But what was he to do? His first thought was to go to Glen Carrah, and find Naomi. Suddenly he remembered his father, and sat down hard upon a rock. He had laid his father at the foot of the barricade. He might still be alive, but...

Jonathan was running for the barricade. He tripped and fell hard; his legs had been too stiff and sore to answer his will. He lay on the rough rock for a moment, gathering his thoughts, and then proceeded more carefully, walking with a limp. He came to the barricade and began to search for Barnabas.

The little hope he had dwindled swiftly. The scene was almost unrecognizable. The violent wind from beneath the falling slab had blown holes in the barricade, blasting the stones as far as several paces up the valley. Boulder-sized shards from the crash had inflicted further damage, and in two cases crushed a man to pulp. Almost every man Jonathan found was either dead or unconscious. A few groaned and spoke incoherently when he bent over them.

Jonathan did not find Barnabas. He went all along the barricade, and saw things he would always wish he could forget. At the end he sat down on the ruined barricade and stared at the ground, feeling sick. He was the commander: he was sure he could not simply lie down and sleep. There must be some task that was his duty, if only he could think of it. While trying, he suddenly realized that he was starved and thirsty. He found what was left of the supplies from Petrag. There were full water skins, and he drank, slowly, lest he vomit. As the water gently trickled into him, it seemed to bring new life. He stood up, and thought of Aaronkal. Tulbur would be there, and Ilohan... no, Ilohan's corpse. But it would take an army to recapture Aaronkal. Perhaps he should sleep, after all – but before that, he must learn if any Norkaths were left alive. He found a sword, and set out across the slab of fallen rock.

High above him the sun over the cliff tops still shone on the dust and seemed to give the valley a glorious ceiling of glowing gold. Higher still, hawks soared in a limitless blue depth of sky. In the shaded air beneath, the dust hung heavier, shrouding the Norkath camp in a gray haze. The fallen slab across which Jonathan walked was broken in many places, but still it blessed his eyes with its smooth cleanliness: it was not littered, as so much of Petrag was now, with the ruins of the bodies of men.

But Jonathan did notice a pile of dark bundles far off to his right. He went to them, still walking slowly and stiffly. He was only half prepared to find them bodies, since he did not see how anyone could have died there. But they were bodies, horribly shattered and broken, so that he believed they had fallen from the cliff with the great slab. Arrows protruded from some of them, the shafts broken by the violence of their fall. Two bodies at the top of the pile had not been as badly shattered as the others. Jonathan turned them over, trying to understand what had happened to them. And he recognized them: Tharral, and Mer. He fell to his knees. "They should have been in Ceramir," he cried, so loud that the words rang and echoed in the valley. "I sent them to the Cloth of Joy. Why are they dead now, at my feet? Why?" He bowed his head and wept. It seemed to make the whole victory – if it was a victory – into a mockery and a farce.

Chapter 17

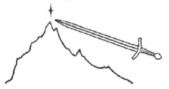

The Sons of Mortal Foes

JONATHAN KNELT FOR A LONG MOMENT BY THE CORPSES of Mer and Tharral, stunned by the inexplicable tragedy. At last he gathered both their broken bodies in his arms, stood up with a great effort, and thus heavily laden he continued toward the Norkath camp.

A man on a great black warhorse rode slowly out onto the slab to meet him. He held the banner of the Fist of Iron in his right hand, but there was a white flag affixed below it. He stopped not far from Jonathan, and called out in a clear voice that was yet somehow strange and unsteady, "I, Andokar the son of Fingar, King of Norkath, humbly request the commander of the army of Karolan to accept terms of surrender."

A wakening wind from Karolan swirled and thinned the dust that hung in the valley, and Jonathan could see the speaker more clearly. He did not set down the corpses, but he came forward, slowly yet without a limp, until he stood before King Andokar of Norkath. "Lay down your arms," said Jonathan.

"I have none," said Andokar.

318

Jonathan looked intently at his face, and then slowly scanned his whole person, and his horse. Finally Jonathan said, "State your terms."

"I and all the forces under my command will lay down our weapons and return to Norkath," said Andokar. "I will pledge that now, throughout my reign, and forever, Norkath will be at peace with Karolan. I will make a changeless law that no successor of mine may ever cross Karolan's borders in war, or seek to conquer her by treachery.

"In return I ask that my life, and the lives of my soldiers who remain, will be spared, and that our wounded will be tended. I ask that the King of Karolan will make the same pledge of peace to my land as I make to his. I ask no more.

"It is well that you do not, dog's son," said Jonathan. "Do you think it is a simple matter to make peace with men whose homes you have burnt, and whose fathers, brothers, sons, and friends you have killed? By all justice you should die where you stand. But I will not kill you – at least, not yet."

He knelt on the smooth stone, and laid the bodies of Mer and Tharral gently upon it. He acted as though he had forgotten the existence of Andokar, as though he were alone with the broken corpses of his friends. He pushed their hair gently back, and arranged their limbs so as to hide the brokenness of their bodies. He took off the cloak he wore and spread it over them to hide the blood and wounds. "Mer... Tharral..." he whispered, "shall I let you go unavenged? Shall I act as though the wonder of your love was nothing, a treasure that can be shattered at will with no payment or punishment required? Shall I do this?"

He stood and faced Andokar again. The young king had not moved. "The man is Tharral," said Jonathan. "He offered me hospitality when he was dying of hunger, and he saved the life

319

of my prince when I could not protect him. The woman is Mer, who tended the worst injury I have ever taken, and comforted me in my folly and my fear. They were good, and brave, and merciful. They were husband and wife, and loved each other with a love such as seldom graces this dark and treacherous world. I have seen her choose to die with him, when leaving him to die alone would have saved her. They had a daughter, Jenn, who doubtless is dead or dying now, whose love and goodness, had she lived, would have grown as strong. They are dead."

"They were among those who pushed out the rock which brought you victory," said Andokar. "In love for my father, who is now in hell, I ordered my archers to kill them. They are dead, and yet they have triumphed. Would that they were living."

"So you say, now, whose hands are red with their blood," said Jonathan. "And should I spare you? Barnabas, my father, who surpassed yours as clean iron surpasses rotten wood, is dead. Prince Ilohan, who might have led this broken land into a time of joy and beauty such as we have never known, is dead. Thousands whose faithfulness and bravery put you and your father to shame are dead, and should I spare you?"

Andokar was silent. Jonathan drew his sword. "I will die a man," said Andokar. "I will not beg for life, or cry out, or flinch from your blow. Yet you will harm yourself if you kill me."

"Foolish words," said Jonathan. "You say you will not beg, and yet you beg, and give weak reasons why I should not kill you. No anger the world has ever known has been hotter than mine. No strength in all the world could save your life..." Jonathan suddenly paused, thinking of Naomi, and then continued, shaken, "...save one, perhaps, whose name you will never know."

The sword slashed through the air with all the force of Jonathan's agony and rage. The stroke could have killed a horse and man together. And yet, even as he swung, in the back of Jonathan's mind there rang Naomi's words: the second promise she had asked for. He knew what she would ask for now, and he gave it to her. He pulled the blade back perhaps two handbreadths only. The shaft that held the banner of Norkath broke in two with a loud crack, and horse and man staggered beneath the rebound of the heavy oak pole. Then Jonathan threw his sword down and leaned forward with his hands upon his knees, panting and trembling. Andokar regained control of his horse, rubbed a red welt across his neck where the tip of the blade had just touched him, and held the much-shortened staff of his banner with as much dignity as he could.

Jonathan straightened slowly. "Other goodness than your own has saved you," he said coldly, controlling his voice with an effort of will. "The banner of Norkath deserves that disgrace and more. Concerning your terms of surrender I say this: I am not the King of Karolan, and I cannot answer for his promises. But as for that part of your request which I have power to grant, I will grant it, if you add one pledge more on your own side."

"What pledge is that?"

"Promise to aid me today and tomorrow, in all that I plan to do, and after that to go to Norkath and never return to Karolan unless the king himself shall ask you."

"What do you plan to do?" asked Andokar.

"Since you have surrendered, I do not think Aaronkal will be held against me. I plan to ride there and kill Tulbur, the traitor. I will learn the fate of Ilohan, my friend and prince, and bury him in honor if that can be. I will free the captives, end the rape of Karolan, and start its healing."

"With these things I will gladly help you," said Andokar. "The first token of my help is this: I know what has been done to King Ilohan, and I will tell you. He is in the forget-me-not at Aaronkal. My father asked Tulbur to show him the king's head; Tulbur refused, and my father forced him to explain the reason. I heard it with my own ears, for I was in the council of war that we held at Aaronkal. Therefore it is possible that His Majesty is still alive."

"Get me your fastest horse, and come with me to Aaronkal," said Jonathan, with warmth and triumph displacing the controlled coldness in his voice. "If Ilohan lives I forgive you all your father's crimes, and pledge I will never revenge on you your own! Hurry! He may be on the very point of death!"

"Yes, but wait until –" began Andokar, but Jonathan cut him off.

"I will not wait!" Jonathan cried. "I do not care! Bring me a horse, and come with me to Aaronkal!" He ran past Andokar as swiftly as his soreness would allow. He plunged into the camp of Norkath, glanced around a moment, fixed on a likely horse, and untied it swiftly despite his bleeding fingers. Then he was on the horse, holding the reins. High above, he could see the sunlit dust that roofed the valley beginning to roll back in an awakening wind from Karolan. The valley of Petrag stretched out before him, calling him to fly down it like the wind.

Then he saw two guards, standing nearby with drawn bows aimed at him. "We're not all dead, horse thief!" said one. "Dismount if you want to live."

Jonathan began slowly to dismount. He realized he did not even have a sword, and was confused and ashamed of his own folly. "Faster!" said one of the guards, and drew his arrow back to the head.

"Disarm, guards!" came the voice of one accustomed to command. The guards looked reluctant, but obeyed swiftly. King Andokar rode into the camp.

"Beware, Sir," said Andokar to Jonathan, "of acting when you cannot think. I will ride with you to Aaronkal, but I will carry my banner with a white flag, and you must carry the Stone, Sword, and Star. Otherwise you – and therefore I also – stand far too high a chance of being shot by one side or the other on the way."

Jonathan was ashamed again of his foolishness, but he saw the wisdom of Andokar's words. He was silent for a long moment, trying to collect his weary thoughts so as to commit no more follies. Finally he said, "I will do as you suggest, Andokar, and I thank you. But do not call me Sir. I am only Jonathan, a blacksmith of Glen Carrah, and not a knight. Commander of the army of Karolan I am, since there is no king, prince, or knight to lead it, but that may soon be altered. As I give no courtesies to you, even so I expect none from you. I will not call the killer of my friends a king, and you need not call a peasant who hates your father's name a knight. I go to find a banner. Be ready to ride when I return!"

Jonathan rode back to the cliff. To his surprise, he saw one of the warriors of Karolan coming forward to meet him. The man saluted when he drew near, and Jonathan recognized him as one of the miners. "I am looking for our banner," said Jonathan. "I must go and free the prince."

"I have found the banner, Commander," said the man. "I searched for it when I arose." Jonathan dismounted and followed him to a part of the ruined barricade, where the man lifted something reverently from a depression that had concealed it. It was a long, twisted branch of firewood, but from the end of it hung the banner of Karolan. The Stone, Sword, and Star was ripped and blackened with blood, but it was still recognizable. "Take back our proud standard, Commander," said the man of Petrag. "Whether we have won or lost, we have not dishonored it."

"We have won," said Jonathan. "Victory is ours, and undying honor. But alas! How few have lived to delight in it!"

"I think that many who lie as still as corpses are living nonetheless," said the man. "Sleep can seem more precious than life. When the slab fell and we were thrown down on the rocks, the blow seemed a fair lullaby to many of us – I among them, only I have wakened earlier than most. But it was your courage and strength that held us to the fight, and now, unsleeping, you ride to free the prince. We all know he must be dead – but we are not, which also seemed impossible. Have you any order to leave me?"

"Find a blanket and sleep, brave friend!" said Jonathan with a smile. "And remember that we all – not I alone – have done a thing that no man would have believed, had he been told of it. Farewell, and may the life you won be all that you desire."

Jonathan turned his horse from the low cliff, and guided it cautiously over the cracked stone slab. He was terribly weary, and the reins burned in his blistered hands, but he had an aim, and a hope. Ilohan might be alive, and nothing short of death would keep Jonathan from finding him. Naomi was safe, and he would return to her. The sunshine on the western wall shone brighter and lower down the rock with every passing moment. The fresh wind and the blue sky lifted his heart with their beauty. He had come unbroken through the hellish night.

When he reached the place where the bodies of Tharral and Mer lay, he dismounted and stood looking at them for a long moment. Them, his father, and thousands of others. He bent to recover his sword. He straightened slowly, but then swung himself into his saddle in a swift motion. There was still one friend he might save. He would ride faster than the wind.

When he reached Andokar he saw that the Norkath prince had found new staffs for the banners. Jonathan took the Stone, Sword, and Star, while Andokar carried the white flag above the Fist of Iron. When all was ready, they remounted the horses. "For Ilohan; for love, joy, and freedom," cried Jonathan, "ride!"

Jonathan wanted to ride the whole distance at the furious pace of a cavalry charge, but Andokar held him back. "You will kill our horses!" he said. "The farms are burned below, and we will find no others. Ride hard, therefore, but do not forget that the road is long." Thus in the desperate ride they balanced the fear of arriving too late against the limits of their horses' strength – and balanced it as finely as they could. The wind blasted in Jonathan's face, and the valley walls echoed the thunder of hooves. His heart stirred with the old exultant joy, the joy he had felt beneath the Cliffs of Doom, or when galloping to the war with the men of Petrag.

But Jonathan was weary. His thoughts fell from the joy of the race. He feared the unknown future, and doubted he could find the strength to do whatever he would need to at Aaronkal. All seemed like a dream in his deep weariness: the sound of hooves, the clean, fresh wind, and the bright morning light. He thought of his father, lying dead on the cliff, maimed and buried in rocks or other corpses. He thought of Ilohan, and wondered what four days and three nights without hope or water would do to a man: whether he could survive unbroken; whether he could still be the prince of Karolan's hope. He thought of Tulbur, whose vast treachery bewildered him. He remembered his own words to Ilohan, about an archer on the battlements of Aaronkal. He thought of the coming winter and the vast number of the dead; of burned farms and of starvation.

*   *   *

On the eastern cliff above Petrag, Jenn cried frantically as she struggled to free her hands from Mer's knots. Despite the chill air on the cliff top, she was sweating. She was hot with grief and desperation, and the world around her did not seem real. She knew it was now empty of her mother and father. They were dead, and they had been her all. She saw everything through the burning veil of her grief, and all seemed merciless and strange. This agony could not be a continuation of the life she had known, she thought. That life was shattered, yet she still existed – and was still tied to the tree.

Suddenly her right hand slipped through the knot and was free. Her left followed easily, and she fell forward, not caring to catch herself, onto the cold rock before her. She lay there panting for a few moments, and then stood up, free. She suddenly thought her mother and father might only be hurt or trapped, and she ran to the cliff edge to see. Her hope was never more than partly alive, and when she stopped at the brink and looked down, it died forever.

She fell to her knees, not caring how the rock hurt her. Everything was gone. Everyone was dead. She stayed there, still as stone, for a long time. She was cool then, no longer frantic, no longer crying. Despair claimed her.

If despair does not know joy, it also does not know fear. Jenn started climbing down the cliff. Her one thought was to find the bodies of her mother and father. She was light, strong, and cool, as if all her feelings had frozen into the one passionless decision to climb down the cliff. She climbed with skill and grace, but absolutely without care for her own safety. She chose the route of her climb thoughtfully and well, but did not hesitate if it took her within one small slip of certain death. She did not look out or up, but only at the rock where she placed her feet and hands.

She had almost made it down when she finally slipped. Her feet lost grip on the narrow edge where she had placed them, and her handholds were slippery and small. Her hands were ripped hopelessly away from the rock. She was still too high to have any real hope of surviving. Her only sensation as she lost her grip was one of relief, of tension released. She was glad to abandon herself to the cool air and the hard, cold rock. She was following the only ones she loved.

She heard a sound from below as she dropped: a sharp, tired sound, the sound of a weary man suddenly hurt. And then she struck. The impact was hard, but she did not feel her body breaking and her soul flying free as she had expected. Instead she felt something firm but not hard behind her back, and strong arms like iron around her chest. The arms gripped so tightly at first that she could not regain the breath that had been forced out of her on impact. Soon, however, the grip loosened, and the arms were only dead weight as they lay across her chest. She relaxed the wire-taut tension that had come unbidden into her body, and opened her tight-shut eyes.

She was lying on her back, looking up at the sky. The hands of the arms that held her were large and strong, but bloody, and gray as the hands of no living man should be. She understood then that she was lying on top of a man who had caught her, and that he had fallen backward without releasing her. She wondered why he did not move or speak. Looking at his hands, she wondered if he were dead. She pushed the hands aside, and rolled sideways off him onto the rock, marveling that her body was whole, and still obeyed her will. She knelt, and looked at the man who had saved her.

He was very broad shouldered and strong, but not unusually tall. His clothes were well made of strong cloth, but were now ripped, bloody, and smudged with ash. His face looked very pale, but the expression was kind.

Mer had been among the women who tended the wounded after King Thomas's invasion, and she had taught Jenn much of the knowledge that brings power to hold men back from death and heal them. Jenn remembered her lessons well. She placed her hand gently across the man's mouth. Immediately she felt the warmth and moisture of his breath, and knew he was alive. She stood, and looked him over carefully. Blood was seeping slowly onto the rock beneath his left foot, and from the thigh of that leg a piece of splintered arrow shaft protruded. She set to work, as careless of her own destiny as when she was climbing down the cliff, but less despairing now as the work absorbed her, turning her mind outward to another's pain and peril.

When Therinil and the women with her arrived at the battleground, they first found the shattered bodies of their husbands, and of Mer and Tharral. There were few among them in whose hearts there was no longing for the fate of Mer – who alone had refused to leave; who alone need not now face a life alone. Then they found Jenn asleep, her head against the chest of a Karolan warrior whose wounds she had expertly bound. The sight was like a single candle to them in a world of barren cold and darkness.

Therinil feared no Norkaths, for she believed they all lay dead beneath the stone. Yet she did not push back the dark hood that veiled her beauty, for she felt it was a fitting emblem of her life henceforward. She would be veiled, cloaked, barren and concealed. No one would ever look with burning vision into the center of her heart, as Yalron had. Henceforward she had herself, and she belonged to no other. Yet at the same time she had lost herself, for Yalron had been her, and she him. She knelt beside Jenn and put out a hand to touch her tangled hair. Therinil was sure that she herself would never now have such a child. She had longed to be a mother. Her heart wept for the years she had hoped to spend with Yalron. But she refused to yield to despair.

She would live, and love, and bless, and not wish to recant her choice and die with her husband. The road would be hard and lonely, she knew, but it was the right road for her now, and she would follow it. She would never curse God for making it her path. She would lean on him for the strength to travel it.

That day those eight young women of Petrag saved uncounted lives. They gave their own strength to save the weak and wounded from the grave. They were like angels to the weary, broken men. But for them, scores more would have been widows by the falling of the night.

*　　　　　*　　　　　*

Down in the farmlands of Karolan, Jonathan shook his head and fought his weariness, struggling to see the road ahead through aching eyes that longed to close. Autumn seemed to have changed to winter in the two days since he had led the army of Karolan up to Petrag. The trees were bare now, and cold wind swirled the dry leaves piled high upon the ground. In the westering sun, even leafless trees cast a deep forest shadow on the road. The chill air seemed to seep into his bones and sap his strength.

Both Jonathan's horse and Andokar's were lathered with sweat, and near the end of their strength. Andokar considered suggesting to Jonathan that they slow down, but then kept silent. Every moment lost rendered Ilohan's death more likely, and despite Jonathan's pledges, Andokar believed his own life might well hang on the King of Karolan's. It was indeed a time to ride horses almost to death, and he knew Jonathan would resent any word of caution he might speak.

In his silence Andokar was wise. Jonathan was awake only by the effort of his iron will, and that was wholly bent on saving Ilohan. Anyone who crossed or hindered him would face furious and instant anger. He was too weary and too desperate to be patient, and with every step of the journey he had seen more of Norkath's evil.

Every farmhouse along the road from Aaronkal to Petrag had been burned. Sometimes the forests or fields had caught fire too, and nothing was left but charred logs and blackened ground. Again and again Jonathan suppressed an impulse to reach for his sword and kill Andokar. The destruction had been so wanton, so useless, so utterly inexcusable. And there, riding beside him, was the king of the people who had done it: their representative, their master. Sometimes Jonathan shied his horse away from him as if he were some loathsome creature.

Andokar saw this, but reacted to it not at all. He kept his face blank, covering over all that passed through his heart: the bitter self-reproach; the sense of endless shame; the feeling of being marked forever. The thought was often in his mind that he should have killed his father, but he did not accept it. He had loved Fingar, and could never have murdered him. Never – even had he known, years ago, all the evil that would come of his father's life.

Jonathan leaned forward suddenly, surprised by a tremor that had passed through the straining body of his horse. The rhythm of the animal's breathing had changed. It had become faster, shallower, almost frantic. "Only a little longer," said Jonathan soothingly, leaning near the horse's ears. "Do not die yet, horse. Hold on. We are almost there. Do not die. Steady. Keep on."

Jonathan raised his head to look around at the country, hoping they were indeed close to Aaronkal. They were passing through an oakwood, but he could not tell how far they had to go. The gray bulk of a stone building appeared ahead, and as they approached Jonathan saw that it was a chapel. Streaks of black soot marked where fires had been kindled against the walls and door, but the rampaging soldiers of Fingar had made no real impression on the iron-bound oak and sturdy stone.

Then at last they passed out of the oakwoods – and the great field of Aaronkal lay before them, somber in the long sunset shadows of the castle and the trees. Jonathan reined in his horse. The animal shuddered deeply and then crumpled to the ground. The blacksmith clumsily jumped clear and began to stumble forward, feeling weak and foolish on his own sore feet. Andokar reined in beside him, but his horse had been more carefully chosen and did not die.

The field was dotted here and there with fires, and there were many tents. The ground seemed covered with prostrate men, lying in ordered rows, their bodies twisted in strangely awkward positions. Far more men were lying than standing, but even those who stood were a sizable army. They stood at attention like watchmen, armed with bows and spears, and spaced at regular intervals all over the field. Jonathan gazed in weary confusion, puzzled by the strange, stiff patterns of the prostrate men.

Andokar experienced no such confusion: he knew the situation already, and had, in fact, been one of its authors. He spurred his horse forward into the center of the army, holding the standard of Norkath high against the cold blue sky. The watchmen looked up at him in astonishment. He stopped at the center of the strange encampment.

"Men of Norkath, my loyal subjects," he called, loud enough for all to hear, "we are defeated. My father the king is dead, and the army he led is no more. I have, however, secured pledges of your life and freedom from the leader of triumphant Karolan. Free your captives, and lay down your weapons at the castle wall."

For a moment, the Norkath army made no move to obey. Andokar sat straighter on his horse, and called out in a voice he tried to make more like his father's, "Men of Norkath, we have given you a command! Must we now consider the penalty for ignoring it? Or do you think we have inherited our father's throne but not his power?"

The standing host of Norkath stirred then to frantic action, slashing free the thousands of Karolan prisoners they had guarded. When that was done, they marched somberly up to lay their weapons at the foot of the castle wall. They had expected Fingar to return in triumph, with thousands of soldiers and untold wealth in gold. Instead his son came alone, and they still could not grasp the whole meaning of the dire news he brought. They had changed in a moment from a triumphant army waiting for its spoil to a defeated band hoping to slink away unharmed.

Jonathan thought vaguely of gathering and arming a band of newly-freed Karolans, but in his weariness it seemed the laborious task would take too long. They were weak with hunger, and chafed and numb from their bonds. Jonathan searched in his mind for words of blazing courage with which to rouse them, and found nothing. Instead he took one of the Norkath bows himself, and shot an arrow over the battlements of Aaronkal. He shot another, and then another. There was no sign of answering archery.

Jonathan ran up to the great gate of Aaronkal alone. The portcullis was not down, but the gate was shut and fastened. He knocked against it with the hilt of his sword. There was no answer. He took the sword in both hands, and struck the oaken gate hard with the blade. "Open, in the name of justice!" he cried.

A man with a large, pale, bearded face looked out of an arrow loop in the stone. "Steward's orders, shut against all comers," he said in a voice such as an irritable innkeeper might use toward an unwanted guest.

"Fool!" roared Jonathan, anger now giving him words. "I'll burn the gate down and hang you by your hair above the flames! As for the steward, rivers of blood cry out to be avenged – and vengeance shall find him."

The man stared for a moment, while Jonathan's anger rose like a storm. Finally the gate opened swiftly. Jonathan hung back a moment to make sure there was no ambush, and then ran in. The guard fled down a side passage, and Jonathan followed him.

Jonathan was sore and weary, but he had muscles born of a thousand joyful runs in Glen Carrah, and feet now winged with fury. The guard had no chance of escape. Jonathan tripped him from behind. He fell hard on the stone floor and lay there gasping out feeble pleas for mercy. Jonathan grasped the thick cloth of the man's cloak, one hand on each shoulder, and lifted him. He shoved him roughly back against the wall, and held him there with his back to the stone.

The guard's arms hung limp as he gazed into Jonathan's blazing eyes, just a handbreadth from his own. He was terrified. He looked at the blacksmith's face, and saw a man whose nature was like fire, and who was absolutely, desperately intent on one goal. If he, the steward's guard, resisted that goal, he would be killed without hesitation, mercy, or regret. He had never seen anyone look as Jonathan looked now. The sight frightened him so much that he could not speak or move.

"Where is the steward?" asked Jonathan.

The guard's lips only shook.

"I will kill you if you do not answer me," said Jonathan.

"The steward is gone. When he saw the Prince of Norkath alone, he told us all that we were lost. Then he took off his robes, put on rough, brown clothes, took a fast horse, and left. The rest of them left too. I stayed because I... I am... I..."

"Do not lie," said Jonathan.

"I stayed because I do not ride well," said the guard, "and I was afraid of being captured fleeing."

"Would that Hell were real, so Tulbur might burn there!" said Jonathan. "Where is the prince?"

The guard trembled, but did not say anything. Jonathan's iron grip on his shoulders tightened, bruising him through his cloak. Blood was spreading through the fabric, seeping from the blacksmith's ravaged hands. "I should kill you," said Jonathan. "The prince is my friend. Tell me where he is. I am not patient."

"I... I..." the guard's voice was a frightened squeak. "I do not know where he is."

"Are you lying?" asked Jonathan.

"No! No... I swear it... No!"

Jonathan looked at him coldly for a long moment, and decided he was speaking truth. "Prince Ilohan is in the forget-me-not," said Jonathan. "It should be in the dungeons. You will take me there."

"Yes, yes!" squeaked the guard. "I will take you there! Follow me!"

Jonathan drew his sword. "If I even think you have betrayed me, I will run you through," he said. "Stay just ahead of me, or I shall think you have betrayed me. You know already that you cannot run from me."

Jonathan followed him down the passage, through a heavy oak door, and down a spiraling stone stairway that led to another oak door – the door to the dungeons. The guard stopped at the door, which was green-black with the damp and mold of countless years. Jonathan kept his face expressionless, set like stone, but his sword point, held just away from the guard's back, trembled with the power of what he felt.

"Open the door," he said coldly.

The guard turned a terrified face back toward him. "I do not have a key," he whispered in a frightened gasp.

Jonathan pushed the sword forward until it touched him. The guard jumped at the touch, and flattened himself against the dungeon door in abject fear. "Swear you are speaking truth," said Jonathan.

"I swear it! I swear it!" said the guard in a high, rapid voice.

"I will need something heavy to break down the door," said Jonathan. "Where in this castle is there such a thing?"

"There are battle axes in the guard rooms."

"Can you take me there, or are they behind another door to which you lack a key?"

"I can get there. Please… please to let me turn around."

"Go," said Jonathan contemptuously, drawing back his sword blade. "Lead me to the guard rooms. Quickly!"

They climbed back up the stair very fast indeed, the guard anxious to do anything he was bidden. The guardrooms, located on either side of the great gate, proved to contain exactly what Jonathan wanted. There were rows of great, heavy battleaxes, ordered in increasing size. Jonathan took the heaviest he could find, and sheathed his sword. He turned to the guard. "Do not imagine that you are harder to kill with an axe than with a sword," he said. "I will follow you as before, and kill you as before if you play false. Go back to the dungeon door."

The day outside was dying fast, and already the great hall was quite dark. The dungeon stair, however, was lit by torches. The guard stumbled quickly down it ahead of Jonathan, and stopped with a bump at the door. "Sit down against the door," said Jonathan. "Do not dream of trying to wrest the axe from me."

The guard obeyed him, and looked fearfully up at him as he prepared to smash the door. The ancient, damp oak crunched back at the second tremendous blow, and the third sent the whole door back into the passage beyond. The guard scrambled backward into the darkness like a crab. Jonathan removed one of the stair torches, and handed it to him. "Take this," he said. "Stand up and show me where the forget-me-not is."

Jonathan shuddered as he walked down the rough, dank dungeon passage. It was a palpably evil place, a place where fear and death had long held sway, and where life, love, and goodness had been broken or left to rot. He felt in his heart that it would be too late, that Ilohan must be dead. He did not react to this feeling, except to ignore it and defy it, and carry on. The guard stopped at a blank spot of the wall after the seventh cell.

"There... there should be a... Sir, please do not kill me, I speak the truth. There should be a cell here. It is gone. It was the eighth cell, the cell with the forget-me-not. Please, please do not kill me! It is true, I swear!"

Suddenly another voice echoed in the dark, dank passage, a deep, loud voice full of despair, with no life in it. It was exactly the voice one might expect of a dead thing. Not an ethereal dead thing, an enchanted ghost, but something dark, strong, and evil: a thing that might creep up through the ground, leap out, and haul down living creatures to join it in death and in the grave.

"I know what has become of the eighth cell, and who is there," said the voice. "Woe is me, fallen creature now of darkness, doubly prisoner, never to be freed. To my undying shame, I know." The guard fell in a heap on the floor, extinguishing the torch. Jonathan felt his heart jump inside him as it seldom did, and he backed warily against the wall wishing he had a stout companion near.

"Who are you?" asked Jonathan.

"I am one who betrayed a betrayer, and failed, and thus am lost. Who are you?"

Jonathan, his thoughts strongly rooted in fearless common sense, was rapidly losing the terror that had gripped him. It was a fear alien to his nature. The voice seemed less dead now, and Jonathan gained in confidence that he was speaking to a living man.

"I am Jonathan of Glen Carrah, friend of Prince Ilohan, mortal enemy of Tulbur," he said. "I have come to rescue the prince."

There was a silence, and then an astonishing, heartfelt sob from the darkness. "Come to rescue... Come to rescue... Oh God, how can it be? Oh God... do you care for men, then, against all hope? Or does he come late, only a mockery..." The voice from the darkness was wild now with mingled grief, hope, and wonder: clearly the voice not of a ghoul but of a man tortured by his thoughts.

"Shall I free you?" asked Jonathan. "Can you help me?"

The reply was nearly a scream. "Yes, yes I can help you! Free me! Free me now!"

Jonathan got another torch from the stairwell, and compelled the terrified guard to hold it. He went quickly to the door of the stranger's cell. It was made of stout iron grid work, but Jonathan doubted it would resist the battle axe. He looked into the cell by the light of the torch. A strong man, between youth and middle age, sat there on a low stool. His head was bowed upon his hands.

"I am going to free you," said Jonathan. "But if you play me false, I will kill you."

The man stood and walked calmly to the door. "I am Benther, son of Tulbur," he said. "I followed my father so long that I will never be free from guilt, or free from pain. Yet in the end I fought for Ilohan, and was struck down. You can see the blood in my hair. Ilohan was my best and only friend, and I betrayed him. Now I want his rescue more than my life, more than my hope which is gone, more than my joy which is dead, more than my honor which is lost. I will not play you false."

"Stand back from the door," said Jonathan. "It seems I am fated to help and be helped by the sons of my mortal foes. So be it." The axe blow struck the iron lock with terrible force and burst it asunder. The shards flew and clattered against the rough dungeon walls, and the door swung slowly inward.

Benther came out. Jonathan stood aside warily, his axe uplifted, to let him pass.

"Give me the torch," said Benther. Jonathan nodded to the guard, who gave it with a trembling hand. Benther paced up and down the short space of passage between his cell and the cell seventh from the door. He counted his steps carefully, and then bent down to look at the wall near the floor, at a place directly between the doors of the two cells. He shifted over one step and looked again. Then he looked up, and his face caught the torchlight. Jonathan never forgot its expression: humble relief and gratitude, intensified beyond the range of words. The expression passed in an instant, and he was as he had been while searching; urgent, quick, and cold.

"My father has carried out his plan to seal the door of the eighth cell," he said. "I have found the boundary of the new work. We must break through the stone wall to reach the cell. After that we will open the forget-me-not, but it may be too late."

"It will not be," said Jonathan simply, and began to assault the wall with the great axe. Rock fragments bounced and splintered against the passage walls with alarming force. Each blow produced a deafening crack that echoed dreadfully in the narrow passage. The axe swiftly grew dull and chipped, but it could still break the rock. Gradually Jonathan's mighty blows hollowed a rugged crater in the wall, two handbreadths deep. This crater broke the integrity of the wall, and he began to blast whole rocks clear of the mortar that held them in single blows. The damage spread rapidly before his fearsome assault. Benther or the guard could have killed him easily if they had had weapons, for he thought of nothing but demolishing the wall. Instead they stood and watched him in awe and fear.

Jonathan's hands were in dreadful condition, and his grip was slipping from his own blood. He was deeply weary, and wondered how thick the wall could be. He thought he should have broken through by now. Anger at the ugly stone that kept him from Ilohan kindled like a great fire, and he attacked with even greater force. Whole rocks flew through the air fast enough to break bones. He gasped for breath between his mighty swings. The axe head was beaten into a rugged hunk of iron, barely a memory of its former keen shape. The air of the dungeon passage was thick with choking dust.

The axe head suddenly went through the wall. Jonathan held the handle and stared in astonishment at the dark hole, panting hard. Then he withdrew the axe and attacked the stone again. The wall, now penetrated fully, disintegrated before his fury. A last set of mighty blows brought most of it down in a heap upon the floor. The hidden cell lay open before them. The iron lid of the forget-me-not was clearly visible to their right.

Jonathan paused a bare instant, catching his breath, and then plunged through the ragged opening into the cell. Iron bars fastened down the lid of the forget-me-not, but no locks or chains secured them. Jonathan pulled on them, and each came free with the loud, groaning screech of rust on rust. Then Jonathan put forth all his strength to lift the great iron lid. It did not move. He looked wildly around the cell and saw a large iron pole: a lever, clearly made to fit through rings on the lid. In an instant he had used it and was kneeling beside the open forget-me-not.

Benther was bending over his shoulder and staring. The guard, to whom Benther had returned the torch, was still in the passage, and little light reached the forget-me-not. Jonathan's heart was pounding terribly. All he could make out in the pit before him was the outline of a human figure. He reached in, lifted the motionless form in his arms, and brought it out into the torchlight.

It was Ilohan. Of that there could be no question. But the face was dreadfully pale, and the uncovered hands that touched Jonathan's as he held him were cold. Ilohan looked dead. And yet he looked different from any dead person that Jonathan had seen. His body was not broken or twisted by violence, nor marred by disease. His face was peaceful, and his eyes were closed. Jonathan said nothing, but he brushed swiftly past Benther and carried Ilohan out of the cell. He ran with him down the passage, up the stairs, and out into the great throne room of Aaronkal.

Jonathan gazed round in weary amazement when he entered the throne room. It seemed full of a great confusion of firelight, noise, and people, when he had expected darkness and silence. He knelt down in the midst of it, neither caring nor able to make out what was happening. His only care was for the burden in his arms.

He laid Ilohan down on the floor, where the light of fire and torches fell strongly. He bent over him, wanting to reach out his hand and feel for breath as he had done long ago with Rennel, but lacking the courage. He could not bear to find out that Ilohan was dead. He was not brave enough to move his hand. He knelt there, weary and afraid.

Ilohan opened his eyes. His voice came in a harsh, unnatural whisper. "Jonathan... It was not you, I know." He smiled. "Lord, have you brought him, then? No, no, it is..." His hands moved suddenly, weakly, and his eyes opened wide with surprise, "I live! Jonathan, how –"

"Water!" roared Jonathan, waking at last from his frozen wonder. "Bring water for the prince! The prince is alive! Water!"

Jonathan's voice was bursting with joy, and irresistible in the power of its command. Scores of people looked around immediately for a means to obey. Yet it was Benther, pushing through the crowd, who first brought a large mug full of water.

Jonathan pushed it back, still distrusting him. "Drink half of it yourself," he commanded. Benther winced as if he had just been wounded, but obeyed instantly. Jonathan lifted Ilohan's head, Benther held the cup gently to his lips, and Ilohan drank all that was left.

Andokar ran up to them and looked at Jonathan. "Is this King Ilohan?" he asked. "Is he alive?"

"Yes," said Jonathan. "You spoke truth, and I was not too late."

"Thank God," said Andokar. "Thank God! I feared – I feared many things which did not come to pass. I have disarmed my three thousand, released your starved fifteen thousand, and fed many of them. I have sent men into the country around Aaronkal. Many farms are undamaged, and the people of them have come by scores and hundreds bearing food for our former captives. Have you any other orders for me? I would depart as swiftly as may be for my own country, for…" he broke off and briefly hid his face, "…for it is a dark time for Norkath, and if I delay – or even if I do not – I fear what the people will do. I return having lost a score and seven thousands of men, and having gained nothing."

Jonathan knew now that the noisy, crowded room was full of loyal men and women of Karolan, released from bonds and fear, but the hubbub still bewildered him. He was dazed with exhaustion and with joy. Ilohan lay on the stone before him, motionless, still weak and pale, with Benther also near him. Andokar stood by, awaiting Jonathan's orders. Men, women, and children crowded round from all sides bringing water for their prince.

Jonathan felt that he could not think, and yet he must think. Andokar had asked an important question, and was waiting for his response. He tried to think through the things Andokar had said. The only fact that loomed in his mind was what he had found out himself: that Tulbur was alive and free. "We must not leave Aaronkal unguarded, since the traitor has escaped," said Jonathan. "Therefore I must order you to find Karolan soldiers who have eaten and have now some strength; arm them with some of your cast-off weapons, and set them before the gate. As for departing to Norkath, for my part you have thus far fulfilled your pledges, and may go – but because I am not the prince, I must ask you to await his judgment in the morning. You need not fear: he is a wise man and a merciful one, and may confirm forever the words of peace we spoke at Petrag."

Andokar bowed deeply. "So be it," he said. "I will obey you."

Jonathan felt the full force of his exhaustion, now that the effort to think and speak clearly to Andokar was past. He turned to Benther in desperation. "I am at the end of my strength," he said. "I hope you are faithful. Where is there a bed for the prince?"

Chapter 18

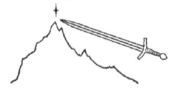

To Comprehend Our Triumph

THROUGH THE DARKNESS OF THE COLD NIGHT IN PETRAG a single horse passed swiftly. On its back were two riders, a girl whose dark brown hair glinted in the moonlight, and a man behind her in the saddle. The man held the reins, and did succeed in controlling the horse with them, but he seemed almost too weak to keep himself in the saddle. They spoke a little in quiet voices, heads held close together that they might hear.

"I think you saved my life, Jenn," said the man.

"I know you saved mine," said Jenn, "though I did not much want it. I thought that if my mother and father died, I would die with them. Then my mother tied me to a tree and I could not follow her. They died without me. I saw… and I tried to climb down the cliff. I fell, and you caught me. I bound your wounds as my mother taught me. Still you should not be riding, but you are, and you are taking me with you. Why did you not want to leave me with the miners and their wives and the other soldiers?"

"I am glad to hear you speaking and wondering, now," said the man. "At Petrag, grief seemed to have taken both your voice and your will. I am taking you with me because you took care of me, and I want to love you and take care of you. I have a wife who will want to do the same when she sees you."

"But who are you? What is your name?"

"I am Barnabas, the blacksmith, from Glen Carrah. If you do not want me to take you to my home, I will not. I can bring you back to the miners. Surely there is a man among them, with a good wife, who would want you. But Jenn, I want very much to care for you, and I would be distressed to give you up. Will you be my daughter?"

"I do not know," said Jenn. "I want my mother and father. I do not want to live without them. I think I want to die, even now, but I know it is wrong, and I am sorry; you were very good to save me. You are kind, but you want me to be your daughter, and I am my father's daughter."

Barnabas was silent for a long time. Jenn had spoken steadily, breaking her long silence, but he felt that she was still numb with grief. Her words had betokened no recovery, no sense of a future that might yet hold joy. He imagined that many who cried frantic tears were yet less stricken than this calm and silent girl. She did not care what happened to her; nothing could ease the pain or repay the loss. He took both the reins in one hand, and hugged her close against him. She was stiff and still in his arms, and did not relax to his embrace. "I can see some of your hurt, Jenn," he said. "I am sorry. I am deeply, deeply sorry."

There was a long silence. They had left the valley now, and the land was open and brightly moonlit all around them.

"Tell me again where we are going," said Jenn.

"We are going to Aaronkal, the great castle, to look for my son, Jonathan. One of the soldiers told me that he went there."

"So Jonathan, the man who led the army, is your son. He is very good, and very strong. Do you love him?"

"Very much."

"I had a brother, once," said Jenn. "He would have been strong and good, like Jonathan. I loved him very much. When he died I was too sick even to say farewell."

Barnabas was again astonished at her calm voice, and the depth of grief he felt behind it. "Lord," he prayed silently, "heal this child, and in time lift her up to joy. Bless her sorrow and her love, and give her hope in you. Please give her to Hannah and to me, if that will bring her highest good. Be with her, and guard her from all evil."

For a long while both were silent. The wind was cold, and they were riding fast across the high, open meadowland below Petrag. It was gray and silver in the cold moonlight. Though the moon shone full, they could see many stars in the crystal night. Barnabas found it easy to trust God, though he had little strength and less knowledge of how the beautiful journey would end. "I thank you, Father," he prayed. "Please, let it be so always. Bless the days to come, and make them days not of sorrow but of joy."

"Have you been praying for me?" asked Jenn suddenly, breaking the long silence.

"Yes, partly," said Barnabas. "But how did you know it? I spoke no words aloud."

"I knew," said Jenn. "My mother and father used to pray like that, quietly, but I could tell. Mother prayed very much when we were together on the cliff, before she left me and died. I think she prayed only for me, and forgot to pray that she would live. But I prayed for her, and God did not listen to me."

Barnabas prayed for her again, intensely, pouring out to God his love and his compassion. "God listened to you, Jenn," he said aloud. "He always hears you, and will always love you. You must not forget it whatever happens. But I know," he held her close against him, "I know it can be hard to remember, or believe. I am sorry. Dear Jenn, I am sorry."

There was another long silence. They rode down the last of the open meadow, and into the first patch of forest. The moonlight shadows of the branches flashed swiftly past them, and the night seemed closer, more urgent and dangerous, but still beautiful. "Barnabas," said Jenn, "I will always be my father's daughter, and my mother's. But if I must also belong to someone on earth, I think it is good for that person to be you. I think terrible things may soon happen inside of me. Will you take me, and care for me, even then?"

"Yes, Jenn," said Barnabas. "I will." There was joy in his heart. He knew that she would find her grief, and that she would not always be so calm and kind. He knew that he was taking a great responsibility, that he could not know what lay ahead. Yet he rejoiced, for he and Hannah would have the privilege of loving Jenn, and by the blessing of God she would grow up strong, faithful, and free. He knew it.

*   *   *

"You have had enough to drink now? You are sure you are not going to die?" The room seemed to spin around Jonathan in his great weariness as he spoke the words. Only two things remained steady, but they were all that mattered. One was his left hand holding up Ilohan's head. The other was his right, with which he held the cup to Ilohan's lips.

"Yes, Jonathan, I am sure," said Ilohan. "I am weak, but I am not thirsty now, and I am stronger every moment. I am not going to die. You must not fear for me. But you are hurt, Jonathan, and very tired. You must sleep, but I must know some things from you first. Are we in danger now? Has

Karolan been captured? Or have we won, by a miracle from God?"

Jonathan was reassured by the calmness and returning strength of Ilohan's voice. It was a great relief to finally release the iron command he had held over his weary mind and body for so long. "We have won... we are safe..." He sank down onto the stone floor beside Ilohan's bed and was asleep.

Ilohan looked up at Benther, who was standing just in front of the closed door of the tower room. "Bring a blanket to wrap around him," said Ilohan, "and bring me some bread, if any can be found."

Benther opened the door to leave, but Ilohan stopped him with his voice. "Sir Benther," he said, "I thank you for defending me. I forgive you for all that is past, and I trust you now. Prove worthy, and God will bring you joy."

Benther bowed deeply, and passed out into the hall, shutting the door behind him. The short hallway and the stairs below it were crowded with people: men, women, and children of Karolan, all waiting in subdued wonder outside the room of their prince. Scores of voices begged Benther for news as he made his way past them. "He is well," said Benther. "He is no longer thirsty, and has asked for bread."

There was a surge of joyful exclamation, loud despite the people's earnest desire not to disturb their prince. "How much did he drink?" asked a small boy in eager curiosity.

"Fourteen mugs of water, full," said Benther, smiling down at him.

"He is of no great strength, then," said an innkeeper. "I have seen men drink that much beer in one night, and they had not been half dead from thirst."

Benther looked at him steadily and seriously. The whispered chatter in the hall quieted. "He is of great strength," said

Benther. "Could you spend four days in a forget-me-not, and come forth sane?" The innkeeper backed away against the wall, and Benther passed on down the stairs.

*   *   *

"Wait here, Jenn, and do not get down from the horse. If you hear me cry out, ride away and do not look back. Go to Petrag."

Barnabas gave these instructions in a whisper, in the last oakwood before Aaronkal. It was very dark, for the thick branches blocked most of the moonlight. Barnabas turned to dismount, but just before he did he felt a small hand grip his shoulder tightly. "You are not going without me," said Jenn. "Unless you tie me to a tree as my mother did, I am coming with you. I will not be left."

"So be it," whispered Barnabas. "Stay with me, and make as little sound as you can."

They dismounted together, and walked slowly down the path. Barnabas limped badly, and Jenn did the best she could to support him. Their feet made little sound on the stone of the path, but it was autumn. Every few steps they would hear the crackle of dry leaves beneath their feet, and know that any watchful guard nearby had put a hand to his weapon and was straining his ears to hear more.

Barnabas saw the end of the oak wood, like a black archway opening on the silver expanse of the field. A man with a spear was silhouetted in it, standing perfectly still. Barnabas stopped suddenly, and Jenn imitated him, motionless and silent at his side.

It was too late. The watchman had heard them. He looked intently toward them, and said, "Who goes there? Speak, in the name of Prince Ilohan!"

"I am Barnabas, a soldier of Karolan," said Barnabas. "I have with me a girl who is an orphan of the war. I have come from Petrag to find my son, Jonathan of Glen Carrah, who was the commander of our army at Petrag."

"Why did you come along so stealthily, then?"

"I did not know if Karolan or Norkath held the castle."

"Well come, then, Barnabas of Carrah. You may pass." The guard stood aside, and Barnabas and Jenn walked out into the moonlit field. But they had made only a few steps on it when the watchman stopped them again. "Stay! You have not come from Petrag on foot, certainly not wounded as you are. What say you to that?"

"It is true. We left our horse thirty paces back in the woods, to move more silently."

"Stay where you are, and I will see if you speak truth."

The watchman returned a moment later leading the horse. "I ask your pardon for my doubt," he said. "Ride to the gate of Aaronkal, and ask for your son. I had not heard of him before today, but it is by his orders that I watch. From what I have heard, he must indeed be a great warrior and commander." He helped Barnabas and Jenn to mount the horse. They rode fast across the silver field, through the sparsely scattered tents of the Norkath army, and up to the great gate of Aaronkal.

The gate was well-guarded, but stood wide open, with firelight and torchlight pouring out from it onto the dark field. The guards required Barnabas to give up his sword, but they knew where Jonathan was, and one of them offered to show the way. They passed through the great hall, which was full of people – mostly asleep – and firelight, and glorious warmth.

They went through other doors and other rooms, and finally climbed a long stair – slowly, because of Barnabas' wounds – and arrived at a closed door. The guard knocked very softly, and Benther instantly opened the door from within. A moment later Barnabas was kneeling beside his son's sleeping form.

Jonathan was lying on his back on the floor, well wrapped in a thick blanket. His breathing was slow and even, and there was a smile upon his face. His right hand had slipped free of the blanket, and Barnabas could see his terrible blisters, all encrusted with dried blood. Barnabas looked up at Benther, who had resumed his place at the door. "He is not wounded?" he asked.

"No, except for his hands, which you can see," said Benther.

Barnabas bowed his head and wept quietly for a long time, his tears of joy and thankfulness falling down on Jonathan's blanket. "Father," he prayed, "I thank you, I thank you, I thank you. This is beyond my hope. That both of us should live... Lord, let me never doubt your love again, and may I love you more each year, forever. My son is alive, because you have protected him. And we go back to Hannah together, in triumph. It is so much more than I have ever merited. And now, Father, I ask for still more. Jonathan is alive. Draw him to yourself, that he may live in joy and love forever, and that there may be no barrier left between him and Naomi, his beloved. Oh Father, bless them! Bless them as you have blessed Hannah and me! How I thank you."

Finally Barnabas stood up, slowly and stiffly. Only then did he notice the bed in the room, on which lay the sleeping form of Ilohan, prince of Karolan's hope, alive. "Jonathan would not sleep anywhere else," said Benther. "He tore open the forget-me-not, and rescued the prince, in time."

Jenn had been standing patiently nearby, but now while Barnabas stood speechless, she took one of his strong, calloused hands in hers. "You must now eat and sleep," she said. "I will tend his hands."

"After which you must sleep yourself," said Barnabas wearily. "I thank you, Jenn."

"There is food below in the hall," said Benther, "and I will show you a room where you can sleep."

*   *   *

The long moonlit night wore on. Its stars shone cold and bright on the shaken, wondering land, and on sleepless men and women watching for the dawn. Some were sleepless with numb despair, some with tremulous hope, and a few with triumphant joy.

The Morning Star rose bright in the cold, clear air. First it was low, a diamond among the bare trees, but soon its intense white fire burned high in the eastern heavens. The dawn surged in behind it, clear blue light sweeping up the sky. The lovely moment came when the beauty of day and night shone together, stars still diamond pinpricks in a firmament of deep blue dawn.

In that moment, Ilohan awoke. He opened his eyes and saw his room illuminated partly by the dying coals of his fire, and partly by the dawn seeping past his shutters. He felt alive, and the feeling was so unexpected and so good that his eyes filled with tears. He rolled over in his bed, delighting in every sensation. He looked down at the floor beside his bed and saw Jonathan, wrapped in a warm blanket, with his hands carefully bandaged in white cloth. The blacksmith was still soundly asleep. Ilohan wondered what heroic things his friend had done since they had parted at Petrag in the darkness before the dawn. He did not even try to guess; it was beyond him, like so many other things.

He slid his bare feet down to the smooth stone floor, and rose from his bed. He marveled that he could stand and walk, and breathe clean air. He marveled that he was free. He went with hesitant steps to the window, threw the shutters wide and leaned out through the thickness of the wall. The breeze was cold and fresh, and on his left the Morning Star was still bright in the brightening dawn. The barren trees below him were cloaked in a white gauze of frost, soon to sparkle like diamonds in the light of the rising sun. Farther away he could see the dead gray patches of burned farms, but also many stubble fields that were not burned, and rising smoke that was from chimneys and cooking fires, not pillage and destruction.

He gazed at the mingled beauty and disaster, but his mind was not on the land before him. Instead he was filled with the thought of prayer. He remembered how its golden light had shone for him in the dungeon, defying hopelessness and death with power come from God alone. He could never lose what those days had given him: a faith reaching Heaven, confirmed by God forever.

The experience had not been ethereal or dreamlike in any sense. It had become more real than the solid rock walls around him. The very fact that he stood now, sane and free, was proof that God had come to him in that dungeon, held him and blessed him. "I am with you always." Christ had carried him and saved him from despair as surely as Jonathan had broken through the stone wall and rescued him.

He looked out on the cold and lovely morning, and knew that life was beyond his understanding and his strength. He knew that his crown had been won at a terrible price, and that he had to lead the people who had paid it. Karolan was free, but there would be thousands of new widows and orphans, and new graves for men who should have lived to labor and to bless their loved ones and their land. There was Norkath, defeated but not destroyed: a weak, embittered foe that could wage a war of stealth and murder now that its great assault had failed.

Ilohan saw all this with clear vision, and was not dismayed. "I thank you, my Lord," he whispered into the chill morning air. "I thank you. You have never left me: do not leave me now. You have heard my prayers. Hear them still. You have done great things beyond my hope. Do them still…"

The east was white, heralding the sun. The Joy of the Dawn, the song Veril had sung while he recovered from the plague, rang in Ilohan's heart. This was a bright dawn, and there would be a brighter. God loved him and was with him through all the darkness of the past, and of the future. He turned back into his tower room to face the day, and all it would contain of darkness and of light.

Jonathan was still asleep, and Benther was gone. Yet he could see the signs of his old friend's care. A basin of water stood near the fire. Beside it was a royal robe, and two other things that gleamed in the soft light from the window. Ilohan picked them up in disbelief, for he had been sure he would never see either of them again. One was the sword of Kindrach. The other was the crown of the Prince of Karolan. He lifted the crown reverently in the dim morning light, and read the inscription once again. "As your days, so shall your strength be." He set it down, tears glistening in his eyes. "It is true," he said, "but, my Lord, it is your strength, not my own. I will love you forever."

*　　　　　*　　　　　*

"Jonathan. Jonathan, please wake up. The prince needs you in his council, and you have slept almost a whole night and day."

Jonathan stirred and opened his eyes. Jenn was shaking him gently, but stopped when she saw him awake. His eyes focused quickly, and he recognized her. "Jenn!" he said, astonished, "I thought you were dead! It is wonderful to see that you –" he stopped, seeing that to her, nothing was wonderful. "I am sorry," he said quietly. "I thank you for waking me."

She nodded to him wordlessly, then walked to the far side of the room and stood there facing the wall. Jonathan did not try to comfort her, but instead focused on the task of getting up. He felt at first that he must be too sore to move, but he gritted his teeth and somehow managed to stand. He looked out the window, and saw that it was already dark. He was shocked that he had slept so long, and so soundly. He did not remember even the shadow of a dream, but felt that he had fallen out of the world for all the hours he had been asleep.

He looked around the room. A small loaf of bread, a pitcher, and a basin for washing were waiting for him beside the fire, as were fresh clothes. He walked haltingly across to them and ate the bread ravenously. As he finished a long drink from the pitcher, Jenn turned around, wiping her eyes. "Of course you will want to dress," she said. "I will wait outside the door, to show you to the council room when you are ready."

"I thank you, Jenn," he said. She nodded to him again, and then made for the door, but when she reached it something made her look back once again. He met her gaze. Tears shone in her eyes and on her cheeks, catching the light of the fire and candles in the room. "I swear to you that I tried to save them,

Jenn," he said, "and there is but one loss in this war that seems to me more grievous than theirs – that of my own father. But they are heroes, and their love was true to the last. You are worthy to be their child."

He saw her try to say something, but in the end she only left the room, closing the door gently behind her. Jonathan took a long time washing himself with the warm water. He was terribly sore, and he could not move his blistered fingers without stabs of pain. The knowledge of his father's death lay like a leaden weight in his stomach, still only half believed. He knew that thousands of good men lay dead along with Barnabas among the cold rocks of Petrag. Yet he himself was alive, and Ilohan was alive, and Naomi and his mother and Glen Carrah were safe. The war had not twisted him; he was still free and strong and capable of great love.

The warm water in front of the fire felt wonderful to him, washing away filth and blood, and soothing sore muscles. He washed his matted hair, and pushed it back so that the water streamed out of it to fall splashing on the floor. He dried himself and put on the clothes that had been laid ready for him, noticing as he did so that they were the garments of a Knight of Karolan. He felt he had no right to wear them. Yet he supposed for one night, and at need, he might wear the clothes of a rank that was not his.

He opened the door and stepped out. Jenn was waiting for him, dry eyed and ready. She guided him unerringly through several passages and stairways to a stout oak door. She opened it and went in ahead of him, leaving the door for him to shut.

The room was warm and welcoming, lit with torches, candles, and a bright fire burning on the hearth. Prince Ilohan stood in the center of the room, beside a table of polished oak that was set with six chairs. Jonathan noticed vaguely that Jenn had already taken her seat, and that Benther, Andokar, and a Knight of Karolan he did not recognize were also seated. But his attention was fixed on the Prince of Karolan, standing to welcome him to the place of honor at his right hand.

Prince Ilohan was reigning at Aaronkal at last. In his heart, Jonathan had always known this was how it should be, but still he could scarcely believe it. His friend wore the ruby-studded crown of Kindrach as a crown should be worn, and the robe of royalty hung down from his shoulders as if he had been born to wear it. Yet in his face Jonathan could see humility and sacrifice such as have seldom in earth's history been coupled with a crown. Jonathan could not guess what the years would bring, but he knew that Ilohan would rule Karolan as few – if any – had ruled her before. Healing, justice, hope, and freedom would be the marks of his reign.

"Jonathan, take your place at our council feast," said the Prince of Karolan. "You are the man of all men most responsible for the rescue of Karolan, and I thank you with all my heart. In justice this crown I wear should be yours, but I know you would not accept it."

"The crown is yours, Prince Ilohan," said Jonathan. "May you wear it long and joyfully." Jonathan took his seat with as much grace as his soreness allowed, and then looked round the table in the short silence. Jenn was clothed in a white dress, with her brown hair clean and combed. Her face was still and sad, but bore no trace of hatred or complaint. Only her eyes gave some hint of her pain.

Benther was clean from the filth of the dungeons, and dressed as a knight of high rank. He looked hopeless, yet determined – an odd expression, but one that Jonathan felt he could understand. Here was a repentant traitor, determined to hide nothing that he had done, and spare himself no punishment.

Andokar looked weary and anxious. He sat erect, but nevertheless Jonathan felt he was ashamed of his crown, a silver circlet set with emeralds, and of the green-gold robes of Norkath royalty.

When Jonathan looked at the last person at the table, the knight who sat on Prince Ilohan's left, his mind raced in confused circles until at last he reached out a bandaged hand to steady himself against the table. The strange knight rescued him from his quandary. "Jonathan, my son," he said, "I thank God for your life."

"Father!" cried Jonathan, heedless of the others in the room. "Father, I searched for you in vain at the barricade, and I knew you must be dead. I knew it, but you are alive! I have joy unrestrained!" Suddenly Jonathan knew that they had won joy. A pall of grief had been hanging over him, ready to flood his heart as soon as he acknowledged his father's death. Now it never would. They would return to Glen Carrah together, bringing news of joy. His eyes filled with tears. "Father..." he said. "I wish that God were real, that I might thank him."

"We have fought together, and we have won," said Barnabas. "You are a great warrior, and a son who brings his father joy. And God is real, and someday you will thank him." That would always be their point of disagreement, Jonathan thought. In that one thing, he was not the son his father would have wished for. But the knowledge did not dim his joy, nor block his love. He was a man now; his choices were his own to make. His father understood that – and rejoiced that he had become the man he was.

A silence fell in which all looked at Prince Ilohan, waiting for him to start the feast. For an instant, Ilohan did not realize that he must do something. He felt very strange, as if he were Mudien of Ceramir, or King of Karolan... But he would be King of Karolan, as soon as he arranged his crowning. He was already king in all but title, and for all his future life people would look at him just as the members of this council looked at him now. He would have to lead them, and by the blessing of God he would.

"I thank each of you for the good you have done, for my people, and for myself," he said. "I have called you together tonight because each of you knows a part of the story of what has passed, and each of you sees a part of the hurt that must be healed. I am sorry for the pain that this night may cause you, for the things you must say and the things you must hear. Yet I need to know all that I can of what has passed, and what I must do to lead my people well. I will soon ask each of you to tell me your part of the story. But before that I welcome you to the first banquet I have held at Aaronkal. I hope you will eat as much as you want, and think not on the evil that has come to pass, or on the good that has been broken, but of the evil that has been prevented, and the good that has been saved. Friends, I would not mock your grief, or slight your hurt, but the outcome of this war has been far better than I hoped, and if it is possible I would ask you to share my joy."

Ilohan nodded to a page who stood by the door, and the page smiled and opened it. Servants entered with platters and bowls of food, and bottles of wine, and served the feast with great good will. Despite the bread he had eaten upon waking, Jonathan was intensely hungry. He knew he must not eat too fast, or too much at first, but the food smelled like paradise and every bite seemed to bring him new strength. It was very good, even by the standards of men not starving. There was rich stew of beef and root vegetables, and there was fine, pale honey, and crispy cakes of brown bread quite different from any Jonathan had had before. There was also a creamy fish soup with savory spices. Jonathan did not think to wonder how Ilohan had obtained such skilled cooks and servants in a castle that had been deathly empty after Tulbur's flight, until he heard the prince explaining it to Andokar. When Tulbur had revealed his treachery, all the loyal servants in Aaronkal had fled or been driven out to hide in the surrounding villages, but now they had returned with joy.

At last even Jonathan had eaten his fill. Servants cleared away the last of the food and drink and then departed, leaving the council in privacy. Immediately a new, almost frightening atmosphere of seriousness fell upon the room. They had now to face both the hurt of the past and the challenges of the uncertain future, and there was no turning back.

It was an astonishing time, the like of which Jonathan had never seen before, even at Eleanor's council in Ceramir. The stories were told simply, briefly, and, for the most part, steadily. But no one was safe. Each one heard, that night, facts that stabbed like daggers, told calmly by an eyewitness.

Ilohan told his story first, the story of his journey to Ceramir and back across the mountains, and of his imprisonment and rescue. Jonathan clenched his bandaged hands in fury when he heard what Tulbur had told Ilohan before imprisoning him. Nor was his face the only one that filled with anger at the steward's enormous betrayal.

Barnabas told what he knew of King Thomas's efforts to gather enough swords to defeat Fingar. He told of his own imprisonment at Aaronkal, of Joseph's bravery and of his death. Jonathan made no sound or motion when he heard of it, but silent tears came into his eyes, and unashamedly he let them fall. Barnabas went on to tell a little about the battle of

Petrag, and then he spoke of his waking up, very weak from loss of blood, in a sheltered alcove of the barricade after the battle. He told how he had seen through his weakness and confusion that a girl was climbing down the cliff. He had staggered toward the cliff, seen her fall, and run forward with more strength than he had imagined still remained to him. He did not remember having caught her, but he told how he had regained consciousness later on and had found her kneeling beside him, having bound his wounds with skillful hands and saved his life.

Andokar told of his father's greed, and of the terror in which he held his knights and servants. He told of the march to Aaronkal, planned and timed with help from Tulbur. He told of the great pincer movement of the cavalry, and of the charges of Jonathan and Metherka that blocked it. He spoke briefly of the march to Petrag, and the long, long battle. He told how he had refused to fight, but at the last had tried to save his father when he saw the mighty rock slab tilting outward. He told how it had fallen, and killed Fingar and all his army, and how he himself had sent his archers back to Norkath and then surrendered to Jonathan.

Jenn spoke softly and calmly of Jonathan's orders to her parents, and to the eight miners. She told of Therinil weeping on the cliff edge, and of the decision to stay and try to pry out the rock. She told of the long, long work, the departure of the miners' wives, and the time when she and her mother were left alone on the cliff. She told how her mother had departed, and how she had at last freed herself and gone to the cliff. She began to speak of what she had seen, but suddenly her voice choked and she stopped. For a long time she sat perfectly still and straight in her chair, her face composed but pale, saying nothing. At last Ilohan asked her if she would rather the next person spoke, than finish her own story. Jenn nodded wordlessly.

Benther told of his own gradual surrender to his father's treachery. He made no excuses or apologies for what he had done. He said that Tulbur had not told him his whole plan at once, but that as each part was revealed he had accepted it. When at last his father had described his plan to kill the prince, Benther had acquiesced in silence. He had acquiesced until he saw his prince trapped and condemned to die. There Benther stopped his tale. He took from his cloak a banner emblazoned with his family crest, the Whipping Willow. He ripped it across and threw it into the fire. "So ends our knighthood, and our honor," he said.

Jonathan told of the border sighting of the invading army, of the race to Aaronkal, and the charge he had led. He told of his strategy at Petrag, and of the glorious, desperate bravery of the Karolans. He told of Fingar's last charge, of the falling of the mighty slab, and of Andokar's surrender. He told with cold fairness of Andokar's wisdom. He told of the lone guard at Aaronkal, who had let him in, and of the report he had heard of Tulbur's flight. He told of his rescue of Ilohan, and of Benther's help and kindness.

There was a long, shocked and weary silence after this last story was finished. It was late in the night. The whole course of the war, with examples of the lives it had broken, lay before them all. The healing would be long and slow.

Ilohan looked all around the room, ready to ask each person there what counsel they could give him for his rule. He never spoke the words. Jenn was missing. He saw that Barnabas had noticed it at the same moment.

The blacksmith stood up quickly, grimacing at the pain of his wounds. "She must have slipped away during Jonathan's story," he said. "Your Majesty, I beg leave to go and make certain all is well with her."

"It is yours," said Ilohan. "And Jonathan may aid you,"

They left the council room together. Jonathan ran to Ilohan's tower room, while Barnabas went back to the room where he and Jenn had slept. They met again in a hallway a moment later. Both rooms had been empty. "I am afraid," said Barnabas. "She was at the edge of Hell."

"The main gate, then," said Jonathan, and ran in its direction.

When Barnabas arrived there a few moments later he found his son questioning one of the guards. "A girl in a white dress?" the guard was saying. "Brown hair, pale face, brown eyes – crying? Yes, I have seen her. She was wearing a heavy cloak, though, also. She said, 'I must have a fast horse, the fastest you have. I will bring him back. My mother and I were separated when Fingar burnt our house, but I have just heard where she is. I must go and tell her I am safe.' I asked if it were not better to send a messenger, but she said, 'no, only seeing me will comfort her.' She said she could ride fast and well, and begged me for a horse. With the tears standing in her eyes I could not refuse her. I hope I was not wrong."

"You were," said Jonathan shortly, "if it is the girl we were looking for. Send fast horsemen on all the main roads that leave Aaronkal, to find her and bring her back. Tell them to disregard her tears and cries, but bring her."

"Wait," said Barnabas. "If she does not come willingly, I fear she will never truly be ours."

"If she does not come, willing or no, to you or someone else," said Jonathan, "she will die in the cold. I would save her life before considering her wishes."

"So be it," said Barnabas. "You are right now, but in future beware. You cannot always save those who are free."

A moment later five horsemen galloped away, one for each of the main roads that went out from Aaronkal. Jonathan and Barnabas stood silent at the gate for a moment.

"I must join the search," said Jonathan at last.

"So must I," said Barnabas decisively.

They took two horses, and rode swiftly away to search the open country between the roads. Both went in the direction of Petrag.

Chapter 19

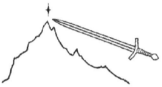

Home to Glen Carrah

GRAY DAWN CAME, WITH A COLD, STRONG WIND, AND the sky threatening snow. All the searchers had returned with no success. It was as though Jenn – and her horse – had disappeared from the face of the earth.

Jonathan and Barnabas sat wearily on weary horses before the gate of Aaronkal. "She could be in Petrag, or half way to Norkath, now," said Jonathan. "You are right, Father, that we cannot always save the free. How I wish it were not so! I would like to kill whatever makes it so!"

"I wanted to bless her," said Barnabas quietly. "But there are others we must bless, and the joy of homecoming will quench this sorrow. We have done all that we could, and must leave her in God's hands and her own."

Jonathan's hot blood rose at the words, and he wanted to say that they should search for her forever. But then he thought what that would mean: endless days of riding, with tiny hope ever dwindling, and Naomi back at Glen Carrah, waiting. His father was right, and he acquiesced with a weary smile.

A page came through the open gate and told them that the prince desired their presence. They dismounted quickly and followed him, Barnabas limping badly and leaning on his son.

They found Ilohan in his tower bedroom. He met them at the door, and motioned them to soft chairs that he had set for them. The fire was warm, and he had hot drinks prepared for them.

"I wish with all my heart that she had been found," he said, "and I am deeply sorry for her loss. For her father and mother's sake, I owed her anything good that I could give her. Alas that she has put herself beyond our reach! Yet now I would speak of other things."

"Your Majesty need not ask our leave to do it," said Jonathan, "though such courtesies may make you better loved than any who has ever worn that crown. Speak; we listen willingly."

"I have told you," said Ilohan, rising in mock anger, "not to use my royal title – and now you flatter me besides! Nevertheless I forgive you." He sat again with a smile. "Now first, I request your counsel, which last night you had not time to give. What things do you feel should be done toward Karolan's healing? Secondly, I wish to knight you both for bravery on the field of battle."

"I thank you for this high honor," said Barnabas, "but does not the law say that field-knightings must follow the battle immediately, and be performed upon the field itself?"

"Far be it from me to disregard the Code of Karolan," said Ilohan, "but the Code makes provision for battles where the king or prince is absent. Men may then be knighted for bravery within twelve days. They must observe the knightly prayer vigil, but nothing else is required."

"As you will not disregard the Code of Karolan, dear friend, even so I will not pray." said Jonathan. "I cannot speak words to a God I know does not exist. It would be a mockery and a lie, no deed for a true or an honorable man. I cannot hold a prayer-vigil. I thank you from my heart for the honor you wished to give, but it cannot be."

Ilohan bowed his head. He raised it again to look at Barnabas. "May I not at least knight you?" he said.

"I counsel you against it," said Barnabas. "Your Majesty must do as you wish, but I am a blacksmith, and wish to remain so. I think I would be but little use to you as a knight."

"I will not command you against your will," said Ilohan, "though I am sorry."

"I thank you, Prince," said Barnabas.

Ilohan was silent for a long moment. At last he said, "My second purpose has not been achieved, and cannot be. What of my first?"

"I do not think I can counsel you," said Jonathan. "In all things, save your lack of hope for your own life, and perhaps your willingness to sacrifice yourself, you have shown more wisdom than I have. This only I will say, though I know it is needless: remember the people of Petrag. They gave abundantly to their own hurt. They gave their blood and lives, their food, their firewood, and their oil. Of the firewood they kept no reserve. It must be replenished at once, or they will suffer cruelly from the cold."

"I counsel you to trust God absolutely in all things, and to cling to the gift of prayer through everything that ever happens to you," said Barnabas. "Search diligently to succor all who have suffered in this war, especially the widows and the orphans. Do not be dismayed, feeling you owe your people a debt you can never repay. We did not fight for a man called Ilohan – we fought that a free Karolan might be ruled by a wise king. All you must do to repay us is be that wise king – with all the blessing and wisdom God will give you. Try to bless as many people as deeply and as truly as you can, but remember that the free can put themselves beyond your power to help them. Never try to make slaves of them that you may save them. Hold forever to two things, which seem contrary but in the grace of God are not. The first is humility. The second is confidence. Let no one turn you from the paths you know are right. But what have I been saying? I have said many words, dear Prince Ilohan, and I think they were wise, but now in my weariness I cannot remember them. Forgive me." He laid his head back against the soft wool cloth that covered his chair, and closed his eyes. He was deeply weary, and he had been presuming to advise a prince.

Prince Ilohan looked at him for a long while, and tears shimmered in his eyes. "Your counsel is true, and beautiful, and I will follow it," he said. "Barnabas, I hope you are awake to hear me. You spoke with wisdom that I know God alone can give. I thank him, and I thank you, with all my heart."

Barnabas opened his eyes, and drank deeply of the good warm drink that Ilohan had provided for him. "I have heard you, Prince Ilohan," he said. "I thank you for all you have done for us, and I thank God for whatever we have done for you."

"I have done nothing for you, and against my nothing are arrayed the immeasurable risks you have taken for me. You will not accept the knighthood I offered you. Is there anything else I can give you, not in payment, but merely in token of my friendship and my great regard for you?"

Barnabas felt strength and alertness returning to him. He smiled at the prince, with the joy of homecoming shining in his eyes. "I want nothing more than a fast horse, and – if Your Majesty can spare it – payment for eight swords I made for King Thomas, though they are probably buried now in the sword-pits at Petrag. Tulbur's guards stole them from me when I came to the muster at Aaronkal."

"It is the right of each king, is it not," said Ilohan, "to set the price that he will pay for swords? The royal treasuries are indeed not what they were in the days of Konder. Will you accept whatever price I deem fair?"

"Indeed, Prince Ilohan, I will gladly, even if you set that price at nothing."

"Do you pledge your word on this? No matter what the amount?"

"Of course, Your Majesty, why –" Barnabas stopped suddenly with a strange expression on his face.

"You have seen my trap too late," said Ilohan, "and now I can burden you with gold in some small payment for all that you have done. I know you will accept it, since your word is pledged." At the shocked expression on the blacksmith's face, Ilohan could not help himself: he laughed aloud in the morning stillness.

"I surrender, Your Majesty," said Barnabas, laughing also. "But I plead that you will be merciful, and not make the burden too great. If I am killed by robbers on the road home, my blood will be upon your head."

"I think I will remain innocent of your blood, Barnabas of Carrah," said Ilohan. "Jonathan will, I suppose, ride with you, and wounded though you are, few robbers should dare to face two such warriors." Ilohan turned to Jonathan, and became serious. "What can I do for you, best and most faithful of friends?" he asked. "You have my prayers now and always, and likewise my love. Yet I would give you something more."

Jonathan hesitated for a moment. "I have always dreamed of building a cottage for Naomi and myself at the top of Glen Carrah," he said. "It comes to me that perhaps the time for this is here at last."

"What would you need to build the cottage, to build it easily and well?" asked Ilohan.

"I would need five wagonloads of oaken beams, a great saw, and a thousand of large iron nails," said Jonathan.

"I will send them to Glen Carrah as soon as may be," said the prince, "and may they bring you and your beloved joy. Now sleep a little, if you will, and I will have horses prepared for your departure."

"I thank you with all of my heart," said Jonathan.

*   *   *

Jonathan and Barnabas walked out the great gate in early afternoon, and went down the cold stone steps to the field. The gray and windswept sky still threatened snow. Their short sleep had not fully refreshed them, but they were eager to be on their way. Prince Ilohan himself awaited them near the gate, with two magnificent horses. The first flakes of snow began to fall as they reached him.

Ilohan embraced Jonathan there beside the horses, and then helped Barnabas to mount. There were tears in the young prince's eyes as he bid them farewell, but his voice was strong and full of courage. "I am losing my most faithful friend and my wise counselor in a single day," he said, "but I wish you both joy. Aaronkal will always be open to you, and in time of need I may ask your help again. I know that however far I look I shall find none more faithful. Jonathan, never forget that I am Ilohan your friend and brother first, and Prince Ilohan your leader second. May God go with you, and bring you joy. I know that I shall need his blessing here."

"He has given it, and will give it," said Barnabas, "for God does not forsake those he loves. Farewell."

"Farewell, Barnabas of Carrah," said Ilohan. "Farewell, Jonathan, best of friends."

Jonathan looked straight into Ilohan's eyes. "Farewell, my friend and brother," he said. "Farewell, prince of the brightest years Karolan will ever know." Before Ilohan could dispute his words, Jonathan smiled, turned his face to the path before them, and spurred his horse away through the bitter wind. Barnabas followed, and Ilohan was left standing alone on the field before Aaronkal, thinking of Thomas.

*　　　*　　　*

Barnabas and Jonathan rode late into the snowy night, and stopped long after dark at an inn a good distance from Aaronkal. The ravages of Fingar's army had not extended so far west, and the inn, though crowded with returning soldiers, was well managed. They slept soundly in blankets on the floor, and woke to greet a clear winter's dawn. Still eager to hurry forward, they set off before sunrise, taking time only for a hasty breakfast and a hot drink beside the innkeeper's hospitable fire.

The day was cold and crisp beneath a pale blue sky. The trees, newly stripped of their last brown leaves, let the sun shine brightly through the tangled intricacy of their bare branches. The drifts of leaves now half-shrouded in snow made a beautiful brown-white carpet for the forest floor.

Now and then they met other travelers on the road and hailed them with the news of Karolan's victory. Many had already heard, but some had not, and Barnabas and Jonathan delighted to see their wondering joy. As they traveled farther from Aaronkal, those who had already heard grew fewer. They pressed on, their own hearts light and full of hope. The days of their journey were days of ever-increasing joy, spent in a world that both had felt would never be. The war that had loomed so long on the dark horizon of their lives had passed away.

On a clear afternoon when the early snow had melted but the air was crisp and cold as winter air should be, Jonathan and Barnabas made the last turn of their journey, and looked straight down the small stone path that led to home. The sun shone brightly through tree branches ahead of them, and though brown, gray, and blue were all the colors of the world, still it was beautiful. The very shapes of the gnarled oak trees were familiar to them, and the sound and feel of the wind spoke of their loved home. Jonathan's heart beat hard and fast, and his joy soared. Naomi was waiting: their love had weathered the storm. This winter would be to them as joyful as the brightest spring.

Barnabas was more sober, thinking of what he would have to tell Naomi, but his heart overflowed with gratitude that he would see Hannah again. He had not lost his mortal life; he was coming back to her, and their joy would be great. He knew she had prayed for him. He had known it a thousand times, a thousand ways. He would tell her so, and she would smile, and drop her eyes a little, ashamed of being praised for what God had done. How he loved her!

It was Jonathan, riding ahead, who first saw something strange, something not belonging to the land that he knew. He spurred his horse forward, curious and vaguely worried in the midst of his joy. There was a dark stain or shadow far ahead to the left of the road. His fear rose as he rode farther and saw it more clearly. At last he cried out and spurred his horse to a furious gallop.

He reined in in full view of the glen he had loved, and sat like one turned to stone. For a moment he could not take in the black desolation before his eyes. This simply could not have happened. There should be a cottage there... a sheepfold... a wide field of frosty brown grass. Not this charred and empty wasteland... Empty... He averted his gaze to scan the gray cliffs of the outcrop that bounded Glen Carrah, and the cold blue beauty of the cloudless sky. There was no help to be found there.

He dismounted and ran to a well-remembered yet unrecognizable place, fell to his knees and reached out to touch black fragments of charred oak. This had been Joseph's cottage. Not only the cottage but the whole of the field where Naomi had used to tend her sheep was burnt, burnt to black ash all the way to the cliffs. Jonathan reeled with fear and horror. His own soul, he felt, was burning in agony as the glen had burned. Yet he acted through the turmoil of his thoughts, with all his usual strength and speed. In an instant he was back on his horse, galloping for his own home. "Naomi!" he cried as he rode. "Naomi! Please come to me! Naomi, Beloved, we have won. Naomi! I swear that I will find you!"

Barnabas had seen all that his son had seen, and the one thought that reigned in his mind was the thought of Hannah. He was far ahead of Jonathan now, for he had not stopped at Joseph's cottage. If Hannah was dead then his life spared at Petrag was a heavy gift. If Hannah was dead, the days to come were dark indeed. His horse thundered down the hard stone path, and he saw far ahead of him the empty spot beside the road where the cottage he had built had stood. All the mighty sweep of the Glen behind it was burnt: all black, all ash, sweeping up to the mountains. "Father," he said as he galloped toward the ruin. "Father... Father..." His prayer could get no further; he could find no words to say, and only the name itself connected his aching heart with the God whom he knew, somehow, still lived and cared.

Then he saw one small gray figure standing in the midst of the black desolation; standing alone on the ashes of his home. He drew closer and he knew it was a woman. Closer still, and he knew her brown hair was shot with gray, and she was of the same height and build as... He was off his horse; he was running, limping, and then Hannah was crying in his arms. His tears mingled with hers as they held each other close, while the ruin of their life stretched wide around them.

Jonathan galloped up, his horse's hooves spraying ash into the clean air. He dismounted and ran up, then stood still beside his parents for a long moment while both of them cried and could not speak for their tears. Jonathan's own eyes were dry as desert stones. At last Barnabas released Hannah, and she embraced her son, with many tears but no words. Jonathan hugged her tightly, loving her, feeling that her loss would have destroyed his world, but not yet knowing if his world was destroyed. "Mother," he said, "please do not doubt that I love you. I love you! But Mother – Mother, where is Naomi?"

She released him, and turned her face away from him, that he might not read the answer in her eyes. "Come with me," she said, still sobbing. "Come with me, Barnabas my beloved, and Jonathan, my son. I will tell you what has passed here, unless you tell me we must fly at once."

"We need not fly," said Jonathan, in an expressionless voice. "We have won, and Karolan... and I thought Karolan... and the rest of Karolan is safe."

"Who did this?" asked Barnabas.

"A band of Norkath soldiers," answered Hannah in a steady voice, as she led them back north and west across the path, to where the village had once been.

"And they will not return?" asked Barnabas.

"I think not," said Hannah. "Why should they? Nothing is left."

Not far ahead was a blackened stone wall about waist high. It had been the wall of a sheepfold in the village. Hannah led Barnabas and Jonathan around behind it, and there they saw a small wood fire with a piece of goats' meat roasting over it, and several children wrapped in warm blankets lying nearby. The wall offered them some shelter from the cold, strong wind.

Barnabas looked at it, and looked at his wife. She had cared for children who were not her own, and had made for them a home and shelter in the wreckage of war. This was what she had done out of the ruins of her whole life, in a world where any tomorrow could have destroyed her. He took her hand in his, and knew that more things than battle can temper souls, or prove them true. Hannah was proven. He knew the days ahead were dark, and their hopes were not fulfilled. But he felt her hand in his, and gave thanks with all his heart that she was with him, to face at his side whatever was to come.

Then he thought of more immediate practicality, and said, "I must go and bring the horses, dear Hannah. They are fast and have not known us long. I must not let them stray."

"I will go," said Jonathan flatly before Hannah could say anything. She watched him go and then swiftly return and tie the horses to a tree. Then he came and sat beside her in the shelter of the wall. He looked at her, and she turned away, pierced by the anguish in his eyes. She would willingly have died to change the past of which she had to tell him.

Barnabas sat beside her and put an arm around her shoulders. "Please tell us, Beloved," he said. "God will hold us through whatever we must hear, and you through all that you must say. Please tell us what has happened."

The warm fire crackled and the wind whispered mournfully in the bare trees through a long silence. Then Hannah took a deep breath of the cold air, and began her story. She spoke calmly, and gently. Each word seemed to carry her love and sorrow, yet the story was clearly and simply told.

"Two days before yesterday," she said, "Naomi and I woke up in the bright morning in our cottage. There were four children with us. We were caring for them to help their mothers, and to calm their own fear of the war. Naomi was restless, and the day was unusually warm and bright, so she went back to Joseph's cottage and led the sheep far up into the glen to graze on the dry grass. I was left to watch the children alone. Our cottage was warm and safe, and they were happy with me, and all was well.

"In the afternoon there was a strong wind from the north. It whined against the cottage and rushed and rustled through the grass. I went outside to see if there was a storm coming. The sky was clear, except in the east, where there was smoke. It was the smoke of Joseph's cottage burning. I had not recovered from the shock of seeing that, when I heard the sound of horses galloping. I looked on the road and saw them coming up from the east. I knew that they were Norkath by their red banner. For a moment I could not think or move steadily. I looked up into the glen, as if that could give me safety. Naomi was far away in the golden grass, with her sheep around her. Then my shock passed and I ran back into the house.

"I had no time for anything. I caught up the crossbow and the youngest child, and made for the well. I called the older ones to follow me. We climbed down the ladder, and I pulled the cover across over us. By that time the Norkaths had reached the village. We could hear the shouted orders of their leader, and the screams of our friends who had nowhere to fly.

"We went all the way down to the deep alcove of the well, and huddled there in the cold darkness. The children were very frightened, and so was I. My only comfort was that I thought Naomi would escape, because she was so far away up the glen and could run so fast. I thought we might be found, and I would not be caught without resistance, so I prayed and loaded the crossbow.

"We could hear the Norkaths still shouting and breaking things, and the women and children of the village still screaming. Soon we heard a loud roar, and I knew it was our cottage burning in the strong wind. The children were very good; they trusted me, and made no sound. In the end it was I who betrayed us, not one of them.

"I remembered that the wind was strong from the north, and I thought it might carry the fire from the houses into the grass of Glen Carrah, and burn Naomi. I had to know, so I pushed the children far back into the alcove, and climbed up to the mouth of the well. I lifted the cover a little, and looked south, up into the glen. What I saw hurt me like a blow. There was a wall of fire roaring up into Glen Carrah, moving faster than Jonathan can run. The flames were as high as an oak tree, and looked hot as a forge. It was not kindled from the sparks of burning cottages, I think, but rather by Norkath torches on purpose to burn the glen.

"I felt sick. I would have died for Naomi, but I could not save her. The cover was suddenly torn from over my head, and I turned around to see a richly dressed Norkath knight with a bloody sword in his hand. There was vileness in his face. I think he would have tried to take me alive, not kill me, but he had no chance to show his choice. The loaded crossbow was in my hand, and I shot him. God was with me, and the bolt pierced his heart.

"He tried to swing his sword at me, but I blocked it with the crossbow, and it fell from his hand into the well. He said, in a husky, marred voice, "But I am Cygnak. Cygnak the brash. Cygnak never sleeps. I keep safe, and I..." He crumpled beside the well. I looked around, and saw no other Norkaths near. I pulled him into the well. The splash of his falling was loud, but the roar of Carrah burning was far louder. I could feel the heat on my face. I pulled the cover back across us, and went back down to the children. They were trembling and crying, and so was I. I could do nothing but hush them as best I could, and pray. I prayed for a long time.

"Some Norkaths came and pulled the cover away from the well. I thought we had no hope, but in the late afternoon light they did not see us. One of them, the leader I suppose, seemed to be accusing the others of murdering Sir Cygnak and throwing him into the well. When none of them confessed, he said something about hurry, and justice, and judgment. It was hard to hear his words because of the echoes in the well. In the end he put the cover back across us, and we did not hear anything more.

"I waited until we were so cold that I feared the youngest child was near to death. I held him under my cloak, and climbed out of the well. It was dark, but some coals were left of the burned houses. I brought the other children out, and we came here. I made a fire from the coals. In the morning God gave us a foolish goat. It walked near our fire in the dawn twilight, and I shot it with the last crossbow bolt. We have lived here as best we could for two days. Tonight when I heard Jonathan calling Naomi, my heart was healed and broken all at once, and I ran out to meet you both.

There was a long silence. The clear, cold twilight was falling fast. Jonathan stood up without a word and began walking with a firm, even tread in the direction of Glen Carrah.

"Where are you going, Jonathan?" called Hannah with tears in her voice.

"I am going to look for her," said Jonathan.

Hannah got up and ran after him. "Jonathan, beloved son, please do not go. You can only break your heart yet more. She is dead – no one could have lived through that fire. Even you could not have outrun it. You cannot find her. Oh Jonathan, please stay. Please…"

But he turned away from her and went on without a word, unless he spoke the one phrase that seemed to her to float on the cold air between them: "I am sorry."

*   *   *

Hannah went back and sat beside Barnabas. She let her head fall forward, and covered her face with her hands. He pulled her gently toward him, and she rested her head on his lap. "You have not failed, dear Hannah," he said. "You have not failed. There was nothing more or better that you could have done. You are as brave and as worthy of praise as any of the men who died defending Karolan at Petrag. Do not reproach yourself, Beloved. Not one in a thousand would have done what you have done; none could have done more."

Hannah let go of the long control she had held over herself for the sake of the children, and she cried long and freely, while Barnabas held her. He held her while her sobs shook her, and his own tears fell silently into her brown-gray hair. They cried for the daughter they had lost, and the son whose life seemed so strongly tied to hers. They cried for the war, which had cost

379

so much, and won so little. They cried for the dead: the brave, the beautiful, the loving who had been broken by Fingar's brief yet hideous assault. They cried for the bereaved who were left behind. There was no hatred in their tears; no self reproach. When their crying ended it left behind a comforting, still peace, like the wet, weary earth lit by a soft sunset shining through clouds after a storm.

The fire burned low, and the goat roast above it was cooked well. No one felt like eating. Even the children were hushed beneath their blankets.

Finally Hannah said, "I suppose the Norkaths took the women and children to sell them in Cembar?"

Barnabas, whose thoughts had been following a different path, was silent for a moment and then said, "I think so; in Bratca most likely. How many cavalry were there?"

"Three score, perhaps more."

"Yes, that is enough to take them all. But were there no bodies in the village?"

Hannah shuddered. "Two," she said, "both children, and both horribly burned. Yet had there been more dead, I think I would have found them. Surely the rest were captured and sold."

"It is better than death, I suppose," said Barnabas. "We should take these children to an inn."

Hannah nodded, but her thoughts were not on the children. "I suppose they have already been sold?" she asked.

"I do not know," said Barnabas. "Yet Bratca is two days' ride from Carrah, and I have heard that slaves are auctioned there but once in a week. Most likely they are unsold yet. But Hannah, we cannot gather an army and try to assault Bratca to free them."

"Would our gold be enough to buy them all? It was not taken; your hiding place was too secure."

Barnabas embraced Hannah again. "You are hopeful and persevering, Beloved," he said. "But our stock of gold would scarcely buy three slaves from Cembar, and those captured must nearly be three score. In any case we would be caught ourselves if we ventured across the border."

"If we were known as Karolan we would be. But is there no disguise that might protect us? Is there no way we could find the gold to buy them back?"

Chapter 20

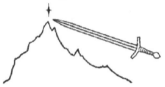

Of Gold and Novrak Poison

IT WAS LATE MORNING THE NEXT DAY WHEN A LARGE
wagon, pulled by four strong horses, left an inn near the castle
of Kitherin and lurched and clattered its way up the stone road
toward Glen Carrah. Its two drivers were among the most
outlandish characters who had ever passed that way. The man
was dressed in a long robe of black cloth, and a white turban
was on his head. A gold belt around his waist held a scimitar
whose hilt was worked in silver in strange designs. The woman
beside him was dressed all in white, in a long sleeved robe that
reached her ankles. A turban of a different form covered her
head, and a scarf passed around her face and left little visible
but her eyes. She wore a silver belt on which was hung a
slender, single edged dagger. Of the entire assembly, only the
wagon looked commonplace, for even the horses' manes were
cut in a form very foreign to Karolan and the nations that
bordered it.

"Perhaps we should turn back," said Hannah. "I will never
forgive myself if we are captured."

"I will never forgive myself if we leave the women of Carrah
to be sold as slaves in Cembar," said Barnabas. "Surely the
gold of Prince Ilohan's gift was intended for no other cause

than this. God will be with us now, as he has always been before, whether we succeed or fail. I am very thankful, dear Hannah, that you persisted in showing me that this must and could be done. Do not be afraid."

"God grant that these clothes indeed resemble those of a distant land the Cembarans know of, as the innkeeper told us – and that with the prince's gift our gold will be enough," said Hannah.

Barnabas raised a bottle from the folds of his robe, and stared at it thoughtfully. "To use this would indeed be a desperate act," he said. "Yet if we find in time that the prince's gift is insufficient, we can at least consider it. As for the clothes, we have but little to fear, I think. Bratca is only a minor slave market. They will not, there, be used to the sight of foreigners from distant lands, or familiar enough with them to penetrate our disguises. My fear is more that no one will understand the words the innkeeper tried to teach us, or that our manner of speaking them will reveal us."

They practiced the unfamiliar words a while, mostly the words for numbers that they might call out to purchase slaves in the auction. Finally Hannah said, "You have heard my mournful story, dear Barnabas, but I have not heard yours. How was Karolan rescued, and why did the prince give you all this treasure in gold? Tell me, Beloved, and do not let us wait years as we did before. I do not think the shadow of any story can oppress us now. I already know the outcome is far better than I feared."

And so he told her, as they drove their wagon boldly on toward Cembar, and night closed in around them. He told her the story of courage, sacrifice, and answered prayer: the story of Karolan's rescue. He told her of his part in it, and her son's.

And she was right: it cast no shadow over them. Yet as she listened, she cried.

In darkness they reached the deserted waste that had been Glen Carrah. They stopped the wagon and walked through the ruined village, holding torches. Blackened remnants of houses appeared like piles of bones on the ashen ground. Jonathan was nowhere to be seen. They called loudly for him, but were answered only by echoes. Barnabas left a bag of food beside the anvil in his ruined smithy, on the bare chance that Jonathan might return there. Then they climbed wearily back up on the wagon, Barnabas very stiffly because of his wounded leg.

"Oh God, my Lord," said Hannah, "guard my son, and do not let him be destroyed by his despair. Protect him from himself... from his own agony."

Barnabas shook the reins of the horses, and the wagon rumbled on into the gathering darkness. Man and woman alike were silent for a long time. Finally Hannah said, "So Jonathan, our son, led the army of Karolan through a hopeless night, to triumph in the morning."

"Yes," said Barnabas, with joy and pride in his voice. "Men followed him because he held to hope and courage with iron strength. The army did not waver until we had no more strength to fight – and even then we fought on, until the last dregs of force and will were spent. Then Fingar gathered his troops for one last deadly charge, and the stone fell."

"And all those who had helped to push it died?"

"Yes. Every one... except... except poor Jenn, who would have been our daughter."

There was another long silence. The wagon was passing through deep forest shadow, and trunks of tall trees loomed on both sides of the path. Presently Hannah took up the conversation again as if it had not paused.

"We will see Jenn again," she said with calm certainty. "Would that the same were true of Naomi!"

Barnabas took her hand and pressed it gently. "We will see her again," he said, "when we go to her. And, though we wish her back on earth so intensely, would we, if it were in our power, choose now to force her to return here?"

"For Jonathan's sake, if God had given me that power, I would use it," said Hannah. "As he has not, I must rejoice in Naomi's joy, and entrust Jonathan to him as... as I have always had to do before. Maybe this loss will turn him toward God, but... but I fear intensely it will only..." she gripped tightly the calloused hand that he had extended to her, and said no more. The outlandish clothes kept her warm, despite the coldness of the winter air. Beyond the rumbling and creaking of the wagon the nighttime forest was silent, still and safe. Its calmness seemed to seep into her, as a whisper from its Creator.

Hannah remembered words she herself had spoken, long ago in the warm, safe bedroom of a cottage that was now black ash. Of the story of the future she had said, "It has a happy ending." That had been while there was still some shelter around her life. The shelter now was shattered, and she saw more clearly her own fragility. She thought of the story Barnabas had told. She thought of the prince's gift, of Jonathan's disappearance, and of the strange journey they were now taking. The terrible realness of choices struck her: the realness of their consequences both foreseen and unforeseen. But despite all this, her faith would not allow her to deny what she had said, or wish the words unspoken. In God, the ending would be happy – it must be, or all his promises were void.

"Why did the stone fall, Barnabas?" she asked suddenly.

"I suppose we can never know with certainty," he said. "But I will always have in my mind a picture of what happened. No man knows for certain what he will do when his life falls to ruins in an instant, and women also cannot know this. Yet those who have lived faithfully and honestly when all was well may find themselves heroes when the shattering moment comes. I think Mer, when she had tied her daughter to a tree, climbed down to her husband and pushed with him against whatever lever or wedge they finally used to pry out the stone. I think that she, being the last to come, was also the last to die. I think her hands alone were on the lever when the slab finally ground forward to Norkath's destruction. So I think, in one sense, it fell because Mer was true while her world broke around her. I know another woman who was as faithful."

She looked across at him, smiling in the darkness. "The slab fell because God willed it so," she said. "And for that reason also four children and one woman were saved, of all of Glen Carrah." They were silent a long time as the wagon rumbled along, and then she spoke again. "In the darkest times still he shows his love for us."

Barnabas held her hands tightly. "Yes, Beloved," he said, "and we shall have need of that knowledge."

*   *   *

Jonathan took a tremendous breath and plunged into the icy stream, black now with the ash that had polluted it. He was deeply cold, and everything was black and wet around him. He would have died of cold long ago, swimming in the chill river, if he had not now and then climbed out of the water and run with dogged strength along the ashy banks of what had been the Carratril, until the running warmed him. He was fast and powerful, and his despair had not lessened his physical strength. He plunged again and again into the dead river, searching for what he did not hope to find.

Now he swam beneath the trunk of a huge tree that had fallen into an eddy of the stream, where the bank was undercut. The place formed a perfect trap for any object washed down the river, and wood and brush from other trees had collected there. Jonathan felt all along the underwater surface of the logjam. His hand touched something the like of which he had not yet felt in his search. A shudder went through him, and he surfaced gasping.

He took another breath and swam down again into the icy blackness. His memory, intensely focused now, led him quickly to the thing that he had touched before. His hands told him that it was indeed what he had sought and feared to find. He put forth a great effort, and pulled it clear of the logjam. He kicked hard, and came to the surface starved for air but with his burden still in tow. He clambered panting onto the shore, and dragged it after him. The corpse was stiff and cold, white in the darkness. He saw clearly that it was a woman's. His heart already felt dead within him, and this further confirmation only piled more stones upon its grave.

He thought the hair was brown, while the dress was brown or black. He knelt beside it, unmoving, unseeing. A light rain was falling. He was below Glen Carrah, where, naturally, the body of anyone who fell into the deadly torrent of the upper Carratril would come. The banks of the stream were wooded here, and the trees stood dark and tall all around him. The chilled lethargy in his limbs told him it was time to run again, but he did not move or care.

Behind his closed eyelids he saw what he remembered: Naomi, running, with the wind in her hair and the sun in her face, with love and laughter in her eyes, and the grass of Glen

Carrah blowing around her. He knew every detail of how she had looked, and how she had moved. He would have known her among a score of thousands.

He opened his eyes and looked down at the stiff, twisted corpse before him. Was the hair brown? Was this the wreck of what had once been Naomi? He reached his hand out and grasped a lock of the pitiful, wet hair. He looked at it closely in the faint light of the overcast sky. There was a whisper of lightning far in the north, a distant bolt behind the clouds, and the strands of hair in his hand showed black as charcoal, not brown-gold as Naomi's had been. The face, too, in the feeble flash of light, was not the one he had known and loved. He pushed the body unfeelingly back into the Carratril. It splashed awkwardly into the dark water with the horrible stiffness of a corpse, and floated past the logjam and out of sight down the stream. Jonathan stood up, dripping wet and shivering. He turned his back on the Carratril, and ran back up to the ashes of Glen Carrah.

He ran until his lungs burned and his legs ached with it. He let the pain wash dully through him, vaguely hoping it might distract him from his deeper agony. Nothing merely physical could do more than add a single cup to a bucket already brimming over. He stopped at the place in the glen where, that morning, he had found the burned fragments of bones. There were many, more than one human body could supply, and he had guessed that he had found the remains of Naomi's sheep. Whether he had found her ruins too he did not know; the bones were burned past identification.

He lay down on the ash and looked up at the starless sky. Lightning flashed dimly above the clouds. He let go of the remnants of his hope. It did not matter that he had not found Naomi's corpse. She was dead. It was vain to search the world for her, for she was gone. Her life was lost and broken, never to be recovered or remade in any way. The fact that the dead body had not been hers only mocked him. It might as well have been. He himself was as good as dead. Worse than dead, because the dead are no more, and know no loss. Joseph had died for her, and failed. He himself had fought for her, and failed. Failed. Failed... Everything that had been beautiful was lost and dead. "I make my choice between ashes and stars," she had said long ago. All that had been stars was ash.

At Petrag, Jonathan had held the hope of five thousand men. He had been the reason they did not despair. His burning words of hope and courage had spurred them on. He had seemed to them more than a man. Yet at that time he had thought his strength might be enough to win freedom for Karolan and for Naomi – and that even if not, he would die as the bravest of the brave, felled by evil beyond his strength after a battle that would be remembered forever. Now he knew that Naomi, his reason for fighting, almost his reason for living, was dead, and he had failed. He had failed to protect her. He had failed at the one thing, above all else, that he had been absolutely determined to do. And so hope, to which he had once clung with iron determination, flew away from him as gently as a butterfly startled from summer grass. It left him alone upon the ash, beneath a starless sky.

He was cold. His leather cloak, the only thing he had which was not wet, was far away down the glen on the foundation of his father's ruined cottage. His eyes were closed, and everything was dark around him. His mind formed lying images of where he was, and he seemed to look down on himself from some great height, and see himself lying on his back on the black plain. The figure that he saw was pale and weak. It had surrendered. It had not the courage to carry on.

He was too tired and despairing to shiver, despite the cold that sunk into his bones.

The thought came into his mind that he was going to die of cold, and he was vaguely surprised. He had thought, in the past, that if Naomi died he would have to live life without joy, but he had not thought the sorrow would kill him. He had thought his own vitality and courage too great for that. Now it seemed he had been wrong. He was going to break, now, as Eleanor had broken, except that there would be no rescue for him. It was excusable, he thought. He had done so much that had been at the edge of his strength and will, that perhaps it was inevitable that he should break at last. The collapse need not have been fatal, but the fact that it would be mattered little. He did not want to live.

It was cold. He was aware that things were going wrong with his body as he grew colder. Soon he would not be able to think or move; then he would die. The sound of the wind was in his ears, mingled with the faint swish and gurgle of the Carratril far away. In his mind there was a picture of himself leading the Karolans at Petrag, roaring out his flaming words to urge them on. Yet somehow his present state was also in the picture: he was lying dead on a black field, with the cold wind around him, yet he was also urging on the troops as their indomitable leader.

He heard his own voice, saying words he never in truth had said, "Only cowards let go life before they have lived it all. Only cowards surrender before they have used the last of their strength. You are a coward, Jonathan, a coward! Eleanor was shattered when her strength gave way, when she was wounded and sick and starving, when she had given more than her all through pain and hopelessness and despair. You are whole and would be well, if you but warmed yourself.

Coward! So quickly to let despair take your life! Coward! Unwilling to live through the pain your life has brought you. Unwilling to stand up and keep fighting for the good that is left!"

The weak, pale figure on the ground said, "Why? What reason is there? Why live in a world without joy?"

"I give no answer!" roared the leader of the army of Karolan, "It is cowardice and folly to ask the question. Stand up and fight!"

In answer to that order, he struggled on the ground, and woke himself up from the nightmare of delirium to the nightmare of reality. Jonathan, very cold and sick, stood slowly up on numb feet on the great black slope of ruined Glen Carrah. He was one person now, and the horror of the nightmare was passing away from him, though it still clung like a heavy mist in the hollows of his mind. He began stumbling down Glen Carrah, in the direction he thought the burned cottage lay. With his chilled and weary body, every step was difficult.

He wondered sometimes why he kept walking. Yet whenever he thought of that, he remembered the question, 'Why?' in his dream, and was horrified that it applied in reality. He trudged haltingly on, caught between two horrors. The first was that he, Jonathan of Carrah, had actually been near to giving up and dying of cold. The second was the horror of the future he must face if he lived: the long, unlighted days without Naomi's love; the facing his parents again and trying to think what to say; the weary care of ensuring he survived the night; and the pain of the next numbed, exhausted step down the ashen remnants of the glen.

At last, after thinking in despairing cycles again and again that he would never reach it, he came upon the ruined smithy, and leaned gratefully against the anvil's iron bulk for a moment. His dry leather cloak was nearby, as was a pile of firewood he had gathered the night before, and a Norkath tinderbox that he had found among the burned cottages. There was also a bag of food he could not remember having taken. He doubted anything he could do would warm his numb hands enough to handle flint and steel and light the fire, but somehow he found the strength of will to prove his doubt was wrong. He stoked the fire high and then stood by it while he ate. He wrapped his leather cloak around him, and fell into a deep sleep beside the coals.

*   *   *

"Ought we to wake him?" The voice intruded vaguely on Jonathan's consciousness in the dawn twilight of ruined Carrah.

"We must find Jonathan if we can," said another voice. "Otherwise the prince will be very displeased."

"Then we must wake this man, and ask where we should look for him."

Jonathan now roused himself quickly and stood beside the still-hot embers of his fire. The speakers were two men dressed in the livery of royal servants, and behind them, standing out sturdy and new in the midst of the burnt village, were four heavily laden wagons.

"I am Jonathan," he said. "What do you want with me?"

"We have come from Prince Ilohan," said one of the men, "bringing his gift to Jonathan of Glen Carrah. We had not heard that Carrah was sacked."

"It was, as you can see," said Jonathan shortly. "I will receive the prince's gift with thanks."

"Can you prove to us that you are Jonathan?"

Jonathan's eyes went to his sword, which was leaning against the anvil, but he made no move towards it. "What proof would you have?" he asked.

"The names of your father, your mother, and your beloved."

"Barnabas, Hannah, and Naomi," said Jonathan in an absolutely flat voice.

Both men bowed deeply. "Pardon our distrust, Sir," said one, "we are at your service."

"I am not a knight," said Jonathan, "I do not wish to be called by a title that is not rightly mine. However, I will welcome your service, if you have truly meant to offer it."

"We have, at the prince's own orders," said one of the men.

"Note well the ground on which I stand," said Jonathan. "What can you say of it?"

"There was once a cottage here," said one of Ilohan's messengers.

"Yes. This was my home. Will you help me rebuild it?"

"What of your..." Jonathan met the man's eyes steadily, and the question died on his lips. The messenger closed his mouth decisively, and then opened it again to say simply, "We will help you."

"I thank you," said Jonathan. "Let us begin work."

As the men moved toward the wagons to begin unloading them, Jonathan quietly and unflinchingly unwrapped the bandages from his hands. The skin peeled off with them, but not even a sign of pain passed through his face. "I will need my skill," he said simply, to no one.

*   *   *

It was late afternoon of the next day when the foreign lord and his wife arrived in Bratca. It was plain to all that they spoke little Cembaran. Anyone who noticed that they hardly spoke at all, even to each other, only assumed that this was customary between husband and wife in their distant country. They went immediately to the slave pens, and together they passed up and down the rows of chained slaves, looking carefully at the face of each slave in turn.

They seemed particularly interested in the slaves held by one particular dealer. These were nearly all newly captured women and children from Karolan. The slaver was not surprised at the outlandish nobleman's notice, for some of the women were quite beautiful, and the group as a whole was unusually good stock. He tried to make the splendidly clad foreigner understand that the auction was tomorrow, and that he would sell all his slaves then. It was difficult, but at last the rich stranger seemed to catch the meaning.

The slave dealer then tried to give his promising buyer a suggestion of the prices that the slaves would likely sell for at the auction. This appeared to displease the foreign lord very much, and he yelled Cembaran numbers back and forth at the dealer in a heavy accent until he was quite hoarse.

In the end the dealer had the best of the argument. They were discussing the price of a Karolan woman, for which the foreigner had suggested the scandalously low sum of verkra, two score and ten pieces of gold, but for which the dealer would take nothing less than varbat, twice the amount. They yelled contradicting numbers back and forth with enthusiasm for some time, but at last the foreigner appeared to realize that he could not win, and conceded, "Varbat!" with a sigh. The dealer nodded, gratified, and bowed deeply to the rich foreigner and his lady as they passed out of the slave pen.

It was late that night when Barnabas and Hannah, still disguised, dared to talk things over in low voices inside the wooden shelter of the wagon. "The dealer named five score pieces of gold as a price for Jemra, and she is not even among the most beautiful," said Barnabas. "We will buy some of them, but I do not see how we can buy them all. And the time is gone to try the poison that physician gave us at the inn."

Hannah's hand was at her throat, and she seemed to be holding back some intense and painful emotion. Barnabas was concerned, and took her in his arms as they sat together on the floor of the wagon. "What is it, Beloved?" he asked. "We can only do our best."

"We have tried the poison," she said. "Barnabas, I am afraid. I poured all the poison into the stew that was cooking in the corner of the slave pen, while the dealer was distracted in speaking with you. I thought he would never consent to your price, and it was the only chance. But now I fear that I have killed them all."

Barnabas' heart leaped – with hope rather than fear. "I will never stop being surprised by you, Beloved. Indeed, you boldly took a chance that may save many lives. I have little fear that anyone will die. Was the pot of stew large enough to feed all the slaves?"

"It was," said Hannah, "and was such poor stuff that I am sure it can be intended for none but them. But what if the physician was mistaken?"

"He was no liar," said Barnabas, "and he said the bottle was of novrak poison, enough to sicken three score women and children. I know something of novrak berries, for when I was a child I and some other fools in my village ate some. We were too sick to stand for a day, but none of us died. Thus I think what the physician told us is certainly true: a little novrak poison will sicken a man, but it takes much to kill him. Thanks to you, the women of Carrah will seem deathly ill tomorrow, and the dealer will be forced to sell them cheaply. No, I do not fear that they will die... My only fear, dear Hannah, is that somehow you were seen, and in the morning they will seize you." He held her close, in arms that trembled.

"I paused by the cauldron only once, when the cook had left it," said Hannah. "I stirred it a single time with one hand, while the other tipped the bottle beneath my robe. If any saw, I think it will seem that I but examined the food, then turned in contempt at its vileness. At worst, it is not such a risk as you and Jonathan took for the freedom of Karolan. But what if, rather than selling them cheaply, the slaver refuses to sell them at all, hoping they may recover and fetch a better price?"

"Even then," said Barnabas, "I think we can simply linger here, and be no worse at next week's auction than if you had done nothing today. For the present, we must trust ourselves and our people into God's keeping – and take whatever he sends us in the morning."

*   *   *

The morning dawned clear and cold in the woods near Bratca. The pale winter sun streamed through the barren trees, and cast bright splinters of golden light on the forest floor. The sky overhead was pale blue without a wisp of cloud.

Hannah and Barnabas stepped from their wagon, looking indeed like a lord and lady from a strange and far off land. Barnabas' scimitar swung easily at his side as they walked toward the slave market. Hannah's turban and veil were perfectly wrapped around her head: their form was beautiful, flowing, and as foreign to Karolan and Cembar as a Zarnith song. Her silver dagger flashed the sun at her side, and her eyes shone with hope and fear together. It was not from his father alone that Jonathan's adventure-love came.

Bratca was a crudely built but extensive town of rude taverns and inns, and ruder slave pens fitted with long rows of stakes and chains. Hannah and Barnabas walked through it with their heads held high, but their hearts were dismayed by what they saw. The auction was still a little time away, and many of the slave dealers were only now bringing their slaves out of the pens in which they had spent the night. Hannah could see the faces of many slaves in the pens, as they were chained together in long rows and only then unchained from their stakes to be led away to the market place. In each face she read what every truly free human who has seen it knows: that slavery is an outrage against the human soul. She longed to stop Barnabas as he walked beside her and cry out, "Barnabas, do you see their faces? Is there nothing we can do to shatter this evil?" Yet she knew that if she spoke even one word of the language of Karolan, she and the husband she loved might share the fate she was deploring.

At last they came to the slave market, at the center of the town of Bratca. It was an open, earthen square, bounded by a sturdy wood fence. It was already well crowded with slavers and slaves, and more were coming in all the time through a wide gate on one side. Once again Hannah was stabbed by the faces that she saw. Men and women – mostly women – who should have been free to run, to work, and to love, were chained like animals by a society in which they were no more than animals. She wondered if she could last through this day, or whether there would come a time when she would collapse at the fence, and Barnabas would have to carry her away.

One boy saved her from this fear. He was chained like all the rest, and tears were in his eyes. Yet when an eagle soared over the slave market, its brown wings catching the morning sun, he looked up without envy, lost in exultation in a freedom that he could not share. Hannah followed him with her eyes as he was lost in the throng of other slaves, but his memory stayed with her afterward. He reminded her that there are parts of each human soul that are forever free, unless the soul itself shall choose to bind them.

The sun rose high enough to shine brightly but not warmly on the crowds of shivering slaves, and the auction began. There was a single pedestal made from the stump of a great tree near the edge of the slave market, and a single, very large and muscular man stood on it and surveyed the crowd. Barnabas took Hannah's hand and they pressed forward to get a good view of everything that happened. The large man crouched at the edge of his pedestal, reached down to take hold of the chained hands of the first slave to be auctioned, and lifted her bodily onto the stump for everyone to see.

Immediately cries broke out from the crowd of watching buyers. The numbers rose higher and higher, until she was finally sold. The winning bid was a number higher than any Barnabas had learned from the innkeeper back in Karolan, but he guessed it meant six score pieces of gold. The slave was not of Glen Carrah, and Barnabas was glad: he had been able to learn the nature of the auction before he had to take part in it. The slave woman was lowered down from the platform in the same way she had been raised to it, and she was immediately led away to her buyer. Barnabas noticed that no money changed hands at that moment, and he guessed that payment came only when the entire auction was over.

The next woman lifted to the platform could not stand. Even when the auctioneer raised her and struck her sharply across the face, still she slumped down to a kneeling position on the pedestal. A few cries of very low sums came up from the crowd. There was a moment's silence. Then Barnabas called out, "Verkra!" Another silence fell, interspersed with surprised murmuring. The woman was lifted down and dragged to where Barnabas and Hannah stood. The blacksmith made a foreign bow to the seller, and looked impassively back toward the auctioneer.

Though Barnabas showed no outward sign of any emotion, Hannah knew from the grip of his hand, which still held hers, that he was full of exultant hope. Their wild plan was succeeding. They would free every woman of Carrah... Every woman save one... "Naomi," thought Hannah, "would that we could see you on that pedestal! We would give all our gold for you alone."

*   *   *

"Jonathan, look at your hands. The handles of all the tools are red with your blood. I do not understand how you can bear the pain." It was late at night, and Jonathan and his two helpers were still working on the cottage by the light of a large fire. Jonathan turned to the man who was addressing him, as he stood beside the waist-high wall of the cottage. He held his hands, one of which grasped an iron hammer, close against his sides, and did not look at them. "We will stop work when the moon rises," he said.

"But your hands," persisted the man. "You should not be working." He walked up to Jonathan and reached for his left hand, the one that did not hold the hammer.

Jonathan stepped quickly away. "Go back to your work," he said sharply. He was obeyed.

They worked on, through the long, cold darkness of the winter night. Now and then they stopped to lay more fuel on the fire, which had to burn high to give them light for their work. Jonathan drove his helpers hard, and himself harder. His hands hurt with a burning, throbbing ache. Every blow of his hammer hurt as though he had grasped a rod of hot iron. He was so tired that merely staying awake was a painful effort. He accepted all the physical discomfort and weariness with cold, careless despair. It numbed the deeper pain, and that was all that mattered.

Now and then the thought occurred to him that he had only postponed his collapse; that it was inevitable at last. He considered it in cold abstraction, and concluded that it was most likely true. Eventually he would break – and perhaps the collapse would kill him, or perhaps not. He did not care. All that mattered was that he did it with honor. When he had nothing left by which to hold himself up, he would fall. Life would shatter him, as it had shattered Eleanor. He would like to fall, as she had fallen, helping those he loved. So he was rebuilding his parents' house.

He could not bear to have time to feel, so he would work all day and far into the night, until he could fall out of consciousness almost instantly when he lay down beside the fire. Even then, he was tormented by delirious dreams. He accepted them, as he accepted the rest of his pain. They were, at least, not real. They hid him from the unrelenting grief that awaited him in the waking world.

*   *   *

The stacked and counted gold coins fell in a stream, clanking dully and heavily as they disappeared into the slaver's bag. Barnabas could see the greed in the other man's eyes as he swept them from the table. He himself watched them go as though they were no more than stones. He recognized the fact that he had just paid more than he could earn in a dozen lifetimes, but it had no hold on him. He was free; a slave to nothing. When all the money was paid, he made his slow, foreign bow, and left the slaver to his astonished delight at the profit he had made selling sick or dying slaves. Barnabas raised his eyes to the heavens, blue and clear above bare tree branches that caught the warm light of the setting sun. He breathed a quiet prayer that they would reach the border in safety.

He would have liked Hannah to sit beside him in the open air, as she had done before, but she was determined to go with the other women in the crowded wooden body of the wagon. He shut her in reluctantly, but he knew that she would be like an angel to the women during the long, long journey back to Glen Carrah.

In the darkness of the wagon Hannah could hear the groans of the women of Carrah, sick with novrak poison and with the thought that they were now slaves of a cruel master who would take them far away. Then she heard the crack of Barnabas' whip, and felt the wagon lurch into motion. She sat against a wall with chained women jostling her from either side, and after a few moments' difficult work with flint and tinder she lit a lamp. A few of the women looked up in surprise, but most paid no heed.

Hannah bent low over one of the captives, and turned the woman's face up toward her own. She pulled off her veil and held the lamp so that its light shone clear upon her. "Renna, do you know me?" she asked in a whisper. "Your state is more hopeful than you think."

Renna blinked, and blinked again. She tried to raise her manacled hands to rub her eyes, but could not. Finally she whispered, "Hannah? Hannah, it cannot be you. What is happening to us?"

"You must not cry out, or even speak above a whisper," breathed Hannah, "but I will tell you what is happening. Barnabas and I have bought you in order to set you free, and we are taking you back to Karolan."

Renna was still very sick from the novrak poison. She shifted uncomfortably on the jolting floorboards of the wagon. "The war…" she whispered confusedly. "We lost…"

"No," said Hannah, "we won. The Norkaths who raided Carrah were rebels, or deserters from the great battle. But the army of Fingar was crushed at Petrag, and we triumphed."

"How… How can it be…"

"Do not think of it now, Renna, but listen to me," whispered Hannah. "I am going to unchain first you, and then the others. Yet we must tell them, very quietly and gently, what is happening. We are in a wagon two or three days' journey from the border, and we will not be safe until we reach it. Until then a single Karolan word, spoken too loud, could betray us. I need your help to tell the others. I will unchain them all, but only after they understand where we are, and why we must be silent. Are you well enough to talk?"

Hannah had been unchaining her as she spoke, and now she lifted her gently away from the heavy irons that had bound her. Renna rested against Hannah, groaned and shook her head. Then she pushed herself up to a kneeling position. "Yes, Hannah," she whispered. "Yes, I will help you."

The two women went the round of the crowded wagon, whispering the wonderful truth to each sick and fearful woman and child. As they understood the situation, Hannah unchained them, until all were free. She helped them lie down comfortably on the wagon floor, with blankets she and Barnabas had brought. She spoke words of hope and encouragement to troubled hearts, and put cups of cool, clean water into trembling hands.

Many women in that wagon remembered how Hannah had come to them on the night the call to arms was proclaimed in Glen Carrah. Now she had come again, in the darkness and misery of their slavery, and it seemed to them that her power was greater now to match the greater pain. As the worst sickness from the novrak poison wore off, they fell asleep listening to the creaking of the laden wagon, and knowing that every lurch brought them closer to a free land that might still be their home.

Chapter 21

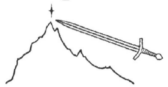

Each Must Face His Doom

"PRINCE ILOHAN GAVE ME THINGS I DID NOT THINK TO ask him for," said Jonathan. "I did not ask for stone and thatch, nor for this gold he has sent to buy whatever more is needed."

"He is very generous," said one of the workmen, wearily leaning against a wall of the nearly finished cottage. "Under him we hear nothing of the scantiness of the royal treasury, which was mentioned frequently when Thomas was the king. But I want to ask you, Jonathan: Do you know how long three men commonly take to build a cottage?"

"No," said Jonathan, "and I do not care."

"Perhaps a score of days," said the workman. "Sir – I mean Jonathan – will you never allow us to rest? We have been working day and night with you."

"You are free to go, if you will. I will work alone. Choose what seems best to you."

There was a long silence. Gray evening twilight filtered through thick clouds that told of snow before the morning. A soft but cold wind blew down the glen, and the burnt ground was frozen hard as stone. Jonathan saw a weary traveler on a weary horse coming up the road from the east. The hooded figure departed from the path, and rode slowly up to the unfinished cottage.

"What has happened here?" asked the traveler in a trembling voice that Jonathan recognized: he was one of the men of Glen Carrah.

"The village has been sacked and burnt by a troop of Norkath cavalry that broke away from Fingar's army," said Jonathan in a flat voice. "The women and children were captured."

The figure slumped suddenly in the saddle at the words, but then straightened again. "Am I the first to return here and ask such questions of you, Jonathan?"

"No," said Jonathan. "Many have come before you."

"And what have they done on hearing what I have heard?"

"I do not know," said Jonathan. "They all rode back the way they came. Each must face his doom in his own way."

"Are you indeed the same Jonathan who led our army to victory in Petrag?" asked the man.

Jonathan fell suddenly to his knees upon the frozen ground. He looked up at the hooded rider, so that the last light of the clouded sky fell full on his face. "I am," he said. "Is it strange to you to find me here?"

"Strange to find you without hope. What of your mother, and Naomi your beloved?"

"My mother alone escaped," said Jonathan. "Naomi is dead."

"Where were the captives taken?"

"I do not know," said Jonathan. "To slavery in Cembar, I would guess."

"Where is Hannah now?"

"Safe," said Jonathan. "I do not know where."

"What would you have me do?"

"Leave this place," said Jonathan. "Act as you think best. As I have already said, each must face his doom in his own way."

The man wheeled his weary horse and rode away without another word. Jonathan rose slowly and stood watching him until he vanished into the dusk. "I will work with you until the work is done," came a voice behind him. He turned to see the workman who had spoken.

"As will I, Jonathan of Carrah," said the other workman.

"I thank you," said Jonathan. "We can finish the chimney before the snow."

*   *   *

The next afternoon a wagon four days out of Bratca, heavily laden and pulled by weary horses, came slowly up from the west and stopped before Glen Carrah. Barnabas stepped down from the wagon seat and came around to unbar the big wood door at the back. The women and children of Carrah came pouring out, their faces sober at the knowledge of the destruction they would see.

The first thing they saw was clean, bright snow, and the second was the golden beauty of sunlit clouds in the west. The whole land was bathed in golden light from those clouds, and the ruined homes were buried by the snow. Then as Barnabas led them all around the wagon, they saw the cottage. It was finished, and smoke came from the sturdy chimney that showed above the thatched roof.

There was no answer when Barnabas knocked upon the cottage door. He pushed it open and went in, followed by Hannah and some others. No one was there. The inside was bare and clean, with no beds, chairs, or tables, yet a cheerful fire burned on the hearth. As Barnabas returned from inspecting the two side rooms, a woman caught his arm and looked anxiously at him. "What can we do to find our husbands?" she asked. "Or... Or have they all perished in the defense of our land?"

"Some have perished, but most, I think, still live," said Barnabas. "I will set out now to ride to the nearest inn and ask for news of them. Glen Carrah is not a place any returning soldier would choose to linger in. Have hope! There is good reason to expect your husband will be among the living."

Barnabas found Hannah and embraced her. "You have been an angel to them," he said, "as I knew you would be. I see no reason why they cannot all stay here while I ride in search of their husbands."

"Barnabas," said Hannah, "who built this cottage?"

"Jonathan," said Barnabas simply. "Only he could have known how our home looked, and matched it so exactly. The prince promised him all the materials he would need to build a cabin for Naomi. She is dead, so he has built one for us."

"And where is he now, Beloved?"

"Would that I knew, dear Hannah! Perhaps he will return here soon."

Hannah looked grave. "No," she said, with tears standing in her eyes. "He will not return soon, and we will not find him if we search for him. He has hidden his grief."

There was a moment's silence, and then Hannah said, in a changed tone of voice, "Shall I send three women to ride the other horses, and seek their husbands at the inns you will not reach today?"

"If any will go," said Barnabas. "Remind them that the land is in some disorder, though it has been saved. They must beware of outlaws on the roads."

Hannah followed Barnabas out to the wagon where he unhitched one of the horses, and led it away from the others. Before he mounted, he turned to Hannah and spoke the grief he felt. "We had two daughters and a son," he said. "Now we have none."

Hannah put a hand on his shoulder as he turned to mount. "They are not lost forever," she said. He turned around and met her eyes. "Not even Jonathan," she said.

He swung himself up onto the horse's back, and rode away across the frozen ash. Hannah watched until he disappeared down the eastern road, and then she went back into the house.

*　　*　　*

Jonathan shunned the roads and walked alone through the cold, barren woods eastward from Carrah. He went fast, despite his weariness and the painful throbbing of his battered hands. His sword was at his side, and he carried the gold that Ilohan had sent him in a blanket slung across his back. He carried also the Norkath tinderbox that he had found among the ashes of Glen Carrah, but nothing else.

He did not know where he was going, or why. He did not care what happened to him. He wanted only to dull his pain. The walking and the cold seemed to do this, together with the ever-changing character of the winter forest. The endless vistas of gray branches and white snow sank deeply into him and quieted his grief.

When night came he curled himself up in a forest hollow and slept until the dawn. He rose in the frigid twilight and walked on. At midday he felt his hunger, and went north to seek the road. He found it in the late afternoon, and bought bread and smoked meat at an inn in the evening. The sight of other people made him uneasy, for he did not know what to say to them, and he wanted neither sympathy nor aid. The barren winter woods embraced and comforted him. Their solitude, their open silence broken only by wind and water and falling snow, were all that he desired. They could not take away his despair, but at least they asked no questions and gave no advice.

He ate sparingly of his meat and bread, and drank clean snow that melted in his mouth. Every day he walked farther east, staying between the mountains and the road. He had no object in his journey, but he did not want to turn back. Going south would have taken him up to the freezing mountains, and turning to the north would have taken him past the Luciyr road and into populated regions that he wished to avoid. So he kept on. He had food enough to last for a week, perhaps more.

The days of weary wandering blurred into one another. Every day his hands grew worse. They swelled and grew hot, and the deep abrasions oozed pus. Any motion hurt. At times he would put his hands in snow, and feel relief as the pain dulled. Yet he was fearful of freezing them, and avoiding the pain seemed to him like cowardice. Most of the time he kept them warm in the pockets of his cloak and pushed on with gritted teeth. He kept going because he did not want to stop, and most of all he did not want to see people.

Sometimes he thought of his parents, and of the grief he must be causing them. He wondered if they would live in the house he had built, or if it had only been a foolish waste of Ilohan's gift. He thought of turning around, and trying to find them, but he felt he could not bear to face them. Even if he died here, in the frozen forest, he wondered if that would cause them any more pain than living with him and seeing his grief. His life was broken, and returning to them could not alter that.

409

He would rather hide his grief – and, if he was to die, his fate – from them and all mankind. He did not want to face a sympathy that could not heal, or to live out his grief to its end in the sight of men.

When he ran out of food he did not look for more. He merely kept walking. The pain in his hands was too severe for him to sleep anymore. He walked without sleep or rest for three days and two nights, hungry, cold, and without hope. Throughout the second night and the third day he found the ground sloping steeply uphill, though he had not turned toward the mountains.

As the third day drew to a close, and the third night gathered around him, he knew that his final collapse was near. He trudged onward, too tired to think, wondering if he had been a coward not to turn around while he still could; wondering if he would, after all, die a craven's death. As he went on through the darkness, he found he wanted another person near to comfort him. Until then he had wanted to be far from all human sympathy, but now he felt he would have given much – if he had had anything – for a kind voice and a helping hand, even if it was only to help him lie down to die.

His sleepless exhaustion blurred his perception until the whole world seemed a confused, waking dream. But a moment came when suddenly, despite the tangled unreason of his thoughts, he realized that he was walking on the road. He saw a tree silhouetted against the starry sky, and its shape struck some dull chord of familiarity in his mind. He lowered his gaze and saw a lighted window, and a narrow path made by footsteps crossing and re-crossing in the snow. He stumbled and fell, and lay on the ground for a moment thinking that the window must have been a dream. His fear of dying a coward brought him to his feet, and the window was still there. He trudged up the little footpath to a tiny cottage, and knocked upon the door. The motion sent stabs of pain through his whole hand and arm. When the door opened, he formed no coherent idea of who had opened it before he took one step across the threshold and collapsed upon the floor.

*   *   *

"Do not move your hands. I will take care of you."

There was love in the voice. Jonathan did not open his eyes, but he thought somehow that he knew the speaker. His hands still ached, but it was a very different feeling than he remembered. It was a pain in which there was a hope of healing. He was aware that he was lying on a bed, well wrapped in blankets. Clearly he had slept a long time. He wondered how long.

"I only want you to eat a few spoonfuls," said the voice. "It is only bare gruel, and has little taste, but it is all I have. Open your mouth."

Jonathan obeyed, and swallowed the spoonful of gruel that was put into his mouth. The taste was bland, but he was ravenous and had no complaints. When he had eaten a score or so of spoonfuls, no more came. He wondered a little at this, but then fell quickly back asleep.

He slept deeply, and his dreams stayed faint and vague. Yet out of them emerged one steady thought, and with it the conviction that it was really true. The thought was that it was Jenn who had cared for him. Just as his mind grasped the idea, he felt himself becoming awake. He rose rapidly through the mists of his dreams, and opened his eyes on reality with a clear mind.

The ceiling above him was old thatch, and the wall beside him old wood. He was comfortable and warm, but weak. The light in the room was firelight. He looked around, and saw that he was indeed in Tharral's cottage. Jenn was asleep in a chair by the fire. A bowl of gruel was at her feet, and several loaves of bread were on the table.

Jonathan laid his head back on the pillow and closed his eyes. He thought about what he had seen. He was sure he was awake: this was no dream. So Jenn had made it back, alone, to the cottage where her parents had lived. And, with the ample supply of grain he and Ilohan had harvested, she was self-sufficient here. It was obvious that she could take care not only of herself but also of him. She might last a year, perhaps more, on the food she had. Surely, in that time, healing enough would come to her that she would let herself be adopted.

Jonathan started to think of his own future, and did not like what he thought. He was ashamed that he had come so near to death without good reason, yet even now he almost wished he had actually died. If he were lying frozen in the snowy woods now, he would not have to consider what to do with his life. As it was the problem remained.

He tried to shift himself in bed, and learned again how weak he was. It occurred to him that he need not make any decision about the future until he was strong enough to take an active part in it. At that moment he felt Jenn's small, cool hand upon his forehead.

"Do not try to move like that," she said. "Your hands will heal best if they stay still for several more days. Yet if you are awake and well enough to talk, tell me what has happened to you. Your blisters, bad as they were, should have healed by now. Instead your hands are covered with deep, festering sores, and when you came to my door two days ago you were nearly dead of cold and fever."

Jonathan was silent for a long moment. "I am almost ashamed to tell you, Jenn," he said at last. "Yet honesty and courage require it. When I came to my home in Glen Carrah I found it had been burned by a troop of Norkath cavalry straying from the main army. My mother had escaped, by great courage and quick thinking. My beloved, Naomi, had been killed. I could say grief drove me mad, but if that is true I am mad still. I un-bandaged my hands, because I wanted to be able to handle hammer and saw with care and strength. I rebuilt my parents' home, with the help of two other men, in six days. Whether my parents will choose to live there, or even return to find it rebuilt, I do not know, for they left Carrah together not long after my father and I arrived, and I do not know where they have gone. After the cottage was finished, I laid a fire on the hearth for their welcome, should a strange chance bring them home in time for it, and I set out walking east alone. Did you say this is the second day since I arrived here?"

"Yes, Jonathan," she said.

"Then that was... Ah, I have not counted the days. Yet it must have been nearly two weeks ago. I had a week's food, but I ran out several days before I reached here. My hands were bad when I started, and grew worse all the way, but their hurt was nothing compared with the anguish of my heart. I shunned places where my grief might be seen, and I sought only the barren woods as my comforter. I cared nothing for my life or healing. Thus it was that I came to you in such an evil plight. I thank you for saving my life, for you ought to have thanks for your labor, however little I may value what you have preserved. Will I recover full use of my hands?"

"I expect so," said Jenn. "It is not as though they were slashed or broken."

"How long will it be until I regain my strength, and my hands heal enough to be used?"

"Two weeks, perhaps more," said Jenn. "You must be very careful. If you abuse your hands again before they heal, you may ruin them forever."

"Where will you sleep during that time?" asked Jonathan.

"In the bed. You are well enough now to move over and make room for me."

"You are not afraid, Jenn?"

Young though she was, she was not too young to understand what he meant. She looked at him very intently. He met her eyes, but found their intensity hard to bear. She was very different from the starved, shivering girl who had opened the door for him and Ilohan so long ago. "Have I any reason to be afraid?" she asked.

"No," said Jonathan, "you have none." He knew he spoke the truth. He did not doubt himself or her. There was nothing he had that he would not have given to protect her life and honor.

The moon, nearly full, shone brightly on the little cottage. The two young people, brought together by their deep sorrow, and by the odd combination in each of great weakness with great strength, slept soundly in the old bed. The pure white snow upon the roof was not more free of evil than their thoughts. The old tree in the woods not far away, that had shattered beneath the weight of ice, was not more broken than their hearts.

*   *   *

The days of Jonathan's healing passed quickly. Neither he nor Jenn spoke of the past, or thought much of the future. It was enough to hold their thoughts in the present: to eat the soft brown bread that Jenn could bake; to see white snow sparkle in the morning sun while icicles shone like diamonds on the trees; and to rejoice as every day showed new progress in the long, painful healing of Jonathan's hands.

Soon there was no doubt that his hands would regain their full strength. He was patient through the long days when Jenn would not let him do anything. He knew that she was right, and, though he could not say why, it seemed very important to him that his hands should heal. Nearly three weeks had passed before she would let him help gather firewood, though for her alone the task was cruelly hard. When at last he went out to help her, his hands carefully bandaged with thick cloth, he rejoiced to find his arms still strong. Tasks that had taken Jenn a whole day and left her sore and weary passed in part of a morning with Jonathan's help.

A week later, when they went out to gather firewood again, Jenn let Jonathan work with only thin bandages. The next day she took the bandages off altogether, and from then on he went into the forest and chopped wood for her every day, gradually building up his calluses. Jenn laughed at the enormous piles of wood he cut and stacked for her, but there was sorrow behind her laughter: she knew without his telling her that he was planning to leave her soon.

Each day the soft, pink skin on Jonathan's hands grew more brown and tough, and he rejoiced that he would soon be able to handle sword or hammer all day long without fear.

*　　　　　*　　　　　*

It was early evening outside, but already dark as midnight. The coldest part of the winter had come. The snow swirled around the little cottage, and Jenn and Jonathan built up the fire and huddled close to it against the draughts of freezing air that came through chinks in the old walls. Jenn knew that Jonathan would soon depart, and she felt she could not bear the loneliness of the tiny old cottage without him. She knew his sorrow had not faded with the passing days, but even in his grief she had thought him still as she had described him to Barnabas: very strong, and very good. Every day she had slept at his side in the old bed. Every day, at least after the first few when he had been weak with fever, she had been completely in his power. He had not touched her, nor made her feel afraid by word or deed. She had not misplaced her trust.

And now he was going to leave her. She said what it had long been in her heart to say. "Jonathan, if when you leave me you go to hope or joy, go with my blessing."

Jonathan turned to her in surprise. Tears glistened in her eyes as they caught the light of the fire. "And if there is no hope or joy I go to?" he asked.

"If there is not, I want you to know that if you say the word I will be your wife. I am young, it is true, but it is not strange in Karolan for girls no older than I to marry, when they have no father." She did not move toward him, or even reach out, but tears fell fast from her warm, deep brown eyes. "I would love you, Jonathan," she said. "I would not seek to win from you the love you gave Naomi, but I would love you as a comforter, a healer, a friend. Jonathan, your answer can be the only real joy I have known since..." She tried not to cry, because she did not want him to marry her for pity, but it was beyond her power. She put her head in her hands and wept until her whole frame trembled with the sobs.

Jonathan loved her, and would willingly have died for her. Yet as he thought of marrying her, he came against an impossible barrier in his mind and heart. Whether he wanted to or not, he could not do it. His heart simply would not assent to the decision. He hated the fact that his answer must cause her more pain, who had already seen pain far beyond her years. But if he married her, he was sure he would not bring her joy. He longed to take her in his arms and comfort her as he told her his choice, but he knew he must not do that. He sat still in his chair, and spoke as gently as he could.

"Jenn, it can never be. I love you, and I know that you are pure and kind. You have saved my life and healed my hands as few others could, and still fewer would, have done. I know that what I owe you I cannot repay. I know that your power to love, and your courage and loyalty are very great. Yet it cannot be. My heart cannot let Naomi go, though she has fallen from the world that is. Jenn, dear Jenn, I am more sorry than I can say.

"I know that you cannot live here alone forever, and I propose to buy a horse and take you back to Glen Carrah. If my parents are there, they will adopt you. If not I will take you to Ceramir, the Cloth of Joy, where there is hope and healing for the deepest grief. Will you come with me?

Jenn raised her face, her eyes now red with weeping, her frame shaken by sobs. "If you do not marry me, if you leave me at Carrah or Ceramir and go away, I am afraid you will die," she sobbed. "Without me you will let yourself starve, or die in some other way. I wanted to show you the value of your life. I wanted to be your reason to keep living. Jonathan, you may leave me, but will you promise me not to die?"

He pushed back her tear-wet hair and stilled her trembling hands. "I will not die reasonlessly, to escape from grief, as I would have if you had not healed me here," he said. "Though life is a heavy burden, I will not take the coward's way and cast it off without good cause. This I promise you, with all my heart, and the pledge shall not be broken. So, Jenn, you are my reason to keep living, for it is to you that I have made that promise. Come with me to Glen Carrah. The hearts of my parents will sing for joy, and I will know that though I may have taken from them their son I have brought them a daughter."

Jenn was still now. Her sobs had ceased and her tears fell silently upon the rough wood floor. She spoke, and it was as if every word were a heavy weight she had to lift. "I should not have asked you to take me as your wife, Jonathan," she said. "I am sorry." There was a long pause and then she went on. "I will give to you the same promise you gave me, that I will not throw away my life. Yet I must ask you to leave me here, and not take me back to be the daughter of your parents. I had that chance once, and I hurt your father deeply when I threw it away. Yet I had to do that; I wanted to be his child, but I could not be. I cannot be still. I will not go with you to Carrah. This is where my father and my mother lived, and this is where I must live. The time may come when I will leave it, but the time is not now. Jonathan, if you will, please leave tonight. You may take the blanket from the bed to make you warm, and all my loaves of bread for food, but if you stay each moment will hurt us both. Please leave tonight. The closest inns are to the north; you can reach them before the dawn. Jonathan, I love you alone among all who live. Please leave me. Please do not stay."

Jonathan stood and laid a hand on her shoulder. "Jenn," he said, "whatever you do, do not fear for me. I will never be the worse for anything that you have done, and the memory of you will always bless my heart. I will take your blanket, in memory of you, but leave you my own, to keep you warm. I will take my cloak and the rest of what I brought here, and I will take half, not all, of your bread with many thanks." He had taken the things he mentioned as he spoke, and now put on his cloak and made a neat bundle of the rest in the center of the floor. He lifted it easily to his shoulder and went to the door. "Farewell, Jenn," he said. "Never in all my life have I longed so much to say, 'God be with you,' but I will not for I know there is no God. Farewell. Farewell, and may you live to see a joyful spring. Farewell." The door shut hard behind him, and an icy blast of air swirled in the room in his wake. Jenn looked hard at the old wood of the cottage door, but it did not open again. He was gone. She ran to the bed and huddled there, crying as she had never cried before. Jonathan's blanket was soaked with her tears.

Chapter 22

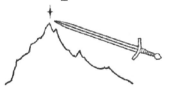

The Symbol on the Box

AS JONATHAN WALKED THROUGH THE SNOWY DARKNESS, his thoughts were in turmoil. He had no regrets about what he had done, but he was intensely angry at whatever fate had made things turn out as they had. He told himself that he was angry at nothing; that fate or destiny were only fantasies that men created in order to rage at them, but that did not help. The frustration only made his anger hotter.

How could it be? How could it be that he, who loved Jenn deeply, must hurt her as he had? How could it be that she, whose heart was broken all over again by his departure, had had to turn him out of her house for his own good and hers? It was so wrong, so devastatingly unjust. They had done the best they knew, and caused pain to each other when they would have given all they had to heal instead. And Naomi, whose life had been more precious than the light of the sun, was dead. And Tharral and Mer, whose faithfulness had been as strong as stone, were dead on the stone of Petrag, and their daughter was left to live alone a life beyond her strength, and to know a grief beyond her years. Glen Carrah, that had been a shining swath of living gold, was burnt as black and dead as the ashes of a pyre. He hated the world. He almost wanted to destroy it, but his love of the beauty that remained in it checked that desire. He wanted to protect the beauty and goodness from the ash and evil and madness that would destroy it. But he could not. At all that he had most intensely attempted he had failed.

He walked on through the dark woods and the cold, snow laden wind. The moment of his departure from Jenn's cottage was still vivid in his mind. He could hear the thud of his pouch of gold as he flung it hastily down in the center of Jenn's blanket. He could see his tinderbox flash the firelight, with the odd Norkath symbol wrought in silver on the lid. Yet the most intense part of the memory was nothing he had seen or heard. It was what he had felt: Jenn's grief and pain echoed in his own heart. He had not dared to meet her eyes in that swift packing of all that he had. Yet he guessed well enough the suffering he would have seen in them.

As he walked, and became more weary, the pain of the memory faded, and his mind fixed on odd, irrelevant details. The gleaming silver symbol on the Norkath tinder box stuck in his mind. He should throw it away; it was a symbol of what had destroyed Naomi, and it was wrong that he should carry it.

It was a symbol of what had destroyed Naomi... Suddenly he realized what that meant, and the world changed. He saw clearly the path that Justice had laid before his feet. Eagerly he chose to follow it, and his will swiftly hardened behind the decision. He had a goal now, and a mission. His hands with their new calluses went slowly to the hilt of his sword, and he walked with a swifter step. The lights of a village and inn shone through the blowing snow ahead of him, and he strode toward them. Sleep, fire, and food would keep him strong – that he might carry out his new intent.

*　　　　　*　　　　　*

It was two weeks later when Jonathan of Glen Carrah raised the hilt of his sword and knocked three times on the heavy oak door of the Norkath castle of Drantar. He had had a long, weary, and mountainous journey to reach it, but at last he had come. He smiled, and looked behind him at the barren oakwoods lit by the rosy sunlight of a winter evening. There was no possibility of failure now. It was over. Naomi's murderer was the master of this place, and soon his blood would soak the newly fallen snow.

Jonathan could see it in his mind: the enemy's sword raised to parry, but futilely. His own stroke would shatter the Norkath blade and kill the scoundrel with a single blow. It would be a fair and just single combat, but the outcome was as certain as the dawn.

The great oaken door opened. A richly dressed steward looked at Jonathan with surprise. "What is your business?" he asked.

"That depends on your answer to a question," said Jonathan. "Is this the symbol from your master's coat of arms?" He held up the tinderbox for the steward's examination.

The steward looked at it closely. "Yes," he said, "that is the sign of the Unbroken Spear, crest of my master's house."

"Then I, Jonathan of Glen Carrah, once commander of the army of Karolan, challenge Sir Drantar to single combat with swords, because he was among those who burnt my home and killed the woman I loved. Tell him that if he is half a man, he will not refuse the challenge of one whose grief he has caused but cannot heal. Tell him that I will face him on the grounds of this his castle, before the setting of the sun."

The steward stood still for a few moments with his mouth open, and then made a swift, slight bow and hurried back into the hall. He made his way up wide, curving staircases and down passages well lit with lines of torches. Finally he knocked respectfully at an oak door gilded with the sign of the Unbroken Spear. "Enter," said the knight of Drantar from within.

The steward entered and delivered his message. The knight rose from his seat beside a stone table, and walked across the room to a broad, barred window. He gazed out over a great expanse of rolling hills cloaked by mighty oakwoods, lit now by the rosy sunset light. Only near the castle were there any tilled fields, clustered close around the great stronghold, Norkath's only outpost in the first eastward breach of the great mountains. Drantar stood looking out at the beauty of the land for a long time, and then he turned to give the steward his reply. "Tell Jonathan of Carrah that I was loyal to my king. I hated the orders I was given, but I had sworn allegiance to Fingar. I am not responsible for the death of Jonathan's lady. In the years to come I will do much to heal some of the hurts of the world, though I cannot bring back the dead. I have no wish to lose those years upon the edge of Jonathan's sword tonight, and I have no doubt that such will be the outcome if I accept his challenge. Tell Jonathan of Glen Carrah that he must leave this place and never return."

When the steward relayed this message to Jonathan, the blacksmith stood perfectly still for a moment. Then anger kindled in his eyes and his hands leaped like lightning to his sword. Fear flashed into the steward's face, for he knew that he at least would die as Jonathan tried wildly to fight the whole castle alone. Then suddenly Jonathan was gone, walking with an easy stride back across the drawbridge and into the woods.

He left no defiance, and no reply. He had thought of a better answer.

*   *   *

"You cannot be Jonathan of Glen Carrah. I do not believe it." Jonathan had heard those words scores of times in the weeks that had passed since he left the castle of Drantar. The man who spoke them now was perhaps a year or two younger than he was, and was sitting across a tavern table from him drinking a tumbler of ale.

Jonathan smiled at him. "Would you follow me if I could prove I was Jonathan?" he asked.

The young man thought it over for a moment. "You say we would attack with absolute surprise, and outnumber the garrison at least five to one?"

"I am sure of it," said Jonathan.

"And the gate will break at the first thrust from our battering ram?"

"It will be a stout oak log with three score strong men on either side." said Jonathan. "The castle gate is oak with simple iron bands. It will shatter."

"The forest offers good cover until near the wall, and there are plenty of large oaks in the woods?"

"Yes," said Jonathan.

"Then yes," said the other man with a loud but not unpleasant laugh. "If you could prove to me that you are Jonathan, I would follow you to capture Castle Drantar. I would see that you get a just and equal combat with Sir Drantar of Norkath. I would watch you crush his head."

"Have you a sword?" asked Jonathan.

"No, but I can borrow one from my friend the innkeeper here."

"Do it then, and meet me in the street before the inn in a moment."

The young man stared at Jonathan in amazement. "Do you mean it?" he asked.

"I do indeed," said Jonathan.

Soon afterwards they faced each other across a few steps of snowy inn yard, each holding a sword. "I will be careful not to hurt you," said the young man.

"I will not hurt you," said Jonathan. "I think that it matters little what you try to do to me."

"Have at me, then, braggart!" roared the man, and the fight was on. A moment later there was a crash of iron on iron, and the young man's blade landed softly on the snow of the inn roof. Jonathan stood still facing his vanquished opponent.

"I am Jonathan of Glen Carrah," he said. "I fought on the bloody cliff at Petrag until my hands froze to my sword. There are few in the land who can defeat me. Even those who can do not quickly forget my strength."

"I believe you," said the young man.

"Good," said Jonathan. "How many more do you think you can recruit to my cause?"

The other man thought for a moment. "A dozen, perhaps more. I know many who spent the war of Karolan's defense as captives before Aaronkal, who would welcome a chance to fight under Jonathan in a just cause."

"Bring as many men as you can, and meet me on the battlefield of Petrag at the next full moon," said Jonathan. "I will be there to lead you into Norkath. We will take a just revenge for the rape of Glen Carrah."

"It will be an honor," said the young man. He bowed and walked swiftly off into the gathering night.

Later that night Jonathan slept in a wooded hollow a good way from the inn. He was comfortable in the wild, and did not like to spend his gold for rooms and beds. He had plenty for food, and his plan was succeeding very well. His name had become almost a legend in the land, and he had seldom found his strength too little to support it.

Sleep did not come quickly to him, though he was warm, wrapped in his blanket with dry leaves piled above him. His mind was too active to slip easily into dreaming. Less than a year before, he thought, less even than half a year before, he had been only a blacksmith's son in Glen Carrah. Now he was a great warrior, preparing to execute a harsh revenge upon a knight of Norkath. There was nothing honorable in all the world that he would not have done to regain the earlier time. Yet there was nothing at all anywhere that he could do to bring back Naomi, his beloved, or the good days that were gone, with her, forever.

He wondered for a while about the justice of his cause. Drantar had said that he had only followed the orders of those he had sworn to obey. But Jonathan did not accept this: given a vile order, it was a true man's duty to refuse, even on pain of death. Jonathan had not a shadow of doubt that in Drantar's place he would have done exactly that. He would have defied the order to burn Carrah, and turned against the soldiers to fight for the women and the glen. He would have stood alone, and would have fallen: his body would have burnt to ashes in the fires that burned the glen. It would have been a hard duty, but he would have accepted it. Drantar had not. His doom was deserved: death in a fair single combat with Jonathan of Carrah.

Jonathan wondered what he would do if Drantar refused absolutely to fight. Kill him in cold blood? No, never. He would take everyone out of the castle and burn whatever parts of structure would take flame – alas, not very much. Then he would strip Drantar in front of all his servants and leave, taking no lives and no captives. Where a man would not face death with honor, disgrace was the only possible revenge.

The excitement and purpose that his plans had brought to his life were pleasant, but as he drifted toward sleep he felt sick at heart. Naomi's death had broken his whole world, and now even the best that he could do seemed somehow wrong. Was this the tribute he would give to his beloved: a dead Norkath and a broken gate – or worse, a naked knight, shamed in the sight of his servants, shivering before his gutted castle? Would this have pleased Naomi? He knew it would not have, and she seemed very near to him in the cold dark night. She seemed lovingly sorrowful over his actions. But she must understand that justice could be stern and hard as well as right. The burning of Carrah had killed at least two women, probably more; the rest were slaves in Cembar. The fortunate among them were menial servants, the unfortunate were concubines of Norkath noblemen or slaves in brothels. One man's death did not satisfy justice, let alone exceed it. Naomi was dead, and would never be grieved by any word of what he did. It was up to him to follow his own conscience, and he loved justice. His mind drifted from these thoughts to dreams of happier times, and he slept at last.

* * *

It was a week later, and within a few days of the full moon, when Jonathan set foot again in Glen Carrah. He hardly knew

427

what had drawn him there, but, with all preparations made for his invasion of Norkath, there was nothing to keep him away. He had had no object, no goal, for those few days, and his feet had taken him here. The glen was white, but not with the lovely roughness of snow on tall dry grass. This snow was flat and smooth, and here and there the ash showed through. There were a few new cottages where the village had once been; it seemed Carrah would not be utterly deserted.

Far down the glen Jonathan could see a trail of smoke from the chimney of the cottage he had built, blown nearly flat in a stiff, cold wind from the west. Someone was living there. Jonathan did not know if he hoped it was his parents or not. He did not know what he would say if he saw them. Soon he would go down and knock at that cottage door, but not now.

He walked slowly across the glen to the Carratril. It was deeply frozen, and partly covered with snow, but he could still hear the swish of water far down beneath the ice. The banks that had once been green and gold with living grass were black and dead: frozen ashes over frozen mud.

He climbed up away from the ice and back to the great, white sweep of the glen. He dug through the snow to find the black ground. It had a strange texture. The ground beneath the grass had been partly dead grass itself, a peaty mixture of dead vegetation and mud. It had burned hot and long, and left a weird, marred soil – as if the earth itself had taken flame. Jonathan doubted anything would ever grow there again. He knelt in the patch of ground that he had cleared of snow, pushed his hands down into the ruined soil, and bowed his head. His tears fell slowly, one after another as if each one had a struggle to escape his closed eyes. The whole of his broken life seemed to swirl around him like a wind across the barren glen. He spoke aloud the grief that was in his heart, in words broken by his tears.

"I am here again," he said. "Once we knew joy here, joy such as must be seldom found in all the world. We were ourselves; we did not know what the days to come would do to us. We were free and joyful and fearless. Our love was as fresh as the dawn, more precious than the purest gold. 'Deep running as the roots that lie beneath us, rich growing as the grain that shows above.' It was like that. It was better than the words can say. And now it is like this. Ashes. This is what I cannot escape. This is a part of me wherever I go, whatever I do. All the rest of my days will be lived on the ashes of our joy."

Here ends the second book.

IF YOU ENJOYED THIS BOOK...

-Tell your friends! This is a self-published book without the advertising budget of a big corporation behind it. If you think it's a good read, spread the word!

-Buy Books Three and Four: _Rain, Wind, and Fire_ and _Darkness Gathers Round_ – which bring _The Epic of Karolan_ to its triumphant conclusion! They're available from www.hopewriter.com, and from Amazon.com.

-You can order Karolan books for a friend or family member from either of the websites above. To contact the author directly, email ariheinze@hotmail.com, or call (832) 622-1114.

-Check the website, www.hopewriter.com, for interesting background about Karolan. News about Ari Heinze's next writing project may eventually appear there as well.